LAST

COMES

THE

EGG

LAST

COMES

THE

EGG

A Novel

BRUCE DUFFY

Nonpareil Books

DAVID R. GODINE, PUBLISHER · BOSTON

This is a Nonpareil Book, first published in 2001 by
David R. Godine, Publisher
Post Office Box 450
Jaffrey, New Hampshire 03452
www.godine.com

Originally published in 1997 by Simon & Schuster, Inc.
Copyright © 1997 by Bruce Duffy

LIBRARY OF CONGRESS CATALOGING-IN-PUBLICATION DATA
Duffy, Bruce.
Last comes the egg : a novel / Bruce Duffy
p.   cm. — (Nonpareil book)
ISBN 1-56792-124-8 (softcover : alk. paper)
1. Boys–Fiction. 2. Catholics–Fiction.
3. Maryland–Fiction. 4. Nineteen sixties–Fiction.
I. Title. II. Series.
PS3554.U31917 L37   2001
813´.5–dc21   00-037574

FIRST NONPAREIL EDITION
Printed in the United States of America

For my parents

and the many others

who raised me.

And for my daughters,

Lily and Kate

I'M GRATEFUL TO

THE JOHN SIMON GUGGENHEIM MEMORIAL FOUNDATION,

THE MRS. GILES WHITING FOUNDATION, AND

THE LILA WALLACE–READER'S DIGEST FUND

FOR THEIR GENEROUS SUPPORT.

SOMETHING IDENTIFIES YOU WITH THE ONE WHO LEAVES YOU, AND IT IS

YOUR COMMON POWER TO RETURN: THUS YOUR GREATEST SORROW.

SOMETHING SEPARATES YOU FROM THE ONE WHO REMAINS WITH YOU, AND IT IS

YOUR COMMON SLAVERY TO DEPART: THUS YOUR MEAGEREST REJOICING.

—CÉSAR VALLEJO, "SOMETHING IDENTIFIES YOU"

LAST

COMES

THE

EGG

390

CUBES

OF

WIND

"NYEERRROOOOO)))))))))))))))WWWWWWWWWWWW—"

That starts it for me. I hear *"NEEEYYYyyeerrrOOO)))))oowww-WWWWwww,"* and suddenly I'm twelve, blowing down the road with the top down in our '62 T-Bird, an aerodynamic teardrop so white and shimmering new it's as if we've flown through a rain.

With the windows rolled up and a white canopy of clouds above, it's domey and thunderish inside, white sun on white seats, as we make our Sunday "bombing run" west around the first completed leg of the Washington Beltway—west, then north up the felty new blacktop of 70S, where the cows and the yahoos roam. In the sunny, hazy-hot August heat our bodies are three erect flags. Houses list. Trees sweep away. Then through wind-creased eyes I can almost see you blowing by—you, my mother, Julie. You were only thirty-seven then, actually a year younger than I am now as I cross this first page. And so, as a sort of contemporary—a brother adult if you will—eye to eye, age to age, I'll presume to call you "Julie." Or so I will now as I begin this admittedly strange line of inner questioning.

So Julie, then. Julie cruising in the dark glasses. Tall, slim Julie with the curly dark hair, the teased dark hair bound in a red scarf. Julie with the arms of a white, pearl-buttoned sweater tied carefully-casually around your neck: For dear life, the spirit clings to you, the sweater's loose arms flapping as I rear up behind you.

"EEEE—Yabba-Dabba-Dooooooo!"

Vroom, an underpass. Ape-hanging over Dad's shoulders, I plow my head into the wind, aiming myself through that sonic warp of glass and wobbling white hood, as we swoop across the last rolling miles of Montgomery County, over the rocky brown steel of the Monocacy River, then past the old red bricks of Frederick, Maryland. Slapping off the back bumper, flapping static strips sap off the electric charge—the zap—of our speed, and it's the same for

me. Frantic to *do* something, crazy with this giddy, near hysterical love that'll
hit you as a kid, I run a couple quick takeoffs off Dad's head.

"*NEEEYYyyyeeerrr-OOO)))))WWWWwwww*"—my flattened palm screaming
off his dark flattop into the piercing blue Pacific.

"*NEEEYYyyeeerrr-OOO))))))WWWWWWWWWUUHhhh*"—my fingers just
grazing the dark, flaring bristles.

God, the *feel!* The incredible feel of his hair, millions of tiny thistly tines
standing on end, firm as a hairbrush in my stubby palm. But more amazing
now, in this sudden light shift, is how *dark* his hair is. Dark as paint—far
darker than I remember—darkly flaring and tipped with light as Dad growls
back at me.

"Okay, hotshot, now sit on down." Grinning back at me in his glinting Ray-
Bans, he even looks like a fly-guy, saying in his roger-wilco voice, "Snazzy
ride, huh?"

"You said it, Daddio!"

Then a glint of gold. Yellow gold in full sunlight, the last the blind can see.
It's the gold of your jangly gold charm bracelet, Julie. Then your wide-eyed
laugh as you pinch my chin.

"No, you mean *Mommio*. Let's not forget whose idea it was to buy this
jalopy, shall we?"

POWER FLOWS IN SECRET AND IS NEVER WHAT IT SEEMS.
In our little family power flows in such a secret who's-got-the-ball way that
I'm always wondering just who's got the power and where it all goes. But in
our house there is one thing still more secret than power—money. So in the
T-Bird now, Dad, the engineer, is correcting your horrendous money gram-
mar, with me the referee.

"So Frank, old buddy, just you remember. When the bill collector comes,
just point him at Mommio, not me."

You spew smoke! Typical! Mr. Think-Small and Dawdle-Around! Mr.
Johnstown-Flood-Kid who picked coal from the smoldering slag heaps, then
hauled it home in his blackened wagon, *Peter, are you going to go through your
entire life dragging that miserable, goddamned coal wagon?*

Love's a long and unflinching study, isn't it, a kid with one eye closed, squinting in the sun? The gold flashes and disappears, merges with an image of your cigarette. Not even that. No, it's just the ash, the ash that I watch in the amazed, vaguely stupefied way that you'll fixate on something as a kid. Just concentrate on the ash, I think, on the ash of the knee bone of the thigh bone of your cigarette. So with the wind twittering like a gnat in my ear, I stare hypnotized at the burning ash, watching how the white cigarette paper slowly browns, then almost imperceptibly abrades away, blowing away like sand in hot, whistling flyspecks that graze my eyes. And so up the ontological chain, from the *gold charm bracelet* to the *ash* to *the mole*, the mole scarcely larger than a pepper grain on the side of your lip—the mole where, with one canny eye closed, in one long, slow burn of pleasure, you slowly pull on your cigarette. And the cigarette winks at me. The burning paper actually *squeaks*, my ears are so sharp. Yes, the ash and the mole, they both wink at me, as if to say we know what life is, you and me. Or you and *I*, if we gotta get snotty, grammarwise.

But a mole, Julie. Such a strange animal word for a splotch, I think. Called a mole because it's all molish dark? Cause it's all burrowy under the skin, in a kind of hole? Don't you see this yet, Julie? Leaking through the mole come a few stray splinters of light, a final expiring wound of light saying what it said to the kid, what it says to the grown man, and what it will always say, *But don't you get it yet, she's dead. Dead.*

You died, Julie. You failed. To the living, the dead are always failures, if only because they have failed to live or stay. But of all the dead, none are more failed than the young dead, especially if the leaver is a mother and the stayer is a child. Our sorrow is changing. Our sorrow is maturing, and the shadow is shortening, not lengthening. When you first died, your disappearance seemed unendurable, yet now when I can feel the ecliptic of your returning—when at last I hit the terminal point of outliving you, snapping-the-whip at thirty-eight—your return seems more unendurable, as it did when I was twelve. Normally, I'm not at all superstitious but now I sure am. Weird nightmares of early death. Or worse, fears that my wife will also die young, dying while I live on, agelessly aging, like a vampire. But c'mon, the vampire's not a monster, he's just an overgrown kid who survived and grew up, only to face the monster of old age.

And here it comes, Julie. After twenty-six years of that strange marriage called death, we'll soon be reunited like Einstein's proverbial twins. Thirty-eight-going-on-forty meets thirty-eight-going-on-nothing. At last, I'll hit that guiltiest, most vulnerable age, older-than-you.

• • •

ANOTHER EXPRESSION PUTS you back in that kiss-my-ass car we bought just before you died.

Spewing smoke and scattering your long fingers, you would say with mock contempt of that class, power thing that so confounded you, *money schmunny*.

To you, money was a form of belief, a kind of adult make-believe about who you weren't but well might be one day, once our ship came in.

Money schmunny. By the age of ten or eleven, like any other kid, I also knew a lot of believing, deceiving mental tricks. I knew, for instance, that if you tilted your head and half crossed your eyes (like snake eyes, sorta) I knew you could see and understand things. Things that formed an oblique picture in the corner of your eye but that maybe you would *die* from—make-believe die from—if ever you faced The Thing too directly.

Like you, Julie, I also knew that if I looked a certain way, glowery or certain, angry or determined, then I wouldn't be afraid. Or at least nobody would *see* us afraid and, therefore, powerless before the plunging storm of life that we could see up ahead, lifting distant trees.

Money schmunny. Under the hammering aerodrome of wind, invincible in our car, I remember that happy sense of foreverness, of time kneading into itself, like great white clouds or shirts tumbling in a dryer. With the sun dangling like a raindrop off one eyelash, I even have a song for this tremendous forever-feeling, *Jim-i-ney-Crack-Corn, and-I-Don't-Care—And-I-Don't-Care—And-I-Don't-Care* . . . Because I don't care, or have to. Because, even if we do pay on time, and even if on the first of the month Dad does sweat and swear, we're special, you say. And so in the snowy, sunlit darkness, as we cruise a "thrifty sixty," the Mole says to him.

"Aww, go on, Pete! Open her up for once! Let's see what she'll do—"

Dad rolls his eyes. He breaks into his exasperated engineer's voice, "Honbun, I told you. There's such a thing as *material limits*. Until we reach the thousand-mile break-in period—"

"—Thousand! Last week you said five hundred!"

"Well, some say a thousand."

"Right! Then three! Then four thousand!"

"My dearrrrr. We'll scar the cylinder walls—"

"Aww, go on! It's supposed to last forever?"

Cylinder walls, material limits—*money schmunny!* To you, this was just another case of Dad balking. Balking like he did the day you spied the Bird in the showroom window.

"Twenty-eight hundred bucks!" moans Dad. "Come on, kiddo, you're dreaming. Look, I'm not taking another barrel over the falls for you. Forget it."

"But, Pe-ter," you hiss in your have-a-little-imagination voice, "Pe-ter, it's a *write-off*. Let the *corp-or-ation* buy it."

The corporation was Gaffney/Dougherty Systems, or G.D.S. Inc., which sold commercial heating and air-conditioning equipment—boilers, pumps, steam traps, giant valves, . . . okay, *big, rusty, greasy things*. Anyhow, G.D.S. had just opened and things were still shaky. Real shaky. Or so *he said*. You, of course, were way more bullish. Why, to hear you talk up the incorporative concept was to feel we'd busted into Fort Knox! Do the In-corp-or-ation, a brand new dance craze, like the Twist.

"It's a *legal* concept," you explained. "A corp-or-ation is simply a legal entity. Like a person. Or rather, a third 'it' type person."

"Hold on," I ask. Understand, I'm ten at the time. "So what's an enty?"

"Ent-i-ty. It's a thing."

"But Mom, you just said it's a *person*."

"I was *likening* it to a person."

"Aww, come offa it, Mamma! If it's your company, then it's you. It's still you and your own money, right?"

"No, no," you insist, you who don't so much as lick a stamp. Invoking this Holy Trinity, Three-Mints-in-Hoakum, you go on, "Can't you see? It's us and not us. And the Corporation can *buy* things for us."

"But what's this entity thing?" It sounds like the Holy Ghost.

"It's *not us*, that's who! It lessens our exposure—legal exposure." You get all giddy. "And if it all blows up in our faces, guess what? We can't be sued! Aww, calm down, Petey boy, I'm just kidding! All it means is that your Dad's smart and we're protected nine ways to Sunday—"

Money schmunny! All it was, was this big scheme consisting of Dad's technical wizardry and his partner Bud's hot air—them and two young gofers and this stacked, broad-beamed young secretary named Shirley who bumped real slow past the men's desks and had just gotten the D-word—*divorced*. "Flopsy," you called her. Flopsy, see, was Bud's "girl" and Bud's *'zecutive prerogative*. Yeah, when push came to shove, Dad had to can his secretary, old, reliable Mrs. Steadman. Poor Mrs. Steadman could take dictation and type eighty a minute, but Bud put the kabosh on that. He said she didn't have Flopsy's *'zecutive tone*.

Anyhow, atop this mighty little corporation, Humpty-Dumpty-like, sits a *Board*. ("We all sit around a big table," you explain. *"Lunch table,"* pooh-poohs

Dad.) Anyhow, as I picture it, you and Dad—the recording secretary and VP, respectively—you both sit over on one side, while on the other side ("completely tipping the balance but your father won't listen") is "President Budworm," plus his treasurer wife, "Whiney Anne," plus Bud's "Uncle Money" and Mac "the Knife" Davis, a lawyer S.O.B. who Dad and Bud both knew, but mostly Bud. And this was called a corporation! Man, it was totally amazing to me, the half-baked stuff adults cooked up.

"Look," you say to me, "you should know something about business, so you won't be a fool, or marry one." So, going to the dictionary, under "corporation," we read *a body of persons granted a charter legally recognizing them as a separate entity having its own rights and privileges distinct from those of its members.* To which you add with a smirk, "So think of it as a fresh book of checks."

Meanwhile, in the showroom of Chevy Chase Ford, it's *Gentlemen start your engines.* In front of this finned barrel with the bullet hood and spoked wheels, the recording secretary is reminding the VP about the well-known Parable of the Fired Executive. You've probably heard it. The guy gets canned so what does he do? . . . *He goes on a buying spree!* He charges up a new wardrobe, eats at all the best restaurants, takes a round-the-world cruise and is no sooner swaggering down the gangplank than he's flooded with red-hot offers. And why?

"Because he's *a winner,* Pete! And again, it's a *write-off.*"

Dad drops his arms in disgust. The beer barrel is tumbling hard for the falls. "Why the heck must you always argue with me? Like the corporation is Daddy Warbucks! Or your Uncle Stephen, huh?" (See, Uncle Stephen was rich and a lawyer. If we crashed at sea, Uncle Stephen was always ready to pull us out of the drink—*you* said.) "Shoot, we haven't even circled the derned wagons, but here we go! Forty-eight months tied to another anthill! . . ."

Give up, Dad! Blocking Dad out, the salesman, Alligator Shoes, Shoes already has you shoehorned behind the wheel, pointing out all the bells and whistles, when Dad muscles back in, "Okay, kiddo, fun's fun." Dad sidles up to Shoes, "Boy, this gal's *stubberrrn.* Now look, I'm in sales myself so I hate to waste a man's time. So let me be plain, friend. This jalopy's way, *way* outta our league . . ."

But even as Dad's dickering, across the glistening floor, by the tall windows of that huge car aquarium, two men start unsnapping latches. And then with a rumbling, they roll back the whole showroom window! Sun and air flood in. Pennants start flapping and Sinatra's ringadingdinging. Spring has sprung.

"Well okay, folks!" cries Shoes, "what say we get a lookkat her *outside,* huh?"

"Now hold on, mister! I don't like these tactics! Not one bit!"

But *vroom,* and the T-Bird bumps down into the lot, its whirring white roof retracting into itself like the wings of a giant swan. And like a thief you run for it, Julie, this thing so you, so new, so white, so destined, that you can hear yourself regaling people at some cocktail party *and they took out the showroom window! Literally. They took out the whole damned window* . . .

"Fine," says Dad to Shoes. "You got the gas to burn, sure, I'll kill an hour. You want my license? My Diner's Club? What?"

"Oh, please," smirks Shoes to Mom, "can we trust this guy, Mrs. Dougherty?"

"Sure, Mrs. Gotrocks," fumes Dad as we roar off. "Just fork over the damned money!"

Dad accelerates, he brakes, he kicks. Diabolically, Dad sets out to *defeat* the power windows. Rolling them up and down, Dad's cackling, "Boy oh boy, wouldn't I love to load test this baby now! In winter, hah! Come January, she wouldn't even *crank!*"

"Right," you say icily. "When it's five degrees, we'll be rolling the stupid windows up and down!"

"And what if the window motors burn out, huh?"

"If-if-if—"

"—if, heck! And these brakes. Hit 'em too hard and you'll be picking your teeth off the dash!"

Power nothing! Cause back at the dealership, wow, Mom! You slap a whole dollar in my hand! "Frank, get yourself a soda and a comic book. Across the street—and *stay* there, you hear? *We'll find you.*"

YOU KNOW HOW sunburn stinks? Because, an hour later, when you both pull up in that loud, lustrous Dreamsicle of a car, that's exactly how Dad smells—I can actually smell Dad's scorched pride as he peers back at me through the rearview mirror, *so how do I look?* Yeah, it's all in my lap now. Because in a Holy-Trinity-type family like ours, I'm the one who's gotta sign for it. Trying to pull you both out of the inevitable post-potlatch nosedive, I'm hugging and kissing you both, gushing, "Wow! *Our car!* Oh, man, I can't even believe it!" *But we're happy, right? But this is really really what we always wanted, right?*

"Frank!" you snap. "Watch the shoes on the seats! That's glove leather, you know. You're stepping on little baby lambs."

Sprawling drunkenly across the seat, staring at the sky, I'm clutching my head like it'll blow away. I can't stand it! Peering back over the white trunk curved like an enormous pearl, temporarily insane, I'm waving at the people, at all the envious thousands, thudding along behind us, *suckers!* It's an inauguration parade. Waving at all these dirty, lesser cars swamped in our white wake, I'm hurling out stacks of thousand-dollar bills, *Ha ha you poor dumb slobs!*

And actually, Dad's relieved. Dad's fleeced but happy, jabbering back at me, "Phew, it took some doing but we beat those pirates! And do you know why, Frankie boy?" Dad's nostrils flare in the mirror. *"Because we walked.* Ask your mother about that one. Can't be too eager, right, Julie?"

"Aww, quit it—"

Then what happens, Mamma? All you do is give Dad a little flip of the wrist but he blows up at you! "Sure! Just give me the big superior act when you were ready to hand the store over to the little S.O.B.! And here, when I distinctly *told* you—"

But then as usual, Pop catches himself. Dad scribbles over this part, turns into the good guy again, "Ennnnny-who, I could see Hotshot was getting worried. Well, he pulls his palms off the table and *smuck*. Two sweaty palm prints!" Dad smacks his forehead. "Why of course, I think to myself, it's the twenty-fifth of the month! Sure, the slob's sweating out his *quota*." Dad whirls around. "You get me, Frankie?"

"He's *twelve*," you break in, "of course he doesn't *get* it."

"What I mean, Frank, the poor slob had END OF THE MONTH written all across his face. See, in sales you got a *quota*. So—"

"—so we *bought* it, Frank."

"*We*." Dad blows smoke at the sky. "After I dragged you out of there. After Hotshot caved in, *we* bought it."

"Frank," you cry, "enough with the power windows!"

"Heck, no," snorts Dad. "Don't you dare roll that price tag down."

It's just a jab. It's hardly anything but with this last poke from Dad, you're beaten, Julie. The flavor's gone. Stomach gurgling, I can feel it myself, the buzz-saw sun mercilessly grinding down the paint and the wind pummeling the fenders with a million tiny dents. And as I feel this, I can feel you subside into that little death of giving up, half of you outside, out in the wind, disembodied, scorning the car as junk, and the other half inside, furiously calculating the poundage we need to inflate the tires into some finally sustainable sense of elevation. You whip around at me.

"And listen, big mouth. Don't you go blabbing that this is a dealer demo."

Dad's horrified. "What the heck are you telling the kid, *what?*"

"I'm telling him how people are."

"So who the hell did we buy it for? *Them?* Why, I've got half a mind to take the stupid thing back!"

But it's too late now—we're spotted. No, as we turn the corner, here's the true test drive. It's the long climb up Corregidor, our raw, just-paved street, one down from Burma (Shave) Road and two over from Anzio, alphabetically all the way up to Pearl Harbor. Bulldozed on what had been pasture outside the shady old town of Taverna, our neck of the woods is called *Taverna Estates,* one of a hundred rude, red-brick subdivisions going up in the cow pastures all around Washington, D.C. To a New Yorker hepcat like you, Julie, it's all "the sticks." Still, for hustlers like us, these suburbs are a gold mine! Because in government offices downtown, every schmo who lives in each one of these little dumps, well, he needs *heat.* Which means money in our pockets, because we sell the junk that makes the heat to keep their lazy fannies warm pushing papers for Uncle Sammy! And see, virtually everybody in Washington—everybody except us—works for the government. All our neighbors do.

So for now, or at least until we move up, well, it's white-bread, economy-size, come-'n'-git-it Corregidor. Corregidor with its cookie-cutter brick split-levels dropped from the sky on bare, green lawns broken only by a few skinny trees. But back then, Corregidor wasn't just a chinchilla farm packed with G-men and pencil pushers. Above all else, Corregidor was a staunchly Catholic street, and here you and Dad had made one fatal miscalculation. Nope, we too were Catholics and it was Lent. So while our devout neighbors had given up sweets, cigarettes, meat, and probably even sex in some cases, here we come, blazing around the corner in your white elephant.

Everything stops.

With a slap, jump ropes fall slack. Arms and pigtails flying, rollerskating girls breathlessly stop. Ramming his chattering push mower up the hill, devout, slick-haired, Mr. Reece stops, as does white-legged Mr. Davis washing his decrepit station wagon, as does your nemesis, fat, bossy Mrs. Feeney, queen of the ladies' sodality at St. Stephen's, shading her eyes in a menacing salute, *So what in God's name has the woman done now?*

Have you ever touched your tongue to the tangs of a dry-cell battery? Cause that's the taste, exactly, that gagging bite of contempt tinged with envy. Dad tastes it. All nervous, Dad accidentally hits the accelerator—hits it as my stomach plummets and my head rocks back with that sickening roller-coaster feeling of being hauled up the rickety, greasy tracks of a ride you could never hope to stop.

Yeah, after you died, Julie, probably a million times I must have ridden—

and re-ridden—the Bird up our narrow, cheesy little street. Dad I'll never forget, the way he almost goes into a crouch, once again squeezing into the old barrel for you, cannonballed for one last long drop down the falls. But hey, I used to think later, it wasn't so stupid of you, buying that car. No, after the funeral—later, once I really thought about it—I decided that secretly *you knew*. Sure, I thought, you bought the car on time to *buy time*, hoping to stretch those seven months you had left into a roomy forty-eight.

Nope, there's no lack of blame and craziness once anybody dies and gets bodily repossessed, even though adults, they all lie like a damn rug about it. But trust to science, naked inventions, and good old American horse sense! Because we came back! Roaring back! No sir, Mamma, once I calmed down and got my head screwed back on straight, we saw the whole stupid sham of what these Catholic cannibal-types call *death*. And we didn't just see it but we *heard* it, too. Why, on that super death frequency, we pulled it in just as clear as I would WERE in Cleveland. *Remember?* Yeah, with death it was just like working the cat's-whisker tuner on my crystal radio, picking up the freak oscillations of some *a-way-way-off* crystal night. Yeah, I heard the news then, and even now I can hear it bouncing off the clouds. Cause that's the first thing about imagining childhood, gang. The first thing, see, is just to re-tune your ear dials to it, working that zithery cat's whisker to this whole, *whole* other frequency.

WHICH GETS TO MY OTHER HALF, my *technical* side. Specifically, principles I'd gotten from Dad—Mr. Fixit in our neighborhood.

Anything that blew, broke, dripped, overflowed, or went on the fritz my Dad could fix. Which figures, Dad being an Eagle Scout, then a Westinghouse machinist in Pittsburgh, then a hurry-up-college engineer in the U.S. Merchant Marine. That was during the war—World War II, not Korea. All these ships were being torpedoed in Long Island Sound, so they really had to crank out the cadets. Forget the English and history and argyle socks, Dad said. They compressed four years into a year and a half, then shipped them out like kamikaze pilots, with just the bare essentials. Telling me this, Dad smiles sheepishly, does the embarrassed nose thing, then cracks, "You didn't need much English to get blown up!"

Down in his workshop Dad tells me all this, the workshop where practically every night, we're fixing a radio or a toaster for somebody. Taking an old vacuum cleaner motor, Dad once even built a flying saucer that hovered over the floor, bouncing off walls while Dad worked the electric cord like a lariat.

"Technically, I know my stuff," says Dad, explaining the piddly degree. "That's what counts, even if it isn't the kind of MIT sheepskin makes the hotshots bow down and say *salaam*."

Of course, Dad makes out like he doesn't care. Like he's only being realistic, all those years dragging his coal wagon and stuffing tin cans and cardboard in his shoes. Still I knew it bugged him—*a lot*. Sure it did, not having the regular sheepskin like those hotshot sweater guys with their pipes. Smoke-artists like Bud, his partner. *Smokicus profunditus*, says Dad. Bud, a classic example of the sheepskin type, forever fiddling with his pipe and blowing smoke instead of shaking his fanny! "Still, you need a front man and a rainmaker," says Dad. "Just put me in back and let me cook. Bud can play maître d'."

Look, it's not like a kid asks to see his old man's *license* or questions his competence. And even if he'd had the real bona fide sheepskin, Dad wouldn't have nailed it up on his wall. Anyway, Dad didn't have to tell me this, especially not in those days with the GI Bill and night-school educations. Not when just about everybody we knew was in basic training, learning how to be middle class.

"You know what makes a lousy engineer," Dad asks me as the lathe spins off a greasy coil of steel. "It's a guy who doesn't know tools—the kind who's too darned good to get down in the grease and tinker. Me, I carry my coveralls in the trunk, and if there's a problem, I'll pull off my suit and climb in 'em in a minute, too. Everybody in town knows that. You get down there in your coveralls with a bunch of steam mechanics, well, brother, it's a whole new ball game. *Service*. Yeah, they buy from Pete Dougherty and they *know*— day or night, Pete Dougherty'll never leave 'em dry docked, not like these other thieves out here."

Reeking of machine oil and that roasted-nut smell of freshly sawed wood, Pop's workshop was a world I never could square with yours, Julie. Down by the squat black furnace, beneath bare bulbs and snaking ducts, here were whole walls of tools. Brute things like his lathe, drill press and fearsome arc welder, blazing blue smoke and showering yellow sparks. Then there were his fine tools, the carefully honed wood chisels, screw tap sets and machining tools, and, finest of all, his watchmaker's things, the hinged magnifying glasses and the graduated screwdrivers in their velvet-lined wallet—screwdrivers hard blued and barely larger than pins, extraordinarily fine, blazing like crystals as he slowly took apart some dusty, long-stilled clock. After sluicing the filthy, time-caked brass clockworks in benzene, he'd screw his black jeweler's glass into his eyesocket. Then, taking out his tweezers, Dad would painstakingly reassemble the thing, gear by gear, spring by spring. I could hear his breath whistling through his black nosehairs. I could smell his sweat blousing out the back of his shirt. Elbows out and nose to the bench, Dad would build it back up like a house of cards, up until it all danced, the gears meshing, the spinnets spinning, the ratchets clicking and the hairspring coiling and uncoiling, pulsing life like a tiny heart. And then with the air whistling out his nostrils, Dad would just sit there watching the clock return to life, watching it astounded, knowing that inside the most ordinary machines lay profundities, and even life itself.

And parts! Wasn't Dad a pig in his parts, hoarding screws, nuts, springs, vacuum tubes, spark coils, mercury switches, diodes, wires and cotter pins, secreting these in carefully labeled cans, baby food jars, Band-Aid tins and cigar boxes. Here whole legions of the junked and disassembled awaited restoration, even immortality, all to be resurrected through some future problem, when some nice little thing snapped, blew, or simply wore out. And the beauty was, Dad, through his thrift and foresight, Dad *had just the thing,* a thing that suddenly soared in value, zooming from junk to a choice red ruby!

Which gets to the hidden nature of fixing. See, these were the days when things were still fixed at home—when things were still *worth* fixing. Still, the process totally mystified most people. It wasn't just fixing they failed to understand, Dad said. What people totally failed to grasp was the hidden nature of *breaking,* which Dad's cardinal rule was, *nothing breaks all at once.*

Think about it! Everything's going fine, when, *fssst,* your clock, radio, fan, or whatever, conks out! And why? It's just this busted pin or burned thingamajigger, but after a few rough shakes, people say, "It's broken," like suddenly it's *all* broken, totally smashed to bits, not one screw salvageable. And not just busted, *hated.* Why, it's gypped and betrayed them! Worse, it's made them feel inept. Whump, into the trash.

Just bugged the hell out of Dad, how people who'd go to any length to save a sick cat or pry a quarter from under the molding would heave out a perfectly good clock or toaster that only needed a little oil or tinkering. Whump. Out on the curb it goes, there for some kid to kick down the street, and people are so haughty and ignorant they don't even know the love and familiness that gets accumulated into things, which somebody somewhere had sweated blood to invent and make for them, and all their lives they'd camped around it like a little fire without ever seeing the soul inside it or anything. People being what they are, they wouldn't even *dispose* of it with any respect, say, in the way they'd burn an old Sunday missal or wrap a poor sparrow in a cheesecloth and give him a decent burial. Whump.

Well, don't worry, because that never happened in our house, and didn't because Dad and me wouldn't *let* that one little thing defeat us! Which it—defeat—didn't crush you if you knew the physical principles, and the breaking characteristics, behind things the way Dad and me did. Then again, we didn't just fix, Dad and me—oh no, we *built*. Together, we'd built our own hi-fi with woofers and tweeters, and, for me, a crystal set that could pull in WERE in Cleveland, and without using one red cent of juice. You name it, we fixed it, and not once—not even when we had an ironclad Sears warranty—did we *ever* call in a repairman, not when there were manuals and *Popular Science* and, most important, scientific method using all the kneebone's-connected-to-thighbone, process-of-elimination, circuit-tracing tricks that we knew.

Still, lots of times the short way—intuition—was the best. Best because, as Dad said, the old *intuo* was a total mystery to most people, who, even if they had it, are too fainthearted to trust it. You know the kind. The people who slavishly follow directions and recipes—who get so bogged down on Step 96 that they miss the whole point, which Dad says is *getting interesting results*.

Well, here. Here's a good beginner example. Boiling an egg.

First, think *materials*. An egg. A lugey in a shell. Clear pus surrounding a yellow eyeball, which, *click!* . . . right you are, *dissimilar densities*. Okay, now you're ready! So throw out the stupid egg timer and trust your own God-given intuos. What you want, see, is to think about heat flow and *easy eggitude*. The idea is to peer down into that saucepan, into the wild jittery bubbles and micro molecules screaming and careening around in bumper cars in that huge atomic soup, *and be inside the egg*.

But you, Julie, you'd roll up your eyes at this craziness. Why, you'd accuse Dad of being "an egg sharp"—merely counting the seconds. But no! Even if Dad walked out of the room or sat reading the paper with that crazy, superior gleam in his eye, Dad was always right on the money with his intuos. And here I can see the other side of your marriage, the happier side, the two of you playing and being silly, Dad being the big Eagle Scout know-it-all and you the gawky girl who stood five foot ten inches tall. Like a kid, coming down off your high horse, you'd get all happy and excited. You'd get inside the egg of loving him, saying, "It's done! Okay, it's done!" And zigzagging his jaw, Dad would raise his eye, *Sure? You sure??* Waiting until you couldn't stand it, when he'd cry, "*Voilà!*" And with one deft whack of the knife, the shell would pop like ice, all the good yellow gook cooked up perfect, because Dad had the hot psych and the intuos. No, Dad knew his materials and Dad knew his heat, which, if it broke stuff down, it also got that soft-boiler, as he'd say, *"organized* real nice in my mouth."

Well, naturally, word spread about such wizardry. It sure did in our neighborhood, to the point that, most evenings, the neighborhood men wouldn't leave poor Dad alone. The blizzard of '58, for instance. Dad worked almost all night, tearing down the Feeneys' furnace when it died. Well, he had to, with seven kids and four running fevers. And after Dad was done, he never took a nickel, either. When people hauled out their wallets, Dad would actually run out of the house, waving his arms in that goosed way he'd get whenever money came into the picture.

Still, at supper it never failed. We'd just be sitting down when there'd be a knock, and not the breathless, birdy knock of a kid. No, this was the slow, heavy, embarrassed knock of the Gumhand putting his greasy paw prints on our perfect turquoise door.

"Stay put," you say with a glare at Dad. "Frank, tell him we're *eating.* And go in there chewing, too."

Forget it. Chew all you want. Clank your silverware, even have company, it don't faze the Gumhand. As the door swings back, there he is, a charred hunk of metal like a grenade in one greasy paw and smoldering white cigarette in the other. He's steamed, too. He's dragged his pride all the way across the street but, for me, he puts on this phony-chipper, Man-to-Kid voice, "Oh, hey, Frank! Say, is your Dad home?"

Desperate as those guys were, Dad could have been a perfect know-it-all jerk, but he never was. Dad never insulted anybody's intelligence. If Dad wasn't actually stumped himself, he'd always make out like he was, soon absorbed like heat itself into the problem. Five minutes later, rattling silver and clacking pots, you'd storm out only to find he'd drifted across the street with John Decker, the Mooch. Or else hopeless Mr. Keith, who seemed to compulsively smash things so Dad could amaze him yet again.

"Now, look, hon, don't get all shook," Dad would say, running back for more tools, "Half an hour, tops."

"Then let them *pay* you, damnit. Well, why not, wrecking our meals and evenings, giving all your hard-earned knowledge away for free. Well, why not, Pete Dougherty? Did you ask John Decker for free legal advice when you were incorporated? Or—Lord knows—would he ever think to offer in three million years?"

Dad starts pacing. His flattop pricks up like a parrot's when he's mad. "That's not the point. Forget it. You just don't get it."

"I get it. You *like* helping people. And yes, that's *nice*. Look, I know you're generous—believe me, I love that in you. And okay, so I wouldn't feel comfortable taking money from them, but come *on*, Pete. After a while it gets ridiculous, does it not?"

Then again, maybe Dad wasn't such a chump. Because another time, I can hear him rail back at you, "Well, thank god I'm here to *fix* things after you break them in this neighborhood! Think of it as the Toaster Diplomacy, Mrs. Impolitics!"

BUT DAD ASIDE, AND CONTRARY TO POPULAR MISCON-CEPTIONS, you do do things for Taverna and other people. Plenty, too.

Like the two years you were a den mother, for instance . . . okay, not much on knots, but still, a pretty good one, I recall, more willing than most to let us run wild and just have fun. Also, despite what The Small Minds said, we had lots of friends—at least, we did outside Taverna. Mrs. Hunter, for instance. Mrs. Hunter, wife of Bob who made it big, bought a boat, had a fling, and that was that. Still, you helped her and her four boys through the divorce.

Our prejudices about "government slobs" aside, we also had friends who worked for Uncle Sam, the Hergots, who were FBI, and the Jowdys, who were ICC—I could go on. You also had one close friend in Taverna—Angelene Pettinelle, a Texas-twanging, cigarillo-smoking, head-turning divorcée and, really, your one true-blue ally. An Ag Department scientist, Angelene lived the next block over with her two girls and her Mom. At first glance, Angelene didn't seem your type, being too Southern, too well educated, too rich and, frankly, too well built. On the other hand, Angelene was a fellow eccentric who spoke her mind. As a divorcée, Angelene was also a semioutcast in Taverna, and you went to bat for her, too. At Taverna Park Pool you raised such a stink that they bent their unwritten rule barring divorcées—*women* divorcées—as members. Even so, Angelene's membership was limited to daylight hours and then only with a Cracker Jack diamond on her finger and her two girls as chaperones. That's the kind of world it still was back then.

YOU SERVED YOUR country, too. In the 1960 election, wanting America to finally get some class, you signed up as a Kennedy organizer.

To hear you, you're a major coup for Taverna's own Elect John Kennedy

chapter. The boss there, this boy wonder named Andrew Morris III—"Andy,"
to you—well, Andy flips when he finds out you're a former executive secretary with great dictation and, even rusty, fifty wpm. And a grammarian! Andy,
Andy, Andy. Yeah, Andy's your ticket—a Yale man and a New Englander, plus
his Dad's some big shot Democrat.

"Poor Andy," you say after your first day. "God, what a mass of illiterates
he has to work with. And Andy's so funny—he's from Connecticut, you know.
Well, Andy's asking me on the q.t., 'Don't they teach grammar down here in
Dixie?' 'Well, I wouldn't know,' I told him. 'I'm from New York.' "

Dad's sure enthused. Yeah, trying to talk you out of it, Dad's saying how
he doesn't need any presidential sideshows—not with him about to launch
his heating company! Nope, buttering you up, Dad's saying how he needs
your oomph, your cheerleading, but finally he gives up. Fine, have fun, he
says, shooting me an *us-guys* wink. Dad knows this JFK stuff will all wear off
in a few weeks.

But he's wrong this time. No, Pop's as wrong about your determination as
he is about the coolness of JFK, with his crinkly-eyed smile, his youth, his
bucks, and that posh Boston accent! And once you tell me the whole story—
especially about PT 109—well, Kennedy's my hero, too. *My Mom's a writer
in the Kennedy campaign, she wrote the Kennedy Klambake recipe.*

Yeah, on the school playground that fall it was war, *The Kool Kennedys* ver-
sus the *Nixon Nazis!* On the merry-go-round, it was the Nixons pushing clock-
wise and us pushing *counterclockwise! Counterclockwise* 'cause we were turning
back the clock from Nazi boredom and the Depression to youth and freedom
and *viggah!* Which Kennedy being Catholic and it being St. Stephen's, we
crush those puking Nixon Nazis! After dragging those crew-cut creeps
through the dust, they look like freshly battered hush puppies, all of us cheering, "KENNEDY! KENNEDY KENNEDY!"

Meanwhile, you're getting home late, meaning dinner's late—late huddled
with our TV trays and TV dinners while you sit glued to Walter Cronkite.

"Look!" you cry one night, "There's *Andy! At the Capitol! My boss!*"

"A real sweater boy, if ever there was one," mugs Dad, seeing the bow
tie. You fling your napkin at him.

"You're *jealous?* Oh yes you are, Pete Dougherty! Look at those flaming
red ears!"

Pop about blows peas out his nose. "I wanth to eatth my dhihnner! In
peath!"

But Dad's petty jealousies aren't what do you in finally. No, after a few
weeks, you're more the girl bringing home problems from school. Nope, it

doesn't sound too good, as I listen upstairs. It doesn't sound good at all, Pop clearing his throat and scuffing his chair across the floor. Pop sounds like he's lecturing one of his Gumhands.

Still, you're no quitter. No, you work harder, some nights not getting home until I'm in bed—so late that you and Dad finally give me my own house key. Then what happens? After maybe a month of this Kennedy craze, coming home from school, I unlock the door and find you at home! Home three hours early at least, pulling off your "torture pumps." God, even your shoes have the Kennedy hens clucking—organizers wear practical flats but not you. "Women not wearing pumps!" you fuss. "That's cute! What, are *girdles* next?"

Gloomily, you rub your flaming red corns.

"Well, I finally brought some efficiency to *that* office. I certainly showed our Portly *Friend* across the street."

"Who, Mrs. Feeney?" I panic. "Mom, you never said Mrs. Feeney was over there!"

"Aww, she just started. And I did ignore her—I tried. Sucking up to Andy because *she's* Irish, as if I'm not. Pig pen Irish, is more like it. And her playing the queen bee, with the sodality dimwits to stuff envelopes for her—"

"—*Mom!*"

"—Look, I've been nice. Too nice. Well, today I set her straight!" Zanily, your cigarette veers off. "*Any*way, Congressman Maines came through the office—his aides all know me now. And *Eunice.*"

"Huh?"

"*Eunice Shriver? Sargent Shriver's* wife? Get with it, Frankie. Eunice, *Jack's sister?*"

I mean, I'm ten years old but at "Eunice Shriver" your eyes flash. "Sure, I've met Eunice Shriver. Listen buddy boy, did you ever think of going to West Point? Or the U.S. Naval Academy? Well, if you do—and with your brains you could—well, if you do, you'll need more than grades. *Pull's* what you need. *Political* pull and your Mamma's got it now, buster. . . ."

Wait! you say. Command decision. One Coke for me and an early Manhattan for you, *thank you very much*. And then, like a scratched record, the story is skipping from Jack to Eunice Shriver, then back to Mrs. Feeney.

". . . Well, Our Friend, *Our Learned and Portly Friend* . . . she's actually asking me this in front of Mrs. Shriver, do you hear me? *In front of our next president's sister* . . ."

I forget the story—not that it matters. Even if the story isn't so funny—and even if it means, as I think we both sense, that you'll soon be through in that office—even so it's funny. You're funny. Your face is funny, and the story, the story's a balloon being blown up, and the balloon is your face going *foof* and *foof.* I've got the hiccups from laughing, and you, you've earned another drink. Then another record plops down. You grab my hand.

"Cha-cha time! Hear it? The natives are restless tonight!"

So we throw on "The Spicy Cha-Cha," then Harry Belafonte, mon, a wild bingo-bongo calypso so I can learn the savage rhythm, the fancy footwork, of us being micrometeorites on the outer-outer orbit of the Kennedys *but dot where you start, mon!* And then an even faster record plops down. It's the tintinnabulating, deafening "Mambo in Drums!"—faster because it's really a *war dance* we're doing, seething at Mrs. Feeney's crack about how working for JFK was the only Catholic thing you'd ever done. And there she is! It's Fatso out on her stoop, wondering what's all the noise about. You rip open the blinds.

"We show Fatso who's *Cath-o-leek.*"

"Mom!" I yell over the marimbas. "C'mon, what are you *doing?* Who cares about Mrs. Feeney?"

"Aww, doan be such a ch*ee*ken! Dance, mon! You wan' go buck-buck-buck through life?"

And the floor shaking and the Belgian crystal ringing in the china closet, the toppling live weight of you, a romping grown woman, ripe with the sweat breaking in stinging salt needles through your dress onto my burning palm. The door booms back. It's Dad.

"Julie! What in the *h* are you two doing?"

"Aww, loosen up, sailor! Have a drink! Join de native, mon!"

Let him glare, the old grouch! Upping the power, you give him your thousand-watt, I'm-stone-sober stare. "We're *dancing.* I'm showing Franko how to *dance.*"

So, egging me on, you and me, Julie, we turn it into a surprise party. Dancing and drawing right angles, we yell, "Okay, Volcanohead!" and "Ouch, what a grouch!"—pushing Pop over the hump until, with this crybaby wince, he actually starts laughing... laughing in that way which makes my balls itch as he slugs back his second retro-rocket martini.

But hey, just like in social studies, there's checks and balances in the family system of government. At supper later, we're the Three Bears, everybody in their bear chairs and the drinks all even-stevened. Happy? Why, I'm Garry Moore on *I've Got a Secret.* Keep the party rolling, that's my job. Yep, playing host, I'm asking Pop how's tricks at work. Then, to you moping over your dinner, so you won't get all quiet and beaten like I hate—

"So, hey mon!... *Mom!* Hey, de cheeken, she really-really *good.*"

• • •

BUT PEOPLE HAD OTHER REASONS FOR BEING SO EDGY.

People were really spooked that last year. Spooked bad, what with all the H-bomb tests and Colonel Gary Powers getting shot down in his U-2 spy plane and, scariest of all, that fat, liver-lipped nut Khrushchev banging his shoe at the UN, *"We will bury you."*

And fallout shelters. You'd even see them advertised in the *TV Guide*—$995 for this egg-shaped thing with a snorkel and, for entertainment, a pooper stuck smack in the middle of the living room. Well, that does it for you, Mamma. Dad and me are reading the Sunday funnies when you start flapping the *TV Guide*.

"Listen to this, *'Perfect for the kids as a second playhouse.'* They're all nuts! And what are we supposed to do, living six miles from Washington, D.C.? Dig up our backyard? Get a gun and threaten to shoot anybody who tries to get in? Because that's what the Cosgroves are doing." And staring at the *TV Guide*, you know. Shelter or no shelter, if the Big One falls, you'll never make it. Not in a million years.

On TV it was grim, shaved-headed Commie kids running lathes and pulling down steel bomb hatches. Well, the Commies won't bury us! At St. Stephen's they stage full-scale evacuations—early dismissal. Yeah, at 2:00 P.M., revving like huge diesel engines, the yellow air raid sirens start howling. Like crazed yellow bird lips, they wail over the far hills, booming over a thousand identical black-shingled roofs. Roofs which John Meher's Dad, Colonel Meher, says'll go up like grass huts in the atomic typhoon!

"AIR RAID! AIR RAID! Boom! Boom! Boom! *Eeee-yabba-dabba-doo!* . . ."

Like crazed bats, mobs of shrieking kids, stampede through the school doors! Cheering on the missiles! Waving on the Russian bombers, goggled guys in hairy yak-suits streaking through the mushroom clouds! Charging through the spring wind, whooping and laughing, I run the whole way home. And who do I see swimming in the front window with a look of total horror? Crashing through the front door, I run to the kitchen clock.

"2:14! Wow! Great time!"

"Time for *what?* To scare poor children half to death? No-body's go-ing to at-tack."

"Cheez, what are you, a *peacenik?*"

"I'm not a peacenik, I—I just *hate* and I *object* to all this hysteria. *And it won't ever happen.*"

Dad's not so sure, though. At supper, by way of explaining why we're not sinking $995 into some blast-proof septic tank, Dad gets all *intuo*. "Look, I've actually given it some thought. I've read several excellent articles on the subject. You laugh"—he shoots me a warning glance—"but if it comes, I'll pile dirt on the living room floor. That's right, dirt. Dirt's the perfect insulator. Six to twelve inches will do it."

"And then what?" you demand.

"Then we'll go under the house."

"Like worms, I suppose?"

"But Dad," I bust in, "who's gonna have time to haul all that dirt? Colonel Meher says we'll all be vaporized."

"Frank," fumes Dad with a look at you. "I'm sure no colonel said this, and I can assure you *there'll be time*. Don't listen to these Chicken Littles. That's the first public misconception—that the bomb'll just *fall out of nowhere*. That's nonsense. If it comes to that, we'll know in advance. *Days* in advance."

Smoke shoots at the ceiling. "Oh, please, don't insult the kid's intelligence, piling dirt on my good rug. If the bomb comes, I'll drag out the ladder. Then we can all bloody well sit out on the roof. And *clap*."

WELL, AFTER THE KENNEDY HUFF WITH MRS. FEENEY plus the Russians and maybe some other setbacks I don't even know about—well, you have another change of heart. Getting right with the world, you sign up as a school library volunteer, reading to the kids two afternoons a week. But even here there are certain, well, conditions. No, you'll only work with the little kids, you say, little kids being so much more appreciative and better behaved. But now I wonder. Was it because the kindergartners were better behaved? Or was it because they were still too young to judge you, as I was doing?

I remember our last vacation in Cape Cod. In the rec center, they had a little dance where you and Dad chaperoned like Ozzie and Harriet, and I had my first real crush on some girl named Carolyn Penrose, up with her family from Connecticut or some such place. But suddenly the next morning, after going on how proud and excited you were, suddenly you clutch me.

"You'll dump me. Oh, you won't know me, the circles you'll be moving in. Oh yes you will. I know you think I'm a big deal now—that we're big deals—but come on, kiddo, we're nothing. No, believe it, Frankie. We're just small fry."

And something *was* happening, if not to you, then certainly to me. So they wouldn't wake up and think they were bleeding to death, the fifth-grader girls all went to the auditorium to see that notorious film noir, *Menu-stration*. And even us boys, never told dick, even us boys had been warned—warned in the blandest terms possible—how our voices would be getting all gargly and hilarious, on account of our balls stretching out and these nasty fizzies called *hormones*.

But of all the catastrophes foretold—crueler than pimples or even that first splurt of nocturnal Vaseline—of all the scourges to come, nobody had said boo about the ultimate plague, *seeing*. No sir, after all these years of being a go-along gorp, suddenly on the bridge of your nose, they've set these massive new prescription glasses, half telescope, half microscope. Suddenly you're not a kid. No, you're a cyclops, a cyclops projecting a big lighted cone of vision boring like a nail right into the hot nougat center of your swelling boy brain!

Stopped me dead in my tracks sometimes, the world was suddenly so weird and warped and mirrored. I remember sneaking by the library window and seeing you inside, *you*, reading to the little kids. It's like a wavy one-way glass. Suddenly I can see you, a child among children squatting on the floor in your stocking feet, *Look, that's her, that's your own Mom*.

BUT THE LIBRARY wasn't your only change of heart. After years religiously sitting at home in bed with the Sunday paper, you start going with Dad and me—semiregularly—to Sunday mass.

My prayers are answered. You'll go to confession. Receive Communion. Not go to hell. That first Sunday, though, as you and Dad are getting dressed, I hear Dad fussing, and then I see why. Bad enough you're wearing long, black gloves, but here you've got your mink stole, and, worse than that, bare shoulders, sure to scandalize everybody. Inside the church, you dab your gloved finger in the holy water, then up you go, high heels echoing, *dok dok dok*. The pressure drops. Like a cat walking a freshly spread dinner table, you stalk past all our jewelry-less, makeup-less neighbors in their weepy black veils, sack dresses and Catholic flats. *Butting in line*, that's what you're doing, I realize. Butting when here, week after week, month after month, they've been kneeling and mumbling, beating their breasts and denying themselves. Lord, it's an eternity during the consecration of the bread and wine. You can't possibly kneel that long, not you. No, like the old ladies, you kneel half-assed, knees on the kneeler and butt on the pew. Worse, when everybody goes up to take Communion, all you do is sit, a holy reject, your soul melting in a guilty puddle. And all I can think is how I wish you'd just vanish. Just plain disappear.

• • •

I GUESS IT DIDN'T WORK, YOUR LAST HALFHEARTED EFFORT TO BE REINSTATED OR WHATEVER. No, whatever it was, it failed and you shut down with the sleeping sickness.

I guess I first noticed your chronic naps that last summer, around the time your rich Uncle Stephen dropped dead. Not that we ever saw Uncle Stephen. C'mon, we almost never saw him, but this only made Uncle Stephen all the more enormous, especially because he was so loaded. You said he was a second father to you, and if you believed it, I guess that it was true, your real father being long dead. Still, if Uncle Stephen was such a big deal, then how come we never saw him or his big house down in Florida? It was one of those big white hacienda Cesar Romero places that we'd see in the movies, and right in the theater you'd grab me, *Look that's just like Stephen's house.* Yeah, yeah. Still, even if he never invited us, he sent me a crisp ten-dollar bill every Christmas! Of course, it went right in the bank, but I appreciated his trying. At least he wasn't the kind of old creep who sent U.S. Savings Bonds.

Uncle Stephen died during the summer, and that was rough for you. But it really wasn't until school started, once life returned to some schedule, that I truly came to dread your endless naps. Getting home from school that last fall, I'd slam the door hard, then listen for signs of life. Nothing. Upstairs, always the same answer. Always the locked door and the radio buzzing inside like a loose fly.

"Mommm—maa . . ."

First, trying to be cute—*unworried*—I work the puppy ploy, scritch-scritch-scritch. Then, waiting a good minute, disguising my anger, I throw in the whimpers. Finally, I lose all patience.

"Mom!"

I twist the knob, then do the blackboard squeak, dragging my greasy palm down the slick paint. When this fails, I do a quick bongo, I cup my mouth and call in my ghoul voice.

"Maaaooommm . . . are you a s l e e p? *Huuuuuh?*"

Nothing. Nothing but my heart and the whorling seashell sound as I smush my ear against the cool wood. Then I smell it oozing under the door . . . *cigarette smoke.* I start banging.

"Mom! You hear me, so *up!* You open this door right now!"

"I'm sleeping, damnit! I have a right to sleep, now go!"

"Quit being so lazy! Do you hear me? You're nothing but a lazy bum!"

Well, that's it! I slam the front door, then Zorro leap off the porch.

"Hey."

"Hey."

Just some neighborhood kids, Jimmy Ridell and Billy Feeney all acting like they don't see—like people can't see the curtains pulled, or how at five o'clock they'll whisk open again. Oh yeah. Come five o'clock, you're ripping your hair out, smearing on lipstick, then running down the stairs, setting out Dad's salted peanuts and cracking ice for *martooney* time.

But hey, I don't blow the whistle on you, not me. No, after school one day, shut out as usual, I'm in front, out in the street with all the neighborhood kids, playing whiffle ball, running from the popsicle stick first to the skinny tree to the phone pole, then home, tromping on the crushed tomato can. Look, I totally stink at baseball, but this isn't what you'd call a serious game. Really, it's more a baseball form of hanging around, where little kids and girls, and even I, can play. Must be fifty kids, all arguing and whooping it up, when Jimmy Quist cries out.

"Look! A sundae with a cherry on top!"

Cop car, he means. Now this is a rare big deal on Corregidor. Pulling up, two cops give a short *vrrrreennne* of the siren, the car instantly surrounded by jabbering, wide-eyed kids hollering, "Hey, what happened? Hey, can you run the siren again?" Nobody dreams they're here on account of us. But sure enough the cop driving says.

"Hey, gang, look, we really hate to break things up, but this is a public street and we just had a complaint."

"Complaint?" gogs Peter Conway. Peter's thirteen and an altar boy. "Sir, this is Corregidor! You sure you got the right street?"

A front door slams. It's Mrs. Feeney! And, fat as she is, she's bagging it, boy, scared there's been an accident! And she's just the first! All down Corregidor doors are slamming, Mrs. Feeney, then two, then three, then ten other Moms, all asking each other, "What's happened? Who called? I didn't call, did you?"

"It's okay," cries Mrs. Feeney, waving her arms, "nobody's hurt!" But as soon as Mrs. Feeney realizes this, she's arguing with the cops, arms on her hips, mountainous in her blue muumuu embroidered in fake bamboo that says GUAM. She hollers to the other women, "They say our kids can't play ball in the street! Can you believe this? Somebody called the police! On our own kids! The *police!*"

All us kids cheer! See, Major Feeney's a lawyer, U.S. *Marine* lawyer, so she's not afraid of any cops. Boy, have they barked up the wrong tree. Between Mrs. Feeney and the others, they're getting an earful, Mrs. Feeney barreling on, "*Yes,* I understand the law. Look, officer, my husband's a lawyer but come *on.* Five minutes we've been out here, and have you even *seen* a car? No sir, you have not. Not *one.*"

"And anyway," says Mrs. Kearny, pushing in, "this is *our* street. It's not some big state thoroughfare—"

"—Wait, wait," breaks in Mrs. Geisman. "Who complained, officer? We've got a right to know."

Up goes his arm. The cop's pointing straight at our house! And at that same second, the tip of your curtain falls. Well, Mrs. Feeney takes off.

"We see you hiding up there, Julie Dougherty!"

Wading across the street, lardbutt lumbers up our lawn, then stands back, craning under your window box, "Let the *Law* do your dirty work, huh! Get down here this minute, you sneak! How dare you call the cops on our kids!"

Surrounded! Women crowded under your window! Slapping at the front door and jamming the doorbell! In all the excitement nobody sees me frozen there in the middle of the street. Then the shutter heaves up. Out thrusts your head, an angry scrawl of dark sleep hair yelling down at Mrs. Feeney.

"You're damned right I called! And why not? I've got my rights, all day long with this ridiculous racket and the playground not two blocks away! You want a child run over?"

"Sure, lecture us on safety, Sleeping Beauty!" Mrs. Feeney totters back shading her eyes. "And what's *your* kid doing while you're sawing logs up there at this hour!"

"I'm *sick,* damnit."

"Well, you said a mouthful there! Pull yourself together, lady."

"The flu! That's the *flu,* Fatso. You don't see my kid out in the street! Where do you people think this is—*Harlem?"*

"But look!" hollers Beth Foster. "Frank's right here!"

Suddenly, all the kids are hollering and pointing at me as Mrs. Feeney crows, "So whose kid is that, *Harlem.* Huh, Miss Priss? So whose kid is that?"

TEMPORARILY IT WAS BAD, but it woulda blown over if you'd had a chance—if people'd had more time to cool off and Dad and me coulda worked the toaster diplomacy. But no, the elves throw you a White Christmas in September. One morning after the blowup with the cops, Dad looks out into early blue darkness and stops dead. Snow?

Toilet paper.

Punks! They've thrown us a twenty- or thirty-roller! Blowing paper is trailing off the trees and telephone wires, and the Bird!—man, the Bird is *wiped*, one giant wad of squishy pink.

Not wanting Mom and me to see it, Dad's tearing around in his robe and slippers, scooping it up when I storm out into this winter wonderland of blowing rags and snowballs . . . *Punks!* Is there anything more senseless and terrifying than teenage boys before you are one? It's a massacre. Looking around I can't even comprehend the meanness. I mean, my Mom never even called the cops on *them,* but oh no, the pillagers gotta get their mitts into it, for the sick satisfaction! Dad's madder than I am. He hands me a grocery bag.

"Look," he says, "I'm sorry you had to see this, but let's get busy." He looks at me hard. "Well, we don't want your mother seeing this, do we?"

Ghhh! Nasty wet, it's coming up in thick wet hanks, on top of which the sickos probably wiped themselves with it. Hell, they're probably watching right now, getting their sick yuks off Dad doing jump shots, trying to get it off the electric wires.

"Daddy, stop it," I hiss. "Don't you know they're watching?"

"Inside."

"But why? What did I do?"

But it's not me he's mad at. It's like when the hornets got him, the way Dad's wheezing and snorting. And running over, I see it—two flat tires and BITCH BOAT scrawled in white shoe polish across the back window of the Bird. And what good does it do, trying to protect you? Upstairs, you're weeping mad. Just mortified, clutching me.

"Sweetie, I'm sorry! I was so stupid—God, I never meant to bring this on you."

"Aww, stop it, Julie," says Dad. "It happened. You were within your rights." Dad looks at me. "Well, what was your mother gonna do? Stand by and watch some kid get hit by a car?"

And calming us down, Dad explains how it can't last. Taking the long view, Dad's saying how, in time, these hoodlum dopes'll all grow up, and as for the rest, it won't even register a blip on our screen. And in the long view, the American view, we just know Dad's right. Given the time and the good breaks, you and me, Julie, we just know Dad'll make a success of himself. Trade in. Buy up. Move. And in the long view, as Dad describes it, I can see Mrs. Feeney and all that bunch stuck here on Corregidor, stuck like some crummy little grade which seems the whole world until you pass it. And ordinarily in life, as I've already figured out, that's the rule ... *No matter what, you always always pass.*

Not that you don't sweat flunking out, scared to death of French or long division. In the seventh grade you're already sweating the eighth, then high school! Latin! trigonometry! And no wonder, with older kids and grown-ups always trying to scare you, *Oh but this stuff is different. Oh man this stuff is really hard!* But, come on, so maybe Dad's business does go bust—so what? Dad's still got his hands and his tools, and there's always our ultimate Ace, your Uncle Stephen. And if the Big One comes, *we pile dirt on the rug but we survive.* And being a kid, being alive since I was born and not even close to stopped growing, with air to breathe and a whole future ballooning out like a cock to fit me, *I just know all this.*

Still, for the first time, I'm not sure about you, Mamma. For a while, in almost a weird kind of requiem, the kids stop playing ball and the naps stop. Of course, you'd never admit it, but in a way I think you really miss the kids playing ball. Peeping through the drawn blinds, secretly you miss the noise, the life, but instead you crow, "Well, you don't see them playing ball now, do you? At least the Law made some impression."

A year ago, even a few months ago, I wouldn't have questioned your stubbornness, but now I'm angry and embarrassed. Dad, too. As it drags on, Dad's completely exasperated with you, carrying on some feud you can't possibly win. "Julie, the *Law's* beside the point! The jury's *out there!*"

In these last few twilight weeks, in my own toaster diplomacy way, I guess I was trying to fix things, mainly by playing with the Corregidor kids. And by then kids were the only channel of communication open to us. The fix-it business was sure dead. At supper we never hear a knock, except for poor Mr. Decker, a drunk who doesn't count anyway. So for better or worse, I'm your emissary and it's still pretty touchy. "Look," says Timmy Reece, "My Mom says we're not supposed to be mean to you just because of how your Mom is." *No offense your Mom's a jerk,* in other words. Actually, Timmy Reece is being pretty nice, relaying without prejudice an adult verdict. Really, a *Catholic* verdict—Catholic like *The Catholic Standard,* whose inquisitional movie index, The Legion of Decency, gave even Doris Day's *Pillow Talk* a big fat *C* for "Condemned." Well, Catholics had standards back then. Corregidor had standards and their standards, I can tell you, left ours feeling pretty dubious.

Oh, it takes a couple of weeks but then the silent treatment really starts getting to you. Especially when with my *immunity,* I can walk across the street, right into the enemy camp. No, you don't want me ostracized. (I think it's fair to say it killed you, dragging me into this Cold War.) Still, my sudden relative popularity can't help but make you feel, well, dubious. And who were you now? I wondered. Better the old scheming and sarcasm than this new feebleness following me around the house.

"Honey, if you're mad at me, just say so. But for God's sake, please quit punishing me. Lately, you play with the kids across the street more than you ever did."

"They're my friends, and I'll play wherever I want! So leave me alone!"

Stomping up to my room, I slam the door. Then at your faint knock I pounce.

"HEY, ARE YOU DEAF? I'M TAKING A NAP."

"Honey,"

"CAN'T YOU UNDERSTAND ENGLISH? I'M SLEEPING."

How can God stand it to lock anybody in hell? I wonder. It's worse than leaving a puppy to whimper in the basement, but still it's for your own good, I think. And that's the whole idea of hell and purgatory, right? You sweat and simmer until you pay your bills. But then the purgatory business goes on too long. What's wrong with you? You're the mother! Bust in! yell! slap me! Something's sucking all the air out of the room, or maybe I fall asleep. But getting up finally, figuring you've left, I open the door and there you are, wedged in a heap in the corner, leaking and trembling like even your own body's deserted you. Well, I bust into tears, hugging you all suffocated.

"Mom, I'm sorry! I *am*, okay, *but Mom you gotta learn . . .*"

Well, I'd—we'd—both get to feeling bad like this, but then I'd take the opposite view, that you'd purposely broken yourself so you could be fixed. That's right, fixed. And if that was the idea, it worked—partly. The naps stopped, you toned down your dressing (a little), then went back to your library job, reading to the kindergartners. Still, it wore you out, carrying on this stupid feud. And even if it was killing you, you couldn't let Mrs. Feeney and the whiffle-ballers think they had you cowed—no ma'am.

Every time you saw Mrs. Feeney it seemed you had to go out and show the flag. In the way two cats will hump and hiss, you'd both freeze, each waiting before you stretched your full five-ten, then stalked to the car. I think I can see their predicament fairly objectively now, the neighbors, I mean. They weren't bad people. At any rate nobody in the neighborhood had the stomach to watch you dig yourself in any deeper, least of all Mrs. Feeney. Even then I could feel her wanting to walk across the street to end it, but how could she when you weren't ready? No, Julie, what you were asking Mrs. Feeney for, I think, was patience, for the small but finally enormous gift of patience.

I know for a fact Mrs. Feeney wanted to end it, because one day Mrs. Feeney herself called me over, so huge, I saw, that the balls of her feet nearly busted out the sides of her scuffed weejuns. Being military, Mrs. Feeney was one of these *repeater* adults—the type who always said everything twice, especially when she was feeling emphatic about being right, which was her nature. And being marines on top of being Catholic, and especially on account of the Semper Fi and defending the weak—well, Mrs. Feeney had tougher standards than anybody on the Rock. "Hey, what's wrong with you two boys!" she said once, collaring two kids who were beating the crap out of her Brendan. Two on one. That wasn't the marine or Catholic way. So Mrs. Feeney had them square off one-on-one while she reffed. And there as she watched, first one kid, then the other, beat poor Brendan to a pulp.

"Sweetheart, listen to me," says Mrs. Feeney getting her Irish up. "This has gone far enough, but first understand one thing. Because I won't speak against your mother, and *I absolutely do not, and I forbid you to—*"

But this is just Mrs. Feeney's righteous excitability talking. Anyhow, she can see from my face that this is the wrong approach, so she backpedals, "Well, I can't very well apologize. And not out of pride. No, not out of pride, *no—*" She starts again, "Honey, I know how hard this is for you, but it's for your Mom and me to settle—ourselves. What I mean is, it's not your fault. Absolutely it's not your fault. No, don't you ever think that, honey."

The toes of her weejuns are really pushing out now, under the strain. And not just her big toes, but the painful blue squiggles in her freckled white ankles, the pressure, you said, from all those babies plus four duty stations and all that cheap food they eat, what with so many mouths. "I mean, I'm truly sorry—*sorry*—you heard it. With the police. And I never saw you! Nobody did, Frankie. Not until the very end we didn't, honey. Look, I'm not saying I wasn't mad. Oh, I was hot. And yes, maybe I did get carried away, but I've prayed. Oh, I've thought and prayed for days about it. And you know I'm not a meanie, right? Well right, honey!"

"I know." My voice gets all high. "*I know that.*"

"No, no, don't apologize. Not to *me.*" Mrs. Feeney looks up at your window, afraid you'll see and thunder out. "I'm just telling you this so you won't feel bad. Please, please don't feel bad. And you remember, Frank Dougherty, *we like you. Everybody on this whole street likes you.*"

Mrs. Feeney starts backing off. I feel like a rabid raccoon.

"And our door's always open, honey. Day or night. Open for your Mom, too. When she's ready *it's open*. And I pray it'll pass. You can tell your Mom that from me. And I mean that in friendship. *Spiritual friendship*, because honey, it'll pass. I know it'll pass."

BUT MRS. FEENEY SAYING IT WOULD PASS, well, this only meant in a way, in a jinxed way, that it wouldn't pass. And sure enough, not a week later, around five one morning, you wake up with a sharp pain in your navel. And, sleek as a suture, the pain only travels, threading through your stomach, deep into your groin, where you clutch it to you like a baby and your face freezes white.

A red-hot fishhook. That's how you say it feels when I find you curled up in your bed, with Dad sitting beside you, trying to play it all nonchalant. Still, from the way you're curled up and your short breaths, I know it's bad.

"An ulcer," you hiss to Dad. "Bet it's an ulcer from all this mess out here." Corregidor, you mean.

"Do you feel it there, Mom?" Squatting, I'm feeling around my groin, nudging a piece of squiggling gut. "It's right there?"

"Frank." Shooting me a don't-be-filthy look, Dad rousts me out. "Privacy here, huh? I'm calling the doctor."

And when Dad returns ten minutes later, he's all super relieved. He's found his One Little Thing. Just off the phone with the doc, he heads me off in the hall rolling his eyes, "Oboy, I thought so. Yep, it's her appendix. Which just may mean"—he gets all heh-heh—"a little, well, *a little trip to the hospital.* Yep, it just might mean an op-er-ation. But minor. It's really pretty minor." With his finger, Dad pokes my groin, pokes me in this electric, like, *gristle* place. "There. That's the place."

That's the place? But that's a horrible place. "But, Daddy, so they gotta cut her open? There?"

"Per-haps. But it's a completely common procedure."

"But"—feeling the place, which in fact is *attached to my balls*—"but, Daddy, listen."

"I *am* listening—"

"—but if she's—if she's gotta—so, shouldn't we go right now to the 'mergency?"

"Absolutely not. Your mother has no big temperature. There's no big emergency. And Frank, no spreading fear through the camp, okay? You know how your mother is. And you're the absolute worst at getting her upset."

But my mind keeps delaying, objecting. "But Daddy, what's an appendix? I don't even know what one is."

It's like sex, I feel totally embarrassed, but Dad only beams. "Well, that's the good part, Frank. *It's nothing.* I'm not kidding. The appendix is probably the only thing in the human body that serves absolutely no purpose—none. In fact, you know what? She's better off *without it!*"

My crossed legs tighten. I start rocking over the place. "*Better!* So why don't they take out everybody's appendix, *better!*"

"Well," he thinks, "because of the expense. And in fact—in fact, with the astronauts, if I'm not mistaken, they do take them out, and you can see why." His nose crinkles up with the joke. "Kinda hard finding doctors up there!"

I stare at him.

"Frank, it's a useless flap of skin. Like a worm. In fact, if I'm not mistaken, scientists say it's a vestigial bird crop or something." Dad's on a roll now. "You know, from when we were down on our *yawrs,* in the Alley Oop period, eating unhulled nuts and acorns. Essentially, it's a shriveled-up gizzard."

But what do we know? I think. Us or fat Dr. Cleavis wanting twenty bucks when Dad and me will fix your whole TV good as new for nothing! And what's the use in denying it? Outside later, as Dad's helping you to the car, shuffling like you're having a baby, well, right away I can see how bad it is. Everybody on Corregidor sees, the kids going to school and the Dads off to work and the women all saying their good-byes. What tips them all off? I wonder. Because suddenly, kids are craning up like prairie dogs, and the grown-ups, they're turning around, all shocked and embarrassed. *C'mon, it's not all that bad! God, haven't you people ever seen a sick lady before?*

WELL, NEWS TRAVELS. Not three weeks after she was storming the Alamo with the whiffle-ball lynchers, here's Mrs. Feeney at the door, peeping through the narrow window slat. Guilty as all hell, too. "Frank, honey, is everything all right?"

But no sooner do I get rid of her, talking up the Open Door Policy and asking did I get any breakfast, than the phone rings—Mrs. Kearny, naturally all curious, so I torture her too, "Aww, it's no big deal. Dad thinks it's just a stomach bug . . . *but hey, thanks, Mrs. Kearny. Thanks for thinking about us.*"

Meanwhile, I've pulled the *A* volume of the *World Book*, which supports what Dad said about the appendix being a wormy thorn of an organ forking off the large intestine. But then reading along, I see, *"It is very important that no laxatives or purgatives, such as castor oil, be given—"* And, man, I jump! *Wait, he gave her aspirin!* . . . But meanwhile, steering the book around, studying the two diagrams, I notice how the appendix, if you really look, well, actually it's . . . *it's like a dick between two balls.* Completely. And especially in the blown-up, boner version, *b. The infected state,* which—wham—the sight of it strikes the penile nerve splice to my brain! Which it, the penile splice, tells me to pull the *B* volume and see what they've got written up on *bosoms.* Which, of course, there's nothing, but even so it's fantastically exciting, knowing how the writer already read my dirty mind! Like I suppose that *World Book* writer is dumb enough to do a big *boner* spread on *bosoms* like on *Bolivia!* Oh, sure, kid, a giant *World Book of Bosoms* with pictures and facts about how big they can get in sq. mi., like that big seed-calendar blonde leaning over her hoe, *So how do you like my prize pun-kins.*

And look everybody, it's a boy! Stretching out into that purple-headed infected state, practically squeaking he's so hard, it's a wicked hot bone thumping against my leg! And unzipping my fly, hairless and bent, about the girth of one of those fat school pencils, he just pogos out *Hey kids, it's Mr. Pokey and he's got a big show for you today!* And bowing him back to your navel, you stroke him along, thinking, *bosoms bosoms bosoms* . . . flick-flick-flick-a-dick . . . hairless little boy hands working over my sucking white belly and the knobber-end squeezed out like a sore thumb, *flick-flick-flick. Flicker-rick-dick-dick* . . .

But there's plenty more to imagine here than *bosoms.* Bosoms are only the bait, the focusing object, like the dial the hypnotist swings before your eyes, *flick-flick-flick.* The light is red against my eyelids, the blood is hot against my ears, *because what if she dies?* But failing to imagine this, kid, instead, you picture popped-out, baby-sucking bosoms and *life,* which, when you're boned-out like Mr. Pokey now, is beyond doubt. Well, okay. Nothing comes out yet—no sap, I mean—but even so it *burns.* Boy, it burns good, and your head rocks back, and like a sheet in the wind, in flames the darkness falls through you, hurtling down into this hard, unquenchable coal where you aren't little anymore and you *are* big, too. Yeah you are too big, kid, and in here yours is the only will in force. But *guilt?* Nope, not yet! No, this solipsism is so new there isn't even a word for this hot, jetting amnesia that you've discovered like your own soul as a way to forget *Appendix, Peritonitis, Rupture* and all these other *Sees* scaring you half to death.

Because in here, inside the egg of beating your meat, there's nobody sick or unforgiven, and even if your halo is more a lamp shade, in here people *love* you, kid! In here, girls are fussing over you. Pretty, big-mounded girls with creamy lipstick are touching you, they're giggling and asking dirty questions until—real fast, burning like a match—this spurting life flares up, then dies again, but not *him!* Not that red-hot pistol and star of the show, Mr. Pokey! Nope, no sooner does the burning stop than ol' Poke is ready again! and again! *and again after that!* Why, any grown man, he'd *pass out!* Why, he'd spring a nosebleed, but not you! No sir, kiddo, at this age you defy gravity! Why, at this age you're a mighty ant lifting a hundred times his own weight, doing it five! ten! fifteen times! . . . and that's *just for starters!*

Whump.

The car door!

Pokey! Down boy! Fan him! beg him! plead him down! zip! Bounding up, I tear downstairs, then outside to where Dad is helping you in from the doctor's, saying in his forced-cheery voice, "*Everything's fine.* Now come in and I'll tell you what's going on . . ."

"BUT WHY do I gotta spend the night at Angelene's?"

"But you like it at Angelene's," you say. Angelene's the divorced Texan lady around the corner who I mentioned, the one that lives there with her Mom and her two girls, Poo and Kukie.

"And I can't come to the hospital?"

"Not at your age you can't."

"That stinks!"

"Well, I agree but I won't be there long."

Dad's downstairs all hush-hush on the telephone. You and me, meanwhile, we're up in your room packing. "Check-in is at noon," you say, like it's a hotel.

"But Mom, why do I gotta stay at Angelene's? Dad'll be home tonight."

"Yes, but at what hour? Now, no more about it. And you stay down at Angelene's, too. I don't want you roaming back up here, telling the neighbors all about me."

"But Mom, you know they're gonna ask."

"Who asked?"

"Well, nobody—yet. But you know they will."

"So let them, so concerned about me. It's none of their damned business."

It's a sunny day. A perfect day. I know because I can still feel my one eye closed in the sun, and the sun hot on my cheek, the same sun coaxing the musty leather smell out of your alligator bag with all the useless compartments and silken cords that you have neither the patience nor the dexterity to tie. Even at this distance, the strong sunlight powerfully magnifies sight. In the brilliant sun I can see fine dust blowing in currents, the dust like swarms of hungry minnows, gobbling at you, swirling and tunneling through the air. At this moment, I don't at all see myself as a child—no, I feel almost elevatedly calm and mature. Flipping one shoe, I see myself as a calm, martial figure here to steady you, camouflaged in one of those bright, boisterously new outfits that nervous travelers wear when they fly.

"Julie," calls Dad. "C'mon kiddo, we gotta go in twenty minutes."

You sigh. Hunched over the hurt place, you lay your things out like little parachutes, draping, then folding them, tweaking the pleats, then gently draping them in the bag—but wait. No, no, no. For the second time, you pull out everything, then as quickly lose your place again, a long ash dripping from your cigarette. Plop. The ash falls on the floor and you see it. Obviously you do, but you don't bother with it, you can't, and I know better than to say a word. And so, laboriously, the packing resumes . . . panties and hankies, your best "guest" robe. Impossibly, for someone having abdominal surgery, there is even a rubbery girdle, yet with all the astounding literalness of shock I don't remember this seeming ridiculous or touching but somehow profoundly "true"—true, I mean, in an adult way, since obviously a lady needed to be prepared with her lady things. No, what worries me then, I think, isn't so much what you take as how you pack, with all the blind instinct of a bird making a nest.

Dad pokes his head in.

"Hey, they're gonna get you for overweight, kid."

Gamely you try to straighten up for him but can't. "And how do we pay for all this? The hospital bills will sure clip our wings."

"We'll fly. We'll do lots of things."

But Dad's bluster only has the reverse effect—it embarrasses us. As he leaves, you lose your place again. Kneading the same scarf, you panic. Like a broken squeeze toy, your voice gets all high and breathy, "Frank, I'm"— your eyes pinch together—"I'm *really really*—"

"—Mom, you'll be *fine.*" I motion at your stomach. "It's not—it didn't?"

"No—" You make a fist over the spot.

"Well," I bluff, "that's my exact point." But wait, just what is my point? I get squeaky myself. "Hey, you think I'd ever let anything happen to you? Well, *do you?*"

BUT I'M NOT the only one who sees you need bucking up. Leaning in the car with the red, teased-up, hot-tamale hair, Angelene gets purposely un-grammatical, the better to fortify you with Texas grit.

"And I *mean* it, Julie D. Frank's here with us, so don't you worry. Not 'bout *nuthin'*—"

"If you say so, okay, okay. *And thanks, Doctor Miss.*"

"Doctor Miss" was your mock deferential for Miss Dr. Pettinelle—a doctor even though, as I mentioned, she had the little *d* branded on her, one of the scarlet Sisters of Mary Magdalene. Other than your widow friend Huta Lunt—Huta the homewrecker—Angelene was the only adult I was ever allowed to address by first name. And Angelene was an actual doctor, a lady Ph.D. research agronomist at the USDA—the office of bug-resistant, hi-growth corn species or something like that. Anyhow, the "Dr." title was only for work, Angelene said—that and the mail and the phone book so certain "peckerwoods" wouldn't bug her. "Mrs.," on the other hand, well, that was a title Angelene couldn't abide. Why, even living with her two girls Angelene hated it. "Miss Pettinelle, please," she'd insist. Like she needed "Mrs." to protect her from wolves like her boozer runaround former husband! Like she cared about those people who, hearing "Miss" and seeing an older, obviously highly attractive woman, would instantly take her for a banshee reject or a homewrecker, or both! "Who was that?" you asked Angelene once when some man knocked at her door. Angelene rolled her eyes. "Nuthin but a dang pest with a pest question." And, crinkling her lip, Angelene would crack up, showing that gap between her two front teeth that she was too proud to let her banker Daddy get fixed for her. And why? *"Cause I always lakked mysef."*

The Gap. At the pool, Angelene even embarrassed me the way she'd spit water through it, emitting a long, powerful jet split like a stream of pee. Watermelon seeds got stuck in it. Once at a party Angelene caught me staring as she moved her tongue over her big teeth. She made a face. Fixing me in her eyes, she pried up her lip, picked the seed out like a broken filling, then plinked it on her china plate. "Wail, what'r you cryin about? That was lady-like. Ya didn't see me *spit* it, now, did ya?" Angelene was always pulling people's chains like that. Mom said she'd once been a debutante.

Another thing I'll say about Angelene. In her prime then at thirty-five or so, she sure had one serious, solid behind on her. Legs, too. Even as you're leaving for the hospital, I can't help but notice Angelene's slow, solid thrusts up the steps to her little house—her house way up on the "butte," as she calls it. But back then it wasn't just Angelene's butt or her stout calves that kneaded as she walked that got her noticed. "Man, that Angelene is *stacked*," said Stevie Wolper. *Stacked!* I'd never heard that word. Why, it was so super *ballooniary* that Mr. Pokey and me had to go home and beat off to four prime! four prime because the prime was super perfectitude, and four was my lucky number . . . *stacked! stacked! stacked!* Angelene, on the other hand, had a more world-weary view of all this. "Actually, it's called *dee-vorced*," she once explained to me, giving me her shrewd been-walked-out-on eye—the eye and this sorta *sorghum* thing she does with her tongue, same as she'd feel for a stuck seed. No, Angelene had a definite view on life, and she wasn't afraid to share it with a kid, and a horned-out boy kid at that.

Well, Angelene's mother Nellie—*"Nellie Belle"* we call her, after Roy Rogers's famous jeep—Nellie Belle also lived with Angelene and the two girls. Nellie Belle was another howdy type, and she was huge—well, fat—with this bouffant hair dyed taffy, which she gets "done" three times a week along with her nails, which must be two inches long and orange when they're not screaming peach. Nellie's got a brand new Cadillac de Ville and this de-nutted, sumo-sized angora tomcat named Spiffy. Spoiled rotten, of course. Cat's so fat and lazy you'd think he's stuffed—at least until he sees Nellie Belle chugging toward him. Oh shit! says Spiffy. She's brandishing the dreaded dingleberry brush!

But the craziest thing is, Spiffy's got this thing called feline asthma. Which is why you always see Angelene and Nellie Belle smoking out on the porch, for a *cat!* Even when it's freezing, they're both out there puffing away. And not—in Angelene's case—to troll for husbands, no matter what her pecker-wood neighbors may say.

Still, Angelene's a real hawk, perched up on the butte as you and Dad finally say good-bye to me and drive off. Well, as the T-Bird turns the corner, feeling dumped and powerless, I see a pile of fresh dogshit. Dropped by the curb! *As a sign from God!*

Gssshhh.

Feeling sick, I grind my heel in it, thinking this magic mumbo about keeping the shit off you by seeing that it finds my heel first. When Angelene startles me.

"Hey, there's fudge up here. Nellie Belle made a whole big plate, y'know."

Fudge? "Oh hey, do you know what?" I say, switching (around Angelene) more to my Maryland hick self. "Phew, I think I just stepped in dog-doody."

"Oh, did yewww?" Flicking ashes over her shoulder. "Well, walk it off good, but then you come on up here, Stinky. And no moping, y'hear?"

NOPE, NO MOPING AT ANGELENE'S. Still, as an all-ladies house, it's complicated. Complicated as much for the bed and bathroom arrangements as for the furniture, which is totally impractical and unboy-proofed.

Inside, it's like the Ponderosa, with all these bright, brittle, Mexican things. Tall, spindly worm-eaten chairs you don't dare try to sit in, bright serape rugs more slippery than banana peels, plus this loose-boarded, worm-eaten dinner table—supposedly some priceless antique that Jim Bowie probably died on, which groans and creaks ominously as I saw at my bloody steak. They're just waiting for me to topple my crystal water goblet, but surprise. Instead, it's one of their old Indian mud plates—yeah, on my second helping of potato salad, smash! Nellie Belle doesn't care. In her puff-sleeved muumuu and antelope squaw boots, she just guffaws.

"Aww heck, Frankie, fer-get it! They cost about a *dime* down there, in Juarez. Heck, we never break nuthin here nohow. I mean, it's *refreshin* to see something broke for once, buncha sissy ol' girls."

Nellie Belle's real cool about it, but not bossy thirteen-year-old Poo. Poo throws herself a regular hissy fit, plumping out her training bra like we're all impressed with these two Hershey's Kisses she's got. Heck, that's a bra? With the little pink rosebud in the middle. Hell, when I first saw that thing, I asked Poo was it two she had, or three?

"Oh, stopit," hisses Poo to Nellie Belle. "Why be polite when he's just clumsy! He already broke the chair. Can't you be more careful, you little oaf?"

I glare back at her. "The chair's just *cracked*, okay? Spot of Elmer's glue. I'll fix it in ten minutes."

"Poo, hush," scolds Angelene. "Frank's our *guest*, young lady. Anyhow, I don't care about any furniture, goll-lee."

Squinting at the end of the table on his special stool, fat as a buddha, the regular guy of the house, Spiffy, is yowling as usual for more chow. Then, behind us, the canaries go off again, lemon wings beating against the wire bars.

"Birds, I hate 'em!" Silver Indian bracelets jangling, Nellie Belle pretends to swat at the cage. "Simmer down, you two dumb tweets! Only reason we have 'em is to keep Spif amused. Thass right. *They're like cat TV!*" And flapping her muumuu, all square dancy, Nellie Belle starts guffawing like she does when she gets tickled. But this embarrasses the hell out of Poo and eight-year-old Kukie, who both moan and roll their eyes, "Fuuu-dge." That's their name for Nellie Belle. "Fudge, don't be a nut!"

"Ohhhh, so serious," Fudge sasses back. She points at me. "Now him, *he's* serious."

"Um-hum," agrees Angelene, wiping her mouth, "Now, Frank, don't be so serious 'cause I'm telling you, your Mom's gonna be fine. Jus' fine."

Nellie flaps her big arms. "But he's always serious."

"*Him?*" Poo can't stand it. "Frank's the biggest goofball in the whole neighborhood."

"Oh yes, he is serious," insists Nellie Belle. "I always noticed that about him. I've seen that from what Frank says and those big words he uses. And I'll tell you what, Frank—and you can take this or don't from an old lady— but being serious won't get you nuthin in life, nuthin. Honey, you got yer whole life to be serious."

"Oh, come on, Fudge," poohs Poo. "What makes him so serious?"

"Cause he is."

"Oh, please."

Feeling picked on, I burst out with my mouth half full, "Hooth thsrr-ious?"

"God." Poo turns away, her dark bangs slapping. "Just look how he *eats*, serious."

"Dees-gusting," parrots Kukie. "Close your mouth."

"No, no," counters Angelene, squinting. "Frank is a serious boy. Very serious. But, see, Frank, in this house we're all *optimists*."

"You mean the Optimists club?" I ask.

"No, I mean who we are. Ab-sol-utely. Well, come on. Way down deep, you're an optimist aren't you? Your Mom sure is."

I look at Angelene like she's crazy. "My Mom? An optimist?"

"Well, sure she is. She looks at the bright side, always has. What, you mean you don't know that?"

"No, I don't know that." I feel insulted.

"Oh, come on. Don't you think so? Then why do you think she pushed your Dad into goin into business for hissef if she's not an optimist? And why do you think she dresses the way she does? Or has that nice car if she's not optimistic?"

"And worries about money," I counter. "And calls the cops on the kids and gets us in trouble with everybody on the street. That's sure optimistic."

"Well, that was unfortunate, that mess up there, but your Mom had a right. Anyhow, I'll tell you something, and don't you go repeatin' it, neither. They're just jealous of your mother up there. They got their noses out of joint 'cause your Mom has class and aspirations and 'cause she always speaks her mind. But again—and you hear me now—that's her optimism talkin."

Poo butts in. "And that's why you break plates, Frank." Poo's eyes blaze with this formulation. "Because you're the opposite—you're *pessimistic*."

I about knock my glass over, I shoot up so fast. "Hey, I didn't pull a jinx on my Mom with your stupid plate! You shut up!"

Poo's triumphant. "But who said jinxed? *You did*. Which only proves it— *pessimist*."

Boom. Nellie Belle's big hand smacks the table. "And thass enough outta the both of you, cain't have a nice civilized family discussion! And, boy, don't you *ever* say 'shut up' again! Not in this house! Not to any young lady! And specially not to my granddaughter!"

REALLY SPOOKS ME, Poo pointing out that busted plate and what it says about me. And I can't help it. Walking by the bathroom later, I see Ange- lene's bra slung over the shower curtain. Two big nose cones. Talk about Boy TV . . . *stacked! stacked! stacked!* And not only are they way bigger than yours, Mamma, but even you'll admit—actually, delight in—Angelene's being bet- ter educated than you, besides being a big card-carrying Republican DAR lady, which you say gives her carte blanche to act so crazy, on top of which Nellie Belle's loaded. Optimists! Yeah, I'd be mighty optimistic if Nellie was always slipping me mint-new fives and tens, like she does Poo and Kukie. To say nothing of buying herself a new Cadillac every year, and always in some outrageous new color to match her nails, *Hey what about tangerine?* Bolting in, Poo snatches the bra away.

"So take a good look, you pig! Hey, I'm sorry about your Mom, but you better learn some manners if you're gonna stay here."

"Like I'm looking!" I cry, giving her my furdy Alfred E. Neuman *What, me worry?* face. "Hey, lay off, willya? I'll probably be going home tomorrow."

Now, *that's* optimistic. But this is nothing compared to Dad after the oper- ation the next morning. "Flawless," he says. "They got it all. Oh, her tem- perature's a little elevated, but with these new wonder drugs, they'll knock that out quick. And boy, don't they get 'em out of bed fast these days. The nurse says she'll be up walking by tomorrow."

Dad's ready to sit for his orals, all right. Knees pressed together on the set- tee, eating a plate of Nellie Belle's three-bean salad, Dad's really making me nervous, he's so optimistic. The more he's not sweating the "blip" in your temperature and this other piddly test, the more I'm scared he'll jinx everything.

But even Dad's not so sure around the Doctor Miss with her sheepskin. Dropping his eyes, Dad does the unheard of with technical stuff—Dad qualifies himself, actually defers to a lady. And Angelene can't just sit there and be amazed like any normal woman. Oh no, Angelene's gotta be crossing and uncrossing those legs and picking at her gap tooth.

"Dad"—I sling my arms around his neck—"Dad, you gotta get some sleep."

"I agree," says Angelene, getting up. "Men never know when it's time to leave."

"You're right," sighs Dad. "Boy, I get to talking"—he stops himself—"well, after this, I'm going home for a few hours." Again, his eyes guiltily slide off Angelene smoothing her dark skirt, which, believe me, smoothes itself like a Peter Paul Mounds. Beneath Angelene's solid weight the floor squeaks.

"Now, Pete," she insists, knowing his next question. "Look, Frank's staying here t'night and nuthin' more about it."

Poo walks out.

"But Daddy," I plead, "Daddy, you're going right home. Anyhow, I'm going over to the hospital to see Mom later. Well, right?"

It's like he's dropped a wing nut down an engine. He bites his lip, "Frank, let's not push it today. They really dope you up in there. Tomorrow will be better."

But the next day, your fever's up and Dad just phones. No big deal, he says, you're doing fine. But all I hear is the reverse.

"I *am* listening, Daddy. 'K, I know. I *know*..." Yessing him, I see my hand balled in my crotch, and all the Pettinelles—even their damned cat—they're all staring at me. I yank the phone cord around the corner. "Can I please have some privacy?"

"Look," entices Dad, "your mother wants to talk to you." *Mother*, that sounds so creepy. And sure enough, when Dad puts you on, you sound terrible, croaking.

"Oh, I miss you, sweetie. Are you coming to see me?"

"Ask Dad."

"Honey, I know you want to come. I just meant it rhetorically—because I miss you so much."

"Rhetorically schmorically."

"And it's not just your father. There's some rule about kids under thirteen."

"I'll be thirteen in a few months!"

"Then it's fourteen, I can't remember."

"So say I'm fourteen! I'm *tall* for my age. Christ, I'm your own kid!"

Well, you know where that one goes. And when I come back in the room, Angelene and them, they all know. Nellie Belle knows what to do. Making no attempt at being *artful*, which I hate, Nellie Belle says.

"Well, you're in a rotten mood. Fine, I cain't blame ya, so I decided we're all goin to *It's a Mad, Mad World*. It's in Cinerama at the Uptown. You know that theater—the one with that giant round screen zoomin like a rolly coaster?"

Nellie Belle's such a great old lady. She really does take my mind off it. Just scratching my back real soft like I like, talking how sometime maybe we'll all ride down to Texas where you can fire guns in the desert and ride around in big hats way over the speed limit, and their family's all a bunch of locoweeds. But just when I'm calmed down, here comes Angelene all dressed up. Way too dressed up for a movie. And Poo chiming in all phony-friendly.

"Frank, wanna play Chinese checkers?"

"And where are you going?" I ask Angelene.

"First young fella, I don't like that tone one little bit. But since you asked, a professional meeting. You knew that."

"I did not!"

"Well, I heard you," seconds Poo. "You never hear anything, Frank."

"What, you think I'm *stupid?* You're going to the hospital, is where you're going." I drop my arms. "Which is so great! Man, I can't see my own mother but you can!" Afraid I'll start crying, I blow out the front door, "So say *hi* to her for me! And *thanks a lot.*"

"So go on, hothead!" she hollers out into the darkness. Angelene's not the type to chase you or scream—no, Angelene's tough, way tougher than you, Mamma. "Thass right. Ruin the movie for everybody else! But you hear me, boy! Cause you had better be back here by 8:30 or I'm callin' yer Dad!"

MEETING, MY ASS.

Hunkered in the bushes across the street, I'm watching Angelene and Nellie Belle roosted up there on the butte. Sure, both trying to act all unconcerned but both smoking like a couple of chimneys. And Poo knows I'm hiding out here. Tromping out, she hollers, "So spoil everything, Mr. Selfish Brat!" But Nellie Belle bundles her back inside, and sure enough, Angelene gets in her car and turns right—right straight for the hospital. *Wait, it's true Frankie, I had a professional meeting with your Mamma's docs.*

What, are they too scared to tell me the truth to my own face? Like I'll die! or go nuts, or something! And all out of some sick, sugary idea of being *nice*. Nice like they're *nice* to some fat, stupid-assed cat they'll probably have to put to sleep and he doesn't even know it.

Liars.

Man, I feel terrible about spoiling the movies—I *do*, but after the stink I've made, I can't, can't on principle, go crawling back now. So, sneaking around the side of the house, I grab my three-speed and go tooling around. There's nothing like my bike to settle me down. Like you set a bottle spinning, I go all dumb and mindless, circling round and round, then diving down long hills, no hands and my mouth open like a siren. Not that deep down I don't know where I'll wind up. No, hauling up the handlebars, a few minutes later I'm slowly pumping up Corregidor, up to our house, all dead and dark except for one tired lamp on the porch and your old Ford dripping oil in the driveway. And, of course, I've got me an audience. Huddled under the streetlight in the fall coolness, Billy Feeney and the Corregidor clan are all lined on the curb in their stupid baseball jackets, calling, "Dougherty—Aeey—" Christ, they probably know more than I do. They're all waiting on me to say something, to confirm what a chump I am.

Forget it. Dropping my bike, I ignore them. Pretending to be busy, I hustle up the walk like Dad sent me to check the doors or get something. But reaching for the house key that normally hangs around my neck, I remember, *Dad's got it.* Dad took it yesterday so I wouldn't be tempted.

Dad wasn't a dick about it, but still it made me feel grubby. Revoked. That's how I feel now, rattling the door and peering in at the table lamp with the light spread below it like an old newspaper. Then behind me one of the kids calls out.

"Hey, Dougherty, you locked out or just peeping?"

Even if they do play sports and I don't, and even after the whiffle ball mess, I like the Corregidor kids. I mean I *did* like them. Really, they're not bad kids, it's just that suddenly—they're kids. Suddenly, it's pathetic how stupid and really blind they all are. "I'm just checking the doors for my Dad, okay?" Shaking my head. "Man, you guys are really *common*. You know that?"

But now I am stuck. If I'm checking the front door, naturally I gotta check the back. Which is a real mistake in the dark, especially when I'm feeling crazy like this. The glinting trash cans. The dripping garden hose coiled over the wilted tomato plants. Then, yawning up, I see a ray in the sky! Trembling in the wind, firing from my window to the maple tree, it's the vibrating brass wire—the aerial—from the crystal radio set that Dad and me built a couple years ago.

The crystal radio was such a beauty, as an idea. See, with the crystal, you don't even *need* electricity. No juice whatsoever, but late at night you can get way far off places . . . Pittsburgh, Cincinnati, even Chicago sometimes. All on account of reflections off the high magnesium clouds, and also because Dad says there's less *noise*, everyone all safe and snug in their beds and all the electrons and ions skipping like stones off that black forever, way up there in the blowing darkness. The radio impulse was the electricity, Dad said. Really, he said, the crystal set was more like an *ear*, radio vibrations bouncing down from outer space, ricocheting down like the sharp raindrops that you'll hear sometimes, going *drrr-inng drr-inng-nngg*, as they strike the stretched aerial wire.

To get so much for pure nothing! And even better, Dad said, the crystal, like a diamond, would never break or burn out on you, which I thought was so incredibly beautiful, as an idea. Under the earphones, zithering along with my cat's whisker dial, I could tune in all these wild places—say, when you woke up late and realized how you were actually a person. I mean, that you were a person with an actual *idea* living in your chest with a real heart and blood pounding, and *alive even when you weren't thinking about it*. And going even deeper, getting really excited about life as an *idea*, I'd realize how all these millions of other people—folks we didn't even know—they were all alive, too! They were all on the line, talking into this big whumming life of yours, everybody on earth was, all shouting into this big echoing smoke chamber called THE WORLD, which was built like an ear, and Dad and me, as true believers, we strung the radio wire, to listen to it. Up in the chattering leaves, back when I was nine, Dad and me strung it. Dad boosted me up into the maple tree. Boosted me up, then held me by the leg, and so I totally no-hands trusted him that I drove the nail, then pulled the wire till it whined just right in the wind, and I saw you waving to me from the kitchen window, Mamma. With no electricity or faith—for no reason and no hands—you were just doing it, Mamma, and like a crystal, your life was doing it, too, just alive for no reason, in that big crystal science that Dad and me had back then, back when science could still explain life. And floating in life like a huge unquestioned lake, back then we could all still trust it, too, knowing, like cream, that we'd always float to the top.

Boy, really spooks me, that wire. Without even jiggling the door, I bolt!

Tear back around, stop short, then walk out real cool. And here they are, the whole kid neighborhood, daring me to say you're okay. I grab my bike.

"Hey, Dougherty," says Danny Bowman, "so how's your Mom? You seen her yet?"

"Just today for only about three hours. She's doing way better, too."

Silence. All scraping sticks on the curb and dropping long spits. Then Jimmy Rundell drops the bomb.

"So is she out of intensive yet?"

"Who told you that, you bastard? Huh! Who ever said that?"

But Rundell just stares at me with that sick, goony look that kids get when they've got something good on you. "Hey, don't blame me. It's just what I heard, is all."

"Yeah, from who?" I demand.

And look at them all! All scared of my new power! Power that I can feel under my shirt, rippling like a flag of meaty red muscles! It's true. Over at Angelene's earlier, standing bare-chested in front of the mirror, flexing my arms, I saw it. What with this tensing sickness in my stomach, my lungs swelling with sick breaths, and my heart enhuged from pumping—it's knotting me up something heroic like that Charles Atlas dynamic technique advertised in all the comics. Roaring back at Rundell, "Well, for your information she's not in intensive! That's total crap! That's total *bullshit!*"

But even if I plead the Insane Defense, this is bad news, yelling "bullshit" out in public like this. On Corregidor, I might as well be waving a loaded gun, grossed-out kids ducking and squawking.

"Hey, nice mouth!"

"Christ, Dougherty, my sister's here!"

But they can't touch me! Right then I'm on the other side of the state line! Untouchable! Lumbering up like I'll slug someone.

"Well, I'll get real shitty about it! And you can tell your shithead, nosy-assed parents *from my Mom* I said so. *Bullshit!* You like that? I'll tell the whole damned neighborhood. FUCKING BULLSHIT."

BOOM! BLAM! BLAM!

On my bike I am *flying* down Corregidor, then right across Midway, with no lights. And I'm doing it again! I'm making these civil defense plans for my life, same as I did earlier when Angelene patted the sofa, "Now, you come on over here, buster. You're not all that big yet." Seeing I'm half desperate for anything warm and female, Angelene scratches my back real soft like I like it, her long, silvery nails shooting icy zithers *zip zip zip* up my spine, until my fanny wriggles like a duck's. And sure, there's some of *that*—you know what I mean—but it's not *just* that. No, even when good old Nellie Belle squeezes up beside me and starts scratching, all flab upholstered and warm, even with Nellie Belle I'll be doing it, hedging my bets like a bastard, thinking how maybe I could even get used to their stupid cat and the bird—how, if it ever came to that, I'd even love Poo, who I'd protect like my own sister.

But flying along now it's not just the Pettinelles I'm thinking about. Seeing all these other kids' places, I'm thinking, *Hey, I could live there. Or over there.* Hell, I'm so desperate I'd even take the Hannagans', where the kids bunk three to a room and the place reeks of steamy old meatloaf and diaper pails. With that mob at Hannagans', there's always crud on the walls and sticky doorknobs and unflushed turds and the endless crusted snot noses, which everybody passes down like their old clothes. But so what, Mamma? Even if their life is a mess close up, it's not *all* that way. Which if you could see just that, well, maybe your temperature would go down.

In fact, when you step back and really look, it's almost beautiful how everybody sticks up for everybody else at Hannagans'. At Hannagans' they never worry, and never about money, not when they know there'll never be any, what with all those kids and Captain Hannagan's measly army pay. And even if the Hannagan kids go to church in worn out high-water pants and jackets too short and the girls in these old fur-trimmed things from before the war, nobody's embarrassed, particularly. They still all believe, and with so many mouths, the food never goes bad, every crumb vacuumed up in the Wonder Bread Twelve Ways to make these weird, exotic moon gardens called "families," which breed and collect around people, and like a certain smell or a nose passed down, like a penis or a hole, everybody on earth, almost— well, everybody rich or poor or smart or dumb has got one. But living here in Chinchillaville, a family of three is as good as no family. And two is just a bad joke.

Now me, I always despised the brownnoser, *gimme* idea of praying, asking God for things like he's Santa Claus. But now as I ride across the main drag, Shawcross Avenue, well, I am desperate. It's gotta be nine o'clock, at least. St. Stephen's probably won't even be open, but that's where I'm headed, I realize. Still, to tell the truth, I'm hoping to find the giant oak doors locked— you know, rack up an *E* for Effort—but no such luck. Like He's expecting me, the door's wide open! Pitch dark, too. Seeing how dark it is inside, I immediately want to bag it, but how can I without God seeing this as another slap in His Face? Man, it's dark in here! Just a couple of feeble lights up by the altar, reflecting off all the gold and silver. Yguhh, and the holy water is so *greasy* what with all these little kids splashing in it. God, the holy water gets this oily pond scum on it, but I wipe it on like bug repellent, then cross myself. *Boom,* the huge door closes after me.

Look, just because I haven't laid on the big pious bit and I have a filthy mind sometimes, well, that doesn't mean I'm not still pretty religious. *Real* religious when I think about it, and especially with you so bad off. Every day after school I've been coming in here to pray, sneaking around the side so nobody'll think we're desperate or eating holy crow. *So go on!* I prod myself. But heading up the aisle I stop short. It's this old lady. Don't even ask me who she is. On her knees, clutching her black rosary, she's one of these dreary old biddies you always see camped here with the various geezers, praying all day and waiting to kick.

And she's still here, draped in this long, black shawl. Veil, I mean. God, her head looks like it's covered with a swarm of black flies. About ten pews down, of course. Oh no, you'll never see these pathetic old church mice parked up front—no, no, that would be to *presume.* No, to mortify themselves better, they like it way back, in the ninety-third row. Or, better yet, wedged behind a pillar, so mousy pure and thirsting that I hate their guts, knowing where you're headed.

Quit it! Man, I don't want to make it any harder on us, thinking all this. And actually, dark and late as it is, I'm half grateful the old lady's here, figuring I just have to *reason* with God, is all. Because, come *on,* when you think about our predicament, it's pretty ridiculous. *I mean, she only went in to have her appendix out, just a piddly flap of skin! You gonna hang her for that? Give her a crew cut when she only asked for a trim?*

That's Jesus up there, on the Cross. And over there, off to the sides, that's his two parents, Mary and Joseph, each with separate his 'n' hers chapels with brass plates carved with the names of these loaded dead stiffs. Well, I worked on Joseph this afternoon, so tonight I do Mary, up here on her gold pedestal. In her little sandals, she's standing on top of this blue globe. Queen of the Earth, Mary's floating over oceans, above a wrought-iron stanchion holding probably a hundred red and blue holy candles, which you can light to remember someone, reds for a dime, and the large blues for a buck. It works, too. If you light one and look up, you can almost *see* them sometimes up in your head—the Dead, I mean—like if you've ever passed an egg over a candle.

And the candles are so beautiful—I always loved the candles part of being Catholic. Even as a little kid, I loved to melt into the candles, into the eggs and eggitude of people. Hands in steeples against my upper lip, I always felt so warm and pure back then, melting into the bleary red, a deep wine red, and cosiest of all, the fierce blue. Blue, my favorite color and the purest. Blue, which I'd look into, wondering if the holy spirits lived inside the candles or if they sat up in the big oak rafters, inhaling all that good pure holy smoke. I know it sounds stupid and stuck-up, but praying there sometimes I'd feel like an apostle with those annunciated, cherry-red flames licking over my head. That pure.

Anyhow, in front of my eyes, there's probably a dozen candles flickering. Blue lips. Red lips. And for a while I'm doing it, I'm getting the melting, then the glowing egg, I mean that sharp, hot flame in the brain when you can really *see* inside of things. But then I wonder, is this really praying? Or am I just daydreaming when I should be doing all these Hail Marys, shaving off all these days in hell, only you got so many billions left, Mamma, that it's ridiculous! Well, it makes me mad! Getting p.o.'d, I give the brass coin box a rattle, just to check if all these good Catholics paid, which of course they didn't. And looking around then, here's the old lady's giving me the Eye! Like I'm a thief! Yeah, old Mrs. St. Doormat, she's staring me down. So, hunching over, I start praying, *HolyMaryholyMaryholyMary* . . .

And I'm not faking it. Closing my eyes, I am trying—*hard*—but my brain keeps getting stuck, skipping like a record, *HolyMaryholyMaryholyMary*—just looking at the huge oak beams of the ceiling and poor Jesus speared up there, *Come on she'll act better if you let her live HolyMaryholyholy* . . . Meanwhile, I've got old Mrs. Doormat behind me, *God don't her old knees ever give out?* Rigor mortis is more like it. Scrunching down on the kneeler, feeling a wicked crick in my back, I tell myself, *pray harder, are you gonna let an old lady beat ya?* But I can't. Christ, she's beat me out, an old lady, and I feel so worthless. So, sticking a whole quarter in the slot, I start lighting holy candles. Dipping the taper I do up a whole row of blues. Blue, then reds. Red like the sparkly ruby in my crystal radio set, which Dad said would theoretically last forever, singing on the pure radio vibrations. But *thirty-nine* candles? Thirty-nine equals what? Four bucks? *Eight?* Swearing out my IOU, I light a candle for each birthday, until I hit that bluest, reddest, most intensest candle, number thirty-nine, your next birthday. *Aww come on God at least give her till then, huh?*

I've lit up the whole cake for you, Mamma. Inside the egg, I watch the glow of all those years licking up, sputtering with life and time to grow on, red and blue and bluer. Hypnotized, I watch the flame creep up the taper.

Up and up it climbs until with a teary wince, I snuff it in the sand and sniff my singed finger. It smells like bacon.

"Young man!"

It's the old lady! She's right behind me, hissing in her spittly librarian's voice, "Do you want to set a fire? You didn't pay for all those candles!"

"Yeah, I paid." I jump up. "I stuffed a whole dollar in, okay?"

"A dollar! You've lit *twenty dollars'* worth. And at this hour!"

"Look, I'm lighting a candle for my Mom, okay?"

"*A* candle?"

"She's *sick*—"

"Sick? And what's your name?"

"Huh?"

"I said, who are you?"

"And I said she's *dying*, okay!"

It just jumps out. Bawling like a fool I go tearing down the aisle. Then as I hit the doors I hear her yell—actually yell—"*I'm sorry.*"

She's sorry? It's the blackest lie ever, and it's the God's truth.

"BUT THEY SAID SHE'S UP IN INTENSIVE!"

Boy, do I bawl Dad out the next day.

"Who said so, buncha kids? Didn't I warn you the rumor mill would be working overtime? Yeah, she's *sick*—fine, she's not doing so well. But she's not in intensive."

"So, how sick is she?"

"I told you, sick."

"*Intensive* sick?"

"You can't express it in *degrees* of sick."

"Oh, yes, you can, Daddy! What's her temperature?"

"I told you, somewhat elevated." I tell you, it's all in his nose, that wrinkled, Pepe Le Pew nose Dad makes when he tells an off-color story. "Fine," he offers, "she's not out of the woods but she's getting there. And we'll beat this thing, we will." Then he's accusing me, "Good gracious, why are you so pessimistic?"

"I'm not! I'm not *pessi-pessimis*—" Accused, I can't even pronounce it.

"Well, good," says Dad flatly. "Because, I tell you what, we'll lick this thing.

We're gonna win this fight. Absolutely. We'll be out of the woods soon."
Woods! I hate that word—these woods he seems almost grateful to be lost in,
so long as there's still woods to hack through. "And another thing. In case you
hear something else from the rumor mill. Well, I didn't want to upset you yesterday, but while I'm giving you the latest, well, here's some good news. We
got a specialist coming in. Best internal guy in the city, too."

Desperate's what I hear, but all Dad hears is *cheapskate*, glowering, "Derned
right a specialist. You think I stint on anything here? Don't even ask what this
joker gets paid. Or the antibiotics at fifty bucks a pop. But if it takes every
dime we've got, your Mom's gonna have it. You hear me?"

He's ranting. I guess it's overdue, what with me running off and him driving all over hell looking for me. Dad was too exhausted to bawl me out, and
he sure wasn't palming me off on Angelene again. So instead Dad and me
head back to our house, unread newspapers, coffee cups piled in the sink and
your bed peeled down one side—half peeled like he won't even sleep here
without you. That was last night, though. Tonight, on about his third martini,
Dad remembers his twentieth *other* thing.

"Oh, one other thing. If the phone rings, you let me answer it."

"Why? Don't I live here anymore?"

"Frank, c'mon, will you give the old man a break?" Dad pulls me into a
sweaty hug. "Look, it's not you. It's your grandmother I'm concerned about."

Your mother Dad means—Dad's Mom is long dead. God, in all the confusion, I'd totally forgotten all about Grammaw Catty. "So what about Grammaw, Daddy?"

But, patting his pockets, Dad ducks that one. Dad does the Lost Cigarette Bit, his face fidgeting and his arms octopussing around. "I'm just afraid
your Grandmother's gonna call and—and—get wind of—" Christ, his Marlboros are right here. On his bureau. I slap them in his hand.

"So, what's Grammaw gonna get wind of? The specialist?"

Phwah—The Dragon Nose. Spewing smoke, "No, I mean about Mom being in the hospital." Well, I explode.

"You mean you never told her? *Daddy, that's her own kid.*"

"Hey, this is your mother's decision, not mine." Dad looks pretty disgusted
about it, actually. "Look, once your mother's better, she'll tell her."

I start shaking his arm. "But, Daddy, come off it. How can you and Mom
do that to Grammaw? It's just like you won't let me see Mom! Well, *it is!*
Christ!"

"Hey, I've told you about taking the Lord's name in vain."

"Aww, quit changing the subject! Listen, you gotta tell Grammaw. Daddy, she'll never forgive you if she finds out."

"Well, she won't find out. And you know how she gets. The last thing your mother needs is Catty's hysterics."

"But Daddy, what if something happens?"

He grabs me by the shoulders. "I'm telling you, nothing's gonna happen. Nothing except your mother's gonna get better. And when she's better—well, so what about Catty?" And just then Dad faces me with a cynicism and a desperation the likes of which I've never seen, at least in him. "Well, Catty can't very well argue with success, now can she?"

GRAMMAW CATTY was fresh on our minds too. Barely a month before this—in fact, just before you called the cops on the whiffle-ballers—Grammaw had stopped by on her way to Florida for the "winter." One little black suitcase. She was like Felix the Cat with her black bag of tricks. Once she left her dreary railroad apartment on the Lower East Side, Grammaw could live out of that little black "grip" for months, mooching off your clothes, your perfume, your food, your booze, your cigarettes. "Heaven help me," Dad would gripe, charging back to the kitchen to refill her glass, "I can't even keep that old lady in *ice*."

Being as there were no governessing jobs for rich people, she'd left extra early for St. Pete, off to live the winter in a scabby pink stucco gift box with her sister, Rosie, and her brother-in-law, Jack. Cheap fruit! Bingo! 99¢ buffets! What with Jack's VA and mailman's pension, those two were "fixed," Grammaw said. Tanned black with black tattoos, stringy Uncle Jack shot pool and played the dogs, while Aunt Rosie and Grammaw ginned it up, fighting with Rosie's only daughter, Agnes the She-Bitch or "Three Diamond" Agnes. With her stinger mouth, Grammaw had named Agnes "Three Diamond" for her trick of marrying these three rich old Jews who died on her.

Never failed when Grammaw came to visit us, Mamma. First, you'd get mad at Grammaw forever staring at you and idolizing you. Worse was how Grammaw would go on and on about Grampa Francis, dead then for twenty years, not to mention all the other dead people that she'd count like her black rosary beads, dead dead dead. And him. And her. Dead clear back to her parents, who died when she was a baby, first her mother dead in the fevers, and then her Dad, another Paddy dragged out of the mud when a shoring collapsed on some bridge. At dinner Grammaw always starts weeping and crying. It makes your back twitch. Then your stomach thing starts, so you go back to bed, and Dad and me, we entertain the old lady, who keeps rattling her glass at Dad, "Darling, that was great, but next time, *less ice.*" So while Dad's freshening her glass, he tells me a joke about Grammaw! It is so funny that later I just *gotta* tell Grammaw. Oh sure, I'm careful about her little *feelings.* Naw, I make it all vague, like something I'd heard at school. It's what old Ben Franklin said about houseguests.

"Hey, Grammaw, do you know how guests and fish are alike? . . . ER-RRuuNNT"—my game-show buzzer voice—"IT'S 'CAUSE THEY BOTH SMELL IN THREE DAYS." I flash a lame grin. *"Except you, Grammaw."*

"Well, aren't you sweet!"

"It's a joke. *Hey, I was just kidding.*"

Okay, so I'm not kidding. Wanting to avoid the usual blowup, I want her to get packing, but no. Not only won't she take the hint, she ups the juice.

"Oh, I *know* you're just fooling, my darling. And you know what these Eskimos do, don't you? Why, they dump old Grammaw on the sled! Sure. When the old lady becomes a burden, they just drag her out into the freezing snow, *Nighty-night, Grammaw, ha ha.*"

"Grammawww, come on." I'm upset now. "It was just a joke."

"Of course," she titters. "Anyhow, they don't use sleds—not today. No, those ingenious old Eskimos, they just pack the old squaw on the train. *Nighty-night, Grammaw, ha ha ha.*"

"Quit it!"

"But, sweetheart, I was just joking—"

"Grammaw, no offense but shut up. *Please?*" Amazing, the mouth I have with her. "Look, don't have a cow about it, okay? Because you *know* how you get."

No, they don't go quietly, those old Eskimos. With her bulgy eyes and bulldog's jaw, Grammaw's relentless when she seizes on anything. Darned right I worry about keeping Grammaw Catty in the dark.

"SO LOOK," SAYS DAD THE NEXT DAY, "if your grandmother should call. Not that she will, but *if* she does."

"Dad, if you're so worried about Grammaw, then why don't I go back to Angelene's?"

But Pop's talking *virtue.* Pop's scared we'll be taken for freeloaders, plus whatever gets him so antsy around the Doctor Miss. Besides, I'm finally going with him to the hospital tonight, so Dad holds off looking for another place to dump me. Meanwhile, Dad's making a federal case about my answering the phone. Except, of course, when *he* calls to check up on me, like I'll know it's him and not Grammaw! Worse, he's using all that "rah-rah" *we* stuff on me. "We'll both be seeing her tonight. We don't need to call her. Sure, we'll give her a good rest, huh?"

So finally Dad's home. Late as usual, bellowing, "Frank I'm sorry, but I got tied up with this customer. Hey, look at this place! What a sweetie pie you are for cleaning up."

Yeah, yeah. Giving me a big kiss, he's got that slobbery red happy hour face on him, which I wouldn't notice ordinarily, except it's just him and me. Almost slaphappy, he's so exhausted, but I hug him good, grab him a beer, and pull myself up a seat on the toilet like you do sometimes while he shaves.

It's so weird, us being men together, listening while Dad takes a quick "birdbath," swabbing out his armpits and splattering—always—the floor and sink. All shined, pressed, and Brylcreemed, it feels like we're brothers going out on a date, Dad sluicing his face, "I got a big job today"—sploosh—"that's why I was off with this joker"—splorrshhh—"you know, *the old deal dance.* Gotta do the social deal, mmmuum"—burying his face in a towel.

You think I don't wanna be happy for him? That I don't want to get this crap straightened out and have us all be optimists again? And hey, on the optimists account, I'm doing pretty well. Real well until Dad starts in on his partner, Bud. It's real indirect, with Bud, but it's such ulcer stuff that it hardly takes a thing to start it. Feeling screwed, I mean. It's all up in Dad's face, especially his throat. Right up in the old *hocker hopper,* that's where you see humiliated money and petrified hopes of money gone down the tubes. Talk about being lied to. Even before you got sick, I'd heard Dad going on how him and Bud might bust up, but tonight he's really p.o.'d about Bud's finagling and the money Bud won't advance him for some junk Dad sold. Check hasn't cleared. No tickee, no washee—you know the deal.

It's past seven when we finally get going, and the T-Bird's a disgrace. Crud all down the sides. The ashtray clogged and, in the backseat, paper cups and balled up hamburger wrappers.

"We can do that later," says Dad when I start picking up the trash. Then, like I'm six, he's giving me the creepy pinchee-pinchee on the neck. "Hey, you know what I was thinking about today, old buddy? Remember that trip we always talked about, driving clear across the country? Clear to California? . . ."

California! All it does is make my eyes burn—Christ, I'd rather watch adults kiss than make make-believe. Then Pop whips the car around. It's the Little Tavern.

"Stay here, willya? I'll just grab some chow. We'll eat over there."

"But, Daddy, can't we just *go?*" And it's not any tavern, it's this creepy little chapel place, making me feel frantic again. "Daddy, I'm not hungry—"

But out he comes with a steaming bag of burgers, which the greasy, oniony smell makes me feel barfola. And sure enough, as we hit the hospital, Dad slows down. Slows down and his shoulders tense up, so that I can already feel the fading brakes of him changing the story. Forget the Spacious Skies stuff. "We lost almost two days. I'm serious. If the idiots in the lab hadn't messed up that test, she'd be out by now, *out*. I'm just telling you so you can put it all in perspective, Frank. That one stupid test—see, that's what led to all these other little problems. And while we're at it, look, I hate telling you this, but, well, to be honest I thought of pulling your mother outta there. Monday I did. I was all set to put her in GW, but this new guy—that other gazillion-dollar-an-hour so-called specialist I told you about—well, anyway, he warned me against it. Said I'd just be putting us behind the eight ball, getting a new crew acquainted with her case."

"But Daddy, it's all better, right? No more cutting, right?"

The Sneeze Nose. The throat clearing and cigarette fumbling. Look, if you're any kind of a major kid, you can't let your Dad fail, and especially fail to make sense. In fact, if it's a toss-up, it's better—and sure a whole lot more expected—that you, the kid, don't make any sense. And senseless as it is, I see there's only one possible explanation, *You aren't gonna die after all.*

Christ, it's obvious! Absolutely when you really think about it. First off, what with the state of science, *we'd know.* Same as those Early Warning Stations, *way way* before the Big One we'd know to start piling dirt on the rug. And anyway, unless she got creamed by a bus, no mother would ever just go off and "die." Not *die*-die. *Never happen.* Not until she told her own mother. And especially her own kid.

Man, I feel great suddenly. Riding the elevator up, I can just see your room. It's all dark when, *snap!* Wall-to-wall balloons! And you throwing out your arms, *Surprise!*

• • •

CREEPING INTO YOUR ROOM, MY HEART STOPS. You're barely breathing! Under all these spaghetti tubes, green things up your nose, you're fast asleep. Then the nurses see me.

"Oh, hi. Are you Frank?"

They're both nervous, especially with Dad peering at the sugar bottle like it's a carburetor, giving them both the third degree. The older nurse, the one with the bulgy legs, she's just using me to brownnose him, gushing about how wonderful I am, when here my eyes can't focus on you, Mamma. Everything's everywhere. It's all scattered, your dark hair (did they cut it?) and your face, which looks so puffy and sick I can't even remember how it goes. And the smell. Even loud perfume can't dispel that gluey-sweet, curdled-milk smell, like God hasn't humiliated you enough already.

My loose leg's trembling. Then, when I stand on it, the other one starts to jittering. I gotta pee. Maybe it is your hair. Maybe that's it, all flat and crushed over your white ears, so you look like a nun. But then, going up closer—once the nurses leave—I see your poor arms and go blind. *Liars!* Your arms, they're just *sticks*, they're just shriveled black vines, dark veins and fat black bruises from those giant dropper needles they feed you with. I'm pissing through my eyes. In this hatred I can't even speak, I'm watching the sparkling sugar water drip like an icicle into your veins.

"But, Daddy, she can't make it on sugar water. Sugar water's for ants, not people."

"It's fine for now. She's not ready for food yet."

"And what's that whistle in her throat? *Hear it?*"

"Lower your voice."

"Hear it? That *hee-hee-hee* sound? Maybe she needs some water?"

"She's fine—"

"—Or a cough drop?"

Groggy, you wooze around. But when I hug you, it's like falling into a sticker bush. Pain's all over you. Stickers of pain all over us.

"Oww, sweetheart, don't jostle the tubes! God, my arms are killing me with all these needles. The incision, too. No, no, kiss me, come on"—smiling, trying to lift your head—"gimme a good hug. But *careful.*"

Your neck's all greasy. The thick tape on your arm scrapes my ear. Then in that ticklish near-hilarity of pain, *"How's school? Did you finish your science project?"*

And the worst thing is, it's all so normal. I'm chattering along, *Sister said my social studies paper was too short, I got a B+, but I got an A on my English essay.*

Stupid ordinary stuff. Stuff that, before, you'd never have noticed but now you eat it up. Quit it. Don't be so impressed. That's only sick and feeble—old.

But I do it, all the corny quiz-show, sick-people, buck-up stuff. Shifting from foot to foot I play the Brain, which I am sorta, although the nuns say I'm horribly lazy. Impressing the nurses, I let you brag how I'm already reading high school books like *Tale of Two Cities* and *Two Years Before the Mast*. But all the time I'm conjugating my verbs, *She could die . . . she might really could die . . .*

LOOK, MAMMA, I don't want to turn Judas on you. I don't want to be the one to decide you're a goner but who else is there now?

Not Grammaw when she's totally in the dark. And definitely not Dad. And that's what adults, in their arrogance and sentimentality, never see about innocence. What adults never grasp is how ruthlessly clear innocence is—ruthless because it's all so new and unprejudiced *before* the facts. No, kid, there's a ruthless new clarity when you pick up this illicit new power like a loaded gun, wondering, *So are you gonna die?*

It's not like I don't give you every chance to disprove it, Mamma. First, there's how you look. Okay, not great, I decide, but not bad either. Not *all* bad. Not *goner* bad. Besides, you'd tried to fix yourself up for us, wearing your best blue satin pajamas and makeup. Which is a definite plus. Your average goner, she'd never fix herself up like that, not with lipstick and rouge and eyebrow pencil, even if one eyebrow does trail off a bit, like a question mark. Perfume, too. For a sick lady, that's a real good sign, right? Well, isn't it, still wanting to look pretty for her own kid? And not just pretty but *happy*. Pretty happy. Next thing I know, you're teasing me about Poo. Angelene claims I've got a crush on her.

"*Mom*, Angelene's just stirring things up. Poo hates me—"

Rolling your eyes. "Aww, come off it. You know you think Poo's cute."

Still everything's fine—basically fine until, wanting a kiss, you pull me into all the stickers and needles. The jangled tubes, the hissing air. Holding my face, you're peering into my eyes, *Magic Mirror, Magic Mirror.* Well, I spazz out. I jerk away and, with a groan, you see it.

"It's not fair!" You glare at Dad. "Well, it's *not*, for him to see his mother like this. Guhh. All sick and bloated—like a fish."

"Quit it, Mom. You look *fine*, okay?" Then Dad groans at me, groans like I've given away the secret. "Dad, I said she looks fine, okay? What did I say?" But then you start coughing and choking, "*Uckh—Cuu-cc-UUkk—*"

A hooked fish. That's the sound. It's the hollow sound a little fish makes who's gut-swallowed a hook but he's too little to be a keeper. It's fisherman's honor. You can't just let him die. Grab a forked stick! Dig the barb out, *Kkk-KUuckk,* and he flaps. *Guhh-uKUK,* and his sharp fins stab you. Finally, though, you pry the hook loose and slide him back in the water, *Swim.* But he can't swim, he's flopped on his side, and as you stare at him putting slow circles, well, your brain flips a switch. Because hard as you tried to save him, now you're destroying him with big rocks, *Doom! Doom doom!*

"Dad," I ask, getting up finally, "can you get me a drink of water?"

"There's a fountain just down the hall."

Can't he even take a hint? But seeing I'm upset and want you alone, you speak up, "Pete, could you go down and get me a paper?"

Dad knows. Dad doesn't like it one bit, but once he's gone I honk my chair up to the bed—so close I can smell moist, sweet air sweeping out of your lungs. So close I'm staring into the flecks of your eyes and the bruises fluttering in your arms like moths inside a lamp. And you know, don't you? You know I gotta ask you the secret. Because even then you see it's a secret, and it's your secret, which it has to be, with you playing Keep Away from Dad and Grammaw, and even me.

"Mom, don't be mad, okay? Don't tell Dad I asked you this but—"

"—*What?*" Immediately you're on guard. "What's this?"

"Huh?" I hang back. "Well, Daddy said you won't tell Grammaw and—"

"—*won't tell her what?*—"

"—that you're *sick. Just sick, I mean.*"

Prudishly, you pull away. "Right, I'm sick. So?"

"So Dad says you won't tell her. About you being so—"

"—Did your father put you up to this?"

"No."

"Well, forget it. I'll tell your grandmother later. *When I'm better.*"

"Mom, come on, you can't just *not* tell her. That's not right—"

You start sobbing. "*Why are you doing this to me?* I didn't want this, I only wanted to see you."

"Mommm, don't fall asleep on me." So I lay on the puppy noises and slobber kisses, "Mom—come on, all I—all I wanna *ask*—"

It's like hugging loose feathers. Sobbing, you fall all apart in my arms, and I get mad. "Well, you could tell Grammaw. *You* could. And if you don't—*Mom.* Mom, she'll always think it was Daddy who wouldn't tell her and she'll hate his guts. Or wait, I know . . . *you can tell me and I'll tell Grammaw for you.*" You're staring at me wide-eyed. I nod back. "So tell me, and *I'll* tell her,

Mamma. Cause you know Dad won't let me come back now. Quit it, 'cause you know he won't!"

"*He will.* Of course he will. *I* will."

Liar. My chair honks back. Blind I run for the little bathroom. Flush the toilet. Run the water all boiling hot and soak my face, to boil out the tears. Give up. Cause even if I washed my own mouth out with soap, there it is in the mirror, your lie in my face. It's Death sticking his tongue out at me, a kid making horrible faces at himself in the bathroom mirror.

DIDN'T YOU KNOW the secret, Julie? And if you had told me the secret, would things have been any different later? Because when I sneak back out of the toilet, you're half asleep and Dad's back all chipper. Yeah, Dad's saying he just had a great talk with Dr. Whozit, but you, you keep drifting in and out. Paper rustles.

"Here, no pickles."

A cold hamburger. Reaching into the grease-soaked Little Tavern bag, Dad's pulling out supper. Burgers. Fries. Melted Cokes.

"Go on, eat," he prods, eyeing the nurse. "Visiting hours just ended."

But eat right in front of you? It's gross! How can I, watching the sugar water drool down the tube into your arm? Taking a bite, even Dad's nervous. Especially when you roll around and smile at me all drowsy, "Go on, sweetie. Eat. Don't mind me."

Eat? But when I inhale that burnt-onion-fried-meat smell, *whompf.* "Stop wolfing," says Dad but my belly's growling like crazy. I tear into the second burger, then mash it up, thinking, *Eat,* like a mamma bird does for her baby. *Eat,* to chew for you, sleeping again with your fingers stuffed in your mouth, your hurt side resting like a hill on the pillow. And the weird thing is once I've eaten, I can leave. Once I've crammed it all down, I don't have any huge big sense of leaving. Not *leaving-leaving,* like forever. Besides, I think, it's not like we really know, you and me. And how could we know, because even inside this new egg—feeling our faces against the slick, feverish walls—well, what is such a thing as *forever?* Next week? Next year? When I get my driver's license? And even if angels warned us, even if we had all the time in the world to seek shelter, who would ever heap dirt on their nice clean carpet? Even if God said so, who would ever do such a desperate thing?

In fact, as we leave, you look real sweet curled up there, sleeping on your side. Hand on your hurt, you're hugging your secret to you like a new baby as Dad and me kiss your hot face, then tiptoe down the darkened hall goodnight.

• • •

SOUNDS PRETTY LAME, SAYING I FORGOT, like you could just forget your own Mom was dying. But that's what happened, basically. For the next four or five days or whatever, I pretty much forgot the whole thing.

Meanwhile, I'm staying all over hell at these other kid's places—you know, *spread the wealth*. Sure, I've buried the hatchet with Angelene, but even so Dad wants to keep me away from our street, where I'm this freak celebrity. Amazing, how people freeze up around me, bellies pushing against belts and purses snapping shut, all waiting on me to pass like a funeral procession.

But, like I say, you forget, which is natural. There's suspended animation. There really is such a state. Frogs and other cold-blooded things have been frozen weeks, and thoughts way longer than that. But then one night when Dad picks me up at Kevin Reece's, where I've been staying, well, I get a really rotten feeling, then a worse one when Dad switches off the engine, tunneling under some trees, into like this *passion pit*. The Bird's all closed up, and I can't roll down the electric window because, of course, the power's off. Dad doesn't move. Gripping the wheel with his chin on his chest and that horrible thunderstorm smell of fear, Dad starts tugging on me, saying how sorry he is. Hail's smacking the roof but it's just crickets. All I want to hear is more about the *woods* and the woodpeckers and the oak trees, but now even Dad can't keep up that woods business. Nope, that's all down the tubes, and I'm hollering.

"Daddy, goddamnit, I want to go! *Right now!*"

It's amazing. I can cuss in front of him now and everything. Really, I wish he'd smack me, but he just lays there sucking wind, the wheel punched in his chest, wheezing like we've hit a tree.

"She's so sick. Frank, please try to understand. If the worst comes, I want you to remember her as she was."

"Yeah," I sneer, "so how about Grammaw, huh? Grammaw who you wouldn't call 'cause things were so *great!*"

"Well, for your information, I *called* your grandmother. Hey, if it makes you feel any better, I've already been beaten up once tonight. Oh, in hindsight everybody's so smart! Frank, can you even dream what I've been through? Just *tonight* what I've been through? *Me* to change the ice to cool her down. *Me* to monitor the oxygen. *And* Catty. *And* you. Have a heart, willya?"

He tries to hug me but I shove him away. "You and your dumb-assed doctors! Why didn't you take her someplace else, huh? Why didn't you take her to someplace *good?*"

Next thing I know we're back at Reece's and everybody's staring at me.

In the family room *The Beverly Hillbillies* is playing waaang-di-yang-yang, and they're all giving me that *so-did-he-get-it* stare. Well, I bolt. Running upstairs, I dive into four-year-old Robbie's bed, all gritty with cookie crumbs and that good pukey milk smell of little kids. Goldilocks had it right, boy, it's the baby-bed for me. Mushing my face into the pillow, I dive for that beautiful murk before my eyes had even opened, before even my pet turtle had died.

SO IT'S ALL OVER, right? Even if it's not official and you haven't been pronounced, I know it's kaput, right?

Doubtful.

Sure, Julie, Dad knew you were dead, or as good as dead, but how explicit could he be? I mean, it's one thing to tell a kid his Mom *has* died. But to slog into the swamp of prediction, to flatly say his Mom *will die*, that's to feel you've signed the death warrant.

As a father myself, I can understand this now—I guess. Still, I wish Dad hadn't sent me to school the next day. Then again, what choice did he have? Even if you were in a coma, Dad couldn't just leave you. Worse, Dad had people to call and arrangements to make, the biggest problem being how to break the news to me.

But still you wonder... *how could the kid not know?* And all the other kids know. Whispering and avoiding me, every kid in the room—probably every kid in the school—has to know Frank Dougherty is gonna get it. Everybody but me.

And what's so bad? It's not like anybody calls on me or expects me to do any work today. Basically, it's a holiday. I can skate. Sitting at my desk, I'm writing, writing stories, which is this other forgetting technique I'm developing. Face flat on the paper I'm writing this story "My Dead Aztec Brother Bill," which I may instead call "The Halls of Montezuma." It's this cool, *Twilight Zone*–type story about this Larry kid who, after his basketball-star big brother Bill dies in a car wreck, well, Larry starts dreaming in Aztec, then speaking in Aztec, too. See, the Aztecs had this Aztec-type jai alai a million times harder than any basketball, especially since they played it in these feathered headdresses, bounding around like gooney birds. Any Aztec alive today, he'd be the biggest basketball star ever. Not to give it all away, but, see, Larry's speaking in Aztec to his brother Bill—I mean Bill the dead basketball guy, Bill (ZuZu-Chumba). But that's before all this other great junk happens to Larry and Bill. Before they both wind up basketball heroes saving their Dad from bankruptcy... and, see, that's the beauty of story writing. Faster than life can happen to you, and before it can happen, *you cook up all this other good crap.*

Somebody's knocking at the classroom door.

"Let's have quiet," whispers Sister Ruth Marie. Swish, swish, swish. Rosary beads rustling, Sister makes a wind as she goes by. Nuns! both whispering, like erasers across a dusty blackboard. The door shuts. Swish, swish, swish. *What?* Looking up, I see all these blurty kid faces. And here's Sister, a white megaphone pointed at me, "Frank"—normally I'm Mr. Dougherty "Frank, you're to go to Sister John Christopher's office."

The principal! Beet-faced, I jump up. Like I've got a bone on, I'm burning. Hunched over, I'm staring at Sister's pale lips, the air buzzing with cracking chairs, scuffling shoes, whispers. Then Sharon Berger, one of those high-strung, pony-lover girls, Sharon Berger buries her face in her arm and starts blubbering. Which of course starts Teresa Marie Aines, then all these other hysterical kids, *Shut up you idiots. So kill her whydoncha.*

Boom, I'm out the door, no lunchbox, no knapsack, no nothing. Fire bells are clanging. On fire, I'm racing stiff-legged down the hall, *Walkdontrunwalkdontrun.* And what's this? Skidding around the corner, here's Dad in his best dark suit! All shaved and dressed. Just chitchatting with Sister John Christopher.

"Ah, Frank," says Sister, with her sickly smiley parent face, "Frank, your father will be taking you home early today."

"Why?" I pant. Playing dumb, I stare up at them. "What's happened?"

But Dad's already heading down the hall, when I see it. Dad's got my coat and knapsack, *'cause they planned the whole thing.*

"Dad, wait up—Daddy, so what is it?"

"We've got to be prepared," he says, steering me out the door. "We could lose her, Frank. I mean *today.* In a matter of hours."

"Okay—"

Fingers crossed, I say it, but it's just a bluff. It's just a crazy dare, it's not a for-real WORD. Oh, sure, it's scientifically possible. Okay, it's even conceivable, but now Dad's so certain, so stampeded into renouncing you, that with his every breath, I feel like a balloon being blown up.

"Frank, I just want us to be clear"—another big breath—"so it won't be such a shock"—and another—"because she really could die. And I mean today."

But how today? I just can't picture this today. Not today with the sun out and the T-Bird fresh from the car wash, more sparkling and spitefully new than the day we bought it. On a beautiful, clear October day? Today, with shadows in the trees and the sun in the grass? Today, riding in the car with

Daddy like all the times before? Christ, why won't he quit fiddling with the radio, feeling for just the right freak frequency to stick it in?

"So do you understand me, old buddy? About your mother?"

"I heard you."

"I said understand, not heard."

"Okay—"

But here when I'm trying to calm down this heckler hollers out, *It could! It could happen just like that ball that knocked you out!*

Woof. Like a puff of smoke, it walloped off the bat, the ball that knocked me cold two years ago. Kids said I was goofing off, said I never knew what hit me, but that was such a crock. *I knew.* Second I heard the bat I knew there was no use ducking. Glove at my side, I just watched it zooming for my head, knowing no matter what it'd whack me sure. And it was the most amazing coincidence! My head and this tiny ball! Colliding! In a whole ocean of air!

And now even Dad sees the ball smoking across the sky! Getting out of the car, Dad's peering across the street, over the rooftops, toward the hospital. Then, jiggling the key in the slot, again Dad's craning around when we both hear it, the phone! The phone's ringing, and as Dad grabs it I stand there frozen, hollering, *"Is it? So is it her? . . ."*

And I'm hit! Dad drops the phone. Stumbling and splashing, arms spread wide, Dad's running back to catch me but he's too late. Not that I need to cry, really. In fact, I don't feel anything—anything except stampeded into feeling, since I know I'm supposed to feel *something.* And the second I bury my face in Dad's shoulder I feel like such a puking little fraud. Such a little snake and a traitor, crying, *"And she's dead, Daddy? And she's really really dead?"*

It's funny, though, once you get whacked. Even out cold on the ground, you're not *un*-conscious. Faces crowded all around. The kid who hit you pissing in his pants. And in that towering Afterhood, *you can see and hear everything.* Now too. Hovering over it like an angel, I can see Dad crying, hugging my limp little boy's body with the scuffed-up little boy's shoes—the shoes that seem so pointless now, so silly when I'll only outgrow them. *And come on it's not so bad so what's so bad?* Because back when I was born, back when I first got dropped and the doctor slapped my butt and I didn't know where I was . . . *was that so bad?*

And that's a sign, kid! That's a definite first sign, that being-born feeling, especially how snowy pure the light looks, and the long, dagger-legged shadows, like in pictures. And once my eyes adjust to the murk I think, *But hold on! Who said it was really her they pronounced? Christ it could be some other dead lady they pronounced.*

Anyhow, calm down, 'cause we can't lose our heads here! The sky's still blue and the sun's in the sky. And besides, as I'm thinking, how can it be you, Mamma? I mean, how can it be *you* when *I'm* still here?

NOW, YOU ARMCHAIR HEADSHRINKERS, you'll probably say it was all just a "shock" on the poor little guy, why he "felt" this way. Or maybe you'll blame it on some kinda kid *-osis* or *-itus*, which really kills it and, worse, doesn't explain a damned thing.

Because just look what people are asking you to swallow.

They're calling death a *fact*, but if you listen, they're talking about it as a *belief*, and a hypocryphal one at that, when here they can barely believe the thing themselves!

And just think about how totally upside down it is. I mean, you don't walk around *believing* somebody's alive, now do you? Nobody ever asks you to believe people are alive, *they just are.* But, see, with Death, or the *D*, as I come to call it, it's all magnetized just exactly the opposite. Suddenly, in somebody's weird idea of religion, adults are brainwashing and pressuring you to believe somebody's dead. And if you don't just go along, they get real put out about it, too.

Still, who knows? If you'd died clean the first time—if Dad hadn't suddenly switched stories later that afternoon—I really might have bought it, Julie. I might have bought the amazing coincidence story of the phone ringing *just as we stuck the key in the door.*

AS FOR GOING into seclusion, forget it. Right away, the phone's ringing. And then the ghouls start trooping over. Knocking on the door, here's your old buddy, Mrs. Feeney. Just slayed too. Just gaping at me, asking in a whispery, laryngitis voice, "Were you sleeping?" *Bawling* she means. "Oh, you poor sweetheart, I just got the news, but I still can't believe it."

She starts sniffling on me then, but I just stand there all cool in my mind, not about to be stampeded into this hysteria, and especially not by your archenemy. No, just as cool and matter of fact as a cucumber, I say, "Dad's up on the phone. You want me to get him for you?"

"*No, no.*" Mrs. Feeney's eyes get all wide. Then of course she starts repeating herself, "No need to disturb *him* if he's—I can come back. I can certainly come back." But still she stands there, her big toe cracking out of her weejuns, dressed in her blanket kilt dress with the big gold pin. And then I realize she's waiting—waiting on me to feel for her. Tears are what they drink, these ghouls, and man it's *killing* her, to see me acting like it's just another day at the ranch.

"You know," she prompts, "I saw your Mom in the hospital a few days ago. We had such a nice talk finally. A nice, nice talk." Mrs. Feeney sighs. "Ah, sweetheart, we put all that sad old business behind us, I can tell you. Frank, heaven knows, I'm sorry about all that stuff—I am. What can I say? I was wrong. We all were. If only poor Julie had had time, we'd—I'm sure—"

Well, she starts crying. Fanning her face. Fanning it off like a sneeze, she makes me promise to tell Dad she's sending dinner over. She'll shop for us, too, she says, clean, wash, grovel, anything. Then, halfway down the walk, seeing the raggedy grass, she calls back, "Mr. Feeney will be over to cut the lawn later. Tell your Dad that, will you please, honey?"

But the minute I shut the door it hits me, *But wait if the hospital just called so how's she know so fast?*

"But, Daddy," I say, "Mrs. Feeney knew! So how'd she know so fast?"

"You've heard the adage, bad news travels fast? And you wait, you'll see all the people your mother touched. You'll see how people turn out for her."

But before I can press him the phone's ringing again. *"Tommy,"* says Dad ticklishly. See, Uncle Tommy's the head of the clan on your side of the family, up in Tarrytown, New York. Tangling himself in the cord, Dad's doing the old cigarette hoochy-koo, shooing me out. Shutting the door, Dad has to know I'm listening but here he is telling Tommy how they totally botched the operation, lost tests, even gave you the wrong medicine—stuff a hundred times worse than he ever told me. Coming back out later, Dad's looking really beat up, so he washes his face again—he must wash his face eighty times a day now. Then in his nervous-chipper voice he calls me over.

"Well, here's something you'll like. Angelene's having you over tonight." Well, he sees how that goes over, so he starts pleading, "Look, you don't want to be here. Not tonight when everybody's getting in." Grammaw, he means. "And look, tomorrow if it gets too much on you, well, you tell me, okay? I'm not naming any names, but if it gets too much, you just tell me, huh?" He hugs me again. "Look, why don't you go up and conk out for a while, old buddy? You look really sleepy."

Sleepy! Man, when I go outside, the sun's just blazing down. You can't even believe the light at this magnification. Standing there, I'm staring at the light, the light in beautiful big flakes, falling through my fingers. And all I can think is, if you're really dead, then why don't I feel more terrible? If you're really dead, then why do I feel more alive than I've ever felt before?

BUT HERE COME SOME ANSWERS. About then, Father Nivas comes thudding up in the black "Nivasmobile," a smoking police-junker '53 DeSoto so charred and salt-eaten it looks like a giant meteorite on wheels.

Dad's warned me Father Nivas is coming, but first the Padre's gotta park this junkheap he drives. Eeek, stop. Eeek, backing up. Blind as a bat and about a mile from the curb. Squinting out that porthole windshield with those heavy black-rimmed glasses and that wide Mexican face.

Hey Padre Pizza Face!

Even I get grossed out sometimes, how kids'll joke about Nivas's poor pitted face, that and his coarse, greasy hair so black there's a white line on his scalp where he parts it, real low over one ear, like some hick from the FFA. "Whistle pig"—that's another name the kids have for him, on account of how, when Nivas is thinking hard, he'll pucker up his lips, so *gone* sometimes kids'll whistle at him and he won't even hear! Or looking up, he'll wave to some little prick who's only sneering at him. God, I hate that. It's dirty, if you ask me, Father Nivas always having to be nice. And, worse, having to pretend other people are nice while they doo-doo on him.

What no kid can sneer at, though, is his Mexican barrel chest, his big hands, and that scar on his pitted neck that everybody says is from a knife. Also, the washed-out ✳ tattoo he gave himself as a kid on the leather web of his hand. Tacky as hell, but the Padre won't have it bleached off. Absolutely not. He won't deny who he was back in his old pea-picker days, before the Jolly Green Giant picked him.

Deny it! In his sermons, Nivas is always going on about his pea-picker days as a kid in Texas and Arkansas and places. Just lay back in the pew and for three hours he'll regale you something Rio Grande about how him and his dozen brothers and sisters, they lived in this broken-down schoolbus, picking peas and okra and half-rotten tomatoes. Why, even today, the man gags at a fresh tomato, which is why at the church picnic you'll see kids grinning and hissing like vampires, mashing and sucking on these gorshy steak tomatoes, rivers of seeds and slime running down their chins as they walk by Nivas, hoping he'll barf. And as a kid, you love it, jittering and ashamed in that help-lessness of you and a hundred other kids holding a live wire, and even if God sent you all straight to hell you couldn't let it go.

Cockfights and ringworm. Locust swarms, tornadoes, dustbowls and eight or nine floods. Well, if you lived through all that mess, I guess you'd think you were Moses, too. Anyhow, Nivas hated it so bad he finally lied his ass off just to get him three squares in the Maryknolls—conned the superiors, cheated on tests, even ran off three or four times. Which gets to this other big "theme" with him, namely, this cheap, sentimental idea people have about priests, or anybody, being "naturally good."

Hey, lighten up, Jose.

Yeah, the "Poverty Bit" annoys the hell out of people—adults—in our parish, what with Nivas going on about the Other Half and Martin Luther King and those colored marches he goes on. And what a slob! What an aw-ful reflection on us! people say, Nivas going around in shiny suits and cracked black deliveryman's brogans like we don't pay him beans. *And why's he even at St. Stephen's?* people wonder. Well why, when you know he'd be happy as a clam in a leper colony or prison?

Nivas sticks it right back to them, though. Like that sermon he opened with the word *nigger,* which people said was like cussing in church, or bad taste at the very least, even though they almost all of them think it. Or the church Halloween party where, dressed in this masked-bandito getup and banging a capgun, Nivas made a point of "sticking up" the biggest phonies in our parish, shouting, "Haaa, green-go!"

But where Father Nivas really spooks people is in confession. It's the Span-ish Inquisition. Pulling back the curtain, people pray it's the pastor, classy Fa-ther Dolan. Or, better yet, old Monsignor Potter, about ninety and put out to pasture, who you could murder somebody and for penance, like push-ups, you'd get a "gimme-ten"—five Our Fathers and five Hail Marys.

Not Nivas, boy. Pull back the red curtain and you hear that wheezy breath-ing, and then you smell him, not b.o. so much as vegetable musty, slumped with his chin on his chest like it's siesta time. But just try beating around the bush.

"Don' bore me with these *numbers,* saying three times this, four times that. *Why? Why,* you must ask yourself today, why would you want to deny God's love doin this thin'? . . ."

Man, when you slink out two hours later, you know people are eyeing you like a pud-pulling bandit. And, slamming the car door, here he comes. Ambling up with that level pea-field squint, straight off Nivas says, "Frank, you look like you wonder who died today."

Padre Pizza Face. Christ, even God sent the wrong doctor.

BOY, IS DAD ever glad to see him, though—grateful, Dad says, for all the times Nivas dropped by the hospital to see you. Persistent, that's Nivas. The second Pizza Face came in your hospital room he must have seen how disappointed you were, like for you they're sending Bing Crosby.

Knowing I don't much like the guy, Dad shoots me this glowery, don't-goof-around look when Nivas starts praying, and who can pray as hard as Nivas, always making you feel like a candy-assed Christian? When Nivas asks us to kneel, Dad and me naturally take the rug but not Pizza Face—no, Nivas plonks right down on the hard wood, eyes clenched and spewing Latin as his glasses slip down his greasy, pitted nose. Okay, I know he gave you Extreme Unction. I know he's praying for your soul, or whatever, and that I should *feel* more (Dad's looking at me). But, see, the worse you try to feel or pray, the worse it constipates you. It's worse than being at a urinal, trying to pee with all these queers butted up behind you.

"Stick around," says Dad once Nivas finishes his prayers. Then him and Nivas go up to your room—go for what, *confession?* Whatever it is, they're gone a long time, and when Nivas tiptoes out and shuts the door, it's like Dad's been religiously sedated. My turn. Nivas motions me down to the rec room, then whirls around.

"Here." He holds up one big brown hand. "Hit this."

"Huh?"

"Forget I'm a priest. As hard as you can, hit my hand. Punch it."

"Father!"

"Go on. You woan hurt me. Hurt *it*, Frank."

"*It?*"

"Your pain. Your anger."

"But I'm okay. You see me."

"Don' hand me that. Sit down. Please."

The cushion gives a bounce as he whumps down beside me, already sweating—move one finger and the man's sweating. "Frank, let us face the facts. Your mother is dead. This is hard but, believe me, this is for the best. Terrible to say but it is true. She was so sick last night when I gave her Extreme Unction, so bery sick. She could not come back from that, never from such a sickness—no, you would not wish your poor mother to suffer like that. Of that much, my friend, I can assure you today. God was merciful."

So what do I say, how grateful I am? Well, pull down the blast door. Man, I'm ready to wait this joker out—for *days*, if I gotta. But then I think, *Hold on here*. Turn the tables. Interrogate *him*. Ask *him* what really happened at the hospital.

"So how sick was she last night, Father?"

"Bery high in the fever. By then she did not know."

"Didn't know? But Father, if she didn't know, so how'd she confess and get it out? If she can't confess, she can't go to heaven—well, right?"

A full whistle face. Nivas knows he's stepped in it now, just like he knows you never went to church, which that alone means hell. Moving his tongue over his teeth in that Spanish way they do, Father thinks on this, then he says, "Frank, we cannot know this. For anybody to know what God will do. Had your Mom lived after this—well, who knows? She might have been 'nother person, huh? Consider that. Had she lived—and esbecially after such a sickness—your Mom might not have been the same woman you had known before. Why, she might have been better than anybody, a saint, who will ever know? But Frank, God takes all this thin's into account. And, God, I am sure, will take good care of her. *Bery* special care, esbecially in view of her suffering."

Aww, come on! Nobody *gets better* in hell. Look, I don't wanna incriminate you, Mamma, but Nivas's got me so rattled I finally bust out, "But, Father. But you know she never went to church. Well, hardly ever. And that's a mortal sin right there. Missing just one Sunday is."

If you're Catholic you know those gestures they teach them at priest school, Nivas laying his palms out *so-nail-me-up*. "What am I to do for you, Frank? What can I do when I can't give you the simple answers, but only, I'm afraid, the mos' honest and complicated ones?"

Christ, kid, are you blind, *give up*. But, see, in this early concussion state, Mamma, when you and me still don't know where we are, we're still pretty pathetic and confused. Not knowing any better, I'm actually trying to *sway* the guy, "But, Father, no offense, but you know that's no answer. Okay, she—okay, you extreme-uncted her and sure that's good. But Father, what—what if she didn't—doesn't—have any faith? *Before*, I mean. Before she could change anything. So she just goes, boom, straight down to hell? Forever? And that's just tough luck?"

"Please—" The cushion gives another bounce. "Our Lord wants you and your mother to be at peace. Of that I am sure."

Oh yeah Pizza Face no way Jose.

But amazing thing. Like a burp of warm soda, up comes this girl's raspberries voice. Your voice, Mamma, but younger. It's you. You in like your *girl's* voice, the two of us yelling in unison but off-key like you blow a harmonica, *Go to hell and screw yourself Father shithead.*

WELL, YOU KNOW WHAT I'M THINKING as Nivas drives off in a cloud of smoke. Then, as I'm up in my room packing for Angelene's, Dad hollers up.

"Frank, let's both take a little ride. I'll drop you off at Angelene's."

Little ride, I shoulda seen that one. At Shawcross Avenue, Dad swings a sudden right. "Look, we'll just swing by the hospital a minute."

I buck back in my seat. "*Now* I can go, huh?"

"Ten minutes, tops. C'mon I just have to sign some papers—bills and stuff."

"Bills? They kill her and we still gotta pay?"

"Died, not *killed*. Watch your language here. You want to get us sued?"

"Daddy, that's what *you* said and I heard you! On the phone with Uncle Tommy you said it—you said they wracked her up. Operated wrong. Gave her the wrong medicine! *Butchers* you called them."

"Well, if you heard me shooting my mouth off, I'm sorry. But the fact is, they tried. They tried in good faith."

"Good faith? They *killed* her, for crissakes."

"Stop it! This stuff won't bring her back."

"Yeah, but we can sure keep our money! We'll *sue them*."

He gooses the gas. His arms start flapping. "Well, all right. Okay! Since you know, Dr. Merrill came totally clean, *told me everything*. And, yes, mistakes were made but Frank, that's just life. We don't live in a perfect world, and that's just the risk, the huge risk, that doctors take. Anyway, for me to use Dr. Merrill's words against him in court—well, that's just dirty pool. Don't make faces at me. If someone gives you advantage, you don't use it against him, do you?"

It's like it was with Father Nivas. It's not just me talking, at least not the usual me-type me, in my own voice. No, it's you, Mamma, and suddenly it's the smarter, maturer you, too. And like you, I'm scared to death, and especially now when I can feel Daddy falling asleep on me—when Daddy's act-

ing so tired and useless and given-up that finally I'm tugging on him, "*Daddy,*
don't pay them, dooon't! Just 'cause Dr. Merrill says *So sorry, oh gee I messed
up,* but I'm telling you 'cause I'm-a-gentleman-and-a-doc, *so you can't sue me?*
Well, I'll tell you what I'd do if I was your size! I'd spit in his damned face!
I'd punch him in his lying filthy *mouth!*"

Man, Dad hauls the T-Bird over, jumps out, then leans there with both
hands on the trunk. For five minutes as the cars go by, Dad just stands there
looking like he'll be sick.

LOOK, I HAD NO IDEA he was going over to identify you—your body or
whatever so you could go to the funeral home. Not that it would have
changed much. Still, for what it's worth now, I had no idea the poor guy had
that weighing on him.

So here we are, pulling into the ugly back lot of the hospital, back by the
dumpsters, where crushed glass glitters in the sun. Woof, the huge exhaust
blowers start up—the Briggs blowers Dad sells—heaving up a stink of dust
and old bandages. So why doesn't Dad just go in? I wonder. I don't want to
get him upset, but finally I can't stand it.

"Please don't get mad, but where is Mom now? Is she here still?"

His temples bulge. "I don't know. By now I expect she's at the funeral
home."

I don't want another blowup, but at the thought of us not knowing where
you are then, physically, I catch my face in my hands. I'm scared my eyes'll
pop out, Dad ripping Kleenex from the chrome Kleenex box under the dash.
"What? What did I say now?"

"Because you don't even *know* where she is. Like now she's just *anybody's.*
Like she's just *junk.*"

"But that's not true! We have our memories and our love for her, but
Frank—Frank, these are just her *mortal remains.*"

With a cough, the blowers shut off. Now, there's just the ticking leaves and
the light that falls, the light that dapples down like snow on water, falling on
everyone and anything but you, seen by anyone and anything but you. And
you're *remains?* In all the world was there ever a word more ugly and warped
than *remains?*

"Are you sleepy?" Dad asks, naturally thinking I'm sleepy. Sleepy when,
even now, I'll have the happiest little dreams! Flashes of you not gone and
everything like it all was before. Darkly, off one eyelash, the crushed glass
glitters, so that I could be eight, ten, *before.* And it's not so bad, is it? Sitting

there I have these split-second dreams, just the happiest, prettiest little dreams, sputtering like raindrops off my eyelashes.

Dad steadies his fingers on the wheel. "Look, can I tell you something, Frankie? Please honey? So we can just get everything square between us? Can you be old enough and big enough and forgiving enough just to please understand what I'm gonna tell you? Because Frankie old buddy, your old Dad did a very stupid thing today. Are you listening to me? Because I knew your mother would die today, I just didn't know when. So do you see my dilemma, old buddy? My problem was—how? How was I going to break the news to you? That was my problem today—"

"—So??"

"—So all right, I'm getting to that."

"So tell me!"

Another big breath. "All right, about that call we got from the hospital? The call we got just when I brought you home from school? Just when we hit the door?" He almost starts crying. "Well, it wasn't the hospital that called. That was Mrs. Davis."

"*Who?*"

"Our Mrs. Davis. From across the street."

Wake up, says a voice but I can't wake up.

"No, no," says Dad, thinking that I don't get it, "Frank, Mrs. Davis wasn't *peeping* on us. No, see, Frank . . . Frank, I *asked* her to watch out the window. So she could call our house? Like it was the hospital that called?—"

"—Are you crazy! SO IS SHE DEAD YET OR WHAT?"

I lunge for the door handle but he yanks me back, sobbing, "Yes, she's dead! *Officially.* I just got the call. The *real* call."

SO WHAT IF THEY PRONOUNCED YOU at the hospital? Pronounced how? And what does it even mean, pronounced? Pronounced like a word? And besides *the doctors have been wrong before, right?*

And who's so unhappy now? Not me, I can tell you—forget it. No, an hour later Dad's gone off to meet Grammaw's flight and I'm sitting in Angelene's living room surrounded by a whole harem of females. It's like my birthday. Poo, you can tell, thinks I've got an even more outrageous swelled head on me, which is inevitable, all the limelight and this mantle of lordliness descending over me *'cause I've seen so much.* Right off, I eat more delicately and use a higher, more mature class of language, frankly impressing the pants off of Angelene and Nellie Belle, who obviously can't believe how big I'm being about everything.

And you can't blame them for not understanding. First, here's Angelene's thinking I'm *tired*, then here's Nellie Belle's thinking I'm *hungry*, worried why I'm not slobbering over her hot Chihuahua bean dip. "We're having steaks and corn, how about that?" she asks all chipper. Then, looking pretty rocky, old Nellie Belle plunks down beside me and starts itching my back. Meanwhile, crossing and uncrossing those big shapely legs of hers, Angelene cocks her doctor eye on me.

"Sure you don't wanna lay down? You sure had one helluva day."

"I'm fine." To prove it, I hold up my Coke. Not one cube clinks.

"Well, I'll tell you what," says Nellie Belle finally with a nod at Poo, "I think Frank's had enough adults for one day. So, why don't you kids both go downstairs? Listen to some records, huh?"

Whoa! who turned out the lights! Well, you know what I'm thinking. But going downstairs, Poo's being such a damned prude, switching on every light in the place. And straightaway she puts me on notice.

"Look, I'm sorry about your Mom. And I *want* to be nice to you. I do but I'll be darned if I'm creeping around here, kowtowing to you like them." Poo stomps off exasperated, "Well, I'm just telling you, okay?"

Hey, I didn't know. I never had brothers or sisters, so this is all new to me how kids—boys and girls both—all instinctively hate and mistrust you as a cripple, sucking off their parents' sympathy once you've lost somebody. But with Poo there's more to it than that. Instantly, my status has changed. Oh no, even if Dad and Angelene wanna ignore it, Poo instantly sees me for a potential—potential brother. And don't tell me it's too early to be thinking stuff like that. Too early nothing. Once a lady dies, it's like a gold rush on her husband, and anybody who says different is either a doofus or a liar, take your pick.

Anyhow, knowing she's really killed me, Poo turns all sullen—sexy sullen as I eye her slick dark hair and lips, thrilled by her girl's power to hurt me. Man! I want to grab her, tussle, kiss! She walks away! Pulling that feline, I'm-older-sensitive-and-better-bred act, Poo proceeds to totally ignore me. Then, with a swipe and a crackle, a record falls on the turntable. It's the Brothers Four.

"Oh, my favorite!" I sneer, "that hey-nonny-nonny folk crap you like."

Poo doesn't bite, though. On the couch, all tucked up into herself, stringing out her dark hair all sensitive, Poo's listening for about the fifth time to

"Greenfields," which I hate anyway and is driving me out of my mind. Now, "Johnny Angel," that I could listen to eighty times, being kissed by Donna Reed's daughter Shelley F. with her creamy lips, but this? Well, I stare at Poo. I snort. Then, roaring over to the phono, I hit Reject.

"Hey," I holler, "can we please listen to something else?" All I mean is, *Let's tussle.*

"Look, I'm trying to be Christian—"

"Christian?" And I lay on this oaf laugh guaranteed to drive any girl nuts. "Aww, isn't that sweeeet! Yeah, listen to her, Little Miss White Gloves *Christian!"*

But Poo doesn't yell, she *squints.* Just squints and wags her head at me, whispering all disgusted, "God, you are *so* immature! *You are.* And not 'cause I'm older or"—glaring at me looking at her tits—*"all that.* Miss Innocent, huh? Man, you *don't even know!* Sure, your Mom may be gone, but at least she wasn't a no-good drunk and a bum like my Dad."

I grab my stomach. "Oh, Poo-hoo-hoo! Tell it on *Queen for a Day*—"

"Shut your mouth!" Poo jams her face in mine. "What the hell do you know? Did you ever see your Dad belt your Mom in the mouth! Or so drunk you had to hide your baby sister in the backseat, scared he'd crash your whole family into a tree! In boy years, I'm about *sixteen. Twenty* compared to you!"

"Shut up! You just shut up!"

My eyes blow up and I bolt for the laundry room. Slap the door shut, then crawl back into the black cobwebby space between the cement laundry tub and the furnace. Now I'm in for it. Any second I expect Nellie Belle to tromp down the stairs but no, I realize, the record player must have drowned out the racket. And it only keeps playing. Automatically, the tone arm snaps back. Again, with a crackle of dust, comes "Greenfields." The louvered door creaks open.

"Frank? . . . Frank, I'm really sorry. Can I come in?"

Am I faking this too? Leaning against the dripping laundry tub, I'm breathing into my fist, trying to make it sound like coughs, when I feel Poo's fingers cluster across my wet face. Upstairs in the light I'd be mortified but not down here. Down here in the darkness, holding each other, we're invisible, Poo's arms flushed with that sharp, shivery popcorn sweat girls get at my dancing lessons, when we pick partners and the gym teacher, Mr. Hornseck, plays "Green Door," *"who's-that-hiding-behind-the-grrr-reeen-door?"*

And she's so healthy, to feel her. Poo's not dead. Poo's totally alive. She's like leaves all in shivers and her hair smells so beautiful. Why, every leaf of her smells healthy, her hair so fine it gets up my nose till I half sneeze. Only

I keep messing it up, wondering does Poo want me to prove I'm mature by *kissing her right on the mouth?* Well, does she? And if I do kiss her, will she open her mouth into mine, filling my mouth, my whole lungs, with air like a balloon and I'll float straight up to heaven? *Go on kiss her right on the mouth well go on she wants you to* . . . Kissing Poo on the mouth, that would be like blowing a soap bubble, when your breath is instantly surrounded like mercury by a trembling globe of ice and tension, *So go on, you chicken.* And then I do, too. Kissing Poo, I blow myself out into the breath of the bubble, the bubble that trembles before my eyes like a new egg and we're both in it, Mamma, both sealed off and protected forever. Out through my own lungs, through Poo, I blow up you back to life again, Mamma. Clear through Poo I blow you back to when you had dark hair, like Poo, and a willowy frame, like Poo, and all I gotta do, I think, is blow and blow until the bubble of life starts blowing back.

THE

PRESENT

SENSE

GRAMMAW BOLTS UP.

"He's here! Aww God bring him over here to his poor, old Grammaw—*sweetie!* Aww, my boy, my poor poor boy, where have you *been?*" Then catalepsy, the flapping arms, the oddly large, gnarled hands with the long red nails that cage her face, sucking and sobbing, "Aww, God, I can't—*Jesus* . . . I can't even look at him, no mother! Never another mother! Never again to see her alive. Never again my Julie, my one, my only *Juuuulie . . .*"

It's a surprise party. Floating across our living room in the morning sunlight, there's a cloud of smoke, and, beneath it, the huddled barn smell of all your grieving, perspiring, freely drinking relatives. Already Dad's been beat up so bad, and he's so pooped out, that he abandons ship for his room. Down the gauntlet I go, hugged, kissed, gazed upon, stuck with tie clasps and earrings, then smeared with tears and lipstick from various ailing, fleshy old aunts seizing up from creaking chairs, wall-eyed Rose with the polio leg, Marge with the elephantine arm that she cradles like an infant and Alice who kisses me with the teary abruptitude of a Vichy general. The doorbell rings. A pot of drooping lilies flies past me—passed down the family bucket brigade—back to the sideboard to be stacked with other gaudy, poisonous looking flowers, beside which my Uncle Jim, the cop built like a fullback with the red combover, where cool Uncle Jim tends bar with his handsome, philandering brother-in-law and A&P butcher, Dave—"Dog Dave"—or simply the "Bellyman," for Dave's knack of boosting out porterhouse steaks and cold cuts strapped to his belly. Playing the nags, running the girls, it's Dave, happy Dave, with the transistor radio bulging from his shirt pocket and the little earphone dangling from one ear. You think life stops for game three of the World Series?

"Aww, bring him here, to his Gramm-maw-haw!" she cries. Then, once I've been captured, like a sopping dog, she sputters her grief over me. All but burping me, she's softly whacking me across the back with those long arms of hers—incredibly long for her tiny body, and all wrapped in this sticky old lady flesh that clings to my sweaty neck like warm bubble gum. Now seventy-three, Grammaw's a craggy old geisha, heavily powdered and rouged, with deep red lips and the matching nails that—to hear her at least—she paints for no man. A heavy smoker, of course. They're all heavy smokers. Grammaw, though, she'll take Viceroys or Marlboros, Pall Malls, Camels, even Kools—anything so long as they're close and they're yours, and especially when she's always conveniently misplacing her own cigs in the turquoise leatherette pack, the "ladylike" pack with the sewn-on moccasin sparkles. (Well, bare packs are a little *common*, don't you think?)

"Tommy! Tommy!" Lighting Tommy's Camel with Alice's matches. Grammaw waves the match out like a thermometer, then grandly misses the ashtray. Foof! A hydrogen ball of smoke envelops her face.

"Honey," she says, not even bothering to lower her voice so Dad won't hear her, "Honey, I just heard! Only yesterday—*yes-ter-day*." Pop Eyes, I call her behind her back. "Frank, your Father just *called* me!"

"The day before he did," corrects Aunt Till. Till is Catty's virtual sister-in-law, the wife of Grammaw's first cousin and brother by adoption, Tommy Twomey. "Come on, Cats," coaxes Till, "fair's fair. Pete tried twice on Monday."

"*He* says—"

"Well, he called us."

A thin geyser of smoke. "And just in the nick of time! Second I heard the phone, I knew, I just *knew* it was Julie. And I'd meant to call her! So, why? *Why* did I ignore it? Christ, why didn't the Old Sonofabitch take *me*, stupid, ugly old goat! That's sense for you! He takes Beauty and leaves the old Beast."

And like a herd, the women cover Catty, mortified at your elopement—stood up and told nothing. Why, less than nothing, locked out of her own life! Yet how can Catty blame you, Julie, you her hero and, worse, her only child? How can the old woman bear it, to think her daughter would humiliate her own mother like this, and right in front of her own family, dying for two weeks and not a word? Whoops, face check. With a snap, out comes Grammaw Catty's compact, then the blood-red, half-melted lipstick—God, the lipstick would send you up a wall, complaining to her, "Mother, you *apply* lipstick, you don't *nibble* on it like a goat!" Round two. Grammaw waves out another match.

"So who took care of you?"

"Dad did."

"Well, *that's* funny." Grammaw cranes around at the family. "He told me he was forever at the hospital."

"Well, I stayed over at places. Other places. Kids I know."

"But how long?"

"A couple days, I dunno."

"Cats, quit," says Till, but Grammaw pulls away, waving her finger, "I should have known! *Stephen, look what happened with Stephen. Before anybody heard I knew!*" She means your rich Uncle Stephen, your "second father," who gave you away but didn't leave you a dime. Like I said, Uncle Stephen just dropped dead a few months ago. Grammaw had a dream and woke up sobbing. People say it's on account of her being an orphan that Grammaw has this sixth sense—this "fey" sense, the Irish call it.

"Indeed, we remember with poor Stephen," soothes Till. "We believe you, honey."

Grammaw starts back on me. "Well, you at least got to see her. Well, *didn't* you?"

"Once."

"Well then I'm asking you, Frankie. *Did*-your-mother-know-she-was-so-sick?"

"Well, she thought she was getting better," I lie—or am I lying? "Mom wanted to get better, then call you. She knew how upset you'd be."

"Upset!"

"Aww, Cats, for cryin out loud. Cripes, quit badgering the poor kid."

Mopping his jowly, boiled face with a monogrammed handkerchief it's Till's husband, natty Tommy Twomey. It's T.T. himself, the family big cheese, grandly chugging up in gold cufflinks and red suspenders, a seven-and-seven balled in his drinking hand while a Chesterfield expertly dangles between the same two tobacco-stained fingers.

"Aww, come on," says T.T. in his bullfrog's bray, "a week. Three weeks— what the hell's the diff'rance? Cripes, Cats, she was like my own, Julie, but you heard Pete. Now goddamnit, leave it alone now. Pete did all he could."

"Ex-cept call me."

"And you heard that priest, Father Chivas, was it?" offers wall-eyed Agnes, the Religious One. "Julie had all the sacraments. She's in God's hands."

"Wait," I break in, "you mean Father *Nivas?* The slobby Mexican guy?"

"Frank!" scolds Agnes.

Catty waves out another match. "Yeah, him I wanna talk to, too. And not about my first Holy Communion."

"No, you don't, Grammaw," I grin. "Not Father Nivas you don't."

"Sheez." Tommy shoves her empty glass at Dog Dave. "Hey! *Useless!* Fix mother here a drink, willya?"

AND ALL THE CRAP people sent over. Back on the sideboard, it's a flow-ershop/bakesale, topped off with this coconut cake some little bastard jammed his fingers into, a sign to warn me off his Mamma. And look at this. From Dad's partner, Bud, it's this golf-bag-sized urn of flowers, *Condolences and love as always, Bud and Anne.* Boy, isn't that the truth. The biggest always send the biggest.

And flowers are so stupid when they only die and cakes only get stale. And especially when all it does is remind me, stuffing my face with chocolate cup-cakes. Whenever somebody walks by, their footsteps bring down a drizzle of petals and pollen. Look, the pollen's like yellow paint, and I write in it POO. We were making out again this morning, Poo saying, "Okay, you can kiss me but no French kissing." *French kiss why's that French?* I mean, here Poo's break-ing my damn concentration when I wanna go *Green Door.* When I want that bubble of her breathing and being breathed into with that thundery rain smell she gets, *Look you don't gotta build Rome in a day.* Sure, just start with some-thing simple. Poo's ear. *Her ear and the strand of dark hair she hooks over it.*

Poo seems far away now, though. Upstairs, Dad's still asleep, and I'm hav-ing to hold hands with Grammaw—literally, if I don't want her going into another crying fit. But then as me and Grammaw are sitting there, here's Dad, who's looking none too hot himself. Seeing him now, I'm scared Grammaw'll blow up at him but no, I realize, the old lady's too slick for that. No, clasp-ing Dad's hands, Grammaw gives him a wounded, adoring look, saying to the family, "Look at him, not even forty. Not even forty, are you?"

Dad glowers but he eats up the sympathy. "Forty-one, Catty."

"Ten—no, *eight* years younger than I was when my Francis died, God bless his heart. Aww, Pete, Pete, Pete. God, Julie was *so* proud of you. She just knew you'd strike it rich."

"I tried."

"And I know you tried, honey, I know you did."

It's weird with Dad and Grammaw. You'd think Dad would want to run out of there, but instead he hangs around, anything to be forgiven and com-forted, and especially by anything female. "Well," he says finally, "we'll prob-ably see her this afternoon"—you, he means, Mamma—and Grammaw answers, "Well, I won't believe it until I do. And I *can't* believe it, I just can't.

And you were so happy," Grammaw adds. Then, off-key, like a mockingbird answering her own call, she turns it a half note, twists it into a question, "Well, you were happy, weren't you? Sure you were—right?"

Dad can't stand it. He gets up. "Look, Catty, I've got errands to run. Frank, can we talk outside a second?"

Errand schmerand. It's pure b.s. And Dad makes no pretense of it now, anymore than he does to keep calling Catty "mother." God, that's right, I realize. Already, Dad's demoted her to "Catty." It kills the old lady, too. She's lost more face than even she can even smear back on, popping out her compact every two minutes.

"Daddy," I complain outside, "Daddy, why are you calling Grammaw 'Catty' and not 'mother'? You know Mom would hate that."

"Did I?" he pretends, "Well, I didn't mean anything by it." Smiling, Dad hands me a dollar—wow, a whole dollar! "Look, you're not on duty here. What's your friend Paul doing today?"

"Dad, he's in *school* today."

"So play hooky. Ride your bike. Buy yourself something. Be good for you."

"Okay, Dad!"

Hear that? Well, if Dad can call Grammaw "Catty," I figure I can quit this namby-pamby "Daddy" business, which frankly, even before this mess, was on my mind. And riding off, I can hear myself calling back, *Bye, Dad. See you, Dad.* And right then I know I've cut another rope. A big one too.

Well, I take off but halfway there I can feel the handlebars loose, and the chain—the damned chain's slipping, plus the seat's maladjusted and people are staring at me why aren't I in school? It's too much. Ten minutes later I'm sneaking my bike around the back of our house, thinking I'll sneak up and listen to my crystal set, which always calms me right down, muffled under the earphones. Creeping up through the basement I'm peering around the corner, ready to make my break, when here's Grammaw, "Oh, there you are, sweetie." All re-rouged and powdered in her party face, she brightens, *Look we can be gay.* And that's the confusing thing about Grammaw. How tiny she is, then how she can zoom up, on account of anger counts as size. And suddenly there's all this *fun* in her voice, saying, "Let's go upstairs and talk. Just us, huh? Why, I've barely *seen* you, my darling."

I'm such a chump for women. Any idiot would see it coming. With Dad gone, Grammaw makes a beeline for your room, yanks me in, then shuts the door. And right off she's picking things up, and here when I'm worried about *anything*, even a pin, being out of place so we lose the crumb trail back to our old life. And she can't just sniff the perfumes on your vanity, oh no. No, she falls down on her knees, then starts to *feeling* the inner soles of your shoes, which sounds weird, I know, but when I look myself, it's amazing. Inside your shoes there's these big, black footprints pressed in, actual proof of life, like on a birth certificate.

"Grammaw! Hey, come on, that's Mom's *stuff* you're messing with!"

It's the *smell*, it's that b.o. life smell that's what's driving the old hound crazy, and even that's not enough for her. No, plunging both arms in the closet, Grammaw drags out about two dozen dresses, clutches and dances them like a body flopped over at the waist, loose hangers clattering on the floor. Whump, Grammaw collapses back on the bed, with that sick, lied-to look, "She *wore* all these. These were actually *hers* . . ." Grammaw's feet start flapping on the floor. She starts wheezing and panting, "I don't know what I'll do. I—don't—know—what—I'll—do."

I grab her arm. "Well, I know what we'll do. Get the heck out of here before Dad catches us!" But here while I'm rehanging things and smoothing out the bed, here she is snatching things out of your jewelry box!

"Hey, are you done?" I holler. "Are you quite done yet?"

But no, she's not done. Yanking open your top drawer, she pulls out a bandanna, sniffs it—great, a good dirty one, so she wraps it around her neck, for this Ubangi effect, glaring at me, "Don't be foolish, this is my rr-right! *Two weeks* and your father can't call me? Two weeks and this is all I've got left?"

"So, fine! So let him catch you up here. Cause I'm going!"

But what's this I hear up in the upstairs—up in the spare bedroom where you store your mink and all your fancy clothes? Peering around the corner I about fall over. It's Mrs. Feeney and two other ladies—one of them Mrs. Moffitt, I think. And look, they've got all your clothes all piled on the bed! Shoes! Shawls! Petticoats! Christ, they're all rooting through your closets!

"*Grammaw,*" I hiss, "there's women upstairs! Mrs. Feeney and all them. They're ransacking through Mom's stuff!"

Grammaw stares at me. "No, no, they're women from the church. Your Dad said it was okay. They're getting clothes for your mother. For the *service.*" No wonder Dad gave me that dollar! To get rid of me!

"Grammaw," I say, "that's Mrs. Feeney, Mom's archenemy. Do you understand? Mrs. Feeney hates Mom's guts. All those damned sodality women do. What, you don't know what they did to Mom? She never told you?"

"Of course. Of course she told me." The old lady stands there wavering.

"And you're just gonna stand here? When they made Mom a public laughingstock? Well, huh?"

"Stop that! People admired your mother. She was the envy of everyone."

It's the shock. Gotta be. Normally, Grammaw would be up there like a banshee, but instead she's got her compact out, sucking on her lipstick again.
Well, not me! No, I go right on up! And even if I am being insane, I'm not
all wrong, as I look back on it. They've pulled out everything. Armloads of
dresses. Even hatboxes, like they're gonna bury you in a big hat. In front of
the long slant mirror, here's Mrs. Feeney holding up your red ball dress—that
I distinctly remember.

"*Oh, Frank*—" exclaims Mrs. Feeney. "Oh, look everybody, Frank's here—"

Caught red-handed. Slowly, Mrs. Feeney lays down the red dress. Mild
Mrs. Moffitt tittles forward, and poor Mrs. Kearny cranes out of the closet.
And here's Mrs. Ward too.

"Didn't your Dad tell you?" asks Mrs. Feeney breathlessly. "As a favor to
your Dad, we came to help him. To pick out what—what your Mom will wear
the, uh, day after tomorrow? For, uh, your Dad to pick out?"

"And Frank too," adds Mrs. Ward. "To pick out."

"Of course."

"Of course."

"And you know," prompts Mrs. Kearny, "maybe Frank has a favorite. I'll
bet he does. Well, do you, honey? Your Mom was such a snappy dresser."

"Here," picks up Mrs. Moffitt, lifting the sleeves of your beige Belgian lace
with the fancy leaf designs, skeletal leaves like you see on river bottoms.
"Now *this*, this is gorgeous. This is sooo classy, so Julie. You like this one, hon?"

"Or this," adds Mrs. Kearny in a whinnying, don't-get-upset voice. "See,
we've laid all this out. In fact . . . in fact, let's call Pete up right now, huh?"
But starting down the stairs she stops dead.

It's Grammaw coming up the stairs! Full war paint too! Coming up the
stairs, Grammaw's got two of your scarves tied around her neck and three or
four of your bracelets buckled on each wrist. "Why, *hel*-lo," she chirps with a
wondering smile, "I'm Catty Slattery, Julie's mother. And well, well, well.
What's all this I see?"

"Oh yes, we met you," insists Mrs. Feeney with a helpful smile. "Yes indeed. When we first came in? . . ." Stricken, Mrs. Feeney looks at the other
women. "Well, there were so many people, but I know we met Mrs.—Mrs.—
Julie's Mom, right, girls?"

"Yes, of course we did," tinkles Mrs. Moffitt. Easing down the Belgian lace,
she makes a pained face. "We know how awfully hard it is for you today, Mrs.
Slattery."

Hard? she says. Why, just then Grammaw's beaming, and horrified they
all look at her, the poor old thing. Is the old woman in shock? Hard of hear-

ing? Mrs. Feeney pipes up, *"Around here, Pete's Mr. Fixit, you know.* He's given us all *so much help* in the neighborhood over the years, so *well*,"—she looks at the others—"whelp, the least we could do—"

"Didn't she have beautiful things?" says Grammaw all of a sudden. It's like she's skating, sweeping toward the piled bed. "Such beautiful taste she had, don't you think? She was always tall. Always the tallest girl in her class. Model thin." She points at fat Mrs. Feeney. "Now what do you like, my dear?"

Mrs. Feeney's lost. "You mean for, uh, *Thursday?"*

"Or Friday. Or Saturday. I mean for you."

"Well, Mrs.—"

"Slattery, dear. Now, that," she says picking up a black cocktail dress and moving toward Mrs. Feeney, "Well, I don't know, with a little pinning, *et cetera*—well, that might do for you. In a *pinch."* She smiles. "I mean, no sense handing it all over to *Goodwill,* right?" Grammaw beams at her little joke. "God, Julie loved this neighborhood. All the *Goodwill* here. Couldn't stop talking about it. Such lovely, lovely people—"

They're all frozen. I'm frozen. Finally, Mrs. Feeney lunges for the door. "We realize you've had a shock, Mrs. Slattery. And on that note—"

"Shock?" Feeling me ready to bolt, Grammaw grabs my arm. "Oh, no, my dear, I can see you were all busy, busy, busy bees. Why, I'm sure you were all dreadfully curious."

"Ma'am, Mr. Dougherty *asked* us." Blood red, Mrs. Feeney barges for the door, and Grammaw with that knack for the final cut, Grammaw grabs my arm.

"No, don't be rude, Frank Dougherty! *Ladies first!* And thank you all, ladies. *Thank you all,* good ladies of the Church!"

YOO—HOO.

You're here but you're not here but yet I'm here and I can see you but you can't see me and I'll know you but you won't know me, *and I'll be in Scotland before you.*

Here I am with both my eyes staring down at you in the white satin plush, and here I can see you, the *was* you, but you, Mamma, with both your eyes curdled shut, here you won't see me, so I don't know where I am or where that leaves you, *But is that you? the real you?* Oh sure, that's you, but not the *you*-you. And okay, it's definitely your lacy leaf dress with the lace trailing over your spindly wrists but c'mon, this isn't you. Not with your hair cut crooked and curled too tight and a rosary wound around your shriveled hands, *a rosary?* That can't be you.

But first class, though, Dad doesn't stint a dime. No sir, this is Morley's Funeral Home right on Wisconsin Avenue with big white columns and the brass lamps licking real blue flames of gas and everybody but everybody is packed in the Jefferson Room packed with flowers, and all smoking up a storm, so the smoke packs the ceiling. People we barely know. Strangers saying they've known me all my life and people all up and down Corregidor—they've all come in droves, giving me their snuffly, red-eyed heavenward smiles. Everyone except "the Fashion Committee," as Grammaw calls them, Mrs. Feeney and that bunch. No sir, they're not coming anywhere near old Mrs. Congeniality.

Beauty was there—your crazy blond friend Huta Lunt, Captain Lunt's widow. Hubba-hubba, boy! Hula Huta, the terror of naval wives from Bermuda to the Caribbean, Huta had flown in from Key West, on some military transport. Military courtesy, Dad said, most likely courtesy of some tailgunner she'd met at an officer's club with the quarter drinks and the free band. All tanned in her black, sleeveless dress, her silver-blonde hair swept back like a stewardess's, old Huta makes Dad more nervous than Angelene does. No, women *cut* Dad now. Any woman that kisses him, any woman who even breathes, leaves these red gashes of lipstick on his cheek. But with Huta especially it embarrasses me, how hard Dad's trying to impress her, being all suave and ringadingding. Cruising by, I hear him telling Huta about this hush-hush q.t. stock deal he says'll make us a pile and how she, Huta, oughta buy some. Well, I get excited! We'll pay off your bills! Save the Bird, bomb off to Florida and finally get you that good long rest you wanted. But then just as fast I'm scared this stock scheme is something else you cooked up, Mamma.

One thing sure, Angelene definitely notices Dad with Huta. Angelene's trying to snag me but I can't stand it inside the Show Room, and Dad won't let me go outside, so *I keep moving.* I wish Poo was here, but forget that. Except for me, there's not one kid in the whole place. "Mom doesn't believe in it," explained Poo when I begged her to come. "Believe in what?" I asked, figuring it for some Presbyterian crap. Which of course gets Poo all exasperated, "Believe—you know—in seeing people laid out like that." *Laid out.* Like you're some kinda finger food, I suppose. God, I love these damned Presbyterians.

Wearing the same dusty old black mariah she'd buried Grampa Francis in, Grammaw's sure pleased with the turnout. Every few minutes, she breaks down again, saying you were too good because only the good die young and she's the proof, etc., etc. Well, after each performance she heads off to the powder room, then back to the maître d' desk with the brass lamp and the guest register where the people sign their names to the testament, *yeah she's dead all right*. Anyhow, fishing up her rhinestone cat-glasses on the silver chain, Grammaw conducts her latest popularity poll, slowly moving one sharp red nail down the list, from name to name. Once she's done there, she taps the first man she sees for a cigarette. *And* a light, which she says is such an awful failing nowadays in Goddamn and Gomorrah, the way men shirk their solemn lighting responsibilities. Puff puff puff! And not so fast, buddy boy! Then comes the *second tap*. "Dear me, you'll think I'm awful but *might you have an extra, darling?*" What a pack rat, slipping it down her sleeve stoppered with her hankie. I'll bet she's got half a carton wadded down there.

Like I say, I keep moving and avoiding everybody all wanting to back me into a corner and blubber over me. In the men's, I run into dapper Uncle T.T. and Dog Dave tipping off my Uncle Jim's flask, and yep good old Dave has his transistor earphone in, just like in church. "You like baseball?" they ask, embarrassed by the radio. "Look, next time you come up, we're going to a Yankees game. What, you never been to a game!?" I mean they all know I *hate* baseball, but see, this is just life in the *for instance*, people suddenly inviting me out to eat crabs, ride horses, sail boats, shoot real guns. Dad's already warned me, not to stuff myself on the baloney of people's good intentions. That's the problem with people being nice. Sure, they all wanna make me feel better, but c'mon, to only disappoint a kid later? when it's all crap but I'm supposed to yip and jump around so *they'll* feel better?

Well, I don't pee—I can't pee with anybody near me—so again I wash my hands, washing and rewashing my hands and double-checking my hair. Then here's Uncle T.T. following me out into the Show Room. It's a crush now, it's almost *Closing Time*, and Uncle T.T. who can cry on a dime, Uncle T.T. says to Grammaw, "Place looks like damned Mount Vernon." Grammaw shakes her head. "But how will Pete ever pay for it? Ah, Stephen," she sighs. *Ah, money* she means. Yeah, what a year, they say, what with Uncle Stephen, their little brother, dying last summer in Palm Beach. And come to think of it, it was funny, the way you and Uncle Stephen copy catted each other. After Grampa Francis died, Uncle Stephen gave you away, then the very next year suddenly Uncle Stephen got married to Aunt Toody, who was older but she really had the loot and connections. That really stunk, Toody having her housekeeper call you to break the news, and then to say it was a private service! Well, you called back Toody's housekeeper, Mamma! Boy you bawled her out, but Toody still wouldn't pick up the phone, the old bitch, jealous because you were Stephen's favorite and so beautiful. Well, you took off. Took the car and Dad was scared you'd drive to Florida, but of course you didn't go anywhere. No, when you came back, all you did was mope and go to sleep.

And speaking of money, who do I run into when I'm trying to pee (again!) but Bud. Coming out of the john. Stinking the place to high heaven but he strolls out like a celebrity, then corners me while he washes his hands. "Frank," he says, all tanned from his forty-foot sloop, "Frank, you know, you and your Dad are overdue for a sail on *Skip to My Lou*."

Skip with the Loot, is more like it! God, I hate money now. It's all I can do not to spit in his bullshitter's face.

WELL, LIKE I SAY, it was getting to Closing Time, and I can feel everybody wondering, *So does he get it yet? That's she's dead?*

Well sure, there's pretty overwhelming evidence *against*. Life, I mean. And sure. Not being blind I *see* you—*but is that really you laying there?*

Not to be gross but did you ever see a stuffed marlin and believe for a second that it was ever a live fish swimming in the ocean? *That's her you're crazy if you don't think that's her.* But then getting angrier and angrier I get super-hyper-suspicious about how you look. Wrong color lipstick. Hair on crooked. And worse, here's everybody eyeing me like I don't, like I never ever could, feel enough. But what's even left to feel with these piranha? I mean I already feel dead and sick enough without everybody pushing me up to the old choke bowl, saying how much better I'll feel if I only get it out. Still, who knows? If Grammaw hadn't gotten into the act then, it all might have been completely different—you, my life, everything.

All ready to close you up, Father Nivas was there, right in front of the coffin with Dad and Grammaw and me right beside him. God, was it stuffy. It was so packed that I was falling asleep, when I jump! *Water!* Out of a plastic squeeze bottle, Nivas flings holy water on you. Throws holy water on your sleeping face, and the water makes little brown holes in your face like rain in dry dirt. I jerk awake. And look, the water wets and stains you but still you just lay there. But wait, I think. There's more, right? But no. At a look from Nivas, Dad gives the nod to the slick-haired funeral director.

"Stop! Sir! No, wait—"

Shoving the funeral director aside, Grammaw seizes your hunched arms, leans in the coffin, then stumbles back, her lips smeared with thick powder like she's kissed the wings of a giant moth. She glares at Dad.

"*Kiss* her, Pete. Go on, it's all right." Pumping Dad's arm, Grammaw says to the whole room, "It's an old S-kkcottish custom. A *beautiful* custom. Pete! For God's sake, kiss her. Kiss your poor wife." Dad's dizzy. To him, it's like Grammaw's speaking for everybody, asking him if he loved or felt enough or tried enough, *"Pete, kiss her, it's your last chance."*

Well, Dad panics. Jerking around, like he's taking a bow, he kisses you, then rears back. My turn.

I can feel Grammaw's hand climbing in jolts up my arm. Frozen, I look at Dad but, wiping his lips, he's totally gone. My head floods. Like a fire hose, my eyes are spewing pure seeing and your water-speckled face is welling up, a silty pool of gold in the silver plush. I can't stand it. Every eye is on me but all there is is your face, your face so far down it's like I'm peering off a high-dive daring me to dive or die here with you forever. And look! You're wearing your diamond ring! Why, just to impress people? So somebody can steal it? But then this other voice says, *Don't you see it's not her real diamond and it's not her either.*

Well sure, I think. It's just a cheap dare. It's like when kids ask, for a million bucks would you lick up vomit? For a million bucks would you suck a dead dog's dick? *Well would you kiss her if she might wake up?*

Blurry, foreign face I can't kiss you. And not just can't—refuse. Refuse, then taste in my mouth the nasty taste of refusal. And when the slick-haired undertaker moves in to shut you up, right away I can feel it. No air! An unbearable airless pressure packing my chest. And you're sinking, Mamma! Clear down to hell you're sinking, down like a stone, sending up greasy bubbles when, *BOOM!*

With a belch of blue smoke, sliding down the secret chute, you're out! free! *in me!* Pushed clear to my throat, you're inside me and I'm inside you and it's a holy mystery, all right, a secret mystery like Holy Communion. Man, I'm like the cat who swallowed the canary. Father Nivas walks up.

"How ya doin'? Not so hot, huh?" And what's this? I think. Because just then Father Nivas hands me this red metal thing heavy as a chunk of lead. "Here, your mother would want you to have this."

It's a red plaque of the Sacred Heart, and it's really gross, this candy-apple heart burning in a nest of flames. God, that's right, I saw it tucked inside the coffin lid, but before I can think what to do, Nivas is steering me into an empty parlor. With the seam on his pants about to bust and his white socks showing, the Padre sits me down. He thinks I'm upset 'cause I didn't kiss you.

"So what if you din' do it?" he asks, "Does this mean you love her any less? *Frank,* enough the silent stuff, I hab eyes. You feel angry—screwed, okay. You hear me, *screwed.* How could God ever do such a low-blow thin' to you?

An' you know what? Prob'bly, you will never see it, huh? Do you see this?" And with his big finger, he taps the heart. Points to the gash where the Roman spear pierced through, then he pokes me in the ribs. "This wound of our Lord's, it is yours too now. Sooner or later eberybody gets one but you, Frank, you get yours early, huh." His finger circles the heart. There's a crack in his shoe where you can see his white sock, and I can hear the hearse revving its engine. "Frank, do you think Father tells you a simple story? Cause after this, my frien', you must dig down to your sorrow, 'cause I promise you, it is a mystery. And mos' of all, you mus' not lose your faith. Well, come *on*. For you to lose your faith? To lose this one beautiful, everlastin' thin' that connects you to your mother? To lose that would be to lose everything."

And God's inside him? I think. *Go to hell, Pizza Face.* And walking out to the car, I watch my shoes, already steadying myself so I won't break you growing inside me, actually hatching inside me, you might say, like an enormous egg.

BUMPS, I HEARD YOU MAINLY AS BUMPS at first, coughs and bumps, 'cause you were still pretty sick, weak as a baby and sleeping a lot. Some days you wouldn't be up 'til noon, but still I'd feel you there, knotting my stomach and coughing bubbles in my blood, and Dad across the table pretending not to see your old chair sitting empty, Dad would say, "Man, you still have your appetite. What'd you do? Swallow a tapeworm?"

Look, this wasn't some Tinker Bell–Topper–type thing, how you grew in me like a peach pit or the sounds you made and how I took care of you all nothing and forgotten, then felt you swelling up in me, like when I puffed out my belly. Even my shadow showed it. In certain lights, I swear my shadow grew almost a tail, like the blur after comets.

Grammaw, she'd gone by then, which Dad (sounding like she was some old dog we'd put to sleep) said was best for everybody. Waiting for Grammaw's flight at National, we were cooling her off at the Bombs Away Lounge, when she got all messy over me again—you know, the-poor-motherless-boy, how-will-he-eat act. Well, once she goes to the ladies, smirking, I nudge Dad, *nerk nerk,* "Hey, Dad, should we call the Guys in the White Coats?"

"Frank—" Wincing because, even if he had to pretend to be disgusted, it had to feel good to him, for me to say what obviously he couldn't—not in his position, being in pretty rough shape himself and in hock up to his butt. Besides, Dad felt sorry for her, a manless, daughterless, nobodyless old lady dragging her beat-up wire cart through New York City. Grammaw, meanwhile, was working on him, playing the lovable, harmless, broken old coot. Grammaw, she even had Dad back to calling her "Mother." Yeah, for now she'd surrender and go, but you'd better believe she was planning her return.

They were one strange pair, those two. First, you'd hear them bickering, then they're both up half the night, drinking and talking, all forgiven—you think. Anyhow, after my rotten crack in the airport Dad's getting after me, "What the heck's the matter with you? Can you even dimly appreciate how the poor woman feels? And especially when you're the last thing she's got left."

Fine, it was a sick crack. But then I'm thinking, if it feels good to him and it's true basically—so why's it so out of line for me to say it? *Fair!* God, I hate that word *fair.* All those trembling-lipped, lame-assed victim's words like *can't, shouldn't, please.* Forget it! That's not even roughly a concept where we are now, Mamma, down here in purgatory together. No sir, way out here in The World there's only one real question, I've decided, and that's *But is it true?*

Oh sure, people get hurt by a True Mouth but if you ask me they get hurt lots worse by the Mealymouthers. Nope, sitting there in the lounge while Grammaw does her pit stop—well, kicking back in my chair, watching the smoke wheel in the sunlight, I'm thinking how, on account of the Monroe Doctrine and the Reds lying about the missiles in Cuba, JFK had almost just H-bombed the Russians! *Just last week!* Phew! Probably the most exciting thing that ever happened in my whole life and we missed it! Man, I never even heard boo about it until a couple days ago, when it was all over. And here when I could have enlisted! Died for a cause, a hero, instead of limping around here playing nursemaid! In fact, realizing I missed it, I get mad, thinking how naturally they've saved the whole world—everybody but you, killed on the last day of the war! Not that I'm whining, understand. No sir, thinking more in the *positive* like I'm learning, I'm thinking of all the stuff that can't hurt you now! bombs! fires! car wrecks! cancer! TB! . . . or liars. You're invulnerable. Where you are, Mamma, you can laugh at all that shit now. And feeling like Hercules Unchained, I know *I'll always see it this way.* And if I keep building up my muscles like I'm doing—if I get stronger in my mind and do everything right and never take any crap, but mainly if I just love and protect you better, then I know you'll stay and nothing else will get lost . . . *but only if I can make my life perfect as the most Perfect Host.*

SO, GRAMMAW LEFT but still it was pretty dicey, what with you on the critical list and Dad in a three-alarm state. Meanwhile, Dad and me, we try to play *Boys and Fathers*, with him playing the Daddy and me the boy, just like before.

Nope, the new world wasn't working, so it was only natural that Dad would run back to the old one, back in his old sea days. And, starting off it's fun swabbing floors, doing laundry and cooking in the "galley" of the U.S.S. *Dougherty*. We've got some hints for old Heloise. Like adding lemon juice to the syrup from fruit cocktail—sure it tastes like spit but you save on frozen. Or the miracles of Kayro starch, which can stiffen a shirt or double a navy bean soup cooked on the hock of a picnic ham that Dad'll shave three meals out of first. Sweating over the bubbling pots, peeling potatoes, we're the two mess mates—"mess cranks," they call them at sea. Yeah, Dad's ornery old Big Crank, and me, I'm Shorty. Barging toward the sink with the boiling spud kettle Big Crank hollers out, *"Hot stuff, Shorty! Hot stuff coming through!"*

We even have a weekly menu—typed. Every Sunday night Dad tacks it up.

Mess: U.S.S. Dougherty
Week of November 16, 1962

Monday

Hamburgs w/ cheese
Crank's famous Fat Fries
   Cheezeball fritters
String beans
cXXookies
Milk/Bug juice/java

Wednesday

Ham 'n' redeye
   Cole slaw
   Masher poe-taters
   'n' redeye
Jello w/cling peaches
Bugjuice/milk/java

Friday

Fried smelts

Tuesday

Fish sticks de Mme. Paul
Dittoxx Crank'sfries
Garden salad
Bakked apple
Milk/Jungle juice/java

Thursday

Pigs in Blxxxankets
Baked beans
   Fried potato patties
apple cobbler
   Bugjoice/milk/junket

Saturday

Ham Hash

Sunday

Navy bean soup

Boom boom boom! beating out the durable dough for biscuits. Squashing out that chewy sourdough smell with little poofs of flour, Crank says, "Boy, we've had a real shocker, haven't we, old buddy? Boy, we've had ourselves a real shockeroo. You never think life'll turn out this way, but boy, it does—in spades. And—and all you can do is go on. Well, *right?* Am I right? And we'll make it. Well, come on, you know we will, right? We'll make it, right?"

So sure I *agree* with him, but mainly I just feel stupid, watching the poor guy getting ready to blow. It's like when Dad eats Chinese mustard. Sucks the breath right out of him, "HOO!" Coughing, then getting even redder in the face, "HOO—boy! . . . I mean, *hoo!*"

What can I do? Either way I'm screwed. If I just look at him crying, it means I'm cold, and if I look away, it means I don't care. Staring in disbelief Dad starts chucking dirty dishes into the sink. Don't ask me why my crotch is always itching these days. But here I am with my hand stuffed down my pants, when Dad whirls around.

"What *is* it with you fooling with yourself down there? Now quit your infernal scratching and come dry!"

MEANWHILE, GRAMMAW'S CALLING two or three times a week—collect, of course—to see how sad I am. The old lady's really creeping me out, telling me her dreams about you and asking can I find certain things of yours, then like *describe* them for her and other junk I'd rather not go into just now. Talk about the cat that swallowed the canary!

I mean I don't want to be rude to the old lady, but she breaks my concentration. Concentration, that's the ticket. See, thanks to the mighty Charles Atlas Dynamic Tension Technique, I'm massively getting my mind and my muscles all concentrated.

How does this work? you ask. Well, suppose your left arm jumps out and tries to stab a bowie knife through your throat! But *jah!* your right hand grabs the left! Hands vulcanized together, Righty and Lefty, Life and Death, they're locked in one mortal death grip! Guhh! with these great groaty scribbly little *veins* popping up on your arms and your palms kneading, Righty and Lefty are making these great, squirty hand farts! And Death is winning! Poor Righty's grunting and quivering, when, *kah!* He gives Lefty a judo flip and stabs the D to Death!

But you, Mamma, Miss Powderpuff, Miss Jack Lalanne flunk-out who never did so much as a sit-up, you *hate* this fire-breathing Atlasizing about improving ourselves—about us coming out winners instead of wieners, and screwers instead of screwees! Wanting to help Dad, see, I leave out my Charles Atlas book ("FEEL GREAT!!! SUPERCHARGED!!!!"), but Dad's not the Charles Atlas type. Seeing all these wedge-headed, oiled-up winners in their French ball-grabber suits, Dad's hollering why am I wasting my money on SUPER PEP!!! THE NEW YOU!!!!!

So go on, I think. Sit downstairs with your adding machine chunking out zeros and weeping, but not me! I haven't given up! My body is my Alamo! No sir, every morning the second my feet hit the floor here's Charles Atlas breathing fire, *Look, if you do everything right and save your allowance and don't let her squander it and NOTHING STUPID HAPPENS—*

But even as I'm hitting the stratosphere of FEEL GREAT, we've got these setbacks draining the air out of you. First off, Dad sells your old Ford Fairlane, which by now I can't stand to look at anyway. Three hundred dollars to appease the Aztec god Popocatepetl. I thought that would be it but with Christmas coming Dad surrenders the T-Bird, too. One day he drives off, then comes back with this clunker '57 Studebaker! Christ, he swaps our white Palomino for a gluebucket—a stupid old six-banger with a three-on-the-tree, pig ears for fins and, on the front grille, these tacky stars fizzling down, *stars!* And all up Corregidor, all but advertising how lame we are, Dad's clanging gears, *Clang.* Wud wud wud *Clang.* Wud wud wud . . .

SO IT WAS GETTING ON TOWARD CHRISTMAS, with the early winter darkness when, normally, all I want to do is burrow down and think about blizzardy big snows and Santy Claus.

Back in those days, before the weather changed, Washington always got snow in November. One November afternoon it really snowed, I remember. School let out early and in that sheer hypnosis of snow I felt so relieved. Relieved because you, Mamma, you hated the snow and completely disappeared into these fat flakes of happy oblivion. The bell rang. The school doors flew open and I careened into it, a romping dog plowing up to his snout in the stuff, snapping wet flakes off his whiskers!

Well, we got us up a big gang. Look out! Red-nosed Catholic hooligans in wool caps! Snorting and blowing out big yellow hockers, our greasy leather gloves packing ice balls that hit like dum-dums! On Shawcross Avenue, hidden by the dense, black firs of the convent, we're crazed marauders, bombarding cars, then dashing back through the darkened boughs, jeering and pelting the motorists who vainly try to chase us through shin-deep snow and whooshing firs. When out of nowhere Kevin Dun smashes my face with an ice ball! Like an egg, my frozen face busts open and they all just stand there, laughing at me! Laughing when my nose is probably broken and I see blood.

"Dun, you coulda busted my nose!"

"Wisten to him, wittle wussy. *Mwh-wommy.*"

"Talk about my mother, you bastard! Shut up!"

To save face, I flail after Dun, when, *whock!* another ice ball, then a storm of exploding ice as they surround me, stuffing my shirt with snow, then driving me off with rapid-fire volleys, *Fuck you we ain't feeling sorry for you anymore asshole.*

And running. Cursing them but, above all, cursing you, Julie, powerless to protect me. Faster and faster—dizzily—I run so the snow will whirl faster, spinning into the blindness and painlessness and oblivion of snow. All up Omaha Beach and across Midway, I run, then rip open my coat and stand there watching the steam pour out of me, as if I could actually rid myself of you.

As I head up Corregidor later, our house looks so fat and beautiful and gingerbready, all muffled in snow, and not a single print on the walk. Spreading out in one long, perfect loaf, it almost could be the old walk, to our old house. Standing there, I feel sick to spoil it. I wish I could float across it like a ghost and never leave a print.

But then it hits me, I'm late! Gotta sweep the walk. Gotta get dinner ready before Dad gets home, and especially tonight, a Friday. Fridays, see, Dad's always entertaining clients, meaning he can get a little on the, well, happy side. Then I think, *Don't forget the porch light!* Boy, it upsets him when I forget to put on the porch light. Forget the light and Dad acts like I've forgotten him—like I've abandoned him to freeze in Siberia. But who turns on the light for me? I wonder. Because when I open the door, it's just as dark. Sometimes for five or ten minutes I just stand there staring into the darkness swarming over the rug like a massive outbreak of fleas. "Daaad," I call out. Then as a decoy against robbers and spooks, "Maaaa-ooommmm—" And your name tastes so strange in my mouth. To call your name in the darkness is like huffing into a paper bag and tasting my own stale, soggy breath—

"Now, boys!" I holler.

That's the signal! Crashing across the rug, ripping my bowie knife, I seize the lamp, ice flecks flicking off my hair, *snap!* Quick! More lights! For twenty minutes I rage around. Shuck off my wet clothes. Get the oven warmed up and the spud water boiling. Mop up the wet snow so he won't holler about that, too. But here when I've done everything I hear Dad outside. Cussing. I open the door.

"Dad, what's the matter?"

"The light! Switch on the porch light, you knucklehead! Don't you hear me blundering around out here?"

WE'RE IN MOURNING, DON'T FORGET. One night after Angelene finally ropes Dad into dinner, Dad explains it. All this good crap about feeling and prayer and propriety and *finding yourself*. Which of course boils down to one thing—he can't date.

Date! Man, you don't wanna hear that, Mamma. And especially not now, when every day more and more of your stuff is disappearing. Same as a little kid will find his pet blankie snipped away inch by inch, we'll find your shoes gone, then your jewelry box hidden, then a smudged rectangle on the wall where the picture hung of you as a little girl. I loved that picture of you dark-eyed and bare-chested, fingering the St. Christopher medal around your throat.

"Look," labors Dad, "it's no big deal, my not dating. I'm just telling you so you'll know why with Angelene—well, why I'm reluctant."

"But how long's it last?"

"A few months, I don't know." I can feel Dad hedging—he sure doesn't want to condemn himself to any year. "I'll know when I'm ready."

Ready? Ready for what? I mean I'm just *looking* at him, when his eyes bug out and the water works start. You never know what'll trigger it anymore. We'll be making biscuits for dinner. Even telling jokes when "HOO." "HOO," and the cords on his neck are twisting as he eyes me, *Feel something anything willya?*

But it's not just "feeling" Dad and me are fighting over, it's sex. Not that I'm looking for that stuff with him—Christ, are you kidding? Sex, obviously that's the last thing I want to see in him, like with these two-hour, scalding-hot baths he'll take with a couple of highballs and *The Saturday Evening Post*. And if I so much as knock or the phone rings, Dad hits the ceiling. Bugs me worse than your old naps, these baths, and I mean *for hours* . . . cigarette smoke and steam oozing out the cracks of the locked door . . . nothing but the suspicious gurgling of the taps and the seal-like *sworp* of his soapy submerged ass amplified over the downstairs ceiling! Then after all that noise, *nothing*.

Is he dead? Do I call the emergency squad? Finally, with a belch of steam, the door opens! But when I squeeze in he gets all prancy, turning his back so I won't see his Thing. "Can't you give me a second?"—whipping a towel around his hairy, purplish cock, so much thicker and darker than mine. Dark maybe from his doing it with you. Dark from the blood in the dark, where you both did it zip zip zip. And sinking down we both stare at it, Mamma. Sex eyes. Eyes like those weird deepsea lantern fish sunk in holes so black they've spouted lights that dangle over their eyes.

But these ritual Saturday baths are nothing to when Dad starts barbering himself. Out to save $2.00 every two weeks Dad buys a four-piece home barber set (on sale, $5.99), then rigs up this wooden contraption of two mirrors and two droplights suspended between the shower rod and the medicine cabinet. And here, like a trick shot, gliding the electric clippers, squinting and contorting himself, Dad struggles to see clear around his head. God, I hate the vibration of black clippers, *herruuuhh*. The hum makes the gristle inside my nose itch something fierce.

"Look at you," I sneer. "It's all lopsided in back!"

"*Next.*"

I back off. "Forget it! You ain't butchering me! Practice on a poodle's butt!"

"We'll save four dollars a month. Forty-eight bucks a year. More like sixty with tips. Get it through your head, *we're scraping bottom*. Come on, it'll look *good*."

I slam the door in his face.

"Oh," he hollers, "are you so *vain*, little Lord Fauntleroy?"

"Are you so *cheap?*"

"Cheap! Sure, when she only spoiled you rotten!"

"'Cause you only gave her every stupid thing she wanted!"

That's it. He shoves the door open, whips off his long black belt, then wriggles it at me. "Slander your mother, you brat!"

"So hit me! You're not cutting my hair!"

Wagging the belt, he swats me, but awkwardly, not hard at first. The first swat's just a warning, but now he's trapped. Now I'm taunting him with this screw-you, you-can't-hurt-me look, *crack!* This time the belt really bites, but I just roll my eyes, "Oh, maan, you're really killing me." "Then maybe you'll like *this*," he grunts, grabbing my arm. "And this! And this! . . ." But hanging there like a side of meat, I just yawn at him as the belt snaps around my ass and legs. And I win. In disgust, he drops the belt, finally. He drags me down the stairs and shoves me in his barber chair. I don't beg. For the next hour I'm a zombie while he fumbles and scrapes, clips and sighs. And the sickest thing is how he wants to please me now, tickling my neck, wanting us to be best buddies again. And fine, it's a passable haircut, but when I see my own humiliation in the mirror I go to pieces.

"I look like hell!"

"Aww, stop." He rubs his face against mine in the mirror, "Brylcreem. A little dab'll do ya."

I rip away. "It looks like *crap*. Like *total shit*."

He turns sarcastic. "Oh, are those actual tears I see? Boy, do you have your priorities straight. Can't cry a *tear* for his mother but like a girl, Little Lord *Flaunt*leroy has a hissy-fit over a stupid little haircut—"

"—Yeah, well, I know what *you* want! A girlfriend! So go on! Have yourself a *date*, Mr. Cheapskate—"

So he backhands me again, which then of course he's bawling and blubbering all over me. God, it wears me out, but that's Dad now, Delilahing me and him both. And why? Well, I'll tell you why. Because he wants a d-a-t-e.

PERSONALLY, I WISHED HE WOULD HAVE DONE IT— DATED. It wasn't just a dare. Really, it was a hygiene thing, especially if the choice was baths, haircuts and other forms of Catholic nuttiness.

Not you, though. Now you're jealous of any woman, Mamma. Even Angelene, you're jealous of, jealous because she's got her own car and money and, worse, a killer figure swelling under her dress. Jealous even when I'll tell you, *Come on, Angelene'll only get old, she'll only lose it.*

Angelene knows I'm avoiding her. And not just on account of Poo dumped me after a couple of weeks. Only an idiot wouldn't have seen it. Basically what happens when a girls gets tits and high school airs hanging out with these snobby folk types with their stupid SNCC buttons showing the black hand linked with the white! Poo said her feelings had changed, but I guess I half knew it always was a pity thing. Still, for her, Poo was real sweet about it. Sisterly but then that's the other worry, both of us scared to death that Dad and Angelene'll start dating, which you *know* what that means . . .

· · ·

STILL, ON THE SEX-O-METER, even Angelene and Poo are nothing compared with Eddie's divorced Mom, Mrs. Bemis. I'm talking about my new pal Eddie, the air force brat. Eddie with his fractured smile who can cuss you out in six languages. Flattopped, bombs-away Eddie on his rattletrap bike with the bald balloon tires and no brakes, on account of his old man, the Major, is stationed at SAC headquarters in Omaha, Nebraska. Sixteen hours at a stretch, Major Bemis is off in his B-52 Stratofortress flying over the Arctic and Greenland, up so high all you see is white, Eddie says. Eddie's seen some wild shit, all right. In Bangkok, they've got real whores and tapeworms ten feet long, long as snots in fact, which guys slowly crank out of their necks on notched chopsticks. Then in Mojave and places, Eddie's seen all these jet crashes, one guy so burned his skin peeled off like hot bubblegum. Yeah, I guess it was destiny that Eddie and me would meet, two flies landing on the same turd.

Frankly, I'm glad I didn't know the kid during the Castro Cuba Crisis, when any day Eddie just figured his Dad was *going East*—gone for good with his blast goggles and poison pill in case the Commies captured him. I mean the kid's already nuts enough on his kamikaze bike. Standing on the pedals, flying headlong down a hill, Eddie's an airborne boner, when, *Oh shit!* Ramming hard for a car at the intersection, Eddie's mouth pops open like a drogue chute, dragging his scuffed shoes. *"You!"* yells the panicked driver, hammering on his door. "Tell your old man to fix your brakes, you crazy little bastard!" "Sit on this, fuckface!" yells Eddie. And pedaling off with that crooked smile, Eddie hurls a triumphant finger at this dick, this asshole, thinking it's all this Noah's ark world, with the Dads and the Moms, and boys and girls, all going up two by two.

Now Eddie's Mom, she was known as The Gray Fox, being such a hot piece and prematurely gray. Weirdest thing, this old-lady hair set on the wildest leg and butt chassis you ever saw. Burns the hell out of Eddie, all these dogs honking their horns and howling at her, *"Owwwhhh, Grammaww!"*

God help them if Eddie's brother, Ronnie, hears it, though! Talk about Atlasizing—man, Ronnie Bemis can bench-press 190 and he's only in the ninth grade! Ronnie I'd seen even before I'd met Eddie, running in these black cast-iron shoes that weigh fifty pounds each, just bobbing in slow motion, this deepsea diver pouring sweat. It's not anything for Ronnie to sprint five or six blocks after a car, vault fences, even call out a whole carload of greasers! Eddie wishes Ronnie'd kill somebody before he kills him. Eddie's bruised all over from Ronnie, and their front door is nailed over with a piece of plywood where Ronnie put his fist through it. Once it got so bad Mrs. Bemis had to call the police on him, her own son. "Don't let those muscles fool you," says Eddie. "Ronnie's such a total baby about her. Man, in her room you oughta hear the big baby, just begging and whining to her."

Trashy people. Service gypsies, you say, sneering at their furniture that only *looks* expensive, and they bought it dirt cheap overseas . . . jade buddhas, pearl-inlaid tables, mirrored camel saddles and Ming chow dog lamps dangling gold back-scratcher tassles. Aww, shut up, I tell you—Eddie's just showing me the ropes, and Mrs. Bemis, well, after all, she is a live woman subject. Besides, at our house, Christmas isn't looking so bright, but Mrs. Bemis, boy, she is certainly in a holiday mood. At the Pentagon there's a party every night, which means a show for me. Oh, yeah. Getting ready, there's Mrs. Bemis running around half naked, hollering, "Eddie! Have you seen my blue silk?" and "Eddie, darlin', can you iron this, please?"

Total nudist! First day I lay eyes on her she zombies right past me. Just home from work, she's drinking one of those doctored Dr. Peppers she sucks down by the case, her dress zipped clear down the back, clear down to her panties, with her bra strap showing and a nice fat *wide* one, too! Man, I can barely look. I mean I don't want to embarrass her.

But forget that. She's not a bit embarrassed but Eddie sure is. Yeah, a few days later Eddie gets his telltale fractured face. And, looking around, here she is again in her bra and panties! Drifts right by. Never even sees me.

"Eddie, sweetheart, I gotta get outta here or I'm gonna lose my job. Sweetheart, can you iron this skirt for me pll-ease?"

Hey, I'm not that common. I look away. Man, my ears get flame red, then redder still when, upstairs, in Ronnie's room, banging like a washing machine, you can hear Ronnie going *NUMP NUMP NUMP NUMP. Is she deaf? Can't she hear Ronnie beating his meat?*

"Oh, all right, I'll do it!" hollers Eddie. Acting like he *hates* ironing, when in fact the kid loves it. Eddie, he'd learned the ancient art off their houseboy Chop Suey, or whoever, back in the Philippines.

"Well," says Mrs. Bemis in her huffiest Southern accent, "you might wanna, so your Mom can go out *lookin'* lak sumpin tonight. *(nump nump nump)* Thass my baby. Good ol' Steady Eddie."

Steady Eddie—yeah, Eddie eats this up, but then he's scared Ronnie'll hear her, saying to me as the iron heats up, "You better leave soon, you know." He looks at me hard. "Hey, she's got herself a Top Secret Clearance, okay? G.S.-7. That's really high up in the government. You get that high up, you gotta *decompress*, okay?"

Hey, that's her business if she wants to go *National Geographic*. Heating up, the iron pops and gurgles, giving off this good burnt-toast starch smell. Eddie pleats and straightens out the dress like a fresh pizza dough, then gets to work—the kid's definitely got the feather touch. "Hey, you better watch this. Cause soon I guarantee you'll be doing it all, Cinderella. All this Susie Homemaker shit. *Ev-erything.*"

Calms Eddie right down, the seams, the hissing steam. "You know, man," Eddie continues in his cryptic way, "in an A-rab's house, there's them that know to eat the cooked goat's eyeball when it's offered to them, and them that don't." *Huh?* But I nod sagely like I totally understand about A-rabs and goats' eyeballs. Then here's old Mrs. Bemis back, in her tight silk wrapper. Upstairs, Ronnie's finished—with a screech of floornails, the barbells start clanking again but Mrs. Bemis doesn't hear that either—no, she's in a trance as usual, watching Steady Eddie ironing. Her eyes tilt up. The cubes clink and she winks at me. "God, he is the *bestest* kid I've got—" Then she blanks, I guess because she doesn't know my name.

"*Here*—" Eddie hands her her skirt. Mrs. Bemis starts upstairs, stops.

"Eddie, hon, anything you need?"

Eddie blinks—he always blinks when he gets exasperated. "Tuna fish? Did you get the tuna fish for Ronnie?"

"*More?*"

"What?" he gags. "You mean you didn't get Ronnie's tuna! And what about Ronnie's sandwich steaks? . . ." *Clank. Screech. Clank.* "Look," mutters Eddie to me finally, "no offense but you better haul ass unless you wanna watch me get mine beat."

The kid was real matter-of-fact about it. In fact it was just like the ironing, just another job that Eddie had in the house. Eddie's fractured smile. Yeah, I was really lucky, having an expert kid like Eddie to show me the ropes.

BUT BACK TO MRS. BEMIS, well, the first couple weeks I'm invisible to her. But then out of nowhere one day—I guess after Eddie told her about Dad and me—well, suddenly I rate. It's amazing. Calling me into her room—messy as a teenager's—Mrs. Bemis says she wants to get to know me better.

But see, this isn't just a change in Mrs. Bemis. Why, before this no woman would have wanted me anywhere *near* her room, but now, on account of you,

I've become a semihonorary female—a water carrier, sexually speaking. In this sense, Mrs. Bemis isn't being provocative, particularly. Even with her toes spread with cotton balls, painting her long toenails, which I swear could spear somebody, even so she's not really noticing me as a *male* or anybody. No, the lady's just real curious, sucking on ice cubes and asking me all about you, Mamma.

"Right, I've seen your mother." She corrects herself, "*Saw* her, rather." She spits a cube back in her glass. "Fact, I've seen your Dad, too. Real tall, right? Dark hair. Looks ex-mil?"

"Huh?"

"Military."

"Yeah, that's him. Dad was navy."

"Officer?"

"Sure was. Lieutenant j.g."

"Junior grade, you mean?"

What's she doing, trying to cut him down? "No, you're probably thinking air force. In the navy j.g. was a medal, I think."

When here's Eddie giving me a killer look! Mad at me for encouraging her, I guess, plus Ronnie's due back from wrestling and Eddie's terrified what he'll feed him. Well, Eddie throws me out, and it's just as well. Because the next day with Mrs. Bemis I'm a j.g. myself, a nobody again, and life there just swims along, Eddie ironing and Ronnie upstairs cracking the plaster, *Nump nump nump! Clank. Screech. Clank.* . . .

But then the next Saturday night—the Saturday before Christmas—Mrs. Bemis says to me and Eddie, "Look, let's have a little party! Sara Lee. Popcorn. Steak. So whaddaya say, Frank, wanna stay over?"

"Sure!"

But seeing Eddie's face I realize I stepped in it again—bad. Next thing I know Mrs. B's hustling us in her big Chrysler to ask Dad's *direct* permission. Forget just phoning him, like I suggest—at this she gets herself in a proper Southern huff. "What? You think your Dad'll just let you stay, *unintroduced?* No, we'll just ride over and ask him. Face to face."

Burrowed down in his outgrown coat, Eddie's got his fractured face and then I see why. Decked out in short, black, high-heeled boots and a black fur-trimmed car coat, Eddie's Mom looks like Miss December Past, her gray hair hair-sprayed into a bucket of silver ice. And then it hits me, *It's Saturday!* Dad, if he's home, Dad's gonna be in his bath. Or else on the slap happy side or both . . . *or so scared he won't answer the door!*

I pretend I don't have a key. We knock and knock.

"Well!" cries Dad, opening the door finally. "Halloo halloo halloo!"

Dad's hung the mistletoe, all right. As the door swings back Dad's ready to limbo, barefoot in his robe, his dark hair still wet. Steam rising off his neck, Dad plants a wet one on Mrs. Bemis, then says in a frisky slur, "Well, aren't you just the young *dearrr.* Mrs?—That was, uh, Mrs. Buuuh—"

"Bee-mis. But *Cathy*, please. And Mr. Dougherty—"

"—Pete."

"Well, Pete. Obvioussly this idnt the time but, well, I was just *so* sorry to hear about your poor wiiife. Lord, the blow that musta been. I know I was jus' dev-astated when Don and me—that's Eddie's Dad, the Major—when we saw we couldn't make it. So, Pete, I've been there, and I *know*—"

And standing like two stumps in the cold, we know too, Eddie and me. So do you, Mamma. Talk about chumps, *Well what do you think's been going on, you blind dope. Him and that tramp already* know *each other.*

WELL, NEEDLESS TO SAY, EDDIE AND ME TAKE A BREATHER. Meanwhile, there are other bust-ups—bust-ups galore. Dad and Bud, for one. Kaput after January 1, Dad says.

Come to think of it, Dad's own bereavement leave from the Bud mess— I mean his month or so of temporary grace—didn't last much longer than mine did before Dad got clobbered. Some Christmas party they had at G.D.S., stealing files and clients and padlocking doors. "Remember this," says Dad giving me the nightly blow-by-blow, "there's nothing more conniving and desperate than a bum looking to cash out. And *especially* one with two sons almost in college. And a boat! And wasn't your mother gaga over *him.*"

"She was? Mom always said you were."

"Her recollection."

Lately, Dad was always making digs at you like this. Worse, I don't defend you the way I would have even weeks before. Meanwhile, things are sounding really bad with Bud.

"Look, I'm not out to worry you, but if that S.O.B. wins—well, I may have to fold the tents here in D.C."

For Dad this would have been the ultimate humiliation, Bud's running him out of D.C. Then again the part of Dad that was dying—dying out of you— well, that part I'm sure relished the idea of chucking the whole mess. In fact, there was nothing Dad loved more than burning old office files in the fireplace. Building one of his dreary Victory bonfires, Dad would rub his hands, grinning into the yellow roar.

"Hey, over at Mercer Pump? Did I tell you? Vince Panella, their VP of sales, Vince said he'd *love* to set me up in Fort Wayne or maybe even Sarasota. Car, office, secretary—well, how about it, old buddy? Might not be such a bad deal, huh?"

Fort Wayne! Your heart couldn't survive that, Mamma, and you absolutely couldn't stand what Dad was doing to me, so I wouldn't be such a fancy pants. The way I'm growing out of everything, it's a disgrace, the way he has me traipsing around in fraying shirts with my pants hiked up to my ankles. My pants are the worst, forever yanking at my crotch, doing knee bends to pinch up even a fart's-worth of space for poor Mr. Pokey and my teeming, itching nuts! And as I scratch and pull and pester myself, all the while, Mamma, I feel you growing ever more huge and insupportable, like a mass of ice ready to come skidding down a roof.

Thank God Christmas was here. Almost. Time to drag out the old decorations, all the old snowflakes and glass balls. Time to hunker in like bears and forget the whole winter. But no. Instead of putting up the tree, Dad says he's gotta work, says he's gotta write up some new price quotes for Uncle Sam. But what's he doing down in his workshop? He's not at his drafting table making money—no, he's at his workbench fixing a two-buck clock thermostat for Mrs. Guarinello for nothing! Fixing it because it's about the one thing the poor guy *can* fix now. God, I hate it in his shop now, all these broken things waiting to be put back together. Radio tubes. Compression rings. Cotter pins. It all seems so long ago, that stuff. In fact, as I watch him with Mrs. Guarinello's thermostat, it's hard to believe we ever fixed a thing, the two of us. A clock thermostat. Stupidest thing in the world, but Dad's like heat, he's so absorbed in the problem. And Dad likes having me there with him. Nervously turning the black works over and over in his hands, he needs my prodding him. He needs me asking questions until we find that one perfect jewel of a piece that'll explain what failed, that one shining jewel that finally redeems what otherwise is just junk. And really, all anybody wants in life is a little job that needs doing, and a place that means going, and a thing that's worth fixing. And really, in life, you don't *want* any big deal. What you want is something completely ordinary. Ordinary like that Christmas Eve back when I was seven, when Dad and me went real late to the drugstore to get more colored lights for the tree. No big deal. It wasn't any white Christmas.

It was foggy and half drizzling, but he was my Daddy and Santa was coming, and outside, in the rain blurs and streaks, all the kids were safe in their beds, so safe I could have rode with him forever watching the colored lights tingle-tangle in the trees.

Shit, I wasn't even asking for that kind of Christmas. Really, Christmas should have been postponed. Christmas Eve, Dad and me could barely decorate the sawed-off tree he bought, both as sick of feuding over you and who missed you more, as for all the useless crap that fell under the tree the next morning—barely a thing from Dad and, to rub it in, an avalanche from Grammaw and the family. No Christmas sweaters this year. No, this year it's pure cream, *all toys*. But as I spread out my haul, my head feels on fire. *Nothing works*. Suddenly I realize I've forgotten. I've totally forgotten how to play.

Forgotten how to play!? But come on, kid, you remember how, don't you? Laying on your belly hardly breathing? Laying there with only your eyes moving, *living* in the toy cars and the soldiers, the blocks and scattered erector pieces? Noises were the secret. Everything worked by noises. Tunelessly whistling but not whistling? Making these Porky Pig, potato-whistle sounds, *remember?* That way high, flutey theme song that went, *fu-fu, tut-tuuuh, fu-fu* . . .

Because you had to make sounds to do it—*invoke it*. But wait! Because the other trick, remember, was to *blow* on things, especially anything busted or hurt. The absentminded way, like God, I'd put some hurt guy's head in your mouth, if it was soldiers, and if it was trains or cars and any guy wrecked or got killed, then I squeezed him—hard—vulcanizing him so he was good as new.

And it was for real not fake. Fake? These were whole cities, families, battlefields. These were whole worlds you built, and when the work was done, it was perfect, so perfect *that nobody could ever wreck it*. So perfect that the next morning there it was again, proof of life *just like you left it*. Was there ever anything more beautiful? It was the whole world and it was starting like another day, the sun streaming through the windows and the heat blowing through the heat registers dancing the dust while you sat there all dazzled eating your Sugar Pops. It was life itself, and when you shook it, like a snow-globe, the life shook down like snow, blanketing everything, the lawns, the streets and the grateful, happy people, the people all looking up with that snow-falls-forever-on-the-town feeling where everything is protected and loved and nobody can ever hurt it.

But today, boy, that snow has stopped. Today, the ball's broken, and I hold my head. Cause today for the first time in history, I forgot, I've totally forgotten how to play.

• • •

AND THE KILLER IS YOU'RE SUPPOSED TO BE SO GOD-
DAMN HILARIOUSLY HAPPY DURING THE HOLIDAYS. So
maybe it was the buildup, I don't know. Because in church Christmas morning I faint dead away. Feeling my head go to sleep I start to see the black
sleet—whole blizzards of black sleet covering the chalice and the candles
when, *boom*. Down I go, cracking my head on the pew.

Oh, I'd fainted before—in summer, sure, but never Christmas. Growth
spurts, Dad says, and Lord knows I am growing. Then again who *wouldn't*
faint? I think. Who, when they starve you before mass, then pack people
in with the organ pumping and Dad and me, this so-called family, sandwiched between these huge Catholic broods, the Garrigues, the Mackeys
and the Caseys all joy-to-the-worlding... *Boom*.

Next thing I know, I'm in the back of the church, Dad and the ushers
crowding in with fans, water and ammonia poppers. I'm too embarrassed to
go back, but Dad won't hear about me going home. No, Dad marches me
right back up to the communion rail... *and they love it*. What a trooper! I'm
Bart Starr being carried back on the field! Mrs. Feeney... the Kearnys and
Caseys... the Sullivans... They're all just winking and beaming at me. And
back home the next day, there's a new outpouring of stoop cakes, fruitcakes,
and Christmas cookies, plus two dinner invites, which, being in mourning,
Dad naturally refuses. Still, Dad's real decent about my fainting. In fact, Dad
drops the whole subject until the next Sunday when, *tim-berrrr*...

No hero's welcome this time. It's bad. Kids pointing and smirking. Out-
right glares. No ducking it now, not for Dad anyway. After church, on the
stone stairs outside, as Nivas is saying good-bye to everyone, Dad's apologizing for me.

"Well, this time he's going to the doctor, Father Nivas. We'll see if it's
anemia."

"Amnesia?"

"Anemia."

"But what's anemia?" I ask Dad. It sounds bad. Anything to do with doctors.

Nivas shrugs. "If the doctor say okay, we can give heem a special dispen-
sation to eat. *Temporarily*." He looks at me hard. "But I hope this will not be
necessary."

Nivas knows! You bet old Pizza Face is sniffing around. After school, two
or three times now Father's come to the house with the I-just-happened-to-
be-in-the-neighborhood act. So I make tea and feed him some Oreos—he'll
scarf down half a bag if you don't watch him. And he's cool. Oh, he's real low-

key, asking about homework and how am I feeling (duh) and talking about how rough it's been on Dad. But today, though, the Padre's being too cool. Dad, too. It starts me worrying, especially with Dad talking doctors.

"But Dr. Richards won't stick me, will he?"

"They draw a little blood."

"Dad, my pants are a foot over my ankles. Why do I need some quack sticking me when it's just a growth spurt?"

"He's not a quack and nobody's *punishing* you. Or are you trying to tell me something?"

"Yeah, I'm telling you something. I'm telling you I *fainted*. You think I'd fake that in front of five hundred people?"

But that's exactly what Dad's thinking, and so am I.

GODDAMN QUACKS! BLOODSUCKERS! Sucking out your blood in some turkey baster!

Forget it, Jack! Bad enough I got the doctor and next Sunday hanging over me but you're whining how it's your birthday next week and can we please go shopping at the Plaza! Broke as we are! And when you know Dad's forbid it, all the hoodlums who hang out there? *But fine, for you I'll go.* Damned right I'll go, but don't you come crying to me about the remedial-ed types up there, all smoking their Kools and scarfing down french fries to get those cratered-out zit faces so skuz-ugly they can get their fool heads kicked in and not care!

Man, I hate that gray low-pressure zone after the holidays. And especially today, when Saturday's beautiful snow is all dirty and melted and all we've got to look forward to is school next Monday and then, on January 6, your thirty-ninth birthday. For weeks you've been all depressed over it, talking suicide and how nobody loves you anymore. So telling Dad I'll be over at Eddie's, we take the law into our own hands. We hop the Y2 for Wheaton.

The slush is slopping under the bus tires and the change box is rattling. Then I read the sign NO TALKING TO THE DRIVER. Christ! There's nobody else on the bus, and you like me talking to people for you, to keep you company. Besides, I feel sorry for the poor schmo with his half hair and his belly bagging out his belt. What a life! listening to the change rattle! punching transfers and always having to wait, wait *for days,* for some old lady to clamber on, then rummage for her fifteen cents, *plink plink plink.*

And truth be known he's probably embarrassed by this DON'T FEED THE ANIMALS sign above him like he's a dimwit. So pointing at the curbs piled with soggy gift boxes and trees trailing tinsel, I cheer him up.

"Boy, the trashmen sure have *their* work cut out for them, huh?"

He grunts. Scared for his miserable job, probably. So, thinking I'll give him a little excitement, I say, "Wow! So, when did all this snow fall anyway?"

Now I got his attention! He looks around at me like I'm crazy, so I explain how you and me we just last night flew back in from Florida. *Palm Beach* where we'd spent the whole holidays with your rich Uncle Stephen and all his crazy maids, all of us piling into his Cadillac to go to the dogs—the dog track. "... Yeah, we just flew into National last night. We won't be needing any orange juice. Man, at the Palm Beach airport they just give them to you, oranges, a whole big sack! I guess they stole that idea off Hawaii—y'know, with the *leis? Those ropes of flowers?*"

Poor guy. On his salary he probably can't afford to go anywhere, so he's pretty amazed. I don't mind. Passing the time, I'm telling him all about Sarasota, the Tamiami Trail, the Seminoles and other stuff off Grammaw's postcards, on and on until we're both feeling really warm, Mamma. Really rich. Happier than we've been in weeks, actually. But once we hit our stop, just as I'm getting out, the driver says, "Boy, you sure didn't get much of a *tan*, did ya?"

So what are you insinuating, buddy? My voice drops. I get real serious. "Well, it rained a lot. Also, my Grandmother keeps us in when it gets too hot. Plus we're in church. *A lot* she's so religious on the holidays." He pulls the door lever.

"Well, 'air you go, Lucky. Yeah, I sure do envy you, that nice Florida tan."

Lucky! Lucky for him he's gone once it hits me what he's said! Like I've never been to Florida! ... *for your information buddy I've been there several times.* In fact, the more I think on it, it's like he threw me off the bus! Hey, I know, I think, stamping my feet in the slush, *I'll write D.C. Transit!* Say I saw the sonofabitch nearly mow a kid down, running his big mouth!

A car splatters me. Then, after I wipe myself off, I'm recounting our money ($1.73), and you're back to yammering, all worried about money and your birthday present as I calm you in my cool Frank Sinatra voice, *Look pretty girl it's simple e-con c'mon babe somebody had to clip your pretty wings.*

Normally Sinatra settles you right down, but not today. Then we cross the street to catch the Wheaton bus, here's this mum colored lady sitting on the bench. What is it with colored ladies wearing these big Sunday hats on weekdays? It's like the colored lady has a sign over her too, DON'T YOU EVEN

DARE TALK TO ME. *So maybe you like her tan better buddy bet she's been to Palm Beach huh.*

There's plenty of room beside her, but you, Mamma, immediately you're all worried. Big deal. She's more scared of us, probably, but you're all nervous, wanting me to get away she's dirty. Why? She doesn't scare me. So to spite you, so you'll stop being such a baby, I sit there, and then I remember that night, once when we all were out, together, you and Dad and me. This was in the old Ford, back before the Bird, two or three years ago, I guess. I don't even remember where we were going. All I remember is it was cold and late and we were driving down Shawcross Avenue heading up to Shepherd Hills. Well, Dad stops. Leaning across your lap, Dad rolls down your window, then calls out to this colored man hunched in the cold under a street-light, "Hey, it's kinda late for the bus to be coming. Want a lift?" *"What are you doing?"* you hiss at Dad. If we'd stopped for a Martian it couldn't have been any more amazing, and the colored man doesn't look so sure about us either. Crouching, the man peers in, then climbs in back with me and we start off. Dad's really nice. Making him feel comfortable, Dad's going on and on about the bus service. Hat on his lap, the man nods. More to explain why he's out, the man says he works at a hospital but doesn't say where or doing what. I felt a colored boy's head once. It was on the Buck Stummer TV show where Buck plays cowboy songs on his guitar and the birthday kids get to ride Buck's pony, Hootie. Billy Randall lied—I didn't see any plug up Hootie's butt. Anyway, we were sitting on hay bales, and the *feel*. My hand was a flying saucer floating over that colored boy's fuzzy hair. He liked it, too, but then the fat man with the black headphones, he points at me so I stop! The colored man's hair doen't look like that, but his nails are purple so they almost glow in the dark. Once we hit Shepherd Hills, you never saw a man so glad to get out of a car. Well, you watch him hoof across the road, then when it's safe you blow up at Daddy. Risking our lives! And for whom, a stranger? *Who?* asks Dad and you say it's *whom, whom.* Yeah, and what color? asks Dad and you say, *Any* color. That's what buses are for. Yeah, says Dad, and how'd you like to be standing out in the cold this time of night? And that's where he belongs, you come back, *like a fish in the sea.*

Dad's right. You are a selfish baby, so to teach you a lesson I sit right by the colored lady. In fact, I think I'll say "Hi" to her, *Hi!* But wait, I think, if I just say "Hi" the colored lady'll think *I'm* nervous, but if I keep quiet, then she'll think it's all about her being colored and get sore. Lord, they're touchy, these colored people, and always keeping to themselves. Poo would talk to her, I bet. I'll bet colored lady would talk to Poo, too—especially if she saw Poo's SNCC button, and especially if she saw that book Poo's got, *Black Like Me*.

Spooks, that's another word I've heard for them. But why *spooks* I wonder? Is it because they're ascared of spooks? Or is it because they're so spooky around white people? In *Black Like Me*, the man had himself dyed colored, but look, this colored lady could be white, because look how white her hands are on the bottom—white like flounders where she wore the color off, like she scrubbed too hard with Lava soap, *Hey, I know ... we could Lava soap them white like us.*

The sun goes in.

I feel a shiver. As the light dims, I can really see you beside her, down in that, like, underwater place, where the polarized lights and darks that make up anybody's body all go pointing in the same direction, like a minnow school. Please don't faint on me again, *So sit Mamma gwan that's better for you.* And see, colored lady doesn't mind you being here, a white spook like you. See, colored lady's not prejudiced of your kind, so why can't you just be happy out here, licking the air off your face? What do you care about her being colored now? Sick as you are you don't even mind the neighbors much now, and good thing when nobody minds you. And really by now, Mamma, you're almost anybody, only more unawares—less stuck-up and more free, even if it's free only to nod off in the sun beside some old colored lady, *So what's being thirty-nine? Who cares about being thirty-nine ... tennineeightsevensix—*

Brakes screech.

"Honey!" The colored lady yanks me out of the street where I've fallen on account of war wounds I won't mention and I'm overcome by smoke.

A man yells from his car, *"Is he okay?"*

"I *slipped*—" I holler back. Colored lady yanks me hard by the arm.

"Slipped? Into the road wid all these cars! You scared me to death! You awl right, honey? You sho doan look awl right."

"It's the snow. *Thanks.* Man, I guess I just *slipped*, ma'am." And do you see that, Mamma? She won't let me black out and fall under a car. I look around at the colored lady. "Gee, do you know what time it is, ma'am?"

"Noon sumpin. Now you sit on down hyeah. You sho you awl right?"

In my brain, the answer flashes, "I got *sugar diabetes*. Boy, better get some sugar in me. Some *gum*. I'll be right back—"

Dodging cars, I banzai charge across the road, to the newsstand, which frankly I've had my eye on anyway. Darting past a knot of guys at the horno-porno rack, I give the revolving comic stand a twirl, then glance up front,

where the sawed-off owner sits, his bald head cut off by the sign WINSTON
TASTES GOOD. Fat little pipsqueak. Human fly swatter's all he is. He's always
perched up there. Feet dangling off his built-up stool, he looks like a ventriloquist's dummy, peeping out at kids either to buy or beat it. And lazy? Little as this schmoe does all day, he can't even get off his fat duff and oil the
goddamned comic rack! No, he lets it *squeak* to alert him against kids stuffing candy and dirty books down their pants.

So watch me, Schmoe! I flip the kiddie carousel another twirl... "Batman,"
"Classic Comics," "Li'l Archie" ... But up there, whoa! Tucked in the upper racks, all greasy slick and out of reach, yonder's the hard stuff... TRUE
DETECTIVE, ROGUE, ADAM, GENT—magazines with stacked, snarling
molls and unshaved, slugged-up guys bounced off cargo planes and benders
all talking about "Headhunter Hell" ... "I Torched the Torchers" ... "Passion Slave" ...

Staring back, I'm feeling slugged to shit myself, saying to the guy in the
leather jacket with the shiner, *Headhunters and all that ooga-booga shit! Hey I'll
tell you some real true shit, Jack!*

It's that overcome-by-smoke feeling. Back to the smut midget, I'm twirling
the creaky stand when down my leg, Old Pokey unscrews with a snaky slither.
It's Hercules unchained. Slipping my hand down my pants I can feel him all
kinked up in one of those wicked hot dick tourniquets, *don't think about it no
no think think think think about it!*

Man, I'll be glad when I'm old enough not to have public boners. It's terrible and *it's so hard*. Why can't a kid just have a boner in peace? Feeling my
stomach fill like a toilet, I'm having to pretend I'm all engrossed in "Archie"
and not this she-devil squeezing her bazooms out between her elbows!
Bazooms? Man, they're like two king-size loaves of Wonder Bread, Candy Girl
hissing at me and making her frou frous with her lips like she doesn't know
I'm down here looking! *Candy Girl!* Like she doesn't know She's Got 'Em!
Sure she knows. Are you kidding kid? *She likes to show 'em off.* Candy Girl, she's
all swollen and splurting milk like in a girl boner! And goll, these two are
BIG, HARD, JUTTING, SQUIRTY NOBBER-ENDED GIRL BONERS.
Yeah, old Candy Girl with her goo-goo, sex-pot pout face, Candy Girl's ask-
ing me, *Ewww is that Mr. Pokey? Ewww is he all hard from looking at me?*

Rap rap rap!

Spotted! *Down periscope!* It's the little runt up front rapping on the glass
cigar case with his fat gold ring. "You! Boy! You heardt me! *You!*"

Hey, I got my pride! To prove my pure intentions, I tool up to the counter.
(Sideways bent-over, of course.) All bland and cool I slap down thirty cents,

cash, six packs of Juicy Fruit. And he takes my money too, the nasty little runt. Takes it, then mutters to his fat wife behind the curtain, "Yeah, he back dere lookin at the wrong kind mag'zine." Well, out flies Mrs. Munchkin, in her gooped-on makeup and peroxided hair.

"Boy! *Boy!*"

She flits her fat pink nails in my face. "You! *go!* Buy nuttin, get us all ina trouble!"

"I did too buy! I bought this gum!"

"Big Eyes!" She circles her claws around her eyes. "Everybody see you *googlin* de girl!"

I bust out the door. Sucking wind I've got a red hot javelin down my spine, *Human Shit! White trash! Calling me dirty when you people only sell the filth!*

"Ggg-narrff! GunnhHH-num!"

With a snaffling of foil and that good fruity gumstarch smell, I rip through a whole pack of Juicy Fruit. Five whole sticks balled in one gigantic chaw when, looking across the street, I stop dead, *It's you, Mamma.* But no . . . with stinging ice crystals in my eyes, I see it's only that colored lady still waiting across the road, *what you mean you took your own mother for a nigger?* It's like when my balls shrivel up and disappear in a hot bath, when you vanish on me like this. On the brick ledge by the shoe repair sitting by somebody's half-drank soda, pissing through my own eyes, I can't even see *because you are too a nigger.* Pinching in my eyeballs I just sit there, just feeling for my nuts and wishing I was dead, *'cause you should too die you bastard you're a nigger just like her tennineeightseven* . . .

The bus!

Dodging heavy machinegun fire, I just make it, climbing on after the colored woman. *Die, munchkin perverts,* the newsstand is one solid sheet of flame, blown up with bazooka rockets and tracers. Gangway, you punks! you midgets! Swinging down the aisle, I plop down in the last seat, Monkeyman, with my monkey bite and my nasty monkey teeth!

"You, back there! Sit down!"

Oh, man. Now this dick's on my butt too. P.O.'d about I'm standing on the last seat, goofing on the cars behind us, my booger finger jammed up my brain.

"—look! You can't act right on this ve-hi-cle I'ma halfta put ya off."

So put me off, Mr. Dead-End Job that the recruiter poster says pays a whopping $2,300 a year! *But Dad makes more than that right?* But then I cool it. Damned tootin. Seeing colored lady whisper to the driver, I get scared they'll call the cops.

And man, are we honking up the highway! Surging and rocking, in big swells, the bus just barrels through the slush, the humming tires throwing up a gray salt mist and the heat blowers blowing and the wipers slip-slapping. You can barely see through the hot snow sheen. The colored lady's off by herself and I'm thinking that if she gets off I should thank her or at least say good-bye so she'll know I don't hate her. And I would only I can't keep my eyes open. With my arms crossed and eyes half open, I watch the filthy cars surging by, throwing up a blinding slurry of dirt and salt—brilliant in the sun. And almost the minute I stop worrying over you, at that same exact moment I can feel you again, Mamma. I can see the veils of you, then the rubbed-up flakes of light—those flakes of you, I mean, sifting down like grains in an hourglass. Trailing down, the white flakes pile up until you're almost visible, not mad anymore but breathing in unison with me and suddenly so focused and alive that it practically rips my head off!

And boy, do I feel good! *Snarff*—Celebrating, I jam in a fresh stick of gum. Gnash it up, then, gunk, I swallow it. And it's weird when I think about it— I mean that I don't stick my gum under my seat like all these other kids do. Because just feel under the seat, willya? Pebbles of gum. *Millions* of gum pebbles all slimy-slick and greasy. Just run your hand under there—I mean under *any* seat, on *any* bus, and you will know what this country is facing with kids! God, *feel* it, all these knots and smears and squiggles, like the top of an exposed monkey brain! And just don't feel it, *sniff it.* And after you've run your fingers under there, just bring them to your nose and smell—just smell all that collective, peppermint-bubblegum-spearmint *pissedoffedness.*

It's kids' *Braille*, gum. It's a secret code. Running my fingers along the wads I can actually *read* all these kids hating this aimless, rattle trap bus of waiting forever to grow up. And chewing away, suddenly figuring out all this good shit—well, I'm thinking how all this stuff—*the stuff I'm actually thinking*—that this is stuff the likes of which they'd never dare print in their phony TRUE STORIES! And mashing me a fat gobber under my seat, I think, *So what if some kid finds my gum here a hundred years from now?* Yeah, grinning and chewing away with the sun in my eye, I'm thinking how, someday, some other kid'll sniff it and instantly *know* old Kilroy was here. And chewing away like a grasshopper, I am telling y'all—that ancient-assed kid, he was sitting right back here—*today*—just grinning like a bandit and leaving all these fat juicy gobbers of the sheer unvarnished truth! And the beauty is, no clown with his sheepskin will ever be able to scrape it off, Jack, not even with an eight-hundred-carat, rock-diamond shit scraper.

· · ·

BUT INSIDE THE PLAZA, WHOA, IT'S A WHOLE HOODLUM CONVENTION. Hanging out under the wafting, french-fry, caramel-corn wind outside Kresge's, wearing black leather jackets and bright velour shirts, their hair gassed back in great black wings, like Vikings, why there must be a hundred of 'em! at least! Hulking, scary retards, too, yelling at kids, slouched against walls and general she-lacka-lacking—you know, stomping the stacked heels of those black, pointy-toed Puerto Rican fence-climbers they all wear.

Sparks fly. A cigarette, a *lit* cigarette, bounces off the coat of some poor decent kid and all they do is laugh! All the better these dummies have to do, when there's laws and NO LOITERING signs, but the rent-a-cops in their stupid Smokey Bear hats, they're all quaking in their boots. Gimme a billy club! Make me eighteen, swear me in, and I'll do something! You won't see me hiding behind curtains and calling the police.

Sure, Mamma, I said we'd go to Woodies on the far end of the plaza—but how with all these greasers blocking everything? Ward's? Too tacky. Lerner's? Worse. Lerner's is all young stuff, which depresses you more than the expensive stuff until finally I blow up, *tennineeightsevensix . . .*

Head down, I bowl myself down the length of the plaza, past Kresge's, past the drained, trash-filled fountain and the giant red tinsel candycanes where the morons are all congregating, when *huhhh!* this little blond greaser trips me! I slam into a wall of black leather.

"Hey, asshole," yells Blondie. He's showing me his shoe, which the toe could fit in a pencil sharpener. "Lookit! Lookit at my fuckin' *stomp, you scurvy piece a shit."*

Another shoves me in the face. "Whass matter, dipshit? Can't walk straight?"

"Hah! If he had some pants that fit!" Grinning, Blondie points at my spindly, bare ankles. "Hah! Lookit this shit. *Fuckin' clamdiggers he's wearing."*

What is this sixth sense bullies have? Blondie could have made fun of my hair, my ears, anything, but no, he goes straight for the balls, my pants. So all the morons and their girls can laugh! And normally I'd be peeing my pants. Normally, I'd be begging for my life but at "clamdiggers" I go insane, hollering—

"Yeah! So have a big *laugh. Laugh* 'cause I'm an orphan and these are Salvation Army pants! *Laugh* when these are all I got—*merry fuckin' Christmas.* Man, y'all want a real laugh, I'll tell you one. Two years ago, my parents both burned up in a car wreck. Now that's a laugh! It's just a laugh riot, being an orphan!"

It's amazing. Total quiet. Under the rattling red tinsel and blowing paper cups, the whole greaser pack is stunned, even shamed, by the astounding power of this new word, *orphan*. But after the first shock Blondie and all his hood friends are jeering back.

"Shut up!"

"Little orphannn—"

"Hey, fuck you, kid!"

So what do I do? If I run they'll know I'm lying and kill me, so I keep it up. "What, you didn't see the special bus? Yeah they just hauled thirty of us up from Buckeysville for our little Merry Christmas. Man, are you guys ever gonna have a *blast!* Cripples galore! Deaf mutes to laugh at. Blind kids, too."

"Shut up, Mouth!" Blondie stubs out his cigarette on my coat. *"Buckeysville!* So where the fuck is Buckeysville, you lyin' sacka shit?"

My jaw drops. "It's in Buck—Buck—*Buckeysville*, okay?"

"Hah, Bobby! Buck buck buck!"

"Goddamn, Bobby, didn't you know? Buckeysville's in Buckeysville, bwoy!"

My arms fly up. Too late. Blondie smacks me one and I freeze, hands in the air and my knocked-up hair blowing backward. Then through ringing ears I hear the greaser girls crying.

"Aww, quit it, Bobby. The kid's crazy."

"Fuck 'em, Bobby."

"Yeah, I think I hearda Buckeysville, Bobby."

"Aww, bullshit," bawls Bobby, but then this older guy steps in and gives me a shove. "Go on, Mouth, *git*. Don't press your fuckin' luck—"

But Bobby smacked me! With his bare cold hands the punk smacked me when he's probably fourteen! Probably *sixteen*. And it's true, I realize, *I am a half orphan*. Well, after the bus driver and the Smut Midget, once I'm down the plaza a ways, I whirl around.

"Hey, Bobby, Mr. big man giant orphan killer! So go over to Arlington National Cemetery, Bobby! You can piss on my parents' graves!"

I SHOWED 'EM! In triumph, I blow into Woodies and I get straight to work. Check the pay phones, then give the soda and candy machines a couple good kicks. Then it never fails, I gotta wicked pee. But, Christ, inside the men's it's sickening. It's wall-to-wall smoke and stinkola packed with homos and kids lighting up and naturally some sick old fart glued to the seat, coughing and puffing on a cigarette, *heh heh fresh as a daisy*. Also, they're dime stalls, which, even though I can crawl under, the principle burns me up, in a free country. And just take a gander under there. Ripped-up paper. Buttered popcorn cups and crumpled french-fry bags. No, queers or not, I grab the corner urinal. Holding down the flusher handle so it'll squeak water, I think *waterwaterwaterwater* while I count the ceiling holes and say three Hail Marys.

Then my stomach's growling. I'll keel over if I don't get a hot dog in me but you won't hear of it. And then the worst happens. We get stuck in Fragrances.

"Well, hello there, young man. What kin I do for yew ta-day?"

Young man. I hate that. Especially from Sexpot here, squashing her tits over the counter. *Young man*, putting you in your sexual place. Dangling her sex and older age over me, she's just toying with us, saying in this perky, cornpone voice.

"Ke-yant I help ya with somethin' ta-day?"

I bury my face in the lighted showcase. "Thanks, I'm just looking."

She starts guessing. "Gee, Christmas is over so"—her eyes light up—"so maybe it's a certain somebody's *birthday*, humm?"

I stop cold.

"Well," she says, "I guessed one right—a birthday, huh? Okay, second guess. The lady-in-question is not too old? Maybe . . . *your Mom?*"

"How'd you guess that?"

"Oh, just a kinda *way* yuh had."

"Way? Which way?" She thinks I'm queer?

"Mmm, just a hunch."

"Boy," I say to test her, "good guess. Yeah, it's my Mom's birthday. Next week. She'll be thirty-nine."

"Well, that's young. That's still young."

You've seen the model of the Invisible Woman, with the clear glass skin and the guts you can paint? Because in the humming light of the perfume case, just like the Invisible Woman, Miss Guess turns to glass, her skin turns to whitest ghost, *'cause if Washington and Lincoln can still have their birthdays and they're dead so why can't I be thirty-nine? Cause can't you understand goddamnit you're dead ten nine eight seven six* . . .

"Hel-loooe?" asks Miss Guess. "And what's the birthday budget?"

"I've got enough."

"Big spender, huh?"

I stare back at her. "We do all right. I got a paper route and my Dad's in business for himself. We just got back from Miami." But talking up Palm Beach it only gets worse, my eyes itching and watering in the light of the perfume case. God, just then the light's bubbling like warm ginger ale as she dabs her wrist, then holds it out for me to sniff, her wrist white as bone.

"Go on, honey. See, it's gotta warm to the blood to really smell it. With perfume, see, it's half what's in the bottle and half who it's on."

I gag. My legs start to buckle. It's like in church when I fainted, but at the last second I catch myself, I spin away, "No thanks, I'll try jewelry." *It's a joke you're not gonna die!* But still it keeps falling, the black snow like in church, when Father Nivas raises the chalice like a fallen star and the altar bells tinkle, *Wake up wake up or you'll die! tennineeightsevensix* . . .

Whoa, what happened? Whipping around, I see Miss Guess eyeing me— her and this detective lady, so I haul ass, but then again you're having a hissy, asking am I gonna let you be a laughingstock. Asking am I gonna let people cheat you to death like Dad did? But what can I do? I ask.

Steal something.

Shoplift! I've never shoplifted, but then we're in Jewelry, peering in the diamond case smoking like a deep freeze, throwing off its blue-white razzle. And it's all junk. It's pure shit, when I see a clunky pair of rhinestone earrings. $1.99 in the silver shrimp basket and they about skin my balls off when I stuff them down my pants.

Things really go downhill after that.

I'm so sick and panicked I blow every last cent on gum and this dripping chili dog, which the relish is so good and I'm so starved I spoon the stuff out and lick it outta my hand. And look, outside it's snowing again, pure snow, four or five inches before I know it! Totally broke and out of breath, I stamp up the steps of the bus, hollering to the driver.

"Mister! Back there! Just two minutes ago, these hoodlums jumped me and stole all my money! Look, I'm stuck! C'mon, you can see I'm a nice, clean-cut kid—please, sir, it's *snowing*. My old man'll kill me if I'm late."

He doesn't want to hear it. Report it to the rent-a-cops, he says, but what with the blizzard and fifty kids all hollering to get on, he finally waves me back. Hey, I'm not asking anything for free, I'm only asking the driver for his name. So, like Honest Abe, I can send the fifteen cents back and clear my sterling reputation . . . And—and do you know what? Patting under my seat, I feel that familiar wet globber *Juicy Fruit*. It's mine! Same gum, same bus, only a different driver.

Man, what a blizzard. It's blowing all across the road. Raking the car lights, it's blowing in big feathers all across the sky and whiting out the trees. I grab the bell rope.

"Hold it, driver! It's my stop . . ."

Jumping off by the Smut Shop, I barely make the next bus. Man, I'm late. It's pitch dark now, and two seats up there's these three stupid girls giggling at me. Slouching down, I pull the earrings from my pants, clip ons, like diamond snowflakes, all glittery against the steamy glass. *Liar.* The earring jaws snap on my ear. And boy, don't those girls look as I squeeze and I squeeze, *tennineeightseven* . . .

You're begging and whimpering for mercy but that's just tough, Mamma, because you're dead now. Really dead. And the earring only breaks, it's so cheap. It snaps and my earlobe pops like a pimple, blood and broken rhinestones tacking across the aisle. So look at me crying, you stupid goddamn girls. Staring through the stinging ice crystals I jerk the rope, jump down into the snow, then go charging down the road, slipping and sliding and the cold flakes grazing my face because I'm alive, really alive finally, all redeemed and free of you. Have you ever seen your face reflected in a million snowflakes in a blizzard? Have you ever run so fast that—*poof*—you finally explode, one flake twittering among the billions, and all you ever want to do is to fall like snow, free as snow, light as snow, falling and falling forever?

SO THE NEW SNOW FALLS and then that snow's fallen and gone to mush. And when I see the doctor about the fainting (and my suspicious hurt ear), I'm negative—or positive or whatever but fine. *Supposedly*, except it's Friday and I've got Sunday mass hanging over me when I hear a honk. It's Father Nivas in the smoking Deathmobile. As I go up to the car, I'm careful to turn to my left—I don't want Nivas getting nosy about this bandage on my right ear.

"Wan' a lif'?" he asks.

I flash this chirpy, all-American look. "Gee *thanks*, Father, but I'm only going a couple blocks." Again he tries.

"Your Dad says your bisit to the doctor wen' well. This puts your mind at rest, I hope?" He tries again. *"This makes you feel better?"* Hey, if you don't understand Father Nivas the first time—wait. The guy always retranslates himself.

"Sorta." I make a face. "Doctor still doesn't know why I fainted."

He points at the tape. "Accident?"

"Oh *that*," I smile. "Really freak thing. Don't laugh but my *ear* got caught? In a kid's *button?*—"

"Huh?"

"See, a buncha us were *sledding*. All *piled* on the sled? And I—I was on the *bottom*, see? Under a kid's big *button? And we crashed?*"

But he's not even touching this stinker. "It will heal. And the fainting will stop."

"But Father, why am I fainting?" Understand, I'm asking this more as *insurance*, in case I do faint again.

"Frank," he says, "enough always the *why*. Do you go to the doctor to be proved *sick?* No, you go to prove to you that you are fine. So you can jus'— be at peace." But Father winces at this one—too sweet. "Aww, quit the preaching, Nivas," he scolds himself. "Frank, just be cool. Be cool and all will be cool. For *yule!*"

That gets a little laugh from me. Also, it's my *escape* clause, looking at him all super relieved like this has really sunk in. "Sure, Father, I see. Right."

"Don't *right* me." But again, feeling himself pushing too hard, he quits. "Frank, to-day Father has a *cold*. To-day he is, I'm afrai', a little *thick*, so promise me this somethin'. Tomorrow, you will make a good and full confession. Then for, ah, added strength you will please say for your mother five Hail Marys and, for you, a *full* Act of Contrition. And eat a big breakfast—early. Do that and you will be fine." Thudding off, he gives me a crazy look. *"No lie."*

And for a couple hours believe it or not, I really do feel better—or do until I remember, it's *Friday*. God, I hate weekends now. Fridays I got the happy-hour butterflies, first worried about Dad, then worried they've mixed up my test and I've really got a septic ulcer, maybe an infected appendix, when across the road I hear.

"Ayy-eee, Dougherty! Mr. Fainter! Mr. Uhhh—"

It's Geffner, this loudmouth fatboy comedian with his two stooges, Mercer and Dubrow. Geffner thinks he's such a laugh riot, calling me Mr. Uhhh. Raising his arms, Geffner hollers over, all woozy, "Frank, I—I—UHHHhh—" His chubby legs wobble. He faints dead to the ground.

"Real funny, Geffner! Funny as your report card, you ugly fat slug!"

"See you at—*uhhhh—MASS!*"

•   •   •

I SNEERED AT A LOT OF THINGS when the hatred hit me, but you think I'd ever have called my first Holy Communion a load of shit? *At least that wasn't horseshit.*

I was seven, with a new buckle belt, my new suit and my shoes all spit shined the way you liked, to distinguish myself. It was late May, burning hot, the big silver fans whumming the dead, thick air. Way in back while the organ played, Sister Ann Ruth hushed everybody, then lined us all up, first the girls in their lacy white frocks, then us boys in our stiff white shirts and clip-on ties.

"Shhhh. Shhhhhuush," hissed Sister Ann Ruth. Tall was in back so I saw it happen when the first kids got It. Lips pruned out, their faces got all big and red. And when they got theirs they *ran* back to their seats, fannies wriggling and elbows flopping. Then Sister nudges me, *you're up.* Closing my eyes hard, I kneel and stick out my tongue—I lick at it, at the air and the light against my eyes and then I feel the priest, first the air he makes, then the Host landing on my tongue, light and dry as a snowflake. It's God and it's happening! Spit is gollywashing through my mouth. The Host is melting and my mouth is clenched down to hold it, bitterer than even the bitterest, most lemony candy.

Run! Run! My mouth welling over, burning with an actual piece of light, and I'm crying but not crying and alive but not alive and asleep but not asleep and a kid but not a kid, and I am solemnly and heartily not faking it *because because I because I heartily love you my God.* Faking it? Falling down on my knee and mashing my fists into my eyes? Faking *this?* Because why else arc all the beautiful stars falling, and they fall and they fall and deep inside of me, moving like chairs and scuffling shoes, opening up like water, rings into rings, there's all this love and voices and *God's really inside me.* And sucking and worrying on the Host in my mouth, all I want to do is make God's goodness to last, to make it last like a candy forever, *So am I done yet so can I open my eyes yet?*

Finally, my eyes flutter open. I wake up to the big silver fans whumming and the hot sunshine stacked in huge yellow bales against the windows and all the kids and the parents and people who got their Communions, they're all knocked down. Everybody's been struck by lightning, but now they're all slowly waking up and, like a flower, I'm waking up too. *Look at me Mamma it's me again and I'm all alive again Mamma look I'm all woken up from being a baby in my life.* It's tremendous. Everybody in the whole world is waking up, Mamma—everybody except you, I realize. Fanning yourself with the Sunday program that you've folded in a hundred creases, you're awake. Awake, I see, because you've *been* awake. Awake because you never got a Communion to make you go to sleep so you could finally wake up. You said it gave you the heebie-jeebies. It gave you the hives, that heat and, worse, all the people packed in beside you. You absolutely couldn't stand that furnace, not the heat or the glare. That's what I saw my first Holy Communion. "Air, I need air," you hissed, barging over people like you'll be sick, *Frank please it was a furnace in there I was dying.*

"REMEMBER," SAYS DAD, "DROP YOUR HEAD IF IT STARTS."

"Okay—"

"And you're okay?"

"I *said* I'm okay."

"Then sit up."

And that prick Geffner, smirking, waiting like everybody for the big splat! Lord knows where we are in the mass, which is divided into Stand, Sit, Stand, Kneel, Mutter, Sing. Dad snorts all irritated. Pulling my black, red-paged missal from my limp hands, Dad starts madly flipping pages, then snaps his nail to the place, *quia peccávi nimis cogitatióne, verbo, et ópere, mea culpa, mea culpa, mea máxima culpa* . . .

"Now fol-low your mis-sal, will you please?"

"Geez, can you say it any louder?"

The wooden pew is still hard with the cold. The cold wood gives another loud crack as I snuggle down, trying to reattach my life to my body and my body to my soul. Because, like shivering, that's just how the body gets warm, Dad says, shivering to repair and raise itself to the proper life temperature. And as a born do-it-yourselfer I do most definitely want to repair my life—are you kidding? REPAIR THYSELF, that's our motto. And, see, what nobody in St. Stephen's will understand is I'm not fainting for *not* trying. Lord no. I'm fainting because I'm literally *knocking myself out trying too hard to believe.* And look how easy it is, believing! I feel like I've been put back four grades. Watching the little kids, I hang my head in shame. Why, the littlest baby-soul swinging his little white shoes can't even touch the floor is doing it as Father Nivas raises the host like a star and the altar boy tinkles the golden bells, *memóriam Passiónis, Resurrectiónis, et Ascensiónis Jesu Christi, and fuck you God and fuck you too Jesus and fuck Mary and Peter and Joseph.*

The organ blasts, the singing stops and then I hear it again . . . the sound of dripping blood. It's the blood spigot being winched off in my brain. In the pit of my throat, deep in my sinus hollows, it starts, the dripping blood, then the outer space tweetering in my ears. I'm freezing. Then the lights dim and it really starts, Pat. Pat pat. Pat pat pat . . . Over the gleaming white marble of the altar, the soot is falling *the soot we're up to the soot part*. In deepening, nattering swarms, the soot is falling over the gleaming white altar. It's falling over the white back of Father Nivas in his white robes bending over the golden chalice, and as it falls, my neck's getting skinnier and skinnier! so skinny my neck's swimming in my shirt collar! to the point *I don't even have a head*.

Quick, the pain tourniquet! I pinch my leg, *wake up!* Teetering on the brink, I'm digging my nails into my thigh, but christ, now we're past the soot to the *bronze*. Now, *bronze* is all I can see, the bronze in the exact place where your casket stood during the funeral mass, *Stand stand up goddamnit tennineeightsevensix*

"Relax, Frank, relax—"

Dad catches me. Just in the nick of time, too, Dad's cold, rough hand rubbing the blood back into my neck so hard the veins squeak. The blood feels so good—drowsy warm—but god it's embarrassing, Dad saying, "Frank, drop your head. *Do it* . . ." Scrubbing my ears, Dad pushes my head between my knees. Seas surge. Hot as whiskey, the blood's pouring over my brain, but when I come back up for air, guess what? Dad's tugging on my elbow. I can't believe it! People are heading up the aisle for Communion! I made it!

Hah hah Geffner boy! Flashing fat boy a grin I slog up the aisle, but even so I'm pretty shaky, afraid I'll get tranced. Anything'll do it. A lit candle. The flash of gold or even the Host, which is so thin, *so white*, in Nivas's fat brown fingers. God, the man's sweating. The altar boys can barely keep up with Nivas, a giant, murmuring bee, going from mouth to open mouth, Host, murmur, Host, flick! flick! flick! Red tongues. Gray tongues. Smoker's hack yellow tongues, flick flick flick! And, under every gagging mouth, the altar boy sticks that gold dribble pan they use in case the Host ever drops.

Dad nudges me—go. But man, I'm feeling wobbly again, especially with Nivas crammed in my oral cavity. It's like kissing. I always close my eyes when I get it. Well, *normally* I do but feeling sick at the last second, I flutter them open and that's when I see him—the altar boy. As the bastard goes in with his dribble pan, his lip curls, then *Zap!* A blue volt of static hits me on my chin! Well, I jump back and then I'm a sacrileger. It's Christ's body tipping off my lips, then sputtering like a dead moth down on the dirty floor!

What did I do!? Hey, I didn't do it! Temporarily insane I go to pick the thing up when I hear Father Nivas hiss, *"Frank. Leave it—"*

But wait, Nivas saw the kid zap me, right? But no, Father isn't looking at him, he's staring straight at me. And Nivas can't just pick the Host up—not without that ritual scouring they do with probably the bishop and a thousand monks. No, Nivas throws a *handkerchief* over it, hissing at me, "*Frank*, look at me. Pay attention."

And look, he's holding out *another* Host. Meaning I'll be dead if I don't and dead if I do but, obviously, dead a whole lot quicker if I don't. Even the altar boy is looking at me funny—almost advising me, *Just take it asshole they'll never believe you anyway.*

And when I turn, it's a lynch mob, people gaping in horror and Dad blocking me out before I can break for the doors. Forget explaining. After Mass lets out, out in front of the church, Dad and Father Nivas huddle. Then Dad's rushing me down the side of the church, so we can meet Father Nivas in the sacristy, back behind the altar.

"Dad, *listen*—"

"I'm sick of listening to you. Tell Father."

Like I say, the sacristy is behind the blue velvet curtains. Spookier than hell, too, vestments hung on walls like the skinned-out souls and this miniature refrigerator with the lock where they keep all the wine and oil and stuff. Anyway, after the silent treatment, Father Nivas comes puffing in. Pulling off his tasseled black robe, he gives me his blowfish look.

"I cleans'd the place—you know it has to be cleans'd, don' you?" He looks at Dad, in case Dad wants to start. But oh no, Pontius Pilate just washes his hands of me.

"No, you ask him, Father. I can't get a straight answer outta him."

"Dad, you won't even listen."

"So *you* tell us, Frank," challenges Nivas.

"What happens to-day? *Again* to-day?"

I sit there blinking. "What, you mean you didn't see it?"

"No, Frank, enlighten us. Please, what didn' I see today?"

"The static electricity, is what! You mean you didn't see that big spark jump off the pan at me?" I glare at Dad. "I *tried* telling you. I got zapped. Off that gold pan—that gold whatchamacallit—y'know, that *salaver* thing the altar boy holds under your mouth?"

"Oh, come on," groans Nivas. "Lightning bolts I have heard. *Angels*, maybe, but never such a thin' as this."

"It did, Father. Well, come on, it's January. It's bone dry, and you got that red rug that runs all along the altar. Father, I swear—"

"No, you will not swear. Where do you think you are?"

My chair honks back. "Well, all right! I'm not pointing any fingers, and I won't squeal, but you ask that altar boy, *maybe he'll know.*"

Well, that cooks my goose. Pushing open the red curtain, Nivas calls into the empty church, "Alvy, can you come in here, please?"

MY WORD AGAINST AN ALTAR BOY'S, that'd be one thing. But against an altar boy *and* a Boy Scout? That's right. Because through the curtain, in walks this Alvy kid in his Boy Scout uniform, his sash so splashed with merit badges he coulda won three wars. Now, I'm no scout but I know my badges and this kid's already a Star scout—two steps from Eagle when he can't be more than fourteen or fifteen. He's got his hotshot Totin' Chip patch (board certified to carry an axe), and there's his silver patrol-leader's whistle hanging off a braided lanyard. And his kerchief, boy, his kerchief's rolled tighter than a western dude tie, then threaded through this wicked 50-cal. bullet.

What really kills me, though, he's got the *Ad Altare Dei* medal. *Ad Altare Dei*, meaning "toward the altar of God." Just a little gold cross hanging from a slice of colored ribbon, and it tingle tangles in the light—*subtle.* That's what's so impossibly cool about the Ad Altare Dei, how subtle and secret and rare it is. I mean, there's probably only four or five kids in the whole school, probably in the whole state of Maryland, who got one. Strictly the cream of wheat of Catholic youth, *Ad Altare Dei.* Why, even to test you gotta be *asked*, and the tests last two or three days, what with Latin and naming all the saints and feast days—crap like that, mostly, plus be invested in these fierce mysteries so you can stomp around with the Glory in your eyes. Adults lap it up, too. All the old farts do. Hell, drag this kid into the Knights of Columbus Hall on a Friday night and the old drunks'll all be slobbering over him, to the point the kid's blubbering about he's heard the angelic yoo-hoo of a *vocation.* And the kid risks all this on a sick prank? When he doesn't even know me?

He's tall, too. He's nearly as tall as me but more solid. In fact, he looks pretty strong, wide-backed with a cleft chin notched like the claw of a hammer and these black glasses, which one way look gorpy and another like bandit goggles. And his eyes—little cold blue eyes. And his hair, splintery, Woody Woodpecker hair so short and slicked it *speeds.* Boy, was I stupid not to see through the Scout getup. The hair alone should have cued me.

And moody, his jaw muscles bulging in disgust, *Don't make me stain myself by ratting on him.* Man, is he perfect. Too noble to sit when Nivas offers him a chair. No, he'll stand, yessirring and nosirring them both to death—Lord, he practically snaps to attention when he shakes Dad's hand. Pulling his soft, brown Scout hat from his web belt, he lightly slaps it. He flicks off some imaginary speck, then zaps me a don't-fuck-with-me look, which, again, Nivas and Dad can't see, this being on the kid bandwidth.

"So, Alvy," says Father Nivas, "Firs' lemme get this straight. You don' know Frank. Never. No contact. No words, ever? No kinda grudge?"

"No, I don't know him, Father. Oh sure, I've *seen* him in school—he's tall, so he sticks out. Anyway, we never said boo to each other. Well, right, Dougherty?"

"Yeah," I nod, "that much is true."

"Ho-K," warns Nivas. "Already we heard Frank's side, so now you will tell us, Alvy. Wha' happent today?" The kid shrugs.

"What I can say, Father? Honestly, I wasn't paying attention—I mean, not to him, specifically. You know how busy we get up there, Father. But as best I can recollect, well, I guess the kid twitched." He stops. What an actor he is. Oh, this is really hard for him, slapping his hat, "Look, I'm not out to knock your own son, Mr. Dougherty. I'm sure he doesn't act this way in your home, the truth is he's a loud, nervous kid—"

"—And?" prompts Dad.

"—Well, he's a little on the, uh, excitable side. In the halls and stuff? He has these, I dunno, *fits?*"

"And today?" huffs Dad.

"Well, today I'd have to say he—jumped. Twitched." Nivas jumps in.

"What you mean, fit? A muscle spasm? A perhaps on-purpose fit? What?"

"Well, I'd hate to say, Father. Maybe half on purpose and half nerves?"

"*Nerves!*" I bust out. "Sure, make me out the nut case! Like *you* weren't scuffing your shoes."

"Beg your pardon?"

"You heard me!" But now my own body's incriminating me, my voice quaking and my hands spazzing out. The kid just looks at Dad and Nivas.

"I rest my case."

"You wish, Loomis! Cause you zapped me. *On purpose.*"

"Aww, garbage. Total garbage."

"And *why?*" demands Dad. "Why would he do such a thing?"

"Cause I'll tell you why—meanness. That's right. Lots of kids are gunning for me now, and why? Because of Mom, that's why." Well, Dad blows.

"Sure, drag your poor mother into it! Have you no shame?"

The kid turns to Nivas. "Father, I've gotta serve the next mass—Tucker's sick, so can I go now, please?" He turns to Dad. "Look, Mr. Dougherty, I'm really sorry. I heard about your wife."

Nivas perks up. "That's right, you served her funeral mass, din' you?"

"Well, I didn't want to *rely* on that, Father. But as a matter a fact."

"You see?" I cry. "There's your reason! *He served Mom's mass.*"

WELL, IT WAS FISHY, the kid serving your mass, and the more I thought about it, the fishier it all got, too. But then as fast as *that*, I'm thinking that *I'm* crazy, that the zap jumped from me to the pan. Or, crazier still, that somehow you had done it, Mamma—done it to frame me same as those earrings I swiped for you.

Father Nivas is sure no help. Once Ad Altare Dei leaves, while Dad waits outside, Nivas sits me down alone in the sacristy—basically, a confession without the screen. Of course, priests aren't in the blame business, so Father Nivas is saying how, ultimately, proof's irrelevant and it's all between me and God, like it's God I need to convince. Like I can think of my life immortal when Dad's outside waiting to beat my mortal butt. Yeah, Dad's really had it. Bad enough I've spit on God but I've invoked your name, Mamma. Publicly I've dragged out the family shame, so once home Dad drags off his belt, waggles it at me, then *whap!*

"You think I'm—I'm just a fool? That you can shit on me, and your mother, and God, too? . . ."

It's funny, getting beat on. At first your skin flares a million degrees, from the humiliation, but after a few whacks it's only a wind that Dad's making. Really, it's all so blank and stupid the guy could beat on me all day.

The whole aspect of the thing changes then. It's just a belt. It's just a whiff the belt makes, and as for the pain painting me like tar, the pain only makes me that much deader and duller, really. This can't be my actual Dad, it can't be. It can't even be the same God, 'cause what God would get His jollies watching a man trying to break the kid he always fixed before, when he busted his arm or scraped his knee? And it's such a drudging *labor,* having to hate the man and, worse, to know, deep down, it's just a job for him, just a horrible, thankless job. Cause let's face it, Dad would never beat me like this if I was a girl. If I was a girl, the man just wouldn't have that much invested in it. But what makes me the tiredest, and what no adult can possibly fathom,

I'm secretly helping him. By letting Dad beat me, I'm helping us say something we've both been trying to say for months. God, it itches, though. It itches like fire. It's the chigger-itch of old perspired-in wool, but still the ass is mightier than the belt. And there's the nasty truth. In a royal whupping there's always a winner and a loser. And here in the final heat, I'm winning, just staring at Dad, thinking how fucking funny he looks, waving that stupid belt around.

It's a game of chicken and I'm running him off the road. And the guy's trapped—I mean he can't go this far and make *no* impression, so he lashes out—bats me with the flat of his hand. Really, it's nothing. It's just a paw of disgust but I turn it against him. Sprawling back, I topple across the coffee table, and maybe deep down I am hoping he'll save me, that he'll catch me in his arms the way he did the day you died. But no, love doesn't work that way now. Dad can't catch me, and I crack my elbow. Poor Dad. He's white as a sheet but I only sneer at him. So being a man naturally he sneers back.

"Aww, did he hurt himself!"

"Who? By you? No! I'm *fine!*"

Whap! He whips himself! But instead of I can let him win, I only keep laughing until the guy goes nuts. *Whap! Whap, whap,* Dad grabbing my hand.

"*Here!* Go on, you little coward, so *hit me!* You think I killed her, so go on! Hit me!"

"Dad! Are you crazy? *Daddy, stop it!*"

Finally, he knocks himself out, I guess. Slumping on the sofa Dad starts bawling, just sucking his own heart out, looking at me like *I* should save *him*. Pulling me into his heaving chest, like from another life he's calling me his "little Frank," but this only itches me worse, his face and neck all welted up and his sweat stinking like old cheese. And he's so alive! That's what I can't believe. As dead as you are now, suddenly Dad's so incredibly alive, and I've busted him and he can't fix me.

AT SCHOOL THE NEXT DAY, Geffner's all over me, "What, you don't even know who the kid's Dad is—*Alvy Loomis?*" Even before school starts, it's all over the place.

"Yeah," I bluff, "I know who his Dad is—so?"

But the fat boy knows he's got me. Big mouth is broadcasting to the whole playground, "Dougherty didn't even know who Loomis's Dad is, *he didn't even know!* Well, here's a hint, doofus!" Bucking his teeth, Geffner cuts loose from a Thompson submachine gun, *"SPUUuuuD-D-D-D—Budda-budda-boot—"*

"Bullshit."

"Dag, Dougherty, you didn't know? Of all the kids Dougherty picks on Lucky Loomis's kid! A kid who eats up high schoolers!"

Shit, I'd seen Alvy Loomis's Dad—who hadn't, all the Germans that Lucky Loomis had killed? I know you've seen his picture. Everybody has. It's that famous picture of General Eisenhower and these five black-faced paratroopers about to jump on Normandy. Ike's off to the left and there, smack in the middle, there's Lucky Loomis with this wild mohawk and that hard cleft chin. "Well," cracks Ike, "I guess you boys know you're all gonna die tonight." Hardy har har. And Lucky's got the biggest laugh of all. Yeah, grinning away, Lucky Loomis just *knows* he's got that first silver star locked up, same as he knows he'll come through without a scratch, and here when his platoon's all but wiped out, half of them before they even hit the ground. Death always changes the picture. Because for Lucky Loomis to publicly face death and then to live, well, this made him even more alive and lustery with luck—the kind of luck people wanted to touch each year in Taverna's dinky Fourth of July parade, when they drove Lucky Loomis down Mills Avenue sitting atop the backseat of a polished white T-Bird. You heard me right. A white T-Bird, a '62 just like ours with white leather seats and spoked wheels—same car in every respect, except, painted in wicked little black letters on the door, just like a jet fighter, was *"Lucky" Loomis, Commander V.F.W. Post 151.* And highly decorated? In his Veterans of Foreign Wars whites, that man was decorated better than a wedding cake. Gold and Silver Stars galore. The Cross du Gore. Old Lucky had them all, I heard. All except the one everybody said he'd been robbed of, the Congressional Medal of Honor.

No, there was no forgetting that easy grin. Rocking and waving, Lucky laughed and hollered to all his friends. And he threw candy, candy by the fistfuls that splattered like ice on the hot pavement as all us kids cheered and dove for it.

How was I to know it was *that* Alvy Loomis? I mean if you meet a kid named Murphy, do you automatically figure his Dad's *Audie?*

So why did this Loomis kid zap me? I wonder.

Now Sister John Christopher, the principal, had heard about the sacrilege and she knew there'd be a fight. In fact, she threatened to suspend Ad Altare

Dei and me both if we fought, no matter who threw the first punch. Well don't worry, I wanted to tell her. That's not about to happen, because I'm buck-buck-buck chicken. Never mind I'd just stood up to a whole gang of punks up at the plaza. With a gang it wasn't personal, like it was with this bruiser. No, for the next two weeks it's the big Stare-Down, as him and me trade dirty looks in the lunchroom and hallways. I can't take those cold, deep-socketed little eyes of his, though—I always break first. No sir, Ad Altare Dei isn't afraid of me or of being suspended, and he isn't even in any particular rush to settle it, or let me off the hook. No, Ad Altare Dei, he won't go away, won't be tricked, and what's more, I realize *he wants something*. What totally drives me nuts, though, he's got this, like, monkey expression, this way of turning his head when I turn mine, answering every *"Huh"* with a *"Huh?"* then a double-monkey *"Huh."* And every time I look, the picture changes. At first I figure he's just psyching me out, monkey-huhing me. But then I get to feeling these weird sympathy vibrations from him, like the kid knows me, like he has to know me, asking, *Don't you get it yet? Can't you figure it out?*

In class I'll look down and see my hand writing, *Alvy Loomis Alvy Alvy Loomis.* It's crazy. The kid's ruined my reputation, killed Dad, and I'm not even mad at him finally! And some days it's all I can do not run up to him, say I'll forget the whole thing, even take the blame, if only he'll just admit it. If only he'll admit that you're the reason why he sabotaged me, Mamma. That somehow, somewhere, it's all about you.

Even Dad says he's never seen such a snowy, sloppy January. One night around this time it sleets and rains, then the thermometer falls and freezes everything bone solid. *Nose hair weather,* I call it, because you can actually hear your nose hairs tinkle, freezing and thawing, thawing and freezing as you breathe. What's really amazing, though, is how even in the coldest, brittlest cold, the sun can burn so fierce! Out on our front stoop one day I'm running an *experiment*—I'm burning holes in a piece of newsprint with the big mag-nifying glass from the desk drawer. It must be minus ten, our poor shrubs frozen like in plastic, encased in all that ice. In the wind they hiss and rattle, and the air smokes but I keep at it, moving the magnifying glass over the newsprint, boring pinholes—all the Os. A wobbling dial of light! A tiny molten-yellow bead . . . a furious black blotch, the curling smoke, *poof.*

I can't stop it. I can't stop your disintegration, Mamma. Almost objectively, I watch the beam flip like a dime into my open palm. What's the matter, hand? I think. Sissy hand, can't even hold one tiny sunbeam? With all the heat of hell, and you can't even take a single grain of sun? And Dad's right about the heat in cold, and the things you think, even when you're not thinking. Even in all that cold, the sun's sharp as a scalpel. I can't stand it. One prick and my hand jerks in pain. *So go on woman you're dead as a doornail so good riddance.*

HAIRY SHIT, HUH? By now you probably think life just happens to me boom boom boom. But see, gang, that's just in the telling—you can't believe how unbelievably boring my life is half the time. For *days* sometimes, but who wants to hear about that or all the long, dull dead spaces?

Oh, sure some adults do—it's safe—but that's not the way here, at this age. No, at this age the only way to survive is to keep moving, and to move faster the worse life gets. But let's admit it, this is not the stuff most grown-ups like to remember—or not around kids at least. Adults, they'd rather tell you the boring stuff, the sweet, hunky-dory stories that, as a kid, you see clear through, knowing these stories are only meant to make you behave or cheer you up, all boo-hooey because you can't tie your shoe or didn't make the team.

And sure, as a kid you know that grown-ups *mean* well. It's just their lame nature, to keep it all light and happy, and lots of times *you really appreciate this*. Like Dad's remembering hot summer days, getting slivers of ice from the ice man and how good it tasted. Or that time during the Paw Paw Newspaper Drive when Dad got his picture in the newspaper—millions of bundles and Dad on top KING OF THE MOUNTAIN. And I *love* these stories—are you kidding? You can't fault Dad not wanting to tell me the bad stuff, like how his Dad never did a damned thing except read the newspaper, complain about politics and feel miserable. And Dad definitely doesn't want to remember the time that his Dad took him fishing.

No, it was my Aunt Edna—Edna, the crazy one, always dredging up the past—who told me the one about the fishing trip with Dad's Dad. Dad's Dad was so hopeless, Aunt Edna said. Fishing! Dad's Dad couldn't hammer a nail, let alone bait a hook. Why, Dad's Dad could barely drive and didn't even own a car, wearing out his shoes trudging door to door selling coal miners dime insurance. But one day Dad's Mom says to Dad's Dad *go!* Do something with your son! You want him to turn out a sissy, an only boy raised with seven girls?

So with their borrowed poles and Uncle Dick's Model A, Dad and Dad's Dad, they both drive up to the lake. Oboy oboy. It's the first time they've ever been out of Johnstown together . . . up and up they go into the mountains, when wobble-obble-obble, they get a flat! Well, Dad's Dad climbs out in his spotless black suit, the one suit he owns. He stares at the sky, then starts to pace. Never fear! Dad flags down a car, then Dad and the Samaritan guy who stops, they both change the flat while Dad's Dad stands there in his tie and shirtsleeves, blabbing on about Alf Landon, who he hates. "Well, there you go," says the Samaritan. He slams the trunk and they all shake hands. "Yeah, the fish are really biting," he says. "Just keep going, the lake's just three miles." Oboy oboy. But when Dad gets in, Dad's Dad mutters, "This'll never work." And then he turns the car right around and that's that.

But Dad never tells me this fish story, not then. No, we stay with the shaved ice, the paper drive and the Scout overnights where Dad would wade cold streams, eating fresh watercress dabbed with the salt shaker tucked in his shirt pocket.

And these are such great stories. Trouble is, though, they always turn on me, making me think, *So what's wrong with my life?* It's like I'm staring through the wrong end of a telescope. Suddenly I'm feeling small instead of large, and wrong instead of right.

And that's the problem with the stories that adults tell. They're not your stories. They're not your life at all, and they can't be—can't because as you must know by now, the real stories are the ones that adults'll never tell.

BUT IT'S NOT just stories, it's the whole problem of *hearing*. You've never seen worse hearing than in our house now. Ever since Dad whipped me, we've both been creeping around, avoiding each other like two sick, worn-out old men. Then there's the whole boring, stupid mess about Bud—the *last* of Bud, thank God—plus the lawyer-leeches and the doctors and *their* credit bureau's hounding us. In fact, when the credit hounds call, it's my job to act all stupid and half asleep, which I'm so *great* at these days, "Gee, sorry, mister, but my Dad's out working. All these bills we got, Dad's always out working..." Or else Dad's in a lather (I overhear him tell Grammaw) about we might lose the house! My fault, of course, because I'm not pulling *my* weight, financially. "Well, I did it," Dad hollers—if Dad had to drag his wagon through the slag heaps, the least I can do is drag a newspaper wagon. Hey, I tell him, there *are* no *Washington Post* or *Star* routes open—I've checked. Not until 1966, or some paperboy gets run over or grows up.

Offer it up, Dad says, because that's the Catholic way, dragging the old "honey wagon" through life. If that's true, Dad's a saint by now. Offering it up, Dad's cut down to two packs a day. And heh heh heh aren't we the penny-pinchers, pasting down our Top Value stamps in some grubby little book redeemable for a set of junk knives. Oh yeah, Mamma, love to see *you* clipping coupons and going through the newspaper ads—*Hey Dad here's a good sale on ground chuck.* By the time I hit the hay and check the old dipstick Mr. Pokey just sulks, he's so worn out.

Still, I *am* trying to be more Christian, to pray more, and cuss and whack off less. (Although that mortal sin stuff's fairly trivial and overblown, I've decided—I *think* I've decided.) I mean, c'mon. There's gotta be more to religion than just scaring the hell out of kids, right? Fear's no answer. Fear's Communist! Why, fear's just a Chicken Little approach toward God, if you ask me.

Now, I like a lot what that writer Jack London said in *White Fang* about you gotta have a code and even dogs with heart have got one. Revamping my life, I've customized that, generally, plus what Father Nivas preaches about *giving your life over to God.* But when's God gonna happen? I wonder, thinking I just gotta make myself more *famished.* More *available* so I can be redeemed.

BUT IT WASN'T THE CHURCH THAT DREW ME NOW, IT WAS THE NIGGER BRIDGE. This was the black-creosoted, railroad-tie bridge that ran over the B&O tracks, dividing Taverna from Taver-Shep, the little colored town. In our town they really lived on the other side of the tracks, hidden behind the weeds in the low, soot-spattered, crumbly-shingled shanties that slouched away all dejected from us. The bridge rumbled good whenever a car drove over it, which was hardly ever, and down below in the bluestones of the rail bed there were bright swords of sun. It was very dejected and *angry,* as a bridge. Angry because on this bridge, on both sides of the tracks there'd be big battles, whities against blackies! *Riot! riot! nigger aginst whi-ot!* Big clashes! Bluestone rocks zinging like bullets through the high weeds, whole showers of rocks and pop bottles lobbed high, like grenades, for the tremendous *smash* on the shining steel rails. Kids said you never had so much fun, but sooner or later some hothead'd yell, "Goddamn *niggers!*" and all the whities would scatter, because here they come! Down the road it's these huge big *boons.* It's their big brothers, with rags on their heads, pure black, and yelling out the sides of their red mouths! Swinging their arms! big-muscled arms, too, shining like black tar bubbles in the sun!

Okay, so I never did any of this. Not while you were alive I didn't, but I sure heard about it from kids, probably half b.s. but that's what they said. And that's the good part now, doing stuff I'd never have dreamed of before. But with Taver-Shep what started it, I guess, was that colored lady I saw at the bus stop—I mean that day we snuck up to the plaza, when I confused you for colored and you died for real. Almost every day since I've been pedaling over on my bike to scout the colored side. I'll bet that colored lady lives here—her and that colored man Dad picked up way back when. I do know one person who lives here, and that's our colored maid, Mrs. Eppes. Crouched in the high weeds during these scouting missions, I worry Mrs. Eppes may spot me and tell Dad, but deep down I guess I know there's not much chance of that. No, Taver-Shep is like a one-way glass. As a white person, I can look in but they can't see out, as proved by the fact that no colored ever says boo to me, or notices. I stop my bike, I look, then I race home like a demon's after me. It's like beating off. God knows why.

So here I am, straddling my bike, peering over the weeds into Taver-Shep when Whoosh! I feel a wind, then a cuff on the head! It's Alvy Loomis on his bike.

"So where's Mamma now, pussy?"

I'm scared to death but I gotta keep *some* dignity, hollering back, "Look, it's over, Loomis. Hey, I'll forget the whole mess but just keep my Mom out of it, okay?"

"Oh! Big man, huh?" He screeches up, so close I'm trembling, so close I can see his crooked, chipped teeth. "Aww, hell, I didn't mean to talk about your *Mom*. Gawd, look at you. Like you're the only motherfucker in the world who ever lost anybody. You big fuckin baby. *Mommmm-mey*—"

"Shut up! What do you know about losing anybody, you big liar? You—"

Next thing I know I'm flat in the middle of the road. One punch! My mouth's gushing blood, and my blue school pants are torn clear down the leg where they snagged the front wheel bolt of my bike. Toppled back in the gravel, I'm blind. In the sun there's a black circle around Alvy's face, and I'm yelling up at him, at the utter vastness of his power.

"Liar! Ftucking thuckerpunther!"

Between the humiliation and the shock I'm *begging* him to hit me again, but he doesn't cock his fist or taunt me, he doesn't do anything. Arms at his sides, the kid's more dazed than I am, suddenly the emptiest, most listless thing you ever seen.

"Ptth, are you crazy?" I say, pulling out a long string of bloody slobber. "Whatth I ever do to youf, you bathtard, *what?* Loof, you buthed my *teef*."

The handlebars are bent clear around. My leg's bleeding and my pants are snagged in the bicycle chain. He's sure no help. With a grunt, I tear my pants loose—they're torn so bad I have to stick them in my coat pocket so they won't snag the chain. Then from the colored side, whoops and catcalls.

"Ha ha! Get that skinny white motherfuck! Fight! Fight! Big white fight!"

Waving and punching the air, there must be six or seven of them, all yelling and laughing at us. Alvy rears back, *"Fuck you black motherfuckers!"* The trance he's in I doubt he even hears himself say this. Like a cat over a wounded bird, he just stands there staring at me, *Don't you even get it yet?*

Sure, I get it, I get going. Spitting blood, I jump on my bike, *"T'thhh,* I'll get youf, Loofmis! If ith the laffth thing *I dooth*—"

"Oh ho. Look at mister white pussy runnn-hun!"

As I crank off, the kid still stands there frozen. And the jigaboos ain't after him, they're all after *me,* charging down the embankment, whipping rocks and bottles. *HuuuuUUHhhu*—A pop bottle moans by my ear. Branches whip in my face, then I hit the main road, crunching metal all the way home. I never pedaled so far, so fast. My coat's all bloody down the front, and my busted bottom lip's filling like a gravy boat. God, my lip's so fat, my bloody spit splatters back, and adults, they whirl around, shouting at me like I must not know, like it's news, *"You! Boy! You're bleeding!"*

Alvy Loomis had hurled a brick through my life, all right. Once home, I ditch my bike, tear upstairs and stare at myself in the bathroom mirror. I look like a rabbit! My bottom lip is split and my top tooth is wriggling. Spitting blood and humiliation in the sink, I rage at the mirror, until suddenly I'm half laughing and half sobbing, half realizing that I'm free, that I'm alive, really alive, and in a weird way connected to somebody finally.

My wild new life had just begun.

ABOUT

ALVY

WHANGSLAP.

Out the busted screen door comes Lucky Loomis, bandy-legged, older and a lot smaller up close, with that long bean of a face and the famous notched chin. Dad already phoned, so Mr. Loomis knows why we're here tonight, not that there's much to wonder with me looking like Bugs Bunny. No, you can be sure he's been waiting, him and whoever's peeping down from the upstairs window—gee, who? I wonder.

I couldn't believe it when Dad agreed that *we'd* come to *them*. Is that the deal, that losers come to winners? Is that the rule? "Dad, why don't they come to *our* house and apologize?" But Dad, I can tell you, Dad doesn't want anybody in our house—not when we're outnumbered and womanless. Worse, Dad's in a suit, to show them we're respectable and he works late. Not Mr. Loomis, though. Mr. Loomis is wearing bummy old pleated trousers, topped off with a sleeveless T-shirt, paint splattered carpet slippers and saggy white socks. And what's this written all over his upper arms and chest? I wonder. Under the hair it's written in these blotchy white nicks and scars. Written, like, in Chinese when I realize . . . *shrapnel scars*.

"Hi-yah." As Mr. Loomis steps out under the porch light, his eyes flutter real fast between words, I notice. He puts out his hand. "Charles Loomis—but, please, Lucky."

Heads up, Dad! Fine, maybe I shoulda been watching for the punch but right now Dad should be watching to get *niced*. Pushing Dad's hand around in a slow locomotive, Mr. Loomis, see, is one of these *pumper* handshakers, real friendly but also sizing Dad up—it's more like they're injun wrestling than shaking hands. Still, Dad's got Mr. Loomis by a head and a foot of reach—at least. So what if Alvy's two hoodlum brothers are over by the garage tearing down some hot rod, Dad's not ascared of Mr. Big Shot Hero, is he?

But Mr. Loomis isn't playing it tough but *nice*. Why, he's playing Dad like a Wurlitzer, and between Alvy and his brothers Mr. Loomis has had practice, all the fathers he's had dragging their bugged-out losers here seeking satis-faction. And Mr. Loomis is cool, and he should be, a man who's seen his best buddies blown to bits. Even playing it serious Mr. Loomis is semi-amused, his chin dimpled like the butt stem of an apple and the cigarette smoldering in his cupped hand. In Mr. Loomis's face, there's a whole he-man philosophy. We're the gumhands here. It's like Dad and me have come to ask a dumb question, and in Mr. Loomis's eyes here's our answer, *These are boys, Mac. They're total knuckleheads but c'mon are we gonna defang dogs and declaw cats?*

"Yeah," says Mr. Loomis, "the wife told me the boys had a little scrape today. Yeah, a little scrape up, huh? . . ." Trailing off, he turns to me and smiles—smiles like he's General Eisenhower, so that I feel half proud, like *I* deserve a medal. "And how are *you,* son? Well, whatever happened, I can see you stood up for yourself. Good for you. Still, darned sorry to see that poor face. Oh boy. Well, Pete, Alvy told me there'd been some kinda little tiff—y'know. Yeah, I was planning to collect Alvy and pay you a visit"—he quickly papers over that one—"Anyway, come on in. We'll get this thing patched up right now."

Until that night I had no idea where Alvy lived. Dad got their address from the phone book, and when he said Shepherd Hills, I practically shit! Shep-herd Hills, see, is this tough white-trash neighborhood that sits on the muddy rise, really a small mountain, over the colored town, Taver-Shep. Yeah, as our Studebaker groaned up Alvy's steep windy street, I could see why Alvy had ambushed me by the Nigger Bridge. Down at the bottom of the hill, through the kudzu vines and dumped refrigerators, there it was—Taver-Shep, with its dull yellow lights and tall dark keyholes of houses wreathed in wood smoke. Suddenly I felt so stupid! So blind! It was like somebody had handed me a map of the whole world. All my life it had been here for me to see, but I'd never looked, or not from this side, from so high up. Suddenly even the mon-grel name "Taver-Shep" struck me as weird, cobbled out of the scraps of "Taverna" and "Shepherd Hills."

Shepherd Hills was this brick and clapboard development built probably the day the war ended from the smithereens. Compared with our town, it seemed old and countrified, and it sure wasn't getting any statelier with age. On first look, the place mostly felt like an army post, except on army posts people can't run chickens or park trucks on their lawns. Talk about little boxes! These were hard, peevish, clapboarded, low-roofed houses with lawn dwarfs and chain link and wild bushes stuffed in white-painted tires—tires that glowed like flying saucers in our headlights. And the people! What were they doing out on such a cold winter night? Dad kept downshifting to first, the road was so muddy-steep, and as we passed by them, the people stared hard at us, like we'd run over a dog. Spud greasers looking like baby wolf-men. Women with giant scarved heads of curlers and men still in their shop uniforms with name tags that read "Chuck," "Bob," "Junior." And the cars! Bombs and hot rods, plumbing and roofing vans, tow trucks, crab trucks and exterminator trucks, even this one Dydee truck with a giant plastic baby wearing a gold crown. This was where Alvy lived, but with one big difference. Alvy's house was the biggest house on the biggest lot, white clapboard like the others but three times the size, with a garage, a white flagpole and V.F.W. Post 151 just up the road. Nope, right off you could see who was king of Shepherd Hills. The only thing Alvy's house lacked was the howitzer.

What got Dad, though, was the white T-Bird in Alvy's driveway—like I said, a '62 just like yours. It was like we'd found you living in a whole new life, under an assumed alias. Getting out Dad touched the car like a ghost. "Wait? . . . Frank? . . ." Dad has to touch it, to believe it. And he sounds so happy for a second, running his hand along the bumper, feeling for that ding you'd put there.

"Frank, that's not the Bird, is it?"

"No, Dad," I sigh, "that's just another super big coincidence."

"COMEIN COMEIN COMEIN," says Lucky, ushering us in to the peo-ple-packed, fried-chicken-smelling free-for-all where, from dawn 'til taps, the blue TV cackles to itself and doors slam and the phone never stops ringing. But the stunner is the Lucky Shrine. The man's got the goodies, all right. Fastened with a little gold lock, here's a lighted case with his choicest booty, German beltbuckles, skull buttons, Hitler Youth knives, plus this wicked lit-tle black pistol with swastikas on the butt, *but c'mon you could buy these.* But what about this, you Doubting Thomases, this smaller, lighted glass case gleaming with medals cozied in deep blue plush? Points of bronze and silver stars. Polished swords and thunderbolts, angels and victories, until I pull away, realizing I'm cheezing the glass with my breath. Give up, I think. Because if you still doubt these, above the case, here's the prize shot of Mr. Loomis and Ike on D day, and if you still doubt that, here's a shot of them both on a big stage years later, when Ike's president and Mr. Loomis is in a suit wearing his peaked V.F.W. cap. And again, Mr. Loomis is cracking up! Right in front of the president! He's giving President Eisenhower something on a plaque and

Ike's just beaming! Boy, these jokers get famous, then they only get more famous, swapping their plaques and sheepskins and having their big hardy-har-hars while all us spear-carriers stand at attention. It's just like Angelene. Being DAR, Angelene can spit watermelon seeds and scuff her grammar, the same as Mr. Loomis can meet us in his T-shirt, or his underwear, for all he cares. And when I look around Dad's mad at *me*. Glaring why didn't I warn him? *Why?* Because I was protecting Dad, is why! Besides, I figured Dad knew! But before I can explain here's Mr. Loomis shuffling back.

"Pardon me, gents. I'm looking for my Mrs. *Bunnnn—Bunn-neeeyy—*"

And who *are* all these people in here? And rude? Because slumped on the sofa watching TV, here are these two big clods, grown men with sideburns who don't so much as grunt at us. And God, all the noise and confusion! Upstairs, they could be having a dance, all the thumping feet and music. Meanwhile, this big black dog, this streak, is ripping around in circles until the one clod clobbers him, "Git!" Then this little boy runs by—Alvy's little brother, I guess—there's the chin—but the man gets mad at him, too, "Go on, boy. Ain't yuh never seen people before? Now go wash your face." And coming down the stairs, here's this beautiful blonde woman. "Oh, you poor thing," she says to me. "Did Alvy do that to you, honey? God, I am *so* sorry."

But wait, she can't be Alvy's Mom, can she? See, at my age I can't *judge* age, or not in adults. Still at any age she's confusing—the whole house is confusing, not knowing who's attached to who and nobody bothering to introduce themselves. Not to mention Dad doing the phony "after-you" business—so he can get a good look at her butt! No, it can't be Alvy's mother, I think. It must be his older sister—she has the chin and the eyes. And she's not the only sister either. Because a second later, the front door opens and in walks this other blonde woman, another knockout and really built, too, wearing a brown suede coat and black toreador pants. This woman, though, she's not friendly at all.

"Okay, okay, honey," she says to the clod by the TV, "I'm getting Audrey and the baby. Where's Buddy?"

"Buddy's washing his face, now *c'mon.*"

The clod lurches out the door—barges right past Dad, no excuse me, no goodnight, no nothing. At that, the woman looks right at Dad and me, long enough, I figure, that she'll at least introduce herself, but forget that. Instead, she picks a lipstick off the table, winds it out to check it, smears some on, then drifts out like a ghost, calling, "Buuu-uddy honey? You in the kitchen?"

"Hey! You seen my pack of Camels?"

It's this old geezer. I don't even hear him, I'm so entranced with her. He's staring right at Dad, staring at Dad like *he* took his cigarettes. So Dad turns it into a joke.

"A herd of Camels, you say?"

"My *smokes*," glares the old man. "Somebody walked off with my damned smokes." Then here's Mr. Loomis who completely ignores the old geezer, passing him off with a look at Dad.

"Hey, sorry for the wait, gentlemen. Let's adjourn to my study, huh?"

I give Dad a hard poke, but no, he walks right into the trap—the big oak desk, the padded leather chair and the three framed sheepskins. Then, like we're not intimidated enough, here's a tommy gun hanging on the wall, *a real Thompson .45 burp gun.* But the worst is the Green Lamp. Beware that Green Lamp.

"So you're a lawyer," says Dad, getting all quiet.

"Yeah, 'fraid so." Mr. Loomis chuckles, then tells his lawyer joke—something about this lawyer at the Last Judgment who sends God his bill from hell. So Dad, of course, Dad has to tell *his* groaner about engineers "studying" the problem. *A lawyer and he lives in Shepherd Hills?*

"But where's Alvy?" I ask Mr. Loomis. "Isn't Alvy coming?"

"Well, son," says Mr. Loomis squeaking in his chair, "I thought we'd hear your side first."

Son! A classic Bud tactic if ever there was one, first-naming and "sonning" you to death. But before I can even tell my side Dad starts in, playing the lawyer while Mr. Loomis plays the judge. Lord, with all Dad's hemming and whereforeing and it-would-seeming, you'd think it was the wind that hit me! And before Dad can even finish Mr. Loomis has got a deal for us.

"Pete, lemme make things a mite easier here. Naturally, I'll pay for a new coat and a pair of pants. And a dental visit. But as far as the who-started-it stuff, well, let's face it. It's just Frank's word against Alvy's. There were no witnesses."

"Oh yes there were," I say. "Colored kids saw it, Mr. Loomis."

"And I believe you, Frank," he soothes. "But I ask you now, what do we do with that information, son? Do we all drive down to Taver-Shep in the black of night and look for them?" Chomping on his cigarette, he grins. "Might be pretty hard to *see* 'em, for one thing. Anyhow, son, I sincerely apologize. And I'm going to get Alvy down here to apologize, too. It may be hard to believe, Frank, but deep down Alvy feels as bad about this mess as you do."

I look at Dad. "So for no reason the kid can punch me?"

"So what do you want, old buddy? An engraved apology?"

"And the *idea*," adds Mr. Loomis, "is for you and Alvy to quit this nonsense. Pronto."

"Sounds good to me," agrees Dad.

Well, fortunately the door busts open, and in rushes this skinny old woman. Skinny-skinny with a poof of gray hair tied in a scarf.

"Oh, you poor thing!"—sweeping me up in a hug she lays on a big kiss— "Oh, your poor face! Boyoboy, am I mad! Am I steamed! Honey, I don't care what you said, our Alvy had no business doing this to you! *Alvy!!* . . ." Who is she? Alvy's grandmother? She must see I'm confused, because then she says, "Gee, I forgot to introduce myself, sweetheart, I'm *Mrs*. Loomis."

But she's so old! Worse, she's really beautiful. Like I say, beauty is scary and age is obscure enough, but for a woman to have beauty and age, both! And Mrs. Loomis has the most beautiful blue eyes, big eyes and full lips and the whitest skin—skin so pale it glows through her bones in a mortal, slightly sickly way but even this I find weirdly thrilling. And she's so skinny. Skinny as a girl, wearing jeans, a sleeveless shirt and a ruffled apron like she'd just now laid down her feather duster. Wrinkles ripple her face like tree rings and her yellowy white hair is done up in a million crisscrossed bobby pins, then tied in a scarf with floppy ears—*bunny* ears, which is why she's nicknamed Bunny. Okay, so it's a little goofy, this getup, but even then I can see that she was young once, so young and gorgeous that she must have made many a stomach ache. And right away, we're connected, her and me. As I wipe my swollen lip on my sleeve, I realize Mrs. Loomis has just kissed me, and right on the mouth! Right on the mouth she's kissed me like I'm one of hers. A good sloppy one, too.

"Sweetheart," she asks flitting, because that's what Bunny does, see, she flits and kinda *hops* around. "Look, you want an ice pack? Or a Popsicle? Wait, I think we've got one." And even though I know, and she knows, that the Good Humor man has gone for the winter, I really appreciate this because she knows how good a Popsicle would taste in my swollen mouth. Then, remembering Dad, she starts apologizing—that's another Bunny thing, apologizing. Wiping her hands on her apron she's begging us to overlook the house! her hair! the mess!

Then she's thinking.

"Wait, Dougherty . . . Dougherty, don't I know that name? Right! Aren't you the poor man who lost his wife a few months ago? Oh, boy!!" She shoots Mr. Loomis a dirty look. "Look, Mr. Dougherty, our Alvy's a nice kid. A sensitive kid. Star Scout. Principal's list, you wouldn't believe the awards. Not to brag but I could show you a whole slew a stuff our Alvy has won." Rearing back she yells at the ceiling, "Alvy!! You get on down here!!!"

And here's justice! Grabbing me by the hand, Mrs. Loomis pulls me up the stairs, to Alvy's decal-stuck door. The door whips open.

"Yeah what!"

"What! Look what you did to this poor kid, Mr. Tough Guy! Just look at his face!"

"Hey, I just finished it! He started it, running his big mouth!"

"Yeah," I say, "and what were you doing, making fun of dead people?"

"What!!?" Mrs. Loomis hollers down the stairs, *"Do you hear that, Mr. Loomis?"* Grabbing Alvy and me by the hands, Mrs. Loomis drags us both down into the study, where Mr. Loomis has a bottle of Jim Beam out, just then pouring him and Dad a coupla shots. Everybody's yelling. And then here's that crazy old man in his pajamas. He collars Alvy.

"There you are! Like I don't know who swiped my smokes!"

"Hey, don't look at me, Gramps! I ain't the one who puts his teeth in the refrigerator!"

"Here, Poppa!" Bunny whips a pack of Viceroys from her duster pocket.

"Filters!" he gags. He butts me out of the way. "Aww, put a steak on it, you big crybaby."

"Enough!" cries Mr. Loomis, clunking me and Alvy together. "Now, you two knuckleheads are shaking hands. And the first guy who throws a swing'll have Pete and me to deal with—got it?"

Stalking out the backdoor into the darkness, Alvy flips up his jacket collar. I can't believe it. Right behind his house he lights up! He's almost friendly now, saying like a GI to a captured Kraut.

"Want one, ace?"

Embarrassed, I shake my head no. I look at him amazed. "Christ, it was you! You swiped the old man's cigarettes!"

Picking out a piece of tobacco, Alvy says to the sky, "Man, this guy is *swaaa-wift."*

Squinting, he takes a deep drag, blows it out his nose. We're both huddled on the cold picnic bench under the rickety wooden stairs, but even then the kid can't sit still. He's like a baseball pitcher, like a monkey, his hand moving from balls to mouth to nose to forehead. He narrows one rueful eye, then, with a waggle, lets loose one long, greasy, perfect fart. Punctually, a lugey splats between his feet.

"Well now you done it, asshole. You responded. Zactly as predicted, too." Smoke blows out his nose. "Man, you still don't get it, do you? Because amazing as it sounds—and it literally may take you *years* to believe this—but the truth is, ace, I actually did you a favor today. You heard me, a *favor*."

"A FAVOR?" I cry. Alvy and me are sitting on the picnic bench. He jolts up. You'd think he was wearing ancient robes, the way he struts around.

"Dougherty, there's kids all over this town who've been screwed a hundred times, a *thousand* times worse than you—dozens. But you, you go through life, playing the poor little chickee dragging his poor broken wing. Don't deny it, you sorry sonofabitch, I've seen you. And not just me, either."

"Who else?"

"Lots of people. Orphans, mostly, although we got a few bastards, too. What, didn't you know? Man, you *are* in a daze."

"Who?"

"Well, I'm not at liberty to say."

"Not at liberty! What kinda crap is that? And whadda *you* know about orphans? You got a nice Mom. A *great* Mom—"

"And you shut your mouth about my Mom."

I jump up, scared he'll clock me again. "Are you crazy, Loomis? *I like* your Mom. Oh, I love this. You can make fun of my Mom for being dead but I can't say yours is great? Christ, what a goddamned hypocrite you are."

But Alvy doesn't get mad. No, he just starts blinking, he thinks this is so stupid and ignorant. "Dougherty, what I'm saying is, there ain't no comparison. None. Your mother—well, you know what she is. She's dead, which is a whole other category. And understand, I ain't saying anything against her, particularly, as a dead person."

"Not saying anything about her? What a load! What about today?"

"Aww, *that*—hell, that today was just to see if you even had any fight left in you. Whoa, hold on." Hearing something he jumps up. "Look, you stay put, y'hear?"

But I don't listen. When he runs around the house, I follow after him and what do I see but more cars. And that's all I can see, cars—it looks like a roadhouse dance with all the cars. But don't get curious. Next thing I know Alvy's pushing me back. "Hey, it's just some friends of my brothers. It's none of your concern." But five minutes later, again he takes off, and again he comes back disappointed, pinching his nuts to adjust his thinking the same as you'd turn the focus dial on a microscope. Light floods over the lawn. Above us, on the rickety wooden stoop, we hear a cough and a clink of bottles.

"My old man," Alvy whispers. "He's getting a couple more brews." Alvy keeps pinching his nuts. "Your old man a drinker?"

"Well, he *drinks*."

"Like a fish, I bet. And where's he hide his *Playboys*?"

"Huh? Naw, he's real religious. Specially since my Mom—"

But Alvy just cracks up. "Man, what're we gonna do with you?"

Again, the back door opens. At first I think they're calling us back in but it's the dog, a black shadow, racing around the yard, then butted up into my crotch, snooting and waggling. I can't believe his rippling back and knotted forelegs. Fifty pounds of solid muscle. Some kinda bull or boxer mix. His name's Beef.

"Beef!" Alvy points at the big tree. "Beef, squirrel! Squirrel, Beef!" It's pitch dark but at that the dog's shinnying up the tree, ripping and grappling up the bark with his long, sharp nails! Clear up to the crotch of the tree, probably twenty feet, he clamors, then he's all dog exclamation points, peering down at Alvy *whoa! huh! where squirrel!?*

"Man, that dog's an *animal!*" I marvel, as amazed at the dog's brawn as his dumbs. "Man, I never saw a dog climb a tree before!" Up a tree is right. Arms slung through the crotch of the tree, poor Beef just hangs there, mournfully looking at Alvy. "God," I ask, "doesn't he know the squirrels are all in bed?"

"God, don't tell him that!" scolds Alvy. He busts out laughing. "Beef! Get down, you stupid fucking mutt! Ain't no squirrels at night!"

Tearing off hunks of bark, like a small bear, Beef grapples down, then leaps off, panting and looking at Alvy, who's laughing like a fool at the both of us. But boy, Alvy stops quick when he hears a car door slam.

"Just stay here. Stay," he orders, but if he means Beef, Alvy should save his breath—the dog just sits there, oblivious. Coming back a couple minutes later Alvy drops his zipper and pees against the house.

"Boy," I say, "old Beef's some watchdog, huh?" But Alvy's super sensitive about the dog, too.

"Hey, Beef's a great watchdog, but finally the poor mutt gave up. And who can blame the dog, people running around here at all hours? I sure don't."

"So who's the watchdog now? You?"

"Hey, I'm just waiting on somebody. Goddamn you're nosy. You gonna hang around here all night?" He keeps pinching up the power in his nuts.

"Hey," I ask finally, "back in the house before, that was your sister I saw, wasn't it?"

"Who?"

"That blonde lady I saw upstairs? When we first came in?"

He stares me down. "Well, suppose you tell me who you think she was?"

At first I think he's being sarcastic, but no, the kid looks exactly like Beef did up the tree. And the weird thing is, he really wants to know what I think. Why? I wonder. I'm a whole year younger than him. What's he care what a kid my age thinks?

"So you're the baby of the family?" I ask finally.

He raises his eyes. "Possibly yes, possibly no." For the first time ever he actually stops moving. "I guess that would depend. But now answer me this, Dougherty. So who do *you* think she was?"

But again I duck the question. "So how many kids are there in your family?"

"Well, that would also depend."

But just then the second blonde woman we saw—the one with the clod guy—she starts across the lawn. Amazing. She walks into the house next door.

"Well," I joke, "people are sure neighborly here. They just walk into each other's houses, huh?"

"Not hardly. That's her house."

"So she's your sister? Next door? And that was her little boy I saw?"

Then he's giving me the fifth degree. "And did anybody tell you that? Well?"

"Well no, but—"

"—Then why *assume* that he's her kid? I mean, for all you know he could be my little brother."

"But your moth—"

But at this I stop, and he stops. See, kids get embarrassed when their mothers are old, like people think they were accidents or maybe they're a little "off" on account of their Moms had them so late. At least this was true back in those days.

"Look," I ask, "are you picking another fight? Cause if I said anything, well, I'm sorry but you're really putting me on the spot."

Alvy holds his hands out harmlessly. "Look, ace—"

"First, my name's *Frank*, not ace."

"So fine—Frank. Hey relax, man, I ain't gonna hit you or nothing. Not now, and not ever, okay? But listen up, 'cause I got some stuff to tell you. Stuff I've noticed about—excuse me—but about why you're so screwed up. Like I could say, for instance, that you weren't there, *mentally* there, at your mother's funeral, but *I* sure was. Man, I was watching you the whole time while I was altarboying. And where were you, man? I'll tell you where—gone. Present but not accounted for. Hey, do you know what it's like serving at a funeral mass? Oh sure, some old geez kicks you don't feel so bad, but to serve over a lady who died that young, and when she's got a kid? And don't think I'm morbid—hey, I didn't wanna see it, *hell no*. Shit, it wasn't even my turn except this other kid wimped out sick. It was horrible. Your Dad and everybody and especially that old woman crying and carrying on. I never saw such a mess, but hey man, so where were you? Nowhere, that's where. All along you kept closing your eyes—like you'd remember how to cry but no, you never did, never. Not a tear. Which amazed me, man, I must admit."

Well, I fly off the handle. "And what do you know about what I felt? It wasn't my fault!"

"And who said it was? In fact, that's zactly what I'm saying, man. Hell no, you couldn't see it—you couldn't see dick, the shape you were in, but the point, man, the point is *Aky Loomis saw it all for you*. And later at school. At school I was watching too but you never noticed—phew, not you. You shoulda seen yourself, man, your head was bumping along the walls like a balloon."

I get frantic. "So what're you even getting at, *what?*"

"I'm just, *for instance*, talking about what you *think* you know about other people. I'm talking, for instance, about a certain kid, and the kid's just going through life thinking he actually knows his own life, but no. He don't know it—at all. And this certain kid, he thinks he knows about people—like his own family, for instance—but he doesn't know them either, not even close. Like you, for instance. Or hell, even me. And I'll give you the credit. You definitely got some smarts but smarts alone won't do it, man. No sir, you gotta open your eyes and quit thinking like a little kid, 'cause if you don't, man, I swear you ain't gonna make it. At all. Period. And I don't just mean 'make it' with us."

"Quit teasing me. Who's this *us?*"

"And I ain't teasing you, I just can't reveal that yet. Relax, man, all in good time. Right now, you gotta wait, and anything we've said, well, it goes nowhere and to nobody. You swear to God? *Well?*"

"Fine, I swear."

"Swear to *who*, you lying fuck? You even believe in God?"

"Yeah, I believe in God."

"Liar. And do you beat your meat on the toilet seat?"

I stand there burning like a bush.

"Well?"

"Well, not there particularly—"

"Answer me. *Do-you-beat-your-meat?*"

"*Yes.*"

"Well," he nods, "that's progress. But now for the biggest for instance. For instance, do you think it's any fuckin accident, you being here with me? I mean us being here tonight?"

"Accident?" I snort. "You punched me. That was sure no accident."

"*No accident?* Your mother died, didn't she? Was that any accident? And why did I, of all people, wind up serving at her mass? Shit, you say *I* zapped *you?* Hell, I'd say it was the reverse, that you zapped me! And today. Since when do you hang around Taver-Shep, talking how it's all some big accident?"

And this'll sound nuts, but suddenly I can see it too! Here I am looking to be redeemed or whatever, can't even get run over, and *he's right here.* My face! His fist! It's like *Superman,* two meteorites colliding in space ka-pow! thinking so why did he zap me in church? and why did he punch me on a bridge? and why's his Dad a war hero? and why a white T-Bird in his driveway? . . . Well, why if it's not a sign from God saying, *this is the kid.*

Mrs. Loomis is calling us inside.

"So whadda we do now?" I ask Alvy.

"Go home and await further instructions. You'll hear from us."

"But when? Soon?"

"Look, I said all I can, at least for tonight. Fact, if you're fuckin' cool, you won't ask me when, okay? Fact, if you do ask, then you definitely will *not* be asked, do you read me?"

I feel dizzy and woken up, back in the light and the thick smelly heat of the Loomis house. Smoothing my hair, Mrs. Loomis is grinning like she just found that Popsicle for me. The two clods are gone but that little blond boy I saw, well, here he is, bouncing on the beat-up couch. And look, there's a little girl, too. I'd guess she's a couple of years older than the boy—eight or nine, maybe—and here's this third kid, this fat, red-faced baby in diapers who doesn't look like either one of them.

"See," laughs Mrs. Loomis, "I have grandkids, too! Would you like three to take home with you?" Turned to the side, Alvy's palming his nuts again, his black glasses slipping down his nose. It's funny. Inside the house, in the light, Alvy looks almost like a kid again. Even the toughest kid looks smaller and totally different in his own home.

"Well, here they are!" roars Mr. Loomis. Sloshing out of the study, him and Dad are all smiles now, yakking about the war and them both being from Pennsylvania. "Hey, Pete," says Mr. Loomis, "these two knuckleheads may be friends yet."

"They didn't kill each other," agrees Dad. "That's sure progress."

"And we'll have you over to dinner soon, honey," promises Mrs. Loomis.

The little boy's punching Alvy in the ribs but Alvy doesn't notice—Alvy actually seems to like it the way a big dog'll let a puppy gnaw on him. As we leave, Alvy jumps up. At the door he's back to his Star Scout self, shaking my hand, then Dad's, saying how sorry he is and how we're really getting to understand each other, him and me. Funny, I even notice how Alvy's being less articulate, less acute, which adults certainly appreciate, the better to keep you down to size. And Dad buys it, too. More than buys it.

"Well, if you can't beat 'em join 'em," he says as we're going up to the car. "You know, you could learn a thing or two from that kid. He's got a paper route. Now that's a real hustler there."

SO I STAY AWAY FROM TAVER-SHEP BUT TAVER-SHEP WON'T STAY AWAY FROM ME.

A couple days after our powwow at the Loomises', coming home from school, I see a gleaming white car parked out front! Heart pounding I stop dead, but of course it's not the Bird or Mr. Loomis's car. No, it's old Mrs. Eppes's white '59 Galaxie—Mrs. Eppes the colored woman who scrubs our house, but now twice a month, instead of once a week, like before.

Mrs. Eppes's white Galaxie is an auctioned-off police cruiser with two hundred thousand miles on it, but you'd never know that from the outside. Except for the chrome spotlight, all the police junk has been pulled off, the holes puttied, buffed down and repainted so it shines like new. Every Saturday Mr. Eppes and her boys spend half the day polishing it.

No, it's sure not the Bird, but from a distance it's just close enough to drive my heart into my throat. I hate that car for getting my hopes up, although that's not the only reason. See, the other thing about Mrs. Eppes's police special is she bought her car first—in fact, just a few months before we bought the Bird. That even became one of the jokes, that the Doughertys not only strained to keep up with the Joneses but the colored Joneses, too. That's the most depressing thing about jokes. Half the time they're half true.

Well, things being what they were in those days, it was a minor sensation, if not an affront, for a colored maid to be driving her own car, especially on a street where nobody had a maid, or would have had one, owing to that peculiar Amishness of Catholics. Equally provocative was the imperial Mrs. Eppes herself, her white gloves clutching the wheel and her head craned back, not so much driving as being driven in her perfect blue suit and white wicker hat.

Really, the only colored people I'd ever known were Mrs. Eppes and Mildred before her, and even if we had known Mrs. Eppes's Christian name, we'd never have dared to use it. With Mrs. Eppes, I remember, your voice got all high, Mamma. Even the smallest, most reasonable request grew in your mind, until it came out like an embarrassed sneeze. "Mrs. Eppes, could you please clean the refrigerator?"—why to hear you, Mamma, it sounded like you were asking was it possible, was it even *advisable*, to clean refrigerators, waiting in suspense as Mrs. Eppes soberly regarded you, picked up her mop, then finally said in a deep, weary voice, "Very well." Mrs. Eppes was just as finicky about the money we paid her. *Secretly* paid her. The money you left under the candlestick would be there when she arrived, and would still be there while she worked, only to magically disappear when she left. It was like Santa Claus with the milk and cookies. Hard as I tried I never saw her so much as *look* at the money. She was no less finicky about leaving. After she changed back into her blue suit, she would stand by the hall mirror—the mirror right by the candlestick—rubbing lanolin into her hands, getting her ladiness ready to face the white street. "Well, we can't be paying her too badly to drive that car," you said once as she drove off. I knew what you meant. We'd just bought the Bird and it annoyed us, her having a white car—it figured a colored person would want a white car. Our minds played tricks on us like that. Because to us by then we'd bought our white car first.

Well, if this stuff confused me before you died, it was all the more demoralizing now, especially when Mrs. Eppes not only still had and drove her car, but also *owned* it free and clear. But this wasn't the only thing that bugged me about her. Because I also knew how, with Dad's blessing, some of your things were vanishing in Mrs. Eppes's white Galaxie—off to her own forbidden galaxy, Taver-Shep. In fact, now that I think about it, this was probably another reason behind my peculiar scouting parties to Taver-Shep.

It also accounted for much of my resentment toward Mrs. Eppes now. I mean, it was humiliating enough for her—for any woman—to come into our house and see our male filth and incompetence, and especially when nobody came inside now, kids or adults. Mrs. Eppes wasn't just cleaning, I thought, she was snooping! Also, I hated her virtuousness, her woundedness at what she could so clearly see happening to me. Her sympathy depressed me, her advice annoyed me, and her careful attempts at criticism absolutely infuriated me. In fact, after several months of my silence, sullenness and sarcasm, Mrs. Eppes no longer even spoke to me directly. No, between us now, there was always this third person whom she spoke to. To hear Mrs. Eppes, it was as if you had returned to earth as another, highly proper colored lady. Mrs. Eppes sighs.

"If your Mamma could only see you now. You gone wild as jimson, boy."

"And what's jimson?"

"That's a wild, prickly, do-nothin weed."

"What do you mean, calling me *weed?* Don't you have anything better to do today?"

Mrs. Eppes looks at her proper colored lady friend, the wall. "Hoo, got a mouth on him, too, don't he?"

And who was this woman with her head thrust in our oven, yellow rubber gloves on her hands as she scoops out puddles of burning, putrid grease? And how did I square this woman with the lady who would later rub lanolin into her hands, slip on her white gloves, snap her white wicker purse, then calmly cruise off again for two more weeks? No, the grease of life never touched Mrs. Eppes, and I always concocted some pretext to observe this royal leaving ritual of hers before the hall mirror. In her dark, watery eyes with the muddy brown veins it seems I can see the whole impasse of our life now. I can see it even in the tiny piece of dry spittle that hops from lip to lip as she talks, the spittle I focus on so I won't have to think about her leaving.

"You know," she says, "it's a shame with you now. Way back when I used to make you lunch. We used to talk. Way back when you used to be Mrs. Eppes's friend."

"Well, way back when you didn't go calling me a *weed.*"

"Well, I'm sorry. It's not *you,* it's how you *act* lately." Mrs. Eppes looks at her colored lady friend, the wall, then sighs to me. "Well, see you around— I guess."

WHICH GETS TO the unscheduled visit Mrs. Eppes paid us a few days after Alvy punched me.

I guess I was keyed up—distracted—wondering when Alvy and his orphan gang would contact me. Anyhow, we had a minor household accident, a little fire. That's what brought Mrs. Eppes, first to scrub off the smoke, then to generally spruce up the place for Grammaw, who was coming to live with us until things simmered down.

But back to this fire, I don't know which is more dangerous, thinking or not thinking, unless it's reading and being in love!

Mutiny on the Bounty, see, was one of a small pile of overdue library books that you'd left when you died. Already, we'd gotten two typed letters from the library, so finally Dad and me scour the house but no *Mutiny*, and no wonder when I'd hidden it. Boy, the cover of that book was sure a smoker! I can't believe the library even allows it, the sight of brown, black-haired ladies with their naked backs staring at the Englishmen—well, I start reading! Now normally, I never cheat on books, never skip a page, but after about the eightieth flogging and keelhauling, I skip to Christian's girl Tehani with her titties out in Tahiti, which, if I'm not mistaken, is where "titties" hail from. Tehani's not a bit embarrassed. It's completely different from the sex midget's place or even Poo. Trying to forget Alvy, every day I run home to Tehani from school. Certain parts I have to read over and over even to believe they're for real, but as I kiss Tehani and hold and lick those two bobbing, sassy twins of hers, I just *know* we'll live here forever on Titti-Titti!

Anyhow, reading away one afternoon I get hungry—popcorn! So, grabbing the pot, I slop in some oil and corn kernels, then turn the stove on high and *pop!* That hot oil gets me all excited! Tehani can't wait for me by the waterfalls, especially with my hands all greased. Running upstairs I turn on the faucet, let the water run, then tell her now don't be ascared of Master Pokey, boning out of my straining knee breeches. Tehani's laughter is even more beautiful than her fat nipples. Stroking my hair by the white waterfall, she sounds like a little nanny goat, and she's sluiced so slick, and so bad in love with me, that I don't care what yardarm they hang me from . . . when, below, undulating along the ceiling, black mattresses of smoke! Pokey plummets! I tear down to the kitchen! I can't breathe! All I can see is the pot glowing cherry red! Well, grabbing the pot muffs, I switch off the stove, drop the smoking pot on the floor, then tear through the house, opening windows. The pot's still smoking when I come back, so I heave it out into the yard. Oh, shit! It burned a black circle on the floor! But wait . . . *paint, I'll paint it.* And I could have figured out something, but here they come, Mrs. Moffitt, then Mrs. Reece and Mrs. Feeney, then sirens, everybody wanting to know what on earth was I doing and why I never smelled it? Well, there you go—flailing my chicken when I shoulda been minding the Crisco.

Which brings me back to Mrs. Eppes and what I discover when she comes to scrub off the smoke.

Spying her white Galaxie, I don't want to go in and have her embarrass me, but the fact is I'm starved. Besides, the state Dad's in, I'm scared him and Mrs. Eppes will totally empty out the place—especially before Grammaw comes. Luckily, Mrs. Eppes has the vacuum going upstairs, so quick I sneak into the kitchen. It's sparkling, too—wow, I bet we won't even have to paint! But then as I'm hauling out the peanut butter.

"Well, hello, stranger."

"Gee, the place looks great." I mean it, too, but that's not how she hears it.

"Well, thank *you*." Her rag plops in the bucket. "Lord, whatever happent to your face?"

"I got hit." I look at her suddenly. "And do you know where I got hit? Taver-Shep."

"So?"

"So, you live there, don't you?"

"Yes, *I reside* there—so?"

"I got punched by the bridge. You live near the bridge?"

"Who punched you?" she asks suddenly. *Was he colored?* she means.

"Well, a white kid hit me. But colored kids saw it."

"Now, you look here," she huffs, "we already got smart white kids coming down our way starting trouble. You tend to your own"—she sticks in a word—"*life*. You tend to your poor father. And your Grammaw, who needs you now. Lord, talking how colored boys saw you! I'll tell you about a colored boy around our way. Both his parents was killed and he's not acting even half as sorry as you losin the one."

Wait, I think, is this one of the kids that Alvy was talking about? I start peppering her with questions. "So what happened to the kid's parents? How were they killed? When?"

"And that's none a yo affair. All I'm talking about is *you*. You and all your moping and know-it-alling and disrespecting."

"But wait," I say, trying to trick her, "I think I hearda this kid. Is his name Ben Holmes?"

"No, it's not no Ben Holmes, and you can quit fishing too. And while I'm at it, here's some more free advice for you, Frank Dougherty. You stay outta Taver-Shep! Not unless you want more a what you just got."

BUT IT'S NOT JUST MR. CHRISTIAN AND ME READY TO JUMP SHIP. It's an early outbreak of spring fever. The next day, Saturday, when Dad and me are riding over to National to meet Grammaw's flight from St. Pete, it must be seventy-five degrees, which can happen in Washington in late February. Everybody's mixed up, even the flowers. Red buds. Green outbreaks of grass. Yellow forsythia pimples. Nope, as Dad and me drive through Rock Creek Park, it's not just me who's having second thoughts.

"But how long's Grammaw gonna stay?"

"That's your decision until you calm down. A *while* okay."

"But Grammaw doesn't understand a while."

"So think of it as an extended visit."

"But she doesn't understand visit either." Do ghosts just visit?

The other problem, though, is what we gotta pass even to *get* to National. The other night over at Alvy's, when I looked down the steep hill into Taver-Shep and saw how they all three connected, Taverna, Shepherd Hills, and Taver-Shep, well, that was only the beginning of all the connections I'm seeing. Physical connections too, slopping like lava over the whole of Washington. And especially on the trip to National, which I've made a million times hauling around all these freeloader clients, long-lost navy buddies and cousins four times removed. Every spring they show up, all wanting to see the cherry blossoms, the Washington Monument and the Smithsonian. At least they used to.

Dad I've heard give the D.C. tour so many times I could give it myself, but, like I said, it never really hit me until today. Never until now, as we plow out of Rock Creek into the rusty Potomac River light and the Lincoln Memorial so white it makes my eyes ache. Nope, never until today does the switch flip, and this happens when we hit the white marble spans of that beautiful monstrosity, the Memorial Bridge, carved out of that Italian igloo-type marble that glows like ice. It always terrified me, that bridge. Dad says it's a war gift from the Italians, but I'd say the Nazis was more like it. Anyhow, it's not the bridge that's so horrible, it's these huge gold statues that stand on either end, men and women big as steamrollers, and all of polished gold, so they burn like so many suns. Square-jawed, muscle-bound men beating fiery ingots and swords. And after them, massive, sphinx-lipped slave women with harrowed sun rays of hair. As a little kid I hid my face, they were so horrible and cruel! And look at the men, dragging the women across the river, there to be sold into slavery and hell . . . and where else, I realize, but to Robert E. Lee's place, Custis-Lee Mansion, over on the Virginia side. Welcome to your new home, Mamma, Arlington National Cemetery.

Probably a million times Dad's told the story about General Lee's place, but today, when Dad suddenly goes mum and looks up in awe, it clicks . . . *they planned this.* Washington wasn't just a huge historical accident, so a lotta Joes could all get free government jobs. And talk about a stare down, here's Abraham Lincoln on the Yankee side of the bridge. And facing off Lincoln from the Virginia side, here's his foxy old nemesis General Robert E. Lee.

Now, Lincoln's view of the city is nothing to sneeze at, but what a view Lee's got way up on the hill there, on the porch of his mansion with the fat columns! Perched up there on his rocker, old Robert E. Lee could survey the whole of Washington when the Civil War started, the White House, the Capitol, the whole shooting match. Dad loves to tell that story. See, after the Rebs bombed Fort Sumter, for probably a week, General Lee camped out on his porch, staring back at Lincoln staring back at him from the White House, hoping General Lee would take his offer to command the Union army. Talk about pressure! Yeah, creaking away on his rocker, probably half in the bag with his sword dragging on the ground and tobacco juice running down his beard, Lee must have been so depressed and pissed off, being caught in the middle like that. Dad said it about killed the guy, deciding was he a Yankee or a Rebel, an American first or a Virginian.

Well, you know what Lee decided, and you know it didn't turn out so hot for him, once the Yankees dug up his plantation and turned it into the national boneyard. And to think that you—your *remains* or whatever—are up there, one of a million white stones chopping like whitecaps down the hills. Dad's sure upset. Hauling out hanks of Kleenex, Dad's doing this fake guilty sneeze, but not me. As usual, I can't feel a thing, no sensations in my fingers my toes, Mr. Pokey, anything. And I can't win! When I try to edge near Dad so he'll feel better, instead he gets embarrassed. Instead, the whole feeling gets reversed. Instead, it's like I'm mocking him or just feeling sorry for him, and especially when, as everybody knows, even Alvy, I can't really feel anything. Frankly, I wish it would just stay winter—forever. Winter would be easier, I think. Better the winter croup than these warm blowing breezes. Better winter than the whole pointless hurdy-gurdy of spring, with these phoney Jap cherry blossoms that don't make any cherries, and the spring herring and shad that swarm up from the sea to lay their eggs. And why? So they can die flopping on the banks? so only more can die there next year? No, General Lee, I think it's the Confederate flag that should be flying over Arlington. Run up the skull and crossbones, 'cause all y'all dead folks, you have definitely seceded from this disunion.

But it's not just Custis-Lee or the spring today, it's Angelene. I know I haven't said much about Angelene lately, and not because she hasn't been forever asking me down. But see, I've been avoiding her too, the same as the spring or anything else that gets my hopes up. Besides, it's noble staying away—Mr. Christian would do that. And when I do go down to Angelene's house, as soon as I get comfy, she's narrowing her eyes at me, "So how are you two doin' up there?" Which if I say, "Okay," she doesn't believe me, and if I say "Not okay," then I'm only being "negative," or "complicated," which I do believe is a sin in Texas.

Just an hour ago I saw Angelene, in fact. We stopped down to the Butte on our way to the airport—Dad's idea, not mine. "I want to see if Angelene and Nellie Belle can show your grandmother around," Dad said, but right away everybody knew what was going on, Poo looking like she'd just had her tonsils scraped and Nellie Belle getting all tittery and square dancey, like she gets. It's the Heat. It's the Social Season hot upon us. Over at the 4-H, see, they got the spring dances coming up. And I don't mean the souee-type 4-H, I mean the highfalutin Connecticut Avenue variety where congressmen's daughters go and they put on flower and fashion shows and all that crap. Speaking of which, Angelene says to Dad.

"You know what, Pete, the junior formal's coming up. Poo's going. Well, I thought Frank might come, and you and I could help chaperone." Seeing Poo go green, Angelene makes a face at me, screwing up her gap tooth. "Well, yeww knowwww—"

Poo hauls me around the corner.

"What's going on with them?"

"I don't know."

"Wake up. Don't you hear him calling her late at night?"

"Hey, she did the inviting!"

Meanwhile, coming off Memorial Bridge, instead of going left, Dad turns right, and I really panic, *The grave he's gonna go to ask you can he date Angelene.*

"Dad, where we going?"

"Nowhere. I'm just driving. We're still early."

Early nothing! Dad's wanting to pay you a visit—shoot, get it over with, when you know Grammaw will be agitating to go. Why's Dad keep torturing himself? I wonder. Over and over we've been through it, how we should wait for the headstone or maybe Memorial Day—or Judgment Day, seeing how we'd both sooner visit the Gates of Hell.

"Gum?" asks Dad, rattling up his sacred box of Chiclets, which he'll never offer without you asking. Sure, I see! It's the cigarette before the firing squad. I forgot to mention that Dad found *Mutiny on the Bounty* splattered by the toilet, which I'd flush to do the waterfall with Tehani in Titti-Titti. Of all the worst goddamned times, two years too late, he's ready to talk about the Birds 'n' the Bees!

But what a gyp! After all the buildup they don't tell you anything, not really. Sure, about the woman having to spread 'em and the man having to stick it in. Ejaculations. Wild excited night ejaculatory periods creaming all over your bed. Organisms. *But if the man ejaculates so what's the lady do?* God, it's useless, what they tell you. Oh sure, they tell you *that* they do it but not *how.* They tell you *where* but not *why*, much less why you and Dad only had me to show for seventeen years of trying. It takes him two cigarettes.

"Well, now's the time to ask," encourages Dad finally. "I'm sure you must have some questions?"

But is the organism when the man puts it in or when he takes it out?

Why's it called the facts of life?

But what if it gets too big in the lady?

Look! I holler, hoping to distract him. It's that sea shrine to Catholic chaplains who gave up their life vests, then went down with the ship. Iron faces. The astonished look on their faces, leaning on the ship's rail watching the lifeboats pull off, *Stroke! Stroke! Stroke!* And that's Dad now, left holding the old *morality* bag, having to tell me the facts when here he's got nobody to do it *with.* Then comes my favorite subject of all.

"Look," Dad says sheepishly, "look, I don't want to make a big deal over it, old buddy—(masturbation). Everyone does it but it's a sin, okay? So you shouldn't do it."

Everybody does it? So he does it? Is that what he's really saying? It's so ballsy of him! I think. God, what a good guy! Really! Just then I wanna tell him, Look, it's okay—creepy okay—if he whips it a little. And of course, as we park the car at the airport, airplanes zooming in, well, suddenly I do have one question.

"So Dad, are you gonna chaperone with Angelene?"

"It's not a date." He makes a face. "And you know Angelene's not Catholic."

"So?"

"So I'm prohibited from marrying a non-Catholic."

"But does Angelene know that?"

"I guess. Probably."

"*Probably?* But Dad, how's she know? Probably you should tell her!"

But Dad gives me his cat-and-mouse look—this look of weird, beaten-down pleasure. "C'mon, don't get yours bowels in an uproar about it. Now, let's go collect your grandmother."

• • •

"MWAH! MWAH! FRANKIE! OH, HERE THEY ARE AND THANK GOD! Aww, Frankie, YOUR POOR FACE. I'll kill that brat who hit you, I'll wring his neck! And Pete, I was ready to call the cops, honey. Didn't I tell you *twelve o'clock?* Oh, I called and called! Three times I've been around the terminal looking for you. Oh, well. OH, WELLL—"

Call off the National Guard. Man, you've never seen anybody ever play the poor lost old lady better than the Governess in her black mariah outfit with the perfume-doused hankie, the smushed black hat with the gauze veil and her usual three cigarettes going. Not that she's alone, understand. No, to carry her bags she's snagged these two jug-headed sailors, and for her lady-in-waiting she's got Sherry, this butterball, busybody woman who acts like her long-lost daughter.

"I took Mrs. Slattery to Traveler's Aid," Sherry tells Dad. "The poor thing was *so* worried—"

"—oh, but he's here," bubbles Grammaw, "my Frank's here. That's all that counts."

"Catty," fumes Dad, "you told me *two* o'clock."

"Ma'am," says one of the sailors uneasily, "real nice meeting ya, but we gotta shove off now—"

"Oh, but wait! honey!" Hauling out her little red change purse with the plastic window, Grammaw pulls out her show money—the twelve bucks she'll milk till next Christmas at least. "Here—take it—" Waving the money so they'd both sooner die, "Well, you *drink*, don't you? Go on. Lap it up. Like a coupla sailors, ha ha hah."

Red-faced, they both haul ass, the one slashed about the ear with Grammaw's grateful lipstick as she carefully rewads her trick fiver, then turns again to Sherry Baby. Man, the heat Sherry's giving off, you know the woman's a husband hunter. Meanwhile, Grammaw's rummaging through her pocketbook, pulling out one of her eight hundred filched matchbooks and a dried-up ballpoint pen, telling Sherry Baby, "Now please, dear, copy down our phone number so you'll have it. Pete! Pete, dear, what's our phone number again?"

Whatever Dad's "type" is these days, I can promise you that Sherry Baby with her fat baby legs and her white blouse closed off with the gold chastity pin—well, Sherry is definitely not it. Still, Dad's a gentleman about it. Even if it is a joke, Dad's not about to write our number on some dog-eared matchbook cover. So, fishing out his old, defunct business card and silver Cross pen, Dad makes a little deal out of it, writes out our number, presents it to

Sherry, then thanks her. But no sooner does Sherry leave than the old lady sniffs at Dad.

"Well, *that* was a bit forward, wasn't it? Giving the girl your card."

Dad drops his arms. "Whaddaya mean? I was merely helping you!"

It's the old bait and switch. Grammaw looks stunned. "*Her.* I meant forward of *her.*"

"*You* initiated it. I have no interest in the woman! None! None whatsoever and I resent the insinuation!"

But now he's killed her. At this Grammaw rolls up in an old lady ball, muttering to herself, "Well, in my day girls sure didn't take cards from strange men."

"Well," snorts Dad, "in *my* day we didn't pass out phone numbers on balled-up cocktail napkins."

But here we go, I think. It's our old haunt, the Bombs Away lounge! I drop Grammaw's suitcase. "Hey, Dad, I could sure use a Coke."

Dad turns fake natty. "Capital idea!" He turns to Grammaw. "Or is it too early for you, my deah?"

"Oh," she croaks, "would you like to?"

That's the idea, I think, get 'em both iced down real good. And sure enough, for a while, things *are* better, Grammaw telling bad knock-knocks and Dad staring out the big picture window, looking half lost as usual, watching the planes land. Weird, Mamma, I never thought you looked a bit like Grammaw, but now when I close my eyes, old images burn under my eyelids—how, just like you, Grammaw lets the ice cubes clink against her teeth, then how her tongue flicks up at the taste, straining the brown nectar with a final fizzle. It's feeling really dangerous, especially once we pay up, then pack Grammaw into the backseat. Which of course she drags me in beside her, so she can wring my hand. I look at Dad.

"Hey, Dad, don't you wanna go the *other* way?" Look, I don't even know the other way. All's I mean is not *that* way, past Arlington. Dad won't hear of it, though. No, I realize, Dad's load testing Grammaw, driving her past General Lee's place to see if she notices—to see will she crack so we gotta pack her off on the next plane. Notices! Grammaw wouldn't know the Washington Monument if you stood her beside it, but as we pass Custis-Lee, by bare instinct, she's craning back around, looking completely wild, like we left her bags at the airport. It's cruel. Milking my hand, she's pinching the dark of her nose, between her eyes, but she won't dare ask him and I don't dare look at her for fear she'll blow and I'll have to Humpty-Dumpty her back to health, too. Yeah, I'll tell you, it's tough enough not to feel for yourself, let alone not to feel for these chemistry sets called adults which come complete with no instructions.

Run for your lives, everybody. Our temporary new household had just begun.

BETTER A BLIND MAN'S DOG THAN AN OLD LADY'S BOY. Not only is it boring but it's dangerous. It boils up! Especially with Dad always away and Grammaw following me around like the little boy Jesus. And Alvy thinks *his* Mom is old! One of my new jobs is riding shotgun in the cab that hauls Grammaw up to do our weekly grocery shop. Anyhow, on our way up, sure enough, I'll always see Alvy loitering by the sex midget's place or the High's. Suddenly, the kid's everywhere, so everywhere I'm thinking that he somehow masterminded the whole thing, the desecration, the fight, even Grammaw now.

And what a life! Grammaw can't even cook, unless you call boiling cooking. The bubbling pot clanks and foams until the steam's running down the windows. Steaming corned beefs and cabbages and roots. Boiled tongues and chickens that totally disintegrate under blisters of yellow grease. Frying at extreme heat—that's her other technique. Seared beef heart. Fried liver and onions smothered in evil oniony gravies. Coughing and smoking, she's forever pacing, her pink fluff Indian moccasins scuffling across the kitchen linoleum, past the black scorch like the flaming imprint of my butt. Suddenly, Titti-Titti seems a long way off.

And God, does the old lady wear me out. One night, I'm so worn out from her pacing that I flop down in the middle of the kitchen floor. What kind of crazy pervert am I? Because as Grammaw shuffles by, under her skirt I stare in disbelief at the heavens, a giant black widow of hair in the center of her slack, pantyless rump! But night's the worst. Her grief's like an avalanche. In the middle of the night she'll wake me up, her cold-creamed skin hugging my face like a rubber mask as she sobs, "*Do* you remember her now? *Don't* you remember her? *Can't* you remember anything?" As she rocks and sobs over me, of course I can't help but see her old titties hanging out through her chiffon nightgown. Still, like remembering—remembering or feeling anything now—it only lasts a second. The minute I see her old tits it's cauterized, it's erased completely, my eyes foaming over like two cuts doused in hydrogen peroxide.

People on the Rock say we're isolated, if you can believe it. That's the *word* on us, but this just infuriates us both—Grammaw for what it says about her, and me for what it says about my being her damn Seeing Eye dog, which I don't exactly want to publicize. Still, the sodality do-gooders send out the Welcome Wagon—Mrs. Baines and these two other rosary-mumblers clutching some daisies. When I hear them at the door I think Grammaw won't answer, but no, the old lady's way too slick for that. No, straightaway she opens the door and glad hugs all three—just *kills* them with kindness, then leaves them stranded on the stoop with their tough-luck potlucks and their Cross-draggings. Nope, we don't see them again.

Nellie Belle has more success with the old lady. Several times Nellie Belle takes Grammaw out to get her hair blued and her nails done, but obviously these two haven't got a thing in common—Nellie Belle being too rich, too sunny and too hick, besides being a teetotaler. As for Angelene, although Grammaw likes her, Angelene scares her to death. Fishing, Grammaw says to me, "Well, I think Angelene's a little too big for her britches, don't you?" What gets me, though, is the *way* Grammaw says it—like the Wall said it and not her. God, I realize, she's exactly like Mrs. Eppes talking to her invisible colored lady friend. "What do you think of Angelene?" asks the Wall. But when I say that I like Angelene well enough, the Wall replies, "And what does your father think of Angelene?" "Who said Dad thinks of Angelene?" I ask. "Did I say that?" asks the Wall.

Well, I knew something would happen, and sure enough it does. It happens grocery shopping Thursday, after school when the cab comes to haul us both up to the Giant. Please, will somebody stuff a bag over my head when the cab honks? And Grammaw's so gay. On the ride up, she always is, doing her giddy toe tap, saying to the driver, "I'm feeling lucky today—*lucky*." And before I can duck, she's smooching on me, asking the driver, "Do you see this? This is all I've got left! All I have in the whole world!"

"Now, Dave," she says, once she's given him the whole sob story, "now, Dave, I can see you're different—no, no, David, at my age I can tell a few things about people. But then maybe you've lost someone yourself?"

"Phew—" Dave cranes around like a five-car wreck. "You got two hours?"

Twenty minutes later, outside the supermarket, Dave's still going on how his third old lady stabbed him in the neck with a steak knife, then ran off with this clown, but once she gets her kids back they're gonna tie the knot again. The fare's $1.35. It better be within a dime of that or she has a shit fit. Holding out a scad of bills, Grammaw first gives him a five, then asks can he break a ten, then accidentally gives him a twenty, which she snatches back.

"Here wait, *I* know," she tells him. "Gimme back the five"—madly swapping bills when her change purse spills over the floor. *"Did you find it?"* she hollers to me, scrounging over the floor. "Find it, Frank, it's my lucky silver dollar!" Then back to Dave, "Now, honey, when you remarry—well, my advice is to use *plastic* utensils, huh?"

"Haw! That's good, plastic!" Dave refolds his wad, then stops. "Wait, that was—?"

"Change for my ten," smiles Grammaw all sincere. The money's like flypaper in Dave's hands, but finally with a shrug he gives it to her as she elbows me out, "Frank! Grab that cart—"

"But, Grammaw," I ask her outside, "did you give him back his ten?" She's scandalized.

"Of course I did. You saw me!"

"Okay. God, don't have a cow. At least you could tip the poor guy."

"Tip, I gave him his tip—plastic knives. Southern riffraff, I've never heard such horridness." She slams the cart into the automatic door. "And no more guff from you, encouraging these yahoos . . ."

THINGS GO TO HELL in a handbasket after that. Her nerves! her bum foot! her sore back! Then she's gotta pee, pushing the bell so the butcher can escort her back to the Ladies' behind the meat locker. God, she's always having to pee—I swear in a phone booth she'd be asking where's the foo-foo room. And complains? Nineteen dollars for a week's groceries! It's worse than New York, the prices down here in Dixie. And the endless wait for cabs!—amazing, when she never tips anybody.

And when the cab does come, the slob might as well be dragging a rickshaw, Grammaw's bawling him out about she has a heart condition and our ice cream has gone to soup! But he's not taking any crap off her, not this guy.

"No sir!" he barks at me, mad about this giant Coke I've got in a paper cup. "Not in my cab. No drinks allowed."

Well, Grammaw's all over him. "Look, you, he can't guzzle it, and he has to drink. The child has a chronic kidney infection—now *go!* I have a splitting headache."

One fat wrist slung over the wheel, he roars off. And still she's riding him. "Driver!"

"I go by *sir*, lady."

"Well, slow down, mister!"

He jams the brakes. "So which way is it? First, you want go. Now you want slow?"

I grab her arm—what's she doing antagonizing him, an obvious nut? And as we near the smut midget's place, Grammaw knows what she's gonna do. She knows exactly what she's gonna do, twisting the raggedy Kleenex in her hands. At the last second, her white glove whips past the cabbie's nose.

"Driver, stop! Stop there, please—"

"Where?"

"There—"

"Where?"

"*There*—" jamming her finger at him, "*right there*—"

"*Where*, ma'am?" He's playing with her, the bastard! I holler out.

"The *liquor* store, okay?"

"Oh *there*." He grins like he farted.

"A little something for your father." She glowers at me. The purse snaps.

The driver creep taps out a cigarette on the wheel. "Father's Day, huh?" He waits, then snorts, "No, wait, that's June, Father's Day. Okay, lemme guess—today's your old man's birthday?" Waving the match out real slow he hooks his arm back over the seat, then gives me a real funny look. "Yeah, I haul plenty of 'em up here, during the day. The old girls, especially."

"So?" I scowl.

Smoke swats the mirror. His eyes dance. "Well, all those gifts they buy. Every day's Christmas, you know?"

So who does he think I am, this guy? Does he think I'll let him piss on your own mother? God, I hate being a man with women, always having to carry the flag and defend them. And this prick is shoving my nose in it. He's only making me madder and madder, when up front I hear this zippery rustling, *What's he doing with himself up there?* It sounds like pages flipping. Like itching. Hey, I don't want to start anything. Twisting the plastic top on my Coke I feel sick, scared sick what I'll do, then sicker that I won't do anything—that I'll only keep taking it like a big baby. Then the cabbie asks.

"So you discovered the girlies yet?" He waits, nose in the mirror. "You know, you're one good looking kid." His voice gets all high and wheedly, "*Oh, yeah you are.* Bet the li'l girlies go for you, huh?"

"Naw, they don't."

"They *don't?*" He whistles in the mirror. "Well, I know the problem. Too much time around Granny, huh? Um-um-um. So how old are you, li'l buddy?"

"Old enough." I say it to sound tough but instead he's thrilled. "*Old enough to do what?*" Blowing smoke at the ceiling he looks to see if Grammaw's coming. "Um-um-um. Um-um-um . . ."

I've got the top off the Coke. Trying not to cry I've got my eyes closed, *tennineeightseven* . . .

"But look," he asks, like I dreamed it, "at night, when your young cock gets all hard, so what do you do about that, li'l buddy?"

"Nothing."

"*Nothing?*"

"I already told you, nothing," *fivefourthree*

"Well, I can tell you what to do, um-umm. What, you mean you don't know? Doncha, li'l buddy?"

"Yeah, *this!*" I throw my Coke in his face.

"Hey! Hey, you li'l fucker!"

Jumping out, I nearly slam his hand in the door. Man, the whole car's bouncing, like he dropped scalding hot coffee on his lap. And out he comes blinded, mopping his eyes with a sheaf of dirty napkins when his arm whips down. I duck! His silver flashlight smashes against the brick wall!

"Frank!" cries Grammaw. She's just out of the liqour store clutching her bag of wine jugs.

"Thief!" The cabbie points at me. "The kid's a goddamn thief! He tried to steal my change machine. I caught him, so he threw his drink in my face!"

"*He's* the liar, Grammaw! He's nothing but a sicko pervert!"

He levels his finger at me. "Go on, boy! Say that again, I'll kick yer ass!"

A bottle smashes at his feet. "*You!* I saw it all, you sick, fat fuck!"

He wheels around. It's Alvy. Clutching another pop bottle, Alvy walks right up to the guy. "I'm a witness! So are these other kids, you nasty old cocksucker! You had it out of your pants!" He flips a dime at this dark-haired kid. "Randy, call the law on this queer motherfucker!"

Then Grammaw starts in. Bottles clanking, she's shaking the family jewels in the cabbie's face. "I'll have your license, you Maryland filth! *What? What were you doing to my grandson?*"

"Go suck on your gin bottle, woman."

"Hey," yells Alvy, circling behind the guy. "Think you can talk to ladies like that?" He points to the other two kids. "Randy, stick your knife in his tires. Bobby, you run to the pool hall. Get Toby and Shiney. Un-*load* the fuckin' place!" Wild-eyed, Alvy does his ack-ack, jack-in-the-box laugh at the guy. "Shiney, oh boy, man, you are fuh-uucked. The way Shiney is about his Mamma? Man, I'd grab me a tire iron if I was you, I'd get me a gun!"

"Get out! Get away!" The driver fakes at Alvy, then jumps in the cab. *"Dirty liars."* He practically rams a Chevy as he speeds off. Alvy's doing a King Kong number.

"Fake-out!" cries the other kid.

"Total fake-out!"

Running back, the other kid gets serious. "He'll be after your ass, Loomis."

"Let him get in line. Take a number."

Grammaw's hanging against a car, squawking, "What happened? My God!"

"You need to call the police?" calls some man with his wife.

"Thanks, we've got this covered," insists Alvy, who thinks he *is* the police, and the man, he doesn't ask again, thinking we're all locoweeds. Meanwhile, with that astounding reasonableness he can just turn on, Alvy's reassuring Grammaw, "Look, ma'am, I'm sorry about my filthy mouth. Normally, I never cuss around ladies, but hey, you saw the guy." He catches her arm. *"Ma'am?* You wanna sit down? There's the pharmacy. There's a soda fountain inside where you can sit down, get a Bromo? Hey, you okay, ma'am?"

Bottles clank on the curb. Then, of course, Grammaw's got her tippy-toe stance, "Frank, do you suppose there's—there's—there's *a little place here?"*

"Oh! No problem, ma'am." He shoots the other kids a get-lost look, then Sir Walter Raleigh's her into the High's. The bottles too.

"Gee," I mutter when he comes back, "I hearda helping them across the street." Alvy squints at me.

"Hey, shouldn't you be getting her home?"

"Look, I'm handling things here. Christ, so take over, whydoncha?"

"Calm down, I called you a cab—a yellow cab this time. Lemme guess. She's your Mom's Mom?"

"Yeah, and guess why she's here? Because of you, is why." I can't stand it. "You said I'd be contacted. I mean, are you out to drive me totally nuts?"

"Hey, ease up, man, you distinguished yourself today. Definitely. Yeah, you most definitely moved up a notch in my book." He looks up. "Fact, meet me here. Saturday. At the pharmacy, ten o'clock. Yeah," he grins, "I got a special little job for you, man."

Distinguished myself under fire! Like his Dad, Alvy's always handing out invisible medals like this. As for Grammaw, when she comes out of the High's all rerouged and zippy-zippy-zoo, well, she's another person, and Alvy's eyeing me, but real understanding, like of course I realize that her seams aren't straight and her lipstick's on crooked. Still, Alvy likes her, I can see. Alvy can see how funny and spunky she is for an old lady. And God, what a flirt the kid is, pumping her for all she's worth and acting like we just now met, him and me. Suddenly he's got his wallet out, showing Grammaw his Mom's picture and even a lock of Bunny's gray hair tied with red thread. "I'll carry this forever," he says and he's dead serious, too. No kid alive would admit this but Alvy's not embarrassed, he's proud, and as he talks to Grammaw, he keeps looking at me, looking so I know he really understands about the people you can't help loving, and no matter what you're stuck loving them and what else can you do?

"Bye, sweetheart," waves Grammaw to him from our cab. "You've got our number, honey. You come visit us now."

Looking back, I can see Alvy grinning and waving—waving he'd better see my ass back here come Saturday. And look, the spring leaves are just budding! Yeah, clutching her bottles, the old lady's happy and I'm in ecstasy—that is, until the cab drives off and it hits me.

"Grammaw, our groceries! We left our groceries in that other cab!"

SO, ON SATURDAY I'M OVER AT THE PHARMACY WAITING ON ALVY. Killing time I'm checking out the tit-enlargement ads in the back of *True Confessions*, when a rough hand spins me around.

"*Ass*-hole."

Alvy's cracking up. "Hey, don't think about it, pop, it'll go down!" Throwing an arm round my neck, he dances me outside, "Yeah, boy, we got a *task* for you, I'm in *love*. Muum-humm and you're Cupid"—meaning, he wants me to send this girl Charlene, Charlene Sykes, some flowers for him. Fourteen long-stemmed roses. And not no dozen, he says falling into his hick voice, *fourteen*. He's even got a note he's written out. I've got to memorize it so I can recite it to the florist.

> *Charlene,*
>
> *It's been a long time, baby. Fourteen long years, but I can't get you out of my head and you know you can't deny it after last week. I'll be back soon. I must see him.*

"But this is crazy," I say. "So who are you in this note?"

"Obviously I'm 'Anonymous.' You know that famous writer, don't you?"

"But wait, you're sending this girl a love note and here you're talking about *him?* And what's this fourteen years stuff? Fourteen years ago you were just a baby. Besides, how will this Charlene even know who it is?"

"Mystery. That's the point." He stares at me. "What, you won't do it?"

"I didn't say that. I just said it doesn't make any sense."

"To *you*." He sours his mouth. "Look, I'm working the confusion angle. Yeah, and you're coming to dinner at my house. *Tonight.* Yeah, my Mom really wants you over. Anyway, tell your old man that"—he hands me a dime, then yanks this kid bodily out of the phone booth—"go on, call him right now. Say my Mom really wants you to stay over. Don't worry, he'll do it. Are you kidding, he'll be *relieved*. He'll think his problems with you are finally over, whoa!" Making massive maniac faces, Alvy's licking the glass of the accordion door, which I can't look or I'll barf, I'm laughing so hard. And just like Alvy predicted, Dad buys it. Dad even agrees to smooth it over with Grammaw. But still, I'm worried. Who's this Charlene girl? And the address Alvy gave me, 112 Oakwood—I should have noticed the address was Alvy's street, except I never pay any attention to streets or directions. And picky! On the final run-through of my speech, Alvy's fussing at me because I keep saying "going out of my *mind*," instead of "going out of my *head*."

"No, no, no," says Alvy. "He wouldn't say *'mind'*—"

"He *who?* I thought this was you."

"Well, it *is* me. Sorta me. But the point—the point is, I'm creating a whole other person here. Just listen to it, *I'm going out of my head*. Now that's powerful! Hear that and you know, this guy's *hurtin'*. Hear that and you know, he's in *need*. And that's what it's about, need. Look, it's been fourteen long years and she's denied him and lied to him and run off? So here, after she's put him through hell, just when he's found her again, she's still denying him, living high and dry and fake-satisfied in this other life! this big lie! with this big fuckin' jerk! with this asshole prick, but here she acts like he never existed."

"But wait, so who's *he?* So this is a story?"

"No, it ain't no story, this is *life*, goddammit. It's how she's acting toward him. It's her whole made-of-ice act, like she don't remember! Like he's an embarrassment. Like he's just fucking *anybody*, when here she made him a solemn promise, a vow. Well, think about it, man. How'd you feel when your mother died and here all around you were these people who couldn't feel one *atom* of what you were feeling? Well?—" Alvy's like a cyclone stopped in midair. He's actually forgotten what he just said. *"Well?"*

God, he's got me so flustered. "Well, okay! I mean, I'm only reciting it for the florist. It's not like I gotta act it out in some play."

He looks at the sky. "Have you ever read any goddamned poe'try or *any*-thing? Man, I thought you had some fuckin' feeling in you."

"Head. I'm going out of my *head*. Satisfied?"

"Good. And look, tell the florist to send it between five and five thirty. No earlier, no later. Y'know, big surprise. But be *vague*. Vagueness, man, vagueness always pays. That way, people fill in all the holes like they dreamed it all up themselves." He's pacing again. "Man, I'm gonna have to read you some goddamned fucking poe'try. And I mean the good shit, man, the cream. Like, you ever read that Keats poem about the knight—no, no, not the starry night, I mean Sir Galahad typa knight in the knight's armor? Aww, come on. It's only the most beautiful poem in the whole English language." He pronounces it "lang-a-guage." "What, you've never even read the one about the knight? Where this knight's loitering around by the lake? Guy's just heartsick and all the birds are dead and this belle dame girl—belle, 'cause the girl's flat gorgeous, man—she's just as cold to him as ice? No mercy on him at'tall?"

"Oh," I huff, "and I suppose this knight says, 'I'm going outta my head,' huh?"

"ASSHOLE. That was set back in England, but this here, Sir Dickhead, this is set in America, if you ever listened to the lang-a-guage."

WELL, AFTER THIS SPEECH, Alvy flips when I come back from the florist.

"He wants *what?*"

"Sixteen fifty—two dollars for delivery and two dollars for the extra roses."

"Well, I don't got that much. Not on me." The kid's got the pride of Satan. If you said a thousand bucks he'd say he didn't have it on him.

"Look, I know you got your heart set on fourteen but we might swing ten."

"Ten! That's the same difference between 'mind' and 'head,' dipshit." He grabs my arm.

"So where we going? You gonna ask your Mom for it?"

"My Mom? What kinda baby are you? We're gonna hustle it."

And steering me across the back lot, he leads me into "Wally's," this back-alley, two-chair barbershop I've never noticed, even though it's only a stone's throw from Taver-Shep and Shepherd Hills. There's an American flag in the window. Crashing through the door, Alvy hollers.

"Heeee-aaay, Mr. Wallace, it's your lucky day, pop! Alvy's here to whiz some hair for you! Hair today, gone tomorrow, haw!"

It's hot inside. The TV's snowing electric-clipper static and the sun's streaming in, the air aswirl with cigarette smoke and that talcum-powder, burnt-hair, clipper-oil smell like roasted nuts. It's packed, too. All down the red linoleum floor in front of the waiting chairs, there's a white streak where scuffling shoes—white-socked black brogans, police shoes and penny loafers—have ground all the color out of the tile. Flattops, crew cuts and that weird hick combo where they buzz the top, then grow the sides and slick it back—they'll scalp you good for $2.25, and for a buck more they'll give you the hand-vibrator witch hazel tonic. The one barber, a skinny little Italian, stands on a beat-up soda box lathering the ears and neck of a customer before he whitewalls him with the straight razor. But this isn't *the* Mr. Wallace. No, Wallace is the fat, hairy one with his blubber-gut busting out his belted blue barber shirt. Fat? He's got white streaks on his flushed face, he's so fat. Puffing and gabbing and stropping his razor, he's so fat he's slowly scuffed a circle around his chair, his fat bum feet laced in these black ortho Frankenstein boots. Mr. Wallace jabs at Alvy with his scissors.

"Forget it, traipsing in here, looking for a fast buck!"

"Aww, come on," cries Alvy. "I'll sweep up, empty the trash, wipe the goddamned ashtrays, wash the mirror. Hell, for you, Mr. Wallace, I'll throw in the front window! Cheap—three bucks."

"Out, you thief."

"But look at that filthy front window, it's a dis-grace." At this Alvy turns to the peanut gallery. "Man, I ask you gentlemen, is this a goddamned deal or what? Any lower and he'll have child labor on his big butt. Fine. So jew me down, Wallace—two-fifty."

"Wallll-lace," cry the men, all moaning and guffawing, "goddamn Wallace, have a heart with the young bastard."

Wallace flips Alvy the bird, then turns to the fat old baldie in his chair. "Can you believe this goddamn little chiseler?"

Alvy points to the blue disinfectant jars filled with black combs. "Food coloring! That's all it is, mister. Dandruff, scaborilla, crabs, hoof 'n' mouth, mange—man, you'll get it all off Wallace's nasty comb. And what's Wallace even doing, clipping them three sorry hairs of yours? Give me a shot at that dome, sir. I am out*stand*ing on chrome."

Chrome Dome loves it. "Hell Wallace, you oughta pay the bastard to insult your customers. You are outstanding at that, son."

"TWO BUCKS," cries Wallace. "Final offer, you goddamn chiseler. And who's this young stringbean with you?"

Alvy jerks his thumb at me. "That's Frank, my hair whizzer *trainee*. Frank's like the fly in the soup. No charge for the extra meat."

Well, at this they all start whooping. A man eating his own smoke tugs on my arm. "Are you gonna let him call you that? A hunka ole *meat?*"

"Speak up, son."

"No," I say finally.

"No, *sir*," orders Alvy. God, he's dead serious, too.

Mr. Wallace motions to Chrome Dome. "An Eagle Scout, if you can believe that shit."

Alvy snaps to attention. "Trustworthy, loyal, helpful?—*helpful?* . . . Aww, shit, I forget the rest! They's sure a lot of 'em, though!" Breaking into his ack-ack laugh, Alvy rubs the old man's head, then bolts as Wallace heaves a towel at him. And as suddenly Alvy's all business, hauling out brooms, brushes and buckets. Setting up a stepladder, Alvy starts me cleaning the mirror while he sweeps. God, he's fast, he's a hair-whizzer machine. Shoulder blades twitching, Alvy first jabs the broom in short, stabbing strokes, toom, toom, toom, then glides into figure eights so graceful you could fall asleep watching his hair whizzer artistry. Yeah, he brooms up a whole bale of hair, then he starts down on the *dust*. You'd think he was brushing for fingerprints, down on his knees with his whisk broom. Pulling a putty knife from his back pocket, he scrapes up a crud splat, then whisk! whisk! whisk! And touchy? Because a second later he's fussing at me, "Hey, you! You're using up all Mr. Wallace's good clean rags, man." He turns to the peanut gallery. "Now, ain't that sad? Kid's so sheltered he never worked a day in his life—never a lick until to-day. Frank, now looky here. See, you fold the rag into *fours*. Four so you get *eight* full sides, then you work down till you get to the squeak, the *squeak* . . ." And I gotta admit, it's real satisfying to watch Alvy work. And that's the trick to hustling, he says, the squeak, the sizzle, the show. And do you know what? Once Mr. Wallace whisks Chrome Dome off, the guy flips Alvy a fifty cent piece! for insulting him! Hell, I think, at that rate Alvy should have booted him one in the ass.

God, it's murder, though, my eyes tearing with the ammonia and the nasty brown tobacco stink from all that old smoke. Still, this being my first real job, I make that rag squeak. Meantime, it's pretty shocking. Do all men cuss like this? I wonder. I guess I thought it was like beating off, something you quit once you grew up. I mean, on Corregidor I've never heard a man cuss, never, not even a damn or a hell. And not just because they're professional men, I realize, no, these men cuss *'cause they don't know me*. That's why animals eat their young. No sir, once men know you're not anybody's kid they're a whole other breed. And I'll tell you another thing about grown men. When you really listen to them talk, they don't make any more sense than kids do. I mean it. You may as well watch a flock of starlings. They land, they take off, they land again. I can't even follow the conversation. They drip their ashes between their feet. They pull out their unfamiliar reading glasses and cough. Sideburns twitching and jaws bulging, the men stare over their noses at the newspaper, slap it shut, then start jabbering. Everything irritates them. They say it's all a lie in the paper, but when some other man talks, they don't listen but just tug on their ears, all staring at the TV. Then suddenly they're onto something else. But I'll tell you what, though—if they had a bullshitter's merit badge (flies buzzing over a steaming heap), well, Alvy would definitely rate one. Two-stroke engines. Baseball, gallstones, guns, some referendum (whatever that is). You name it and Alvy can pronounce on it. But there's one subject that gets them all whipped up.

"Twelve million of 'em descending on Washington," says this old man slapping the paper shut. "Truck 'em in like Georgia melons."

"Come August."

"Martin Luther Coon, boy."

"Nigger oughta be shot."

"Now, don't say *shot*," wheedles the old man. "Not when there's hanging trees."

What is it? I wonder. God, are they riled up. Alvy too. Polishing the front window, Alvy starts Patrick-Henrying them from his stepladder.

"I'll tell you how you stop that nigger-agitator shit. You jerk their parade permit. And how? Our constitutional right to protect the public safety, that's how."

"And what're you, some kinda lawyer?"

"No, but my old man sure is."

"Well, great," complains the old man, "but meanwhile, the niggers are all saying they got their constitutional right to march their monkey asses down Constitution Avenue. And who we got in the White House but that niggerlovin' Kennedy." *Kennedy?* I think. Wow, I didn't know President Kennedy was for it, but Alvy doesn't care. With the cords standing out in his neck, Alvy's talking about the Supreme Court. And . . . speak of the devil. Right behind Alvy here's this seedy old colored man mooning in the window. Mr. Wallace waves him off.

"Sober up. You ain't getting a red-assed cent offa me."

"Damn, Wallace!" says this young, punchy customer with a lazy eye. "Larry" is sewn in white curlicues on his firehouse jacket—really, they oughta call him "Punchy," with his jughead, rolled-up jeans and black cop shoes. "Wall-ace," squalls Punchy, "call the po-lice on the black sonofabitch!"

"And what good'll that do?" shrugs Wallace. "His sister keeps him. Lock his ass up and here he is, right back again. Git, Hermes! Git on with you!"

Punchy points at Alvy. "It's not you, Wallace, it's the kid he wants. What's the old nigger want with you, boy? You don't give him no money, I hope?"

"Who says I give him money?"

"Then what's he want with you, huh?"

"How do I know what he wants? And since when is my money your business?"

"*Your* money?" Punchy looks around at the room. "You pester Wallace to pay *you* money, so you can give it to some nigger winehead? To run off his good paying customers?"

"Who? You?" Alvy flips Punchy a dime. "Buy yourself a soda, man. About all you patronize here, sitting on your dead ass, waiting on the fire bell to ring."

Punchy jumps up. "You little shitass!"

"Larry, sit down!" Lurching around, Mr. Wallace pops the cash register. "Well, you're finished here, hotshot. And the next time—if there is a next time—you had better learn to curb that big fat mouth a yours."

FIRED FROM MY FIRST JOB! In my humiliation all I want to do is get the flowers and eat, but no—our two bucks are already spoken for. As we pass the rusted trash barrels back behind the Shell station, we hear a whistle. It's that old colored man. His pants are shiny, his coat's all burrs down the back and he's not wearing any socks. That's what I most notice—his feet. His crusted shoes are turned up like rotten shingles, and on his ankle there's a runny red sore the size of a cherry.

"Doan be lookin away from me, Alvy, cause I hurtin out hyeah today, I hurtin real bee-aaad, man." He spits. "Wallace! Fat, back-stabbing Judas muthafucka, makin like he doan know *me*." His finger trembles at Alvy's nose. "And *you*, suckin up to them cracker muthafuckas. You done took my job, man. Thass my own job you took."

Alvy's caught now. The kid is beet red but he won't be embarrassed—so he laughs. Alvy honks, he laughs so hard, playing up to me, "Who denied you, Hermes? You wanna know the truth, I thought it was a ghost! That's right. I heard they planted your black ass. Last Thursday, man." He turns serious. "Well, that's what I heard."

I can't believe it.

At this slur the old man starts twitching and waving his arms and I stare at Alvy, wanting to puke. Calling the old man dead—dead like you're a nigger, too, Mamma—well, by comparison. And worse, to see the kid so barefaced, with this frozen, fake-heartless smirk. I mean, how low-down can you get, calling a man dead when he's alive, and then to smile about it—this was my first inkling of just how far Alvy will go to run away from a feeling. Hermes is all over him, too.

"Doan play me like that, giving me yo dumb-assed grin. Cause I *know* you know better, them screwy ole people you be livin wid."

And Alvy does embarrass. Motioning us around the Shell station, he gets all huffy and sanctimonious, first saying to me, "I was just trying to throw a scare into him, is all," then back to Hermes, "'cause, if you don't eat, they *will* be plantin your black ass," then back to at me, "And don't you be crying about the money, either."

"Who's crying about the money?" I ask. God, whatever the kid does, he lays it on somebody else.

"Well, good," he nods, "'cause I *hate* a money-grubber. And right now my man needs him a fish sandwich from the Good 'n' Quick. Messa tartar sauce. Tomato and lettuce, for the sunshine vitamins? So re-*lax*." (Hermes hasn't said boo.) "Look man, you eat good and I'll give you some T-Bird money. But *only* if you eat, y'hear? Frank, you stay here with him."

"Why me? Gimme the money, I'll go."

"Look at this," Alvy snorts to Hermes. "First day on the job and thinks he's running the damn show. And look at him. The goddamn baby still buttons his top shirt button."

So, off Alvy goes, jabbering about he's St. Christopher carrying the whole world on his back. Well, fine, I'll be sociable. I even unpop my top button— hell, at this rate, maybe I'll drop my fly.

"Turn yo back on me, boy! You either dumb or stupid, one."

I whip around. "I'm keeping watch, okay?"

"Shee-it, boy, what you even doin hyeah? You ain even the type."

"What type?"

"The bad type." Hermes nods. "Now I recorgnize you. I seen you t'other day. You the foo whut jumped out that cab hollerin. Yeah I seen you wif de ole lady. I always be seein her, thinking she all sneaky while you be in school."

Well, I freeze, the idea of him, any colored person being aware of us. "She's from New York. You never saw her before." But at this, the old man just laughs.

"Seen her, shee-it. We drinks under the bridge together. Cept she *Sally* to me."

Well, I stomp off, but then I stop short, scared Alvy'll blackball me as a quitter. "Sir," I blurt back at him, "sir, what did I ever do to you? And here when we're helping you." But he only laughs, rubbing his crotch.

"Mean ol' Greenie—Greenie *boyyyyyh*. Get on home, boy. Yo Mamma callin you."

It's almost an icebreaker, when somebody insults you. And when I tell him I've got no Mamma he softens up, like I'm a seminigger, too. "Oh. Nother orphan, huh?" Well here's my chance.

"Hey, you know a colored lady named Mrs. Eppes?"

"Sistah Eppes! Why, she wipe yo white butt for yuh?" He knows her, all right, turning up his nose like royalty. "Good Sistah Eppes. Tell yuh how the Lord licked them leper's sores clean, but she ain got nuthin fo me."

"Goddamn right—ya blame her?"

Damn, it's Alvy. And just when I'm all set to ask Hermes about this colored orphan kid. Peering into the grease-soaked bag, Hermes groans.

"Whass this white shit?"

"That's *milk*, and you're drinking it. Am I gonna have to watch you eat? Am I?"

I guess so. Pushing back the vines and sumac, Alvy heads down the mud path, down the railroad tracks past the Nigger Bridge, and their side of it too. At first I'm scared they'll jump us, but not with Hermes, I realize. No, with Hermes, we're invisible, going the whole length of Taver-Shep until we hit his camp—a culvert under a kudzu hill, where the coloreds won't have to see Hermes in his little plywood hut. I've sure never seen his hut, not even behind the roofing warehouse, where the hoodlums go to drink and make out. No sir, nobody could ever spot it from our side, not unless they were looking for those empty wine bottles glistening like fat green flies in the sun. But even Hermes has his house rules. Right off, he says no busting bottles, then he gets mad when Alvy starts to light a fire in his fire bucket—see, there's clothes drying on the hill, over our mud embankment.

"Hey, man," he fumes, "use yo damn head, smokin up them clothes so folks be fussin at me." And sure enough some coon kid yells down.

"Hermes, sucking up to white boys."

"Least we feed him," razzes Alvy.

"Wine!"

"*Alvin.*"

You'd think Hermes was at his own dinner table, first hushing Alvy, then chewing out the colored kids until they finally slink off. Then the train whams by not ten feet away, shattering the leaves, and it's so cool. Staring back at Taverna Park, like from the other side of the mirror, I can just see our old dead life over there, that and all the people who once thought they knew me as yours. And from this side, the colored side, you can see we never belonged over there either, not to the church or the pool or the stupid teams I never joined. It's like something snapped in me when I undid my top button—anymore, I never feel I belong anywhere, and Hermes, you can see where he belongs, to say nothing of Alvy. If I'd lived back in ancient England during the dukes and the earls, I'd have been a staunch royalist, but Alvy, even though he'd never admit it, Alvy's even worse—a dictator, a kid king. Still, I'm a real absolutist, like with fish-on-Fridays or beating-your-meat type questions. Damned right. If I ever vote, I'll vote the straight ticket or else I'll renounce the party—all or nothing, that's me. Take those men at Wallace's. If they really believed what they said, they'd get guns and stop that colored march, but what do they do? All they do is complain, without a dime's worth of conviction.

I'll tell you one conviction, though—eating. Once Hermes unwraps the mayonnaisey white sub paper, once he finally lets his hunger go, it's amazing. Hermes bites down. His black jaws shine, and his adam's apple slides up and down. Now, me, I could never possibly drink milk with a sandwich, not without blowing lunch. Milk and bread! Normally, I can't bear to look, but I could watch Hermes eat all day, just to see how his saliva mixes with the milk and the mayonnaise, the bread and the fish—how it all goes into like a soup and there's actual life inside it. And Alvy, see, Alvy is just exactly like me. From the first bite to the last, Alvy absolutely can't take his eyes off Hermes. To me, it redeems Alvy—more than redeems him—for that sick crack.

Once Hermes is finished I jump up. "Look, you're still hungry. I'll get you another."

"Naw, man"—his jaws bulge, he swallows—"naw, I be sick." Then he starts to shake, the shock of the food, I guess, so playing doctor, Alvy wants to check out the sores on his ankles. Hermes jerks back his feet. "Mine yo own damn feets." So what's wrong with his feet? I whisper to Alvy and he whispers back, *They lopped his toes off 'cause of the wine.*

It's all the sugar and diabetes, Alvy says, plus the wine's half formaldehyde. Formaldehyde like in frogs? I ask. And they sell it to poor people to drink? It makes me wanna weep, it's so sick. But sympathy doesn't work. Hermes only turns on Alvy.

"So you gonna tell her finally? You done talked enough. Well, huh?"

I look at Alvy. "He knows about your Mom?" To tell you the truth, at this point I still don't know what the fuss is about, except that Alvy's pretty upset about it.

"Damnit, Hermes, shut your mouth!" Alvy shoves three bucks at him, then stomps off down the bluestones.

"Alvy," I huff, catching up. "Three bucks to make his sores worse? And what about the flowers?" Alvy whips around.

"Fuck your flowers, you goddamn money-grubber. You ever been hungover? Well?"

"*My* flowers?"

But when I run round front, to see him better, Alvy's all red in the face and near tears. "All right, calm down, you'll have your goddamned flowers. Now c'mon, 'cause I'm starved and time's money."

AT THIS RATE WE COULDN'T BUY A SINGING TELEGRAM IF WE SANG IT OURSELVES, but Alvy, driven like a bear by hunger, Alvy finds his next victim, the Cozee Diner, where for fifty cents—for cigarettes—plus hot lunches for me and him, we mop and muck the whole place and knock-knock the bathrooms. What a deal. Bud, the sunken-chested old grill man in the grease-spattered paper hat and the bird-call voice (no larynx), Bud fries us up a lunch something sumptuous, hamburgs, butter-toasted buns and fries, which Alvy hurls a bottle of ketchup on, and steak sauce on top of that. He's a human garbage disposal. Back in the kitchen, just before Ray the dishwasher zaps the plates, Alvy inhales two leftover Dagwoods and half a stack of hotcakes, plus a side of meatloaf and practically the cigarette butts garnishing it. Licking cold gravy off his palm, Alvy's bragging to Ray, "You wait'll I'm fifteen, and I'm the one smashing the dishes in this dump. Aww, don't worry, man, you'll have long moved on. Yeah, I already got the car picked out! Candy-apple '49 Merc, man! A double four-barrel 409!"

With Alvy every dream has a car attached to it. His coffee mug's stuttering—boy, that coffee hops him up bad! Yeah, back out front, he's getting all agitated, telling Colleen, the waitress—not young or great in the face department but really built—he's telling Colleen she oughta leave this drunk, this drywaller, who gambles away all her money and runs around on her. Alvy's a giant snowball, accumulating people's problems. He claims he can read palms. Feeling Colleen's hand, he's tracing the lines and she lets him, halfway between she's his mother and something else. Alvy does all the dirty work, too. The cigarette butts in the urinal, for instance. He picks them right out, *with his bare fingers*, then glares that *he's* not too proud—another sin, my pride, like keeping my top button buttoned. And outside, he drops another dime. Shoulder blades twitching and elbows bowed out, Alvy's playing the jukebox like a pinball machine. Playing it! He's practically humping the thing.

"Alvy," I whisper, "I'm not being money-crazy or anything but it's getting late."

"*Hah!*" He snaps a buzzing fly from midair! Cackling, he lets the sucker go, then snap! another! then another!!

"Whe-ell," cuddles Colleen, "I'll take that coffee cup for ya, hon."

Alvy tears back into the kitchen. "Hey, Ray, here's a bet . . . *three flies, three tries.*"

So after he's won and squandered another dollar fly-snapping, then after he's shot another two hours kissing all the women good-bye—after this he takes me into the old, high-class end of town, there to try his other famed hustling technique, door knocking.

"Here we go," he says, stopping at this huge old gingerbready place. "Doily curtains, man, an old biddy with bucks."

The big porch rumbles under our feet. Shirts tucked in, eyes straight, rap rap rap. As the door opens, Alvy oozes into a pool of humbleness. "Ma'am, we need *work*. We'll mow, rake, chop hedges, pull weeds, wash windows. Anything. And when we're done—hey, you just pay us whatever you think it's worth."

Well, she sends us packing, then the next place we get a man. Forget that. Alvy turns right around. "Men! The cheap bastards'll pay a kid a nickel and call it a fuckin' education."

"Well, that's right," I agree. "We could bust our butts and not get fifty cents."

"Are you kidding? They pay you three times more this a way—women do. And if one stiffs you, you stare at the money, then you hand it right back, 'Golly, ma'am, I can't take this, not if you're not a hundred percent satisfied.' Then you get all hurt, 'Gee, ma'am, I can't stay tonight—I got altar boys—but I can come back tomorrow.' Then you beg her to screw you, 'Please, tomorrow I'll work all day and then you can pay me what I'm really worth.' "

"That's awful!"

"That's not awful, that's business. And that's the beauty of English at work, man. But pay attention, 'cause the trick is to say what *I'm* worth. And remember, it only works with women."

"But why just women?"

"Cause women been hurt more than men, is why. Way more. As you oughta know, asshole." And when the next door opens, it's spooky the way he moons in and sizes the place up. A normal kid can never picture himself anywhere but his own home, but a half orphan like me, or bastard like Alvy, all he can see is YOUR PICTURE HERE. It's a dogs and cats difference, really. It's why a dog will lick his balls and stick by the hearth, while your angling cat licks himself so he won't stick to anything.

Boy, it's hard work, getting people to like you. But finally we snag this old lady Mrs. Vera, who agrees to pay us what we're worth, and we do a great job, too—ain't that enough? But no sir, not for Alvy. No, once we're finished the same kid who just called poor old Hermes dead, here he is, dead serious, showing Mrs. Vera this nasty old rabbit's foot his Mom gave him at age six. Alvy's worn it to the bone. There's barely a hair left on it, and half of that is pocket lint. Who ever said rabbit's feet were lucky? I wonder. It's gross, but Mrs. Vera's old heart is so melted she's gotta show us her grown-up son's room—Wayne, his name is. God, I hate these old kid crypts. Straight off, you know Wayne never comes to visit, but like a mosquito, a woman mosquito, Alvy is asking her all about Wayne, making Mrs. Vera's eyes get all red and blurty. And don't worry, Alvy gets his money—enough for the flowers, with a whole dollar left to blow. But as we leave, with no reason to drag it out, here he goes again, showing Mrs. Vera his Mom's picture and the lock of her hair, like maybe, just maybe, Mrs. Vera knows whose kid he is really.

I USED TO LOVE NECCO WAFERS but now they're uncool, a baby candy. Still, after I order the flowers, damned if Alvy doesn't buy some, and over at his house I see why.

"Alvy! Uncle Alvy!"

From the house next door runs the little dirty-blond-headed, gap-toothed kid I saw that first night at Alvy's—his sister's boy. Alvy swings him over his shoulder like a sack of potatoes, hugging and gnawing on the back of his neck. Eyes closed tight, the boy's squealing upside down in Alvy's arms, air hissing through his teeth as Alvy crows to me, "Hey, this is my own boy, man! It's my spud buddy, Buddy!" But as he swings the kid down, I see Alvy eyeing me to pay close attention here, too.

Little kids. They make me nervous, being an only child. Bad enough they're completely oblivious but they're nasty, too. Why, they'll stick their fingers up their butts just to sniff it, then they'll sneeze and happily wipe their noses on you. Besides, this close in age you don't want to invite unpleasant comparisons by playing with them—or be seen as gooney or stunted, like those weird kids who play with babies. Nope, no self-respecting kid—or no boy at least—wants to be seen within a mile of these lepers, so it's amazing to see Alvy leave himself so wide open. The kid idolizes him. When Alvy pulls out the Necco wafers, Buddy starts jumping and squealing. You never saw a kid get so excited, first making Alvy eat one, then me, then watching us both all amazed. Buddy, I swear he'd rather watch you eat his candy than eat it himself. Laying the wafer on your tongue, Buddy wants to see it dissolve in your mouth, to see how thin it can get without breaking. Holding your jaw, Buddy chomps your mouth open and closed, squealing with those squinty Loomis eyes and apple-stem chin. Buddy's the perfect name for him, too. It sounds stupid but he really is a buddy, for a little kid.

"Yeah, Frank!" he whoops at me, "Frank, do you like Necco wafers in your mouth? I like the brown ones best! Do you like the browns best? Huh, Frank? . . ." And suddenly, thinking I'm his next best buddy, Buddy's dragging me by the hand through Alvy's sister's house, out to show me his Dinky Toy car collection, which Alvy gave him. They're totally impossible together, Buddy pulling me one way and Alvy the other, each wanting to show me eighty things at once. In terms of mess, it's like Alvy's house—times ten. Ironing piled on the couch, strewn clothes and stacks of magazines—*dirty magazines*. Stuff beyond dirty. Scary, too, one with a lady all tied up in a chair wearing a black mask, with a red ball stuffed in her mouth and her tits squeezed out between all these ropes. Buddy brings it to me like a comic book, just like it's normal. Well, I get all proper. Really, I *don't* look, first to set a good example for Buddy, but also because, frankly, the pictures scare me sick.

. . . And books. Stacks. Dirty books and regulars, and in the dining room, by the side door, there's a pink toilet almost like a plush chair for company. Meanwhile, everything's *hey! Hey, Buddy! Hey, Alvy!* Opening this fat book Alvy says, "Hey Frank look, *The Rise and Fall of the Third Reich*—that's Hitler. My sister just read that. And here's *Great Expectations*, which she read in about a day." Alvy leaps over the hassock to another shelf. "Yeah! And here's that book you gotta get, the one with the poem, man, the *code*. It's that Keats poem I told you about, 'La Belle Dame Sans Merci'—*The Belle Dame, man* . . . " But before I can even see it, him and Buddy are both dragging me into Buddy's room. Chaos. Puzzles. Erector sets. Games. Soggy Trix crushed all over the floor. It's like somebody put all the pieces in a box, shook it, then scattered it, but if every pin was in its place, Buddy couldn't be any prouder. Down on the floor, five himself, Alvy's making car sounds for Buddy, which Buddy *really really* wants Alvy to make the car sounds. Like he's learning to whistle, Buddy's practically in Alvy's mouth learning to lay rubber and shift gears, *Errrunh—Errrrruuh-unnh*. Next thing I know here's Alvy's staring at me all disgusted—disgusted like he was at the diner when I wouldn't stick my bare hand down the urinal—and why? Cause I won't flop down on the filthy floor, down into the dust bunnies and soggy Trix crunching like wet sand under my shoes? Lord, that's the sin of sins for Alvy, anybody's thinking they're too good.

"Oh Alvy."

It's Alvy's sister, or whoever, in the doorway. She's in a kimono, barefoot with the longest painted toenails and, God, a gold ring around one toe, *a ring*. Her blonde hair is tucked up the back, long blonde strands falling down and a big cowlicky piece fluffed over her eyes. As she comes closer, she smells like sleep, not bad but *deep*, with the kind of stinky, sexy beauty that shames you half to death. But what kills me is Alvy on the floor, flat on his belly with Buddy, pretending not to see her, a wolf hoping he'll pass for a young sheep. "I thought I heard you," she says finally, totally ignoring me when I'm not a foot from her face. "Mommy was asking if I'd seen you. They're expecting you over there . . ."

It's almost like Mrs. Bemis, I'm so invisible. Worse is this "Mommy" business, and especially when she's a mommy herself, talking in this breathy girl's voice. She never once notices me. Grosser still, she speaks almost over her nose, like those people who act like they don't remember you, then like you don't exist, period. Still, if she ignores me, Buddy pays absolutely no attention to her. Buddy only keeps crashing his cars—louder. Then Alvy glares at me, "This is Charlene"—not my sister Charlene but just plain Charlene. Not that it makes any difference where I'm concerned. When I put out my hand, she doesn't take it—doesn't, because she doesn't have to, because she has these special beauty powers, same as she can talk in this little girl's voice and everybody strains to hear her. I'm getting really depressed again. Sure, she could be Alvy's mother—I guess. Still, she is awfully young. How old do they gotta be after they get their periods? I wonder. Alvy, meanwhile, is trying to talk up all her reading. "Charlene, how many books did you read last week? Three? Four? Hey, you know what, Frank? Charlene and me, we both learned to read by ourselves—just learned on our own. And right at four and a half— right, Charlene?" But the harder he tries, the vaguer she gets and the harder

Buddy runs his Dinky Toys over the puzzle pieces and the Trix. Then here's Audrey, Buddy's big sister, carrying in the baby. Baby Huey is more like it. It's this fat truck of a kid named Bramford.

"Mother," scolds Audrey, "Daddy's gonna be home!"

Just like boys get loud, girls only get more proper the more upset they are. I guess Audrey's eight or nine, wearing one of those thin starched dresses with the frilly fronts. Kicking and squawling, the baby's almost as big as she is, his fat, knobby baby belly hanging out of a grape-juice-stained T-shirt. As for Alvy, he's obviously the last person Audrey wants to see, Alvy being the kind of boy sure to drive her—any girl—nuts, always getting away with murder, on top of he's her uncle.

"Well," sasses Audrey, "Gramma's got your special birthday dinner going for your highness running all over creation! She's already been here three times looking for you. And Daddy's gonna be here. And you know that, *so huh?*"—looking at me so we'll both take the hint to beat it. Then she glares at Charlene, *"Mother."*

Daddy! Mommy! Mother! I can't keep them straight. Buddy either. Wrapped like a monkey around Alvy, Buddy's hollering, "No! No! Alvy can't go! Alvy can't go!"—hanging on Alvy, and Alvy following after Charlene, who just shuts the door on them both. It's weird, seeing Alvy staring at Charlene's door just then. It's one of those rare moments when the kid's at rest, and only then because he's baffled. And Buddy's just exactly like Alvy—never knows when to quit. Alvy has to get mad before Buddy'll turn him loose. Running up to me, Buddy sticks another Necco on my tongue. It's one of his precious "brownies," the chocolates, all sticky hot from his fingers. And why's the kid gotta look so grateful? So *retarded* grateful, and especially when I haven't done a thing and he's not retarded—no, Buddy's smart. It's harder than Mrs. Vera giving us all that money so we'll keep talking to her. I tell you, nobody knows what they're worth.

"You see how smart Charlene is?" asks Alvy as we leave.

"She sure reads a lot of books," I agree. Everything's brains to him.

"Well, she hides her smarts," he says darkening. "Lotsa women do. Look, she just woke up. That's why we caught her like that. She's up half the night, reading."

I change the subject. "Buddy's sure a nice kid."

"Don't just *nice* me. Goddamn, you are a patronizing sonofabitch."

"What's patronizing?"

"It's you, fingering the goods and never wanna buy. Now what time is it?"

"I'll tell you what to buy—a watch. Almost six."

"Shit, we're late! And, you remember what you saw at Charlene's. And you saw how she looks at me."

Looks at him? Looks at him how? Like never? But Alvy can't even wait for my answer. Feeling his rabbit's foot, he barges off for his house—his own house, I mean. Well, supposedly.

NAMES. WHEN I'M INTRODUCED I NEVER PAY ATTENTION TO PEOPLE'S NAMES, or never at first. I mean here we meet Alvy's sister, and her name's "Charlene," the same name I sent the flowers to, but it just doesn't register in all the confusion. Stuck on the idea that Charlene is a girl my age I just don't—I can't—think it's *that* Charlene, or not until Alvy slams the door he's home and I see the place all draped with crepe and balloons. "Whose birthday?" I ask. "Mine," he glares, when it hits me, *fourteen years, baby* . . . "But wait," I ask, "what about Charlene?" Alvy grabs my mouth, "You just *came* from Charlene's, numbnuts. Today I'm fourteen, and this is combat, so wake up." And slams the door again, louder, then he points. Shit! It's Mr. Loomis, face down on the sofa with the TV going. And looking up all annoyed, it's Beef, Beef the dog, waiting on his K-9 relief. Woof! Woof! The family watchdog is home, bellowing.

"MAAAA!! Carol! Lucy!"—these are his other sisters—"What's everybody doing? Why isn't Dad up? I'm starved and I got Frank over." Mrs. Loomis calls down.

"*Frank?* Frank who?"

Running down the stairs, primping, her hair in curlers and bunny-ears flopping, Mrs. Loomis at first she doesn't obviously have the foggiest who Alvy means. But once she sees it's me all healed—well, she has a glad fit, giving me one big sloppy kiss, then another.

"Frankie, what a great birthday surprise!" She shakes her fist at Alvy. "You knucklehead, you. Frankie, you know what? I asked and *asked* this joker did he want to invite any kids to his party, but nooo." She prunes out her face— pure Alvy. "No, just the family, he told me. What, he didn't tell you that tonight's his birthday party?" But Alvy hollers back at her.

"Maa, it's a *surprise* party." But this is just smoke, just blather, Alvy windmilling his arms, "Goddamnit, Maaa, Dad should be up! You gotta wake Dad up."

If it was Hermes, Alvy would be all over his old man, but here Mr. Loomis is a Sacred Cow, taking one of his sacred snoozes, which you could easier raise the dead. Getting no response from his Mom, Alvy hollers upstairs, "Carol, Dad's supposed to be up! And when's dinner?"

"Aww, give your old man a break," hollers Mrs. Loomis, "he's exhausted, the poor guy, EXHAUSTED. That's right, up until two last night confirming Bob Baxter, then slaving here all day for you, YA BIG INGRATE KID—"

Embarrassed, Mrs. Loomis plonks down on the sofa beside Mr. Loomis. She lifts his arm, lets it drop, then pokes at him, "*Luu-cky* . . ." Hamming it up for me, she swats at him with a magazine, getting groans from him and a dirty look from Beef. All sweet she looks at Mr. Loomis, smears his hair, then titters to me, "Anytime, anywhere, that's my Lucky. Why, during the war, the man slept through whole bombardments." Then seeing Alvy stalking, she hollers, "Gwan, look in the oven, Prince Charming. Go see the NICE ROAST he cooked for you tonight." Grabbing my hand, she drags me into the kitchen to peep at the roast, then to marvel at her birthday cake. "That's my handiwork, you know"—the icing looks like it was sprayed on with a hose—"it's not from any store, not for the Messiah here." Again she hollers into the living room. "And where the heck were you all day?"

"Goddamnit, Dad should be up!"

"Don't you curse at me! He'll be up!" And in virtually the same breath, she whispers to me, "And protective of me? Even as a baby. Never let me out of his sight. My other boys, forget it, they never stuck by me like Alvy. Totally different creatures . . ."

Her face, her mouth, it's a magic theater. And she has such a big mouth—beautiful big like her eyes, which are like topazes, if that's not the blue. Mrs. Loomis draws her fingers into a cage, a veil, around her face, like of all the people in the world I'm the only one she could ever tell this to, me who just walked in the door, but instantly I'm family and they can all yell and fight and not even be embarrassed. And just like Alvy did at Mrs. Vera's, I'm hedging my bets. I'm thinking, *Heck, if Alvy doesn't want her I'll take her.* But wait, I think, she's not dying, is she? I mean, the way Alvy talked at Mrs. Vera's, for a second I got scared maybe Bunny was dying. But no, I decide, there's not a speck of death in those eyes, although she is awfully scrawny—Alvy says she never eats. And no wonder Alvy is so fierce about her. You worry for Bunny. You want to protect Old Mother Hubbard, killing herself to protect Alvy and all these grown kids who won't get married or move out. And she's right about Alvy's being an ingrate. Here she makes him a nice party, but all he does is holler he's starved, banging cupboards, wanting her to open him a can of tuna fish, obviously too weak to crank the can opener. God is he spoiled. Because what spinach is to Popeye, that's tuna fish to Alvy, hollering about somebody ate the last can, and nobody even cared enough to buy him more, *"Tuna! Where's my tunnnna fish?"* going off like a siren until all three women—Bunny Loomis, Carol Loomis and Velma Loomis—they all three collide in the kitchen, feeding baby bird.

"No, no," Mrs. Loomis fusses at Velma, cranking the opener, "don't drain the oil off."

"Ouch! I cut myself!"

"Here! Here—" Ripping off the top, Bunny starts mashing it up with a fork. That cheap, greasy, liver-dark tuna, too.

"Maaa, okay, okay," calls Velma. "I know he wants the oil! To keep his coat shiny!" Velma looks at me sarcastically. In that house they're all sarcastic, pushing the can at him, "Here! Here's your tuna fish, ya big goddamn baby!"

Alvy grabs the can! Mashing and gagging, oil and all, he sucks it down. Like a giant greasy oyster he sucks down the whole can, gargling the stuff, when he topples back, "Look! It's CATFOOD! Hhhh-UUCCK—" Gagging and spitting into the sink. "Y'all gave me CATFOOD—"

"We did not!" Chasing him around the kitchen, Bunny's snatching at the can to prove it to me, when Alvy rears back, pointing at all three, "APRIL FOOLS!"

It's too much. As an only kid, I just can't stand all the commotion. And here's Mrs. Loomis chasing after me with a bag of Fritos and a saucer of clam dip, "Frank, eat!" Fritos explode as she tears the bag open. Alvy grabs the food and yanks me upstairs.

"And Dad had better get up!"

"So go on," dares Mrs. Loomis. "Wake him up."

"Dinner's at seven-thirty," hollers Carol.

"Well, Dad had better be up. This kid eats early." As Alvy slams the door behind us, I can hear the women all singing back at him, *"Haaa—py birthday to youuuuuu. PtthHHHzzz—"* Razzberries.

Time to get busy. Alvy bolts the door, switches on his hi-fi, then jams the radio on—loud. I don't know what's more amazing, how tiny his room is or how much he's got crammed into it, from floor to ceiling. But what I first notice are the pictures filling the wall over his desk. Pictures of all sizes, but mostly bitty school pictures the size of stamps—pictures laid out like those pencil lines you see on walls, marking kids at various heights and ages. Ticking along the wall I count eight long, squiggly lines, paired face to face, age to age, grade to grade. Of the boys they all look so alike I'd be hard pressed to pick out Alvy, and then only because his pictures are mostly in color and, of course, don't go on so long. And they all have that Lucky Loomis Chin, the boys and girls both.

"Wait," I ask, "so how many kids are in your family?"

"Eight."

"But you said seven."

"Well, it depends. It could be nine, depending."

"But wait, who's this?"

"Ralph, my older brother. Except he doesn't come around anymore."

"And who's this?"

"Him we don't talk about. He died before I was born."

"Died how?"

"Goddamnit, didn't I just tell you? We don't talk about it."

And stares that stonewalling stare of families, which the bigger the family the harder the wall, because the more the bricks, and the deeper the chinks. The room's like his house. Everywhere you look you only see more. Piss-colored pickle jars filled with some creatures that look like these hairy hard-boiled eggs. And wow, a rack of guns—real guns, plus a German helmet with a bullet hole clear through it, two bayonets and a cored-out grenade. And medical books! Man, when I see these I know he's got him a *Playboy* tucked away, I just know it! But what really gets me stirred up, weird as it sounds, are the plastic figures of the Invisible Man and the Invisible Woman. With their froggy palms facing out and their icy plastic skin, they're standing together like Adam and Eve, their guts painted all different colors and only excuses for Things. I've never seen any kid with both the male and the female Invisibles, and the creepiest thing is Alvy like the Invisible Baby.

And here we go. Picking a pair of binoculars off the table, Alvy cranks back in a swivel chair, then teases up the blinds. Uh-oh! I plop down on his slouchy iron bed with the seasick springs. Definitely, a jack-off jetport!

"Is it a titty show?" I cry. "Huh?? Is it a titty show?"

"Cool your tool, I'm watching Charlene's."

"Charlene's?"

"Not like *that*, you sick bastard, I'm watching for the flowers. Get ready, ace. Any second he'll be home."

"He who?"

"He shit. Hicks. Charlene's husband. Common-law husband, because he sure is that—common."

"So he's your real father?"

"Hicks? I'd kill myself first. Now, listen, downstairs, with the tuna fish?—"

"—Huh?"

"—the can of tuna. Downstairs before. Who tried the hardest to feed me?"

I think a second. "Well, your mother."

"No, of my two sisters, I mean."

"Well, Velma, I guess. That was Velma working the opener, right?"

But Alvy doesn't like this answer. "Velma's only twenty-seven."

"So?"

"Can't you subtract? That woulda made her thirteen. *If* she had me."

"Well, that's possible," I fake, although in fact I don't have the foggiest how old girls gotta be. "So who's the father?"

"*The* father. Like it was some dog . . . Whoops, here we go"—he shoves the binoculars at me—"That's him, Hicks. And he's lit, too. Aww, this is gonna be good, the big, stupid sonofabitch."

Pulling up in a shiny red truck Hicks jumps out in a dirty blue plumber's uniform. God, I recognize him. He's the clod Dad and me saw loafing on the couch that first night. But handsome, though, blond with a big forehead and big, furry blond eyebrows—actually, he looks a little like Tab Hunter, the TV actor. Also, in the light he's younger than I remember—younger than her, I think. Playing Dinky cars on the walk, Buddy doesn't squeal to see his Daddy, the kid totally ignores him, too. Hicks's voice sounds like short, hard coughs. Buddy starts kicking when Hicks picks him up but, running out with a beer, Charlene jollies him up—a little. With her hair twirled in a beehive and her eyes Cleopatraed, she's dressed up in jeans and black high heels, a tight white shirt knotted around her belly. Planting a big kiss, she gives him the baby, then pokes Audrey, who gives him a short, standoffish hug. Charlene seems different now—younger, almost teenagerish, her voice chirping on the loose windowpane. Back heaving, Hicks is still fuming at Buddy. Alvy jumps up, cussing.

"Where are you off to?" I ask.

"Whack off."

I think he's joking but no. Whipping a *Playboy* from under the mattress, Alvy's all business. "Bathroom's just down the hall. Call me the second the flower man shows, hear?"

And fast? Wiping his hands on his pants, Alvy must set a new hand-speed record. He's a new man. Over at Charlene's, meanwhile, they're all inside—eating, I guess. Buddy was none too happy about going inside. But when I tell Alvy this, he blows up, "So what do you expect me to do? Goddamnit, just cool your tool, man. The flowers are coming."

And speaking of tools, Alvy jams the crinkly, still warm pages of the *Playboy* into my trembling hands. Flopped upside down by a fire, it's bonnie Miss January! My first naked lady with all these nipples of tits of bosoms, so fat, so sassy I just know I'll die! Pistoning his fist and waggling his tongue Alvy motions me toward the bathroom.

"Aww, all right—go. And don't be splatterin' the mirror."

"What!" My head's a mushroom cloud.

"You heard me. No splatterin' the mirror. You got your cum, don't ya?"

"Yeah," I lie. "Some."

"Well, if you never had a *Playboy*, you better stick a bag over it. I'm serious! Man, you see them big, juicy hot jugs on her? Tits like those, man, you'll spray like a tomcat. Nine, ten feet—*at least.*"

"Okay!" I gotta bend over, the phone pole I got. "So where's the bag?"

"Huh?" Alvy's crouched by the window again.

"Gimme the bag! The beat-off bag!"

"The bag," he hoots. *"He wants a bag!"* Then he whirls around. "The flowers! He's here!" He snatches back Miss January. "Fuck that! Now, *watch—*"

The flower man rings the bell. Hicks answers. Shirttail out, Hicks is still chewing when the deliveryman holds out the fourteen roses wrapped in white paper. You'd think it was a dead cat. Arms up, Hicks backs away. He points down the street but, with a smile, the man flips the bouquet so he can read the card. Hicks snatches it out. The windowpane is rattling now. The delivery man's backing down the lawn and Hicks is hollering. He slams the door, and as fast is Charlene bolting out the back. Tripping, Charlene pulls off her high heels, screaming with Hicks right behind her, lashing her across the neck and face with the roses, "Slut! You whore! You fuckin' two-timing bitch!" That Charlene is a wildcat. Slashing at him with the spike heel of her shoe, she falls on her back, screaming and scratching and kicking at his balls. Her beehive batters open like the flower paper, in tatters. God, he's knocking the heads off the roses, lashing her until they're fourteen green whips. At freak high pitch, poor Buddy's bucking and running in circles. Audrey runs across the lawn, "Gramma! Grampa!" And all this time Alvy is just watching. Dazed. Absolutely in another world.

"What did you do?" I holler. "Just look what you did!" Alvy leaps up.

"Sonofabitch!" Alvy's embarrassed then. Reaching over his bed, he grabs down his .22—he snatches out a box of bullets from the nighttable, but I bat them away, bullets slipping like ball bearings underfoot as I grab the gun.

"Stop it! Alvy, are you totally nuts?"

Charlene's still screaming, so Alvy grabs his baseball bat, vaults down the stairs, then tears round the front, one step behind Mrs. Loomis who's waving, of all things, a fly swatter. It's like that day in the cab with the pervert. I just hang there frozen, thinking if I just calm down, that naturally they'll calm down. Then here's Mr. Loomis behind me, roaring and stumbling in his stocking feet.

"Goddamnit! Goddamnit all!"

"Outside!" I point. "A man's hitting some lady!"

"*Help*," cries Mrs. Loomis.

She's slipped in the mud. Tearing out the door, I find her flat on her butt, mud all down her back and calling after Alvy—who's crazy. Berserk, Alvy nails Hicks once good with the bat, but it's like nothing, like butter. Wrestling Alvy to the ground, Hicks grabs the bat, hurls it away, then rocks Alvy's head back with two short, fast chops. It's a riot. Next door a fat, beehived blonde woman is inside her car, blowing the horn. Neighbors yelling. Everybody's piling out to see, but then they stand there, all hollering at each other, "I didn't call the po-lice, did you call the po-lice?" And Beef—Beef is barking. Tearing hunks out of the grass with his claws, he's streaking around the yard worse than nutty Buddy, barking and snapping, as poor Audrey bundles baby Bramford screeching to the other house. Finally it's a standoff, Hicks practically crying, and Alvy's sisters screaming at Charlene, and Bunny yelling at Alvy, and Charlene screeching at everybody to leave off, then pleading to Hicks, "Honey, it's a lie, I don't know about any flowers!"

Really, it's over by then, but Alvy isn't finished—not when the bastard busted his Mom one in the mouth. Grabbing a cinder block from the garden, Alvy leaps on the hood of Hicks's new red truck.

"Hey fuckhead, you like this?"

"Touch my truck I kill ya, boy!"

"Touch it?" laughs Alvy. Turning the block endwise, Alvy drags it the length of his hood. "That's for you, you ignorant, coward wife-beater piece of shit!" And Beef, boy, Beef is baring his teeth. Beef is growling now, so Hicks kicks him. Bad idea. Raising the cinder block over his head, Alvy hurls it through Hicks's windshield. The air explodes.

"BOOM!"

My shoulder blades collide. Shucking out a shell from his 12-gauge pump gun, it's Lucky Loomis! Drawing down on Hicks without a word, he marches up on him, the barrel pointed straight at his head. Everybody's yelling now, Hicks, the Loomises, the neighbors. But at the last minute as the cops pull up, Charlene grabs Hicks, clutches him to her, then starts screaming at Mr. Loomis.

"Sonofabitch, I never shoulda come back here! Buddy! Audrey! Inside the house! *Now*—" Then Alvy grabs me.

"Go! Through the woods!"

CRASHING THROUGH the brambly, kudzued woods behind his house, Alvy looks back.

"Jesus, they might lock up the old man. They really might this time. God, he went apeshit."

"It's you they oughta arrest. And you knew, you bastard! You *knew* this'd happen."

"Not like this!"

"*HA Allll-veyyy*—"

It's Mrs. Loomis calling from the edge of the woods. Sweating and panting, Alvy's straining to see if they've carted his Dad off, but he can't for all the people. Brush cracks. A big cop yells out.

"Hey you guys! Come on out here now. Is anybody hurt?"

I'm not going to any jail! Hell no, I'm all set to give up when Alvy grabs my mouth. "Pussy out now and you can forget it." So we take off to a trash dump where Ad Altare Dei is all prepared, and then some. Under a hunk of moldy plywood, rolled in a plastic bag, he's got two mildew-stinking baseball shirts and baseball caps, which we put on. Then farther on, under a brush pile, he's stashed this old bike, all rusty and caked with mud, but the tires are pumped hard and the chain's oiled, ready to go. He's even got five dollars in getaway money wedged under the seat.

"Didn't know," I hiss, "you got your whole escape route laid out."

"I always got my escape route laid out, motherfucker." He's breathing hard, superpsyched. "Get on. Not sidesaddle, Maid Marian. Hop up here. *On the handlebars*."

The bike's got no fenders and no brakes, my balls suspended above the buzz-sawing front tire as he cranks down the mud path, skids down a rain culvert, then swoops down an embankment with these jackhammering ruts. It's killing my butt. Crashing the curb we fall down a whole high dive of streets blowing through stop signs, no lights, no horn and only his sneakers for brakes.

"Alvy, a car!"

Some poor slob about puts his face through his windshield, Alvy calling back through the gushing darkness, "*Fuckyooooooo*—"

The bottom's a killer, though. Alvy's pumping. We're swamped in the slop of our own gravity. We're splashing in our own blood. Wrenching up on the handlebars, cranking and straining, Alvy's wheezing bad now. And he's gotta drive himself like this—literally, he's gotta knock himself out. Head wedged into my back, Alvy's crying that fretting cry of feeling berserk, when you can't make the gears to mesh, or the causes to cause, or the sense to sync. So, shoving me off, he ditches the bike, which he stole anyhow. Then he starts pumping me.

"So what did you see?"

"I don't know, people going crazy." I grab his arm. "Alvy, you gotta go back. You don't, you'll just be admitting it."

He snorts. He honestly can't believe I'm this stupid. "But don't you see? *They'll never blame me.* That way they'd only be admitting it."

"That's sick—"

"That's not sick, they're protecting me."

"Oh, sure."

"You saw my Mom and my other sisters run out to protect me, didn't you? Sure, I stirred things up, but how else do you find out? You beat the bushes—experiment."

"*Experiment?* Get your sister beaten up and your Dad arrested?"

"Hey, *I'm* an experiment, I ain't nothing but a human petri dish somebody pissed in." Typical. He changes the subject. "Haw, man, did you see Hicks's eyes when he saw that twelve-gauge! And Dad woulda, too. Shot him. Goddamn, the only person Hicks is more jealous of than me is the old man."

"So whose father is he?—Hicks I mean?"

"He's that baby Bramford's father—he *thinks*. Hopes. And you saw how Hicks is with Buddy. God, he *hates* Buddy, hates him 'cause Buddy ain't his and 'cause Buddy loves me. God, Hicks is *soo* jealous of Buddy."

"Jealous? Of a little kid?"

"Sure of a kid. Men are insane on boys. Stepfathers especially, and worse if you're a big fuckin' baby like Hicks. He's only twenty-five or so, y'know."

"So how old's Charlene?"

"Way older. Near thirty."

Now I'm really confused. "So who's Buddy's father?"

But again I hit the wall of all this we-don't-talk-about-it stuff. I'm having to race to keep up with him, Alvy's eyes swarming out of their sockets. "Sooner or later, I'm gonna have to kill him—Hicks—you know that, don't you? Or he'll kill me, although—although—basically, that'd be okay. Seriously. Hey, it'd be worth it if it saved Charlene and the kids. No shit, I'd lay my life down for them, fuckin'-A I would, Buddy especially. Even Bramford, man—I feel sorry for the kid, I do. *Sorry?* It makes me weep. Like last Christmas? When I gave Buddy that big dump truck, then I sat there watching him play with it, and I was watching over him, like—like in, y'know, *in a trust?* What I mean is, *It dudn't matter.* Hicks gets me first, well, between my Dad or my brothers, either way he's fuckin' dead. And you saw Charlene. You saw how she looked at me, when I went for Hicks, right? Aww go on, sure you saw, *she knew."*

Knew what? It's like I've got the hiccups, only they're all questions. "But, Alvy, how do you know that your Mom—Bunny, I mean—so how do you really know, know for real, that she's not your Mom?" But as usual Alvy only bats this away.

"So how did you know your Mom was dying?"

"Well, if you wanna know I didn't. *Know*-know, I mean. Not for a long time, really."

"But yet she did die and what were you doing? Well, huh? Well, come on, you musta seen stuff. Warnings? Feelings and stuff?"

"Don't be pointing the finger at me. If you're so goddamn smart, tell your parents. Tell 'em you know."

"But I can't do that. Can't you see? God, it would kill my Mom if she knew that I knew." But when I ask Alvy how he's so sure Bunny doesn't already know that he knows—well, like an ostrich, Alvy's absolutely confident that she *can't* know, that nobody can possibly know that he knows, and that they wouldn't say boo if they did. And that's how things happen in his house. Flowers come, things explode . . . *and that's basically that.* And Alvy's always changing the story, changing it, I guess, on account of the story's forever changing on him. I can't follow it. Saving face, Alvy's saying he hopes his "experiment" will drive Hicks out. But when I remind him that Charlene only took the guy right back, well, Alvy says she only did that for the kids, did it so his Dad (I mean *her* Dad, Lucky)—so he won't get into trouble. Alvy says Lucky's had certain "trouble," which of course he won't specify.

And he's really out to sell me on Charlene. Alvy says she scored off the charts on the Civil Service Test, although she never has worked—here. Just like that Lucky could get her a cushy post office job, he says. Big bucks too— three dollars an hour—but she's too superior, what with her 160 IQ, the biggest in the family next to his. Alvy would say that. Me, I don't know how big mine is—IQ, I mean. Nervous, I ask Alvy, "Is that the test you take with the soft lead pencil?" and when he says yes, I'm scared he'll ask me mine, which obviously is pretty low, if nobody ever told me. Still, even if mine's sixty, I wouldn't let some big dum-dum beat on me. At least not if I was free, white and twenty-one.

Lights! A cop car passes, so we duck behind a wall. Then about five minutes later, we hear a big engine rumble. Alvy yanks me behind a fence as this big, jacked-up, blown-out car passes, this blister-purple, metal-flake tank, with blue-tinted windows, like the eye of a monster fly. It shakes. It rumbles, then, *whoom*, it blows back up the next street. "My twin brothers," says Alvy, "man, they are gonna *kill* Hicks for this. Especially for hitting Mom." I didn't know they were real twins. In fact, Alvy says they're best known as the "Two Flies" because that's how they'll swarm, say, if you break bad or mouth off to some girl, or double clutch or use glass packs or other greaser forms of blatant disrespect. Shoo Flies! As far north as Rockville, south to the Bethesda Hot Shoppes or even the Wheaton Mighty Mo, they've cut a swath, so bad that the Truly Bad send them Christmas cards, Alvy says. Steve could have been all-State in wrestling if he didn't smoke so much, and Scotty, man, Scotty alone can lift an engine block over his head!

"So ask Steve and Scotty," I say. Not having brothers, I guess I glorify brothers and all they could tell and do for you, but this only aggravates Alvy worse, he says it's so naive. Worse, when I say I'm starved, Alvy who wolfed down all the tuna and clam dip, Alvy acts like *I'm* a baby. Complain, complain, complain. But still Alvy takes good care of me, which is a part of the Code. Skulking down the road, he takes me to the Bob-Eat-Shop, this creaky-floored colored store on the edge of Taver-Shep, where the floorboards are mostly held together by the crusty dirt and everything's steeped in murky jars, pink pig's feet, slime-green pickles and beet-colored eggs like eyeballs. I want a hamburger, but Alvy says there ain't no time. No, he says, get a half-smoke, then sends me in because he's way too notorious and famous an outlaw to show his face. No half-smoke for him, though—the colored lady about dies when I ask her for two cans of tuna. *Opened*, but don't drain the oil. "Gwaaard, who it fo, honey?" she asks, "Yo dog?"

Back outside, Alvy's talking to this ambling bug-eyed black kid in a black sports cap. His acne bumps really show in the yellow bug light, and as he talks he nudges the dirt with his sneaker. Wimpy's his name and true to his name, he bums a cigarette and fifty cents, but gives Alvy all the latest rumors, screwing his neck around, saying, "Po-lice done drug two men off, what I heard. Sho did." Well, Alvy takes off, slurping tuna while he figures what next. He's right about the half-smoke, too, it makes my nose wriggle, it's so good, all gristly and popping out of its skin with sweet-smoked grease and barbecue.

"Man," I gush, "it tastes like ground up niggers it's so good." I'm only trying to cheer Alvy up. Really, it's like something Alvy would say, but Alvy's totally grossed out.

"Goddamn, you come down here, you eat their food, so have some decency, huh?"

"But I *like* their food. God, you only said 'nigger' a hundred times today."

"Yeah, but there's a time and a place."

What time? What place? But see, this just proves it—I really do have a low IQ. And Wallace's place, of course, well that's the perfect place to call them all niggers! And Alvy's crack about Hermes being dead—what great timing! What a laugh riot, I think, wondering can people like me raise their IQs? Well, I'm feeling worse and worse, and Alvy's all depressed, when suddenly he asks me, "Listen, when your mother was dying, so when exactly did you know? You knew for a long time, right?" *And he's fourteen?* I think. And he's a whole year older, but he doesn't even know this?

"You know what?" I say. "You've got a lot to learn yourself. And I'll tell you something else I saw. You liked watching Charlene get beat on, I sure saw that."

"*I couldn't move,*" he blurts out. "Not at first I couldn't. Hell, I don't know. Maybe it ain't Charlene. Sometimes I think it's Carol, because Carol never moved away." He's getting all agitated again. "Like last year? In the Fourth of July parade? I've always been in the parade with Dad. Every year since I was born. But last year I ran off so I could see him in the parade. *Apart* from me, you know? So I could just see him as Lucky Loomis the same as anybody else could. So—so I could see if he really was my old man and not a lic—"

"—and?"

He glares. "And it was like seeing Santa Claus? in a store as a kid? after you first know it's all a big fake, the reindeer, the chimney and all that shit."

"But maybe not," I say to make him feel better. "I mean, so just how old is your Mom? Like, I mean, women can still have babies when they're pretty old, right?"

"Aww, quit it! How old's she look? Fifty-five? *Sixty?* Four hundred and sixty? Old as Abraham's old lady, in the Bible?" He shoves me. "So say it, sonofabitch, *How old?*"

"All right—too old."

What'd I do? He staggers back into his own face. He's completely crying, and I'm hugging the kid so he can't see me *not* crying. And I want to cry with him—I try. Squinting, I pinch my ear hard, I pluck out a ball hair and picture you in your coffin—nothing. God, I know I'm lousy at it, love, but still I brother him and love the kid as best as I can. I hold on, I mean, and each time as he sobs, under the streetlight, in the wind, like two very blown-on flames, we both blur down to snuffed nubs of nothing. And that's all you can say about loving anybody, I decide. All you can say is you hung on, and he's so warm, Alvy is. Holding him, I can smell him breathing, but not like Poo or you're in the queers, but more in a dog pack way of licking wounds, when you can taste the wound and the taste is raw meat. Alvy spits. Wiping his face on his sleeve he's got his wallet out, which naturally I figure it's his lock of hair, when he grabs my hand.

"Shit! Are you crazy?"

Fresh blood's dripping down my fingers! He's gashed my hand with a razor blade!

"So you're throwing in with me?" he asks, then with a jab he cuts himself worse. "Cause, if you do, this is the easy cut, man. You throw in with me I swear to God I'll never leave you, *never.* But the deal is, if I need you, then you gotta swear—swear on your mother's grave—that you'll come. No matter when or where or how. No matter who gets fucked. Cause make no mistake, *people will be fucked.* Before this is over, people you love will be fucked, fucked bad, too. But hey, if you're gonna redeem yourself, *you can't help that.*"

The kid really knows how to inspire you, talking how we'll probably get our asses stomped and jailed and maybe even killed and how he believes in Valhalla, to give it some Pagan. It's a full Cross of the Cross ceremony—it's ten times the affair of Communion. First, we wipe blood crosses on our bare chests, then, turning in unison, we piss the Sacred Circle, so not even Death can come between us. Then, to cinch the deal and so there'll be no secrets, in a fury we both jack off. And there it is, the egg. In the moonlight, pants around his ankles, Alvy shows me his teeming white wad, smoking like somebody's breath and with my finger I touch it, all oily slick, then I sniff it as Alvy says, "Looky there, Ace, a million babies right there . . . " And finally, in case either of us dies, we exchange hunks of hair, and Alvy recites "The Belle Dame Without Mercy," because we're both Knights now. Knights with stuff to uphold and all this other grievously good shit.

After that, insane with happiness, we're careening down the railroad tracks when up jumps Hermes! The fire's brimming down in Hermes's fire bucket. Waving a table leg, the guy's totally polluted, calling us twenty kinds of motherfuckers. But once Hermes sees it's us, he's all tickled, cackling, "Well, well, well, gem'mens! Y'all find all y'all's Mammas yet?"

• • •

"LOOK!" CRIES GRAMMAW A FEW DAYS LATER. "He gave her all to the coons!"

I charge upstairs to the guest room—Grammaw's room now—where Dad's moved all your clothes to the spare closet. Eyes squeezed shut, Grammaw's got one of your old hankies wadded in her mouth, sucking on it like an oxygen mask. Not one hanger left. Dad's given every stitch to Mrs. Eppes.

"Call a cab!" she cries. "We're getting her back!"

"Grammaw, c'mon, I don't know where Mrs. Eppes lives. And even if I did, no cab'll take you there, a white lady like you."

Now, even Grammaw's not this crazy, but that doesn't mean she can't raise hell about it. "Boy oh boy, is your dear old Dad hot to trot now! Well, why else throw your mother out into the street? As if I didn't know what hanky-panky he was up to last Saturday—and here when you had me half sick with worry." (At Alvy's swell birthday party, she means.) "Don't you see yet? He's getting ready to bring another woman in here."

Which then, of course, she breaks down again, hanging on me like we're dancing, only she's sobbing. So let Dad have a woman, I think. Any woman would beat this. At least she'd be young—younger than Grammaw. At least she'd be alive. As for Grammaw, she may as well hug the bedpost as hug on me. There's a long mirror in her room, and whenever Grammaw and me do this "feeling" dance, I'll turn her around, so I can see my face in the mirror. *Well?* I ask my face. *So huh?* my face stares back. I glare. I grit. I hang my tongue out. *Well?—Huh?—Well?*—And you know what the old lady reminds me of? A hermit crab. Crawling out of her old, dead old lady shell, she's nothing but a hermit crab looking for another dead shell to protect her gummy little body, and that empty shell is me. Well, screw that. Time to call Alvy. Time for the old switcheroo.

And amazing coincidence. Barely am I gone than the doorbell rings.

"Alvy!" cries Grammaw. "Frank just left, honey! You just missed him!"

"So?" scoffs Alvy, giving her a big kiss. "Who wants to see Frank? Hey, what's the matter, Mrs. Slattery? You been crying?" So Grammaw tells him about Dad's giving away your clothes, and of course Dr. Loomis makes his usual prescription. "So have a drink. G'wan. Anybody would, all you been through."

Grammaw loves Alvy's bluster—the way the kid totally takes over. He's exactly like Uncle T.T. and the Croton men. Yeah, Alvy's got the knack, mixing the sympathy with the cream sherry, which Grammaw buys by the gallon, then funnels into Dad's cut-class decanter for these rare, festive moments that start about two minutes after Dad leaves. Still, even with the "truth serum," Alvy says she's one tough old nut.

"So Mrs. Slattery," he asks. "So, why'd your daughter only have Frank?"

"Well, Alvy!"—giving her little whoopee cushion bounce—"you only have as many as the good Lord allows. I know the good Lord only gave me one, my one, my only—" He cuts her off.

"—so Mr. and Mrs. Dougherty with Frank—they both, uh, *planned* it that way?" But hearing this Grammaw has a fit.

"No, they most certainly did not *plan* it, and this is nothing for a boy of your age to be thinking about! Dear me. My Julie was raised in a good Catholic home, a crackerjack home, and I can assure you she certainly ran one. As I'm sure your mother does."

Whack whack whack. And Alvy's such an asshole with his fishing—the bait's gotta be dead before he pulls it off the hook. "So it was *Mr.* Dougherty who only wanted one kid?"

"I told you, it was the Lord's doing!"

Whack whack whack. Doesn't faze Alvy. Grabbing her decanter for her, he dribbles out an eensy, then a weensy and a teensy. And still the kid's fishing.

"But Frank says his Mom used to run off mad in her car. Real early in the morning. Real sudden. Said she just used to blow off all upset." He waits. "Almost every month."

"Aww, Frank's just a big fibber, Frank's cracked. What does he remember of all that, a little boy? And you! My God, I've never seen such a fresh kid, forever dredging up things."

"Me?"

"Aww, I'm an old woman and who cares. They oughta take me out and shoot me."

"Or sell you to the glue factory."

"You're horrible." She swats at him, but really she loves it and Alvy lays on a big hug.

"Aww, c'mon, Mrs. Slattery, I'm just kidding ya out of it, is all. Hey, I think you're a *great* old lady."

And that's the trouble with Alvy. The kid never knows when to stop. The attic's also in Grammaw's room, and one day I find them having a teddy bear tea party. Looking like the Mad Hatter, Grammaw's wrapped in her sixteen scarves and necklaces, jewelry clattering off both wrists. Rag in hand, Alvy's shining these baby cups and saucers he's pulled from an old cardboard box packed in cedar shavings. I glare at Grammaw.

"Hey, what are you two doing? That's Mom's stuff, not yours."

Under her red nail, Grammaw pops a piece of cedar, whiffs it, then holds it out to me. "Smell it—umm, wonderful. It's real English bone china, Frankie"—she takes an imaginary sip—"F.A.O. Schwarz, buster, the best. And you know who gave these to your mother, don't you? Your Uncle Stephen, that's who. Cost him a fortune, too . . ." Yeah, yeah. To her, every Cracker Jack ring's the Hope Diamond, but when I turn the cup over, damn if it doesn't read "England" on the bottom.

"So who's this Uncle Stephen?" asks Alvy.

"He's my younger stepbrother—nephew, technically. See, *his* mother, well, really, my aunt, she took me in when my parents died. Well, my God, Stephen was a virtual father to Julie. Especially after poor Francis passed away, bless his heart. Oh, every summer Julie used to stay with Stephen in the Adirondacks. And in Rye—Stephen had the most beautiful house there. Oh, such trees he had. Real fruit trees. This was before Toody—" she snorts with disgust—"well, in those days, you see, his mother, my Aunt Mary, lived there with him."

Alvy's feelers go up. "What, no wife?"

"Divorced," I break in.

"*Frank,*" she scolds. You'd think I'd said "shit."

Alvy shoots me a cool-it look. "So Stephen and this Aunt Mary, they had Julie all summer?"

Grammaw glares. "*That's Mrs. Dougherty to you.*" (She's so full of it. Alvy's always calling you "Julie" when I'm not here.) Alvy tries again. "So this Uncle Stephen never remarried?"

A gay flip of the hand. "Oh, he had his—interests. He was one attractive man. Very. And he did finally. Remarry. And she can damned well rot down there, Mrs. Toody Goodshoes. But we won't go into *that*—"

"—Alvy," I break in, "his car hit a tree. Just a few months before Mom—you know."

"Shut your trap," snorts Grammaw. But the next second the room's dancing with sugar plums. "Aww, look at her dear little teacups! But wait, Stephen bought her a little silver service. Little matching spoons. Alvy sweetheart," she moans, "can you find Julie's dear little spoons?" Well, that's it for me.

"No, he can't find her dear little spoons. And all this junk is going back where it belongs—in the attic."

Alvy grins at Grammaw. "*All* of it?"

"Quit it! Grammaw, what is going on here? What's he got stashed?"

"Better *somebody* stash it," snorts Alvy.

"And mark my words, Frank," she adds. "Once your father brings some strange woman in here, she'll refeather her new nest! *And* you, my fine-feathered friend. Oh yes, you'll rue the day I leave."

I stamp my foot. "What is going on here? Damnit, what are you both up to?"

But at this the old bird "brrrs" and blows up her veils. And bloating out her cheeks, she looks at Alvy and Alvy looks at her and nobody knows a damned thing.

BUT AN ORPHAN LOST IS AN ORPHAN FOUND! I slam the front door and Mrs. Loomis comes running. Day or night the door's open. Mrs. Loomis actually gets offended if I knock. If I knock, it's like I'm saying I ain't family.

"Frankie!"

"Mom! So where's Alvy?"

Her jaw drops. "Why, he just now left. Not five minutes ago."

Amazing, these near misses. And Alvy was right about our not being blamed for the flowers. You'd think the Loomises would have found me out, or at least suspected me, as their Benedict Arnold—or chump. And at the very least you'd think they couldn't face me, but no, *they're grateful* . . . I saw the worst and I came back. Oh sure, I stayed away a couple weeks until things blew over. But when I came back Mrs. Loomis did a little dance.

"Oh, I thought you'd given up on us, honey! Oh, I was so mad that day, so upset. And all for flowers delivered by mistake! A stupid mistake from the florist—did Alvy tell you that? Well, fine. We know married people will have their tiffs—fine and good—but that Jerry Hicks, well, he has been told to go until he can learn to curb that awful temper of his. Because we absolutely will not tolerate such a temper, Mr. Loomis and me. And especially around those poor kids."

That's virtually all Mrs. Loomis said, and once she said it, that closed the whole subject. Well, c'mon. With eight kids you had to move on, she always said. Forgive and forget. And just like her—like all of them—even Alvy himself forgot, or at least a part of him did. Hearing his mother's explanation, nodding, Alvy truly looked satisfied, totally satisfied, that justice had been done. It was like Kennedy with those Russian missiles. He'd sent a bomb and now his arch rival was gone, meaning, in Alvy's mind, that he had rescued Charlene—that he was a hero. Sure, Charlene didn't admit it—yet—but eventually, she would, oh yes indeedy. And here is what, at the time, I could never fully grasp with the Loomises. Because no matter how free I was to open their front door, or their icebox, or help myself to Bunny's love, I would never overcome their clannishness. In fact, as I was soon to discover, the bigger the family, the bigger and more unfathomable that clannishness finally is. "I'll say one thing about you people," Alvy once said to me—us Doughertys he meant—"You people sure are excitable. Way too excitable." In saying this Alvy wasn't, for him, being particularly hysterical or accusing, and crazy as it sounded Alvy sincerely believed this. And looking at him I sincerely wondered which one of us, or which family, was the crazier, although, being relative, it was hard to tell. Yeah, relatives and families sure are that—relative. All relatively crazy.

I know I was feeling crazy with Alvy's relatives. Because once I made myself a sandwich and chewed the fat with Mrs. Loomis, well, by then it was time to get to work, scoping things out from Alvy's room. By then, it was getting on May, meaning long, sunny hot days where Charlene would waste half the day sunning herself in the yard between their two houses. Oh, sure, there was plenty of sun and privacy on the other side of her house. In fact, there was more sun there but no, I realize, Charlene *wants* her family to see her out here—wants to lay out right under their noses, the better so she can turn her back on them. And Charlene knows I'm watching, *Ladybug, ladybug fly away*. . . . Old Charlene, she has to know, undoing the spaghetti of her bra, then laying on her soft belly, so that her hiney kneads together, her little gold toe ring glinting in the sun. The sun's good for her, I guess. Good for fading bruises and those long, thin, peeling scabs where Hicks whipped her with the roses, *and it's all my fault*. I ordered the roses, after all. And, see, in a way, I *want* it to be my fault, to prove it's even in my power to seriously influence grown-up events. Still, looking at Charlene I do feel terrible, first fascinated, then just stupid—really, I never know what to think anymore, that is, if thinking even counts as feeling. And Charlene knows I'm watching her, right? I mean for me to snoop on her like this—well, I have to think I'm a really good person. Incredibly good, in fact. Really, I'm her bodyguard, but nobody could possibly know my secret love and how incredibly unselfish and true I am, a knight in arms and the Prisoner of Zenda. It's almost like those days after the funeral, when I was resuscitating you, Mamma. Desperately I've gotta warn Charlene—*of what?* Without delay I must tell her to be nicer to Alvy—*oh, sure*. Before it's too late, I must tell her she's got the wrong idea about me—*oh, really?*

God, she makes me so mad! Fine, so maybe she does have a brainiac IQ, but Lord is she lazy, flopped on her ladybug belly, letting her kids run wild. What a terror that Bramford is. Poor Audrey is forever having to chase him around—doesn't faze Charlene. When Charlene's not reading or sleeping or sunning herself, she's doing crossword puzzles. Whole books of puzzles. Genius ones, too, Alvy says. But one day when she leaves the crossword book out, I sneak down and take a peep. And look. Just like a kid will rip through a coloring book and never complete a single picture, not one is finished! Nothing fazes her. Take Buddy. Buddy lives on Audrey's every word, but then Buddy'll fly off the handle, "Shut up, Audrey! Leave me alone!" "Now stop that, you two!" cries Mrs. Loomis from the kitchen window. . . . *"Charlene!"* So finally Mrs. Loomis runs out, grabs Buddy and Audrey, then glares at Charlene. Forget it. Sulking, Charlene picks up her towel and strolls inside. There's an invisible line stretched across the yard, a feud line, but only Charlene's kids can cross it.

I always carry Necco wafers when I visit. Not because I'm pumping Buddy, particularly, but because I really like the kid, even though he's a total pest and a knucklehead. Buddy loves roughhousing. His favorite game is "El Kabong," where he leaps on my back screaming in his Zorro accent, *"Isss me, Elll Kaa-bonnnnggh!"* So I make like he's killing me, then I El Kabong him. Buddy's like a ball. I hurl him down on the bed, but with that crazy Loomis smile he only bounces back for more, and I just stare at him, at his goofy little crew cut with the whorly twist of hair at the peak—you can see exactly how Alvy must a been at that age. It's weird how I love watching Buddy now. Little kids, they're so goony, never knowing where they are, which is so beautiful. Fart all you want. Buddy doesn't sniff it. Life to him must be like a swimming pool where you forget which way's the shallow and which way's the deep. Don't ask me why the kid loves me so much. It scares me. Besides, I think, he should have kids his own age to play with, which even in Shepherd Hills you can forget it. No Mom's letting her kid anywhere near that nut house.

Buddy is such a little doofus, though. I'll get too rough, then he'll cry—then he wants you to rub his neck for him, and he looks so bravely, stupidly miserable that finally I hug him, which I'd die if anybody ever saw this. Still, if I ever had a little brother, I'd pick Buddy.

The kid's always after me to see stuff in his room, but of course that won't fly. "Your mother wouldn't like that," I probe. "Yeah, I don't think your Mom likes me very much." Buddy doesn't disagree. Another time I see a big bruise over his left eye, so feeling crazy I ask him, "Buddy, did your Daddy hit you? Did he?" "He's not my Dad," he says coldly. "Then who is your Dad?" I ask.

But at this Buddy only hunches up his shoulders—his version of the Loomis Wall—then he jumps on my back, *"El Kabonggghh!!"*

What am I watching for? I wonder. I swear I can't see what Alvy sees in Charlene, except he'll redeem her—assuming, of course, that Charlene even is the one. I really do feel sorry for her sometimes. Other times, though, I hate her for torturing Alvy, who can never stay put, and for Buddy, who can never leave, and for Audrey, who hates everybody and is so mortified about her family, and tired. And sometimes, Charlene reminds me of you, Mamma, especially when you got the sleeping sickness. Furious, I wanna bang on the window, *Goddamnit lady get the hell up.*

Alvy's made me learn by heart "The Belle Dame Without Mercy." I won't lie. I can barely understand the thing, or only in flashes, even though Alvy has told me twenty times what a "sedge" is and a "elfin grot." But, looking at Charlene, I completely understand the poem, because there's the Belle Dame, and here I am "loitering by the lake." *Loitering*—that's a funny-sounding word to use in a poem, like the signs Alvy always ignores. It really surprises me how a big-shot poet like John Keats would ever use such a crummy word in such a beautiful poem. Still, you never know, a poet like that. Keats might really have had a reason for writing the poem that way, maybe so the fancy people would be all annoyed and disgusted but still they'd keep looking. Anyhow, on account of that poem and Alvy, I've been writing more of my own stuff and reading—on our class "bookline" I'm second after Billy Winters, although Winters cheats, reading these lame series books instead of *The Red Badge of Courage* and *Twenty Thousand Leagues.*

Anyhow, getting back to the Loomises', I've looked at all Alvy's pictures and hair samples and stuff. Even blood. A while back Alvy went to pretty gross lengths to collect blood, which I won't describe. To Alvy, now it's all so juvenile and embarrassing now—the whole pretense of playing *detective* with his little police set and microscope. So, loitering, I'd sort of let a quarter roll out of my pocket . . . rolling across the hall, into Velma's room, beside Carol's. It's like something out of "The Three Bears," these two tiny, messy rooms with frilly Ward's credit furniture and the closets jammed with brand new clothes, half with their price tags still on—10 percent off, off of everything, for working at Ward's. And look, Velma, the youngest, has Alvy's picture sitting right on her desk! So she's the Mamma, I think. But then suing for the defense, I think, No, Velma feels she can put out Alvy's picture. And why? Because she's not the Mamma, that's why.

Now, of the girls, Velma is not only by far the nicest but also the best-looking and most stacked. Don't ask me why, but in big families all the kids, and the girls especially, get better looking the younger down you go. (Like soup tastes better the second day, the sperms and various female goos get more *organized* and *practiced*.) Anyhow, this law of descending good-lookingness definitely holds true with the Loomis girls. Lookswise, they run in exactly that order, beautiful, more beautiful, knockout. Now, Velma, by Charlene standards, Velma's not the world's brightest girl—at least not to Mrs. Loomis who measures everything. On the other hand, Velma runs the Ward's credit department—well, practically, Mrs. Loomis says, except for the dum-dum man who sits over her. Fact, Velma is Carol's boss—Carol who's older, who drives the red 'vette and goes to Acapulco and never saves a dime. Carol is *conflicted*, Alvy says. Carol, she could only marry a Catholic but she only loves Jewish men, who are second only to niggers in Mr. Loomis's book. Why, Carol had Jews who'd have set her up like a Heeb Sheena, Alvy said—men who didn't care that she couldn't have kids, they'd adopt! (See, Carol'd had a *hysteriaectomy*, maybe after she'd had him, Alvy thought.) One Jewish guy was even willing to convert but, see, that's the whole problem with Carol, because the more the men flip for her, the more Carol runs away . . . *like maybe she ran away from Alvy.*

So Carol was a definite—a definite maybe. But Velma, well, Velma I semi-ruled out as too young. Velma also had plenty of chances to get married. Chances! Men are crazy to date Velma, but it's like Velma has this polio of ever doing anything except watch the house and be nice—nice maybe to make up for Charlene and Carol both being so irresponsible.

Anyhow, finding my quarter rolled into Velma's room, I'd listen, then quick paw through Velma's drawers before I got a whiff of stockings or panties— then it was off again to the saltpeter mines. Alvy says he's gonna install a time clock in the upstairs bathroom. Oh my God. It's "winsome" Miss April with her two tumultuous Easter eggs going *bonga bonga bonga*. Then here's Mrs. Loomis calling upstairs, *"Frankie, your tea's ready!"*

AND HICKS? Between Mr. Loomis's drunk driving scrapes and Hicks's being on probation (some guy he cut up with a linoleum knife), well, they both were quick to drop all charges. Meanwhile, two nights a week—Mr. Loomis's VFW nights—Bunny takes the kids while Charlene slips off to see Hicks. It's amazing. Mr. Loomis had sworn to shoot Hicks on sight but, so he can save face, everybody in the family, even Alvy, will solemnly tell you that Charlene is out "shopping." I tell you, it's wormy as a Swiss cheese, that house. Everybody knows everything and everybody knows nothing, and all at the same time, too.

Then one night when I'm over, who walks in with Charlene but Hicks himself! The maniac doesn't recognize me, but he makes it a point to say hi to me and Alvy. Beef won't buy it, though. Alvy's gotta drag the mutt upstairs, he's barking and slobbering so bad, but me, I goon around like I haven't noticed. Well, I've got Hicks over a barrel. He's gotta be on his best behavior, and besides, Buddy is climbing on me and this Hicks definitely notices—no, Hicks marks me as somebody to reckon with. "Hey, Buddy, look what Daddy's got," says Hicks, pulling out a new Dinky toy. Big deal, a red '57 Chevy (Buddy already has one), but Buddy starts making car noises and playing with it, mainly so he can ignore the creep. Upstairs, meanwhile Alvy's clocking out of the bathroom, giant red sex hickeys all over his neck. You'd think Miss April would a calmed him down, but he lays right into me.

"What are you *doing* down there? Like I need you making the bastard feel any more welcome! And especially with the twins both pussying out on me!"

That was the other crusher for Alvy, the Flies leaving home for the army—and fast too, June 30, just after graduation. Super coincidence, says Alvy, the two of them enlisting in the airborne a week after Hicks goes nuts. Well, Lucky gives the Flies a twenty-one-keg salute at the VFW, but the truth is, they're both terrified of Hicks—which only goes to show you how it is with highly varnished reputations. Well, Alvy isn't scared. Outside their going-away party Alvy humiliates them both in front of everybody, calling them deserters and prize pussies and kicking in the door of their car. He's still got a black eye where Scotty creamed him.

"Alvy can't stand being left," explains Mrs. Loomis over tea. "Never could. My God, when he was a baby, it was always *'Where Mamma? Where Dada? Where Vel'? Where 'lene?'* If that kid didn't know where you were, he'd go to pieces."

GOING HOME I'VE GOT MY OWN LUCKY PIECE, a Dinky car from Buddy. An MG, too. It's Buddy's best car—brown, naturally—and Buddy gave it to me. Yeah, whenever I get to feeling bad or dirty, I feel Buddy's lucky piece in my pocket, and you see, Taver-Shep is almost the same for me these days. Sundays, pedaling up to Alvy's house, I always cut by Taver-Shep, wondering if I'll see your dress heading to church, perched on brown legs, in your Italian high-heel shoes. They're like the paper doll cutouts, your castoff clothes. Hold them over the air, the light, the dark, the anything. Because now they do go with everything. No matter what, the life shines through.

Now, in Taver-Shep, there's a little Baptist church, really a whitewashed house, with a big white cross stuck on the roof. In the summer heat the trees sway, and all up the road, like mirages, they come, big-armed colored women in wide hats and dark men in black suits and shirts so white against their black skin it actually hurts my eyes. It's like the first discovery of life. Feeling Buddy's car I'm always looking for this certain woman who's gotta be tall and slender, dark but wearing your dress in this other life. And who knows, I think, maybe this colored orphan kid Mrs. Eppes mentioned—so maybe he's inside the church sitting right beside this colored woman who's wearing your clothes, all of them singing so loud it blasts the barn pigeons off the roof.

God, I'm desperate to meet this colored orphan kid, but especially to *recruit* him myself—I mean without Alvy. But how? I wonder. Hermes, that's how. Because hobbling out of church one Sunday, here's old Hermes himself! No question about it. Even in the heavy black suit and sandals with the white socks, you can't miss the limp. Lord knows how many times Hermes been saved like this, late in the month when his VA check has run out. You've never seen anybody more serious than old Hermes when he's sober. Glowering on his sister's porch, he just sits there staring at the bridge, the temptation he fights all day. It's a shitty thing to do, but finally I sneak across, then call to him from the weeds.

"Please just tell me who he is. Or take a note to him."

You know he's scared I'll offer him money and knock him off the wagon. And, frankly, I'm scaring myself, fingering the two bucks in my pocket. But man, that Hermes is tough, hollering back like I'm the devil.

"Ain no such boy, and if they was I ain be tellin you!"

GRAMMAW SPITS AND SLATHERS MY HAIR.

"*He* knows what he's doing, huh?"

"Dad's just getting out." Don't think I never defend him. "Christ, you *like* Angelene. And leave off my hair."

"Come *here*—" Grammaw starts snatching at me again with the comb. "Yes, I *like* Angelene, but Angelene should have more sense, *chaperone*. Like anybody's fooled because it's at some women's club—I wonder what the *club* ladies say about adventuring. That's right, adventuring. That's what it was called in my day, and they called it worse, too. Look, mourning's full *year* for men—for obvious reasons—and two at least for women. Well, at least for women of the better kind. Chaperoning, huh. So who's chaperoning them?"

I jerk away. "Are you finished?"

"Boy, am I finished. Like I told your father, my bags are packed."

"Frank, come on, we're late—"

It's some big to-do at the women's club—Angelene's idea, not Poo's. And the minute Dad and me step out, all suited up and reeking of cologne, I can see Grammaw's right—on Corregidor, it's a dead giveaway on a Friday summer night, and when Dad knocks on Angelene's door—well, forget it. All up and down Corregidor and Midway, people are piling outside or at their windows to see. You'd think it was the Resurrection, Dad publicly declaring, *I'm alive, I'm back.*

"Pete! Frank! Well, look at you two."

Dad's balls fly up into his throat. Bosomed out in black patent pumps and a gusher of red silk, it's Angelene with those big, kicky legs of hers. Ordinarily, Dad gives Angelene this flinchy bow of a kiss—a tortured virtue thing—while Angelene does the grasp-quick, a divorcée deal, like *she's* afraid *he's* afraid she's got homewrecker ideas. Who knows who starts it? Squeezed into the foyer, Angelene spooks him. Bumps him. Maybe accidentally kisses him, but it's through the roof on the Poo-O-Meter. Poo, in this white, woofy thing with patent pumps, Poo's looking at me like I better screw things up quick before it's too late.

Meanwhile, in her red and yellow muumuu, silver Navajo bucklers on both wrists, Nellie Belle's having herself a titter fit. Poor Nellie Belle's a wreck, bringing them two tots of rum, then shooing us out the door where the whole street is waiting, camped out on stoops and hosing down their lawns.

"Here, Pete." Angelene points to her brand-new, sky-blue Coupe de Ville. "C'mon, Pete, let's take mine."

Dad looks at her famished, *Sure baby I can drive.*

But shoot, Angelene's not surrendering the keys to him—any man. Swishing around, she opens the passenger door for Dad, *I'll drive.* It's cruel. It's like not cranking the window down for a dog, not letting the man drive. Worse, Dad's got nothing to do. As Angelene swings her legs in, it's all Dad can do not to slobber over her dimpled knees and stout calves squeezing in with that soft unzipped sound of butt-stretched silk on sticky new leather. Me, I'm crowded over on the far corner and Poo's desperate to go, telling Angelene don't put down the top because it'll mess up her hair, besides which it's so *pretentious*—Poo's new pet word. God, do these new leather seats stink. They didn't scrape all the meat off, I don't think.

Look, I know I probably sound like a total nut, always seeing coloreds everywhere now. But sure enough, as we hit the 4-H with the big white columns and the flags—well, on the lot, under the pink and green paper lanterns, there's a whole congregation of coloreds parking the cars. Cadillacs and Lincolns like you wouldn't believe. And as for the girls, forget it. In their glitter shawls, arm in arm with their Mommies and Daddies, they clip right by you, and to dance with them they've bussed in these bullet-heads from some military school—them and these prep-school dicks, all congratulating themselves how they go to *Choke* and schools nobody's even heard of.

But wouldn't you have lapped it up, Mamma! Inside especially, with that rich, used-up old dark of brass lamps spurting gas and sooty paintings and these Chinese rugs your shoes glide over like butter. And more coloreds, this old Cream of Wheat guy in a shiny tux whispering to Dad can he take the ladies' wraps? Dad's smooth. He slips the guy a whole buck, but with a frozen half smile—right in front of everybody—the guy slides it right back. What, it's rumpled? Mortifies the hell out of Dad but then I see why. Down at the end of the table, her silver glasses hanging on a diamond chain, it's this old bird glaring at Dad—like Lincoln never freed the slaves. Well, I glare right back at her, then look at the colored man, *Hey I ain't like these rich creeps*. And Angelene sees. "Well," whispers Angelene, "I should hope you're not impressed by all this highfalutinness." She winks. "Not that I don't like it. But heck, you feel good about yourself, so you should like it, too, Frank Dougherty. You lak the good life, doncha? Cause you remember somethin tonight. Your Mom was as classy a lady as I've ever known. And you, you're just as good and as smart and good lookin' as any kid in here. *Any* of 'em, y'hear?"

But see, this only confirms it, Angelene's having to say we're just as good. And if that's not plain enough, here's Angelene pushing us up to be *introduced* to this bigwig woman tugging on my pinky, saying how delighted she is, when she can see Dad and me would be better off fixing her boilers. But this just starts Angelene fussing at me again.

"Franklin Dougherty, now just you look at all these cute girls in here. Now, you get on out there and *dance*."

Well, good luck! Dangling off each girl's glove, like a bracelet, there's a little book with a tiny gold pencil so you can sign up—*in advance*—so her Mamma can check your pedigree. The band stinks anyhow, so I drift around, my shrunken pants riding up as I yank them down. When here in a clutch of girls, like in a ballet, here's this real tall incredible blonde *but is she too old, is she?*

It's like a slap, she's so beautiful, all pale in the darkest dress. She's got the longest, throatiest neck and the most beautiful clean little ears. And buds, boy. Real startled nipple buds and big lips and a locket around her throat and these French buckle shoes that you can bet cost fifty bucks. Really, I think it's impacted my balls, all the pressure on me these past few months. I mean, I haven't even *noticed* girls my own age, but here I go, staring at her like a fool when she catches me looking and I spin around, *damn*. And she's dancing! Man, the guys are lining up for her, while I watch the electric punch bowl splurt green sherbet, thinking, Dance, Don't dance, Don't be a idiot, 'cause *you'll never be back here anyhow.*

Then way across the room I see Dad all by his lonesome. Looking real rocky, too, thinking of you. With Angelene Dad can half fake it, but once she gads off, Dad's face collapses into horror, like logs in a fire. You know Dad's bad off, because when he sees me he grins and comes right over. For a minute it's like old times. Flipping a look at this stuffed shirt, Dad jokes, "I'm just dying to ask him, 'Say, old chap, might a fellow borrow your jumper cables?' " Well, I crack up. And looking at Dad just then, it hits me how damn handsome he is. And decent. I mean if you just met him, you'd think, What a good guy! And right now I can see this, but I also can see how tomorrow, or ten minutes from now, I won't see anything good in him—nothing. And it won't die! Even when I think I've accepted it, that this is just how we are now, even so here's that old dead kid dying to tell him, *But I'll love you Daddy I can be your wife for you Daddy.*

When here's Angelene back. Back in a flush, too. Wanting Dad alone, Angelene's fussing at me, "Now *go*. You find a girl or I'll find a girl for ya."

So let her have him. I'm racing toward the doors when I see her again—the blonde girl—and she's on fire in the lights. I know, I'll play a joke on her, I'll sign her card—*then leave*. That way after Alvy and me are both famous dead poets and she's an old lady, the card'll tumble out and she'll think, *So that was him.* And even as I barge up, inside, to class myself up, I'm spewing all this wild, spontaneous poetry, *Oh you love-sick knight-in-arms so woebegone o'er the purpled mountains' majesties . . .*

"Here," I say, "may I sign your card?" Then, before she can say no, I grab her wrist, whip off my name super ridiculously large, then turn away when I feel her hand on my shoulder.

"Well?"

I about fall over. "So, it's now? You mean we dance now?"

Her girlfriends are scowling at me, I'm acting so rude and crazy. But with a little sigh, she lays her face on my shoulder and we start to slow dancing and it's so beautiful and old. It's like we're married, both swaying through whole tunnels of light, and then it's dark, then it's light, and then it's darker. I stumble I'm so rusty. There's little microscopic hairs on her neck. There's little lighty twigs tied in her hair, and in the lights, she's so magnified, so warm and alive, that I'm trembling, listening against her like a wall, when she says, "Frank?" and I jump *how's she know my name? Cause you wrote it on the card asshole.*

"Obviously, you've never been here before."

"*Obviously* not."

"I didn't mean it like that."

"Oh, obviously."

She pulls back. "Gee, don't take it so personally. I know I've seen your mother before."

"Well, that'd sure be news," I grin. "Yeah, that'd be the news of the century."

"I have," she insists, "I've seen her here with your sister."

"Well, if you mean that woman over there, that's not my Mom. That's our neighbor, Mrs. Pettinelle."

"But that is your father, isn't it?"

"Him? Yeah, that's the old man." Figuring she'll only dump me, I say it real Alvy. "Hey, thanks alot for the dance."

"But wait. If you don't mind my asking, so where's your mother?" God, it always stops me cold, the idea that you can be dead but still a real name, that you can still be living in language like in an iron lung. Everybody's clapping for the song. Again she tries. "So, your Mom's home sick?"

"Good guess. Yep, that's it. Home in bed."

She glares at me. "No, she's not."

But how's she know this? I wonder. "Well, you're right," I say after a second. "She's dead but look here. As far as Mrs. Pettinelle and my Dad go, it's okay—socially okay. It's been a year. Over a year, okay?"

"Only a year? But that's no time at all."

"Oh, yes it is. A year's fine. *Perfectly okay.* Check it. Any etiquette book."

She stands there blinking. "What are you even talking about? I meant it's no time for *you.*"

"Look, Miss, when you say a year—well, maybe that's no time for you. But to me, it's like five hundred years ago. It's like the Ice Ages."

"Oh, come off it. You know you don't really feel that way."

"*Feel?* Hey, you don't know the first little *thing* how I feel."

Well, that's it! Heart blowing out my chest I roar off, off into the Men's, my face blazing in the mirror, *She's so beautiful.* God, I wish I had some zits to pick instead of freckles, but instead of I can just stare at myself in peace, here's some poor old colored man. *In the craphouse.* In a tuxedo, no less. Vitalis, talc and cologne line the ledge over the sinks. Step up to the basin and he flips on the taps. Even if you're a kid, he flaps you out a nice fluffy towel, then presents it to you, like a king.

"You gonna wear that mirror out," he says to the wall. His eyes won't look at you directly, except indirectly, in the mirror.

"Sir," I ask, patting my pockets. "I feel like a real asshole, but—"

"Go on, man. You doan owe me nothin."

"Well, thanks, but—but can I borrow a squirt of your Vitalis there?"

His face lights up. "Uh-oh, you see sumpin outside there, huh?"

Drake's his name. And what a good guy, giving me a mint and even a free slap-off with his hand broom. Shaking his hand, all glad and ashamed, I blurt out, "Hey, Drake, you know I don't belong in here. Not in a joint like this. No, it's true." But Drake only does his low, slow laugh, *Come on man you white.*

And the minute I turn my back, back outside, here's Dad dancing with Angelene, saying he can't marry her! My blonde's busy, too, dancing under the lights with this kid in gold cufflinks. So I give him a tap to cut in. The kid smirks.

"Sorry, pal, that's not done here."

Prep school prick! Well, I wait but after she loses him, before I can even explain, she runs over to her mother on the other side of the room, and I'm so desperate I charge over and introduce myself. Mrs. Bayard is her name and she's blonde, too. Silver blonde with a smooth round forehead and this crinkly Chinesy-type dress that trembles when she talks. And *rocks*, boy. Mrs. Bayard's got two and three fat rings each bunched on both her fingers, diamonds and sea-green emeralds and filigrees. We both hit it right off, too. The girl's doing daggers at me, but her Mom's not a bit stuck-up. In fact, Mrs. Bayard's incredibly easy to talk to, and really interested in me. Man, do we get to gabbing, mainly talking about these two pictures. *Paintings*, Mrs. Bayard gently corrects me. Actually, this one picture—*painting*—well, it's been bugging me all night. Not that I couldn't have looked on the brass plate, I guess, but it really looks like that picture of John Keats's girl Fanny, Fanny Brawne, which Alvy showed me in the Keats book. So, like I know this Fanny, I tell Mrs. Bayard, "*Y'know Fanny Brawne? the girlfriend of John Keats the famous poet who died of consumption—well, TB today?"* Mrs. Bayard has the smartest, most curious eyebrows, which curl up when she talks to me. Really, I'm not showing off but she is super impressed, especially when I tell her I write stories and even poems now and again. Lately, I really do think I'll be a writer.

"Well, Frank," says Mrs. Bayard in that polite way she has of guiding you like you thought of it yourself, "wonderful talking with you, but clearly you're here to see Jessica, not me." Jessica! Until then I don't even know the girl's name.

"Oh, Jessica," I ask all nonchalant, "Jessica, would you care to dance?" But then dancing me off, Jessica lowers the boom.

"One dance, then bye-bye."

"Look, Jessica, I'm sorry. I've just been real touchy lately."

"And grossly rude."

My eyes fill up. "Jessica, you're the only girl I've asked to dance tonight. You're the only one I even *wanted* to ask, but if you wanna forget it—well, fine."

But, pulling me back, Jessica nestles her face into my shoulder. In the light blobs, we drift and we sway. Then, on account of the three-song rule, Jessica says we gotta cool it for a dance or two. And you know the love game . . . she frowns and I get mad, then she consoles me, and I glower so she can fuss over me, then she pulls me by the hand, to the punch bowl, where I dip her out a cup. God, I just stare at her. At her bottom lip with the tuck in the middle, the tuck where the lipstick collects, and how her lip sticks to the glass, and Jessica is so funny, taking these proper little sips. Mugging into the cup with a giggly sneeze, she asks, "What are you staring at?" *"At you,"* I say and she says, "Quit. Quit!" and her voice gets all hilariously high, *"Quit staring, Mr. Rude."* And wisps away her hair to watch the other girls all watching us. Secretly, Jessica squeezes my hand, then troops off to the Ladies' with her girlfriends, Sarah, Gerda and Alice Mayhugh. Alice Mayhugh is such a riot. Alice Mayhugh is one of these horsy, maid-in-waiting girls who really know how to talk to boys, and the more the boys don't ask her to dance, the more zany and fearless Alice is, hissing in my ear as they leave for the Ladies'.

"So do you feel your ears burning tonight? Jessie's always had weird tastes in boys."

Laughing, I call after her. "Weird tastes in friends, too!"

When here's Poo, warning me under her breath, "You're just setting yourself up, you know."

"Me? What's the matter? None of these bullet-heads wanna dance?"

But Poo's staring straight at Dad and Angelene. "Frank, I hate to break this to you, but just look where you are. Do you see this place? Look, I'm not being snotty, I'm just telling you the facts. Frank, my mother's a Ph.D., and my grandfather argued cases before the Texas Supreme Court. Not that you're not nice people, but in certain circles, Frank, these things mean something. You think you and your Dad can just waltz in here and instantly belong?" I hurl out my arms, ta-dah—

"Well! here we are!"

So let her barge off, calling me pigheaded and ignorant, when obviously Mrs. Bayard thinks I'm totally charming. So be jealous just because something good happened to me finally! And here's Jessica's back, so I sign her card. Man, I sign the whole thing, then dance her into the last, hot crush of time's running out.

"That's three dances," she teases.

"And they can all go to hell!" I about whoop it at the ceiling.

Nuzzling closer, Jessica asks me, "So how did she die?"

Have you ever cracked a peppermint Life Saver in the dark? Have you cracked it so hard that you see the sparks and taste the burnt flint of your own teeth? Stupidity, I say, she died of stupidity, but wait, Jessica says, you can't die of that. Oh yes you can, I say, they should have written STUPIDITY on her death certificate. Jessica holds me even harder, and I can feel her sweating through her thin dress, so close I inhale all the stray hairs on her head, and the perfume. Secretly, under her hair, I'm tickling the groove of her neck, tickling her like a colt, saying it's all right, when cymbals crash and the lights come on! *And that's all? And that's all there is?*

It's like we've been asleep, Jessica and me. We're both still waking up, when here's Angelene and Dad, then Mrs. Bayard with Mr. Bayard—Dr. Bayard, rather. "He's so inquisitive," Mrs. Bayard marvels to Dad. "Look, maybe Frank can come over for lunch sometime soon." They're serious, too. Dr. Bayard gives Dad his card, but Dad just stares at it like they stuck him with the check. Thank God Dad doesn't whip out his card with the boiler on it.

"Jessica," I say outside, "quick, gimme your phone number." I don't take any chances either—I have her write it on my hand. Then, of course, here's Dad cramping my style, and here when I know I could really make out with her.

Forget the drive back home. Once back at Angelene's, Dad and Angelene are like a bomb ticking—a make-out bomb. Poo runs inside and I go straight down the street, to our pumpkin. Hey, I don't look. I don't even care but Dad must not get anything, because he's in a foul mood, then an even fouler one when he sees Grammaw spooking out the front window. I should know better than to ask.

"Dad, can I please see Dr. Bayard's card?"

"Let's get one thing straight. You're not dating. Not at thirteen years old, you're not."

"Oh, come off it. Since when is having lunch dating?"

"Reee-ally, you must drop over."

"Aww, quit it. That's just you, automatically thinking they're stuffed shirts. And Dr. Bayard gave you his card, didn't he?"

"He sure did, and I put it right where it belongs—in the trash. Man, it's in the genes. Show you the free buffet and just like her, every time, you're drooling over the lobster!"

"Yeah, and just who the hell are you talking about? *Who?*"

He butts the door open. "I just buried a fool. I'll be damned if I'll raise one."

"Fool's right. She married you."

"I'll pretend I didn't hear that."

"Well, don't pretend I didn't mean it."

And didn't I just say I'd be hating him in the next breath—didn't I? Well, fuck you, buddy, because here's the phone number written right in my hand. Jessica Bayard, OL2-9609.

OH, DAD APOLOGIZED, AS FAR AS THAT WENT. Dad said it

was in the heat of my antagonizing him, but it didn't change the facts or stop what Angelene had set in motion. Because a year or no year, neighbors or no neighbors, like it or lump it, Dad had finally decided. Dad was gonna date. By damn, he was gonna have himself a life again, he said.

Not with Angelene, though. Not that Dad wasn't sorely tempted, and not that he didn't invoke the church—over the real reasons. So Dad went on a crash diet and sit-up binge, bought a new suit and, thank God, quit cutting his own hair. Once, to be legit, he tried the Catholic Adult Fellowship, this overgrown teen club for losers, but I knew he didn't want any part of Catholic women—regular Catholic women. I mean he'd married you, hadn't he?

Look, back in those days they didn't have all these health spas and fake college courses, these dating services and online "rooms" where guys and gals can raunch it up. Fix-me-ups, sure, but it was still too early for that stuff to kick in—if it ever would kick in, all the distance Dad had put between him and your old friends. So Friday night was Arthur Murray, "the dime-a-dance," Grammaw called it, while Saturday was the Officers' Club at Bethesda Naval

Medical—"The Homewreckers' Ball." And soon Dad had a whole slew of women phoning him. Like I say, Dad was real good-looking, so meeting women was no problem. Meanwhile, I'm not complaining. Because while Dad's working on his mambo, Grammaw's usually asleep, meaning I get to run wild with Alvy. As for the rest, you sure can't say life isn't interesting. Every time the phone rings, Grammaw wants me to get it, and no wonder, a kid my age being about as romantic as a toilet plunger.

"Is it that belly dancer woman Ranneeesh?" hisses Grammaw. "Don't hush me. You want some goat eater for a stepmother?"

But pulling the phone into the closet, horrified and titillated, I chat up these fortune-tellers, wondering which holds my future.

... Oh, I've known your Dad for years ...

... No, your father and I just met a week ago, actually ...

... Well, aren't you saucy! No, my dear, I've never been married ...

... Where from am I? From Persia. Do you know from Persia? ...

REMEMBER EDDIE BEMIS? Eddie with the Shanghai-bomb Mom who Dad, saronged in a wet towel, all but frenched at Christmas? Eddie was famous now, on account of his brother Ronnie, the muscle man who used to beat on him—well, a few weeks ago, Ronnie hung himself off the basement rafter on a length of electric cord. Were we shocked. We thought Ronnie Bemis had just committed straight hari-kari, like they'd written in the papers. But drunk and retched out tonight, when Alvy drags Eddie back from the Beyond, Eddie breaks down and says Ronnie had had his dick out when they found him hanging. Only Eddie saw it, his Mom being too hysterical. Just before the cops came, Eddie took care of it. Steady Eddie. Eddie put it back in for Ronnie, then zipped him up.

All this stuff came out during the Black Jump, which Alvy says is like that sodium pentathol the Commies use—at least for certain kids. In fact, it's my Jump next, and Alvy, of course, Alvy's the Jump-master, wearing his trophy German helmet with the bullet hole through it where Lucky greased the Kraut owner. The helmet's huge on Alvy's head. In the darkness, it's like a giant bell where the sound megaphones, and the two dark holes are his eyes, and the darkest, in the middle, is the bullet hole. Anyway, Alvy's leaning over Eddie, now in a heap, in the high weeds with the moon on his face.

"I don't want anybody to know!" wails Eddie. He keeps smoothing his right hand over his shirt where he puked. Weird. It's almost like he's still iron-ing.

"And nobody will ever know," insists Alvy, but this is pretty dubious, the rejects we've collected here for my first meeting of the OBC—the *Orphans and Bastards Club*. There's Billy Plumber, whose Dad shot himself and Billy saw him, and Bobby Penny, who was adopted but he heard his Mamma is alive in Texas, and Richie Henson, whose Dad never came back from Korea, and this obnoxious Goerstner kid, whose Dad flew B-17s but he's on wacko disability, living at home—only nobody's home, if you know what I mean.

There's nine of us tonight. We're all at the old abandoned Waverly Sani-tarium, which you can reach by walking the tracks down from Taver-Shep, down to the old overgrown railroad spur, then down a tree-lined, crumbling old road. Way back when, Waverly Drive must have been one beautiful nut house, what with the oak trees, but now the old asphalt's breaking up like burnt gingerbread, filled with dead cars, cinder blocks, smashed bottles, dumped refrigerators and old sofas frothing out their stuffing. Nobody comes here, not even the older teenagers, it's so buggy and nasty. They say the san-itarium's been shut down since at least the war—World War II. Kevin Billings says he once had an uncle here, and I'd say so, judging from Kevin. Behind us the scaling white columns of the sanitarium look like giant dinosaur bones. Upstairs there's bars in the windows where they kept the real loonies, and from a limb, a woman's dress blows above an old pair of pumps—a hex we rigged to keep people out, plus we've pissed everywhere and strung army-surplus wire tied to junk that'll rattle if anybody even touches our perimeter. Trigger-happy Alvy, though, Alvy keeps hearing things. Worse, he's also on about his fourth bottle of Micrin, the crème de menthe of mouthwashes, and some potent shit, too.

"Ssshh!" he cries, "hear it? Whass that?"

Alvy whips out that damned pistol of his, a Hungarian 9mm automatic that mysteriously disappeared from his Dad's cache about a month ago. Alvy's wrapped the butt with rubber bands so it won't slip down his pants—a po-lice trick he learned from some cop at the VFW. The gun throws a flame a foot long.

Goerstner gets serious. "Loomis, you lunatic, put that thing down before you shoot your dick off!" Goerstner is the world's greatest needler. He sends Alvy up a wall, especially that pig-grunt laugh of his, *Erruhh uhhh uhh.*

"Ssshh," orders Alvy, "I just heard it again."

"Guess so, wearing that potty on your head, you psycho. *Errrhh. Errhhh Uhhuuh—*"

Man, what a mess it is trying to start a club, especially with assholes like Goerstner—him and alkie fuckups like Andy Dorman, who's been on his hands and knees since the chicken fights. No, you can see why Alvy's ready to disband the OBC. Tonight, Alvy even supplied refreshments—fifty bottles of Micrin, which is brand new. Now, there's youth enterprise for you! When that introductory free sample of Micrin hit Alvy's mail, Alvy grabbed his old *Evening Star* sack, then went house to house collecting people's free bottles. Micrin miniatures, man! One bottle and you're happy. Three and you're a gibbering idiot, and each sample carries a card that reads, *Smokers! Tell us in twenty-five words or less how you like Micrin and you could win a year's supply of your favorite cigarettes!* We want to write back, *Dear Mr. Micrin, I just love the minty new taste! It's as good going down as coming up! And once I barf I'm all minty fresh to kiss my date!*

Mostly I've been faking drinking, scared about my first Black Jump and worried about Eddie, when Alvy barks, "Dougherty, snap on and stand in the door"—paratrooper lingo meaning *get ready to jump.*

But then Alvy really throws me. He's got an old picture of you, Mamma! You're fourteen, maybe, standing by this old-time white roadster. Wait. There's a man, too. Alvy snaps his lighter. It takes me a minute, but then I see who it is—your Uncle Stephen. But that's all the farther I get. Next thing I know I'm spread-eagled against the big oak tree with Alvy butted up behind me. We're approaching the DZ—the Drop Zone.

"I knew it, you lying bastard! You've been rooting all through our attic! You and Grammaw!"

"*Stand in the door.* Concentrate. On the picture. Because it's *her,* man. See, she was just a girl then." Alvy shows it around to the other kids. "Look how beautiful she was, y'all. Young. Innocent. Hey, *I* woulda gone for this girl."

"God, she was pretty," marvels Bobby Penny.

"*Fifteen deep breaths,*" says Alvy. "And *one*—And *two*—Deeper! Count with me, man. . . . *four*—DEEPER—"

It thunderstormed earlier. The storm drove out all the gnats and mosquitoes, so we'd set off our smudge pots, oil-soaked rags that still choke the place in fumes. The smoke burns my throat, but leaning against the tree, I huff and push out. After ten big breaths, the air's all swirls. At fourteen, the frogs are screaming. At fifteen, my legs are wobbling worse than Elvis—then at the last second, I hold my breath and Alvy bear-hugs me. My head explodes! A torrent of red and gold explodes out my neck, and I fall and I fall forever, then crumple like a clod, and they all stare at me, a dead heap in the trampled-down grass. A circle of boy faces, all staring down at me, *so that's how it looks so get a good look.* Alvy really has to take charge then or else they get nasty—black your eyes out with grease, yank down your pants, even stuff your mouth with dirt. And why? It's because in that dead state, and because of who they are, they hate you then, looking so pitiful and powerless and stupid. Alvy hauls me up by the arms. I can see his Cyclops eye, and it's so beautiful, all the stars and the dark. I swear I can hear the wind whistling through the bullet hole in his helmet. And Alvy's so proud of me.

"You did it, man. You went deep. *Really deep.* Did you see her?"

I don't wanna seem stupid or ungrateful. "Yeah! But just for a second."

"But how old was she?"

Everybody's staring at me. But then the answer comes, *"I wasn't even born yet."* And Alvy likes this answer. This answer is excellent. All excited Alvy says, "But see, you were just an egg, an egg." Right then it reminds me of these pictures—paintings—they have up at the pharmacy, *Great Moments in Medicine,* Dr. Alvy looking around at all his students.

"Don't you see? This is *basic biology.* A girl when she's born, well, in her belly, *as a baby,* she's got every egg she'll ever have. So, when you see a girl—any girl, even a bitty baby—well, inside her she's got every egg that she'll ever make, every egg and all the life in her that she'll *ever have.* Which means"—Alvy's brain's going a gazillion miles an hour—"which means that even before you're born, you were always there with your mother. You were always there and you felt and knew *everything. Well?* Do y'all get it?"

Billy Plumber starts laughing wildly. "Wait! So, like, I got all the sperms in me I'll ever have?"

"Fuck no," sneers Goerstner. "You ain't got a one, jacking your peter in school all day. Ever seen this asshole? All day long he's frigging himself. *Err-uuhhhh.*"

Alvy waves his arms. "Listen, you cretins, I'm making a point! Men *make* their sperms but, with their eggs, women always *have* theirs."

"Bull!" they boo. "Bullshit! Boolashit!"

"No!" he cries, his arms upraised like Moses. "Listen, Frank. What I'm saying is, *you were there.* When all the bad shit happened to your Mom, *you were there, pardner.*"

I stop dead. "What bad shit?"

"Well, whatever happened to her."

"When what happened? Goddamnit, what did Grammaw tell you?"

"Nothing! I'm talking bare instincts, man."

"Drunk instincts," needles Goerstner.

But Alvy doesn't waste time arguing with Goerstner. No, Alvy has other souls to tend to, kids babbling and crying as he goes down the line, bear-hugging each one into a groaning dazed heap. Alvy *is* a doctor, I think. Look, the doctor slapped you alive as a baby, but the doctor couldn't explain to you that *this was life.* The doctor couldn't tell you that this was the life you'd got, and the parents you'd got, and all the breaks you'd got, or ever would get, because the *breaks*, man, these are the boy eggs. Very few people, even adults, can explain this science but certain great kids can, I realize. No, there are certain kids who are *Doctors of Life*, and Alvy Loomis is just such a deep kid. But even so, with Eddie Bemis—and Eddie being so drunk—well, Alvy goes way, way too far tonight. Nobody wants Eddie to jump again, and when Eddie does, he just sits there bawling, and Alvy's all upset, telling him.

"Eddie, don't let them send you to any headshrinker. Eddie, listen, only a kid can headshrink a kid. Your Dad and that air force headshrinker, they'll only make you sicker, man. And admit it. You hated Ronnie. And who can blame you, the way Frank said he beat on you? And hey, was it *your* fault that you were her favorite? Was it *your* fault that Ronnie was a sicko and a musclebound baby? But now answer me this, Eddie, 'cause I swear nobody here'll ever repeat a word. Why was Ronnie's dick out?"

"Goddamn it, Loomis, you drunk," fusses Goerstner. "For Christ's sake, just leave the poor kid alone, like his life ain't screwed up enough already." Goerstner may be an asshole, but he really is a fair kid, I realize.

"Eddie," hisses Alvy, "hey, maybe it felt *great*, Ronnie jacking off while he strangled. But it's like Ronnie's bench-pressing, right? You don't bench-press alone. No, if Ronnie was whacking off like that, well, he'd need somebody, like, *to spot* for him, right? He'd need somebody to catch him before he choked—well, right?"

"Fuck you, Loomis!" Eddie starts flailing and crying.

"Alvy," I say, "you're too drunk."

"Meeting adjourned," hollers Goerstner. "C'mon, Eddie, I'm taking you home."

"Me too," seconds Billy Plumber, then they all leave. Pulling out his pistol, Alvy pops off two shots. Yellow flames in the darkness.

"So go on!" he hollers back, "I hereby disband this fucker anyhow!"

A catcall from the darkness. "Hey, Loomis, *Errrhh-errh-huhhh.*"

Man, I can't take him drunk and waving that pistol around. Another Micrin bottle smashes.

"Alvy, I'm not staying here if you pass out."

So Alvy and me hide the gun, then start down the rotting street. When out of the shadows steps a shadow! A shadow of a shadow in a porkpie hat!

"Evenin, muthafuckas. Hear one y'alls been lookin fo me."

Alvy coils to spring. "Nigger, if I—I was a looking for you, I'd ff-fucking well have f-found you."

"Look," I plead, "please don't mind him. He's just really, really drunk—"

"Sonofabitch." Alvy stoves his head into the darkness, but the little colored dude doesn't back up one inch. "I knew I heard something! You're lucky I didn't shoot your black ass!"

The colored boy just laughs. "Hey, man, I *here*. I *here* for ya, you cracker asshole muthafucka. Jus say the word. But firs, who dis Frank be?"

"Wait, you're him? The colored orphan kid?" I stick out my hand. "Aww, man, I am so glad to meet you!"

The kid stares back. "I ain here to shake hands, 'tupid. Now, what you wan wif me, leavin notes and axin all around bout me an shit?"

Alvy's as confused as he is drunk.

"Alvy, that's *him*. This kid's an orphan. From Taver-Shep. For weeks I've been leaving notes to find him and tell him how to find us."

"Notes?" squints Alvy. "What ya doing, Dougherty? *Ad*vertising?"

"Yeah, man," agrees the colored kid. "Wrappin notes in rocks an shit."

"*Huh?*"

"In rocks he threw ovah to Taver-Shep. Tacked up a sign, too, *a sign*."

"Well, aay, man," slurs Alvy, backing up, "I do sincerrrrely 'pologize for 'at. As a child, he was sheltered, y'know. He's real young. Stupid, basically."

"Screw you, Loomis. I found him, didn't I?"

"Foun *me?* What I want wit chew? Buncha ole white boys?"

"Not white boys—*orphans*."

The kid cracks up, air squirting out his cheeks, *"Gisk, gisk, gisk."*

"But Frank, no colored boys." He looks over at the kid. "Nothin personal, man."

"Sho. Nuthin personal here neither . . . *you cracker asshole muthafucka*."

Alvy loves it. "See, Frank, thass brotherhood. Whass your name, man?"

"Sheppy. You?"

"Alvy. Alvy Loomis."

"Um-hum, I hearda you, asshole."

"Sheppy what?"

"Dwyer."

"You know Hermes?"

"Oh yeah."

"Eunice?"

"Um-hum."

"So where you from?"

"Round." Sheppy pulls an already smoked cigarette from behind his ear. He takes out a wilted match, pops the head under his fingernail, then lights it. "Carolina. Rig'nally."

"North or South?"

"Bofe. Souf, mainly."

"And how old are you?" I ask.

"Thirty."

"Shee-it," says Alvy.

"Naw, thass right. I fifteen but c'lored years count *twic't* fo white boy years."

Alvy's interested now. "So when'd you come up here, man? Name's Sheppy, right?"

"Um-hum. Last De-cember, a year ago. Might leave on out, though. Flor'da, maybe. Nice warm water. Sun. Get me some ole job an a raggedy-assed shack."

"Yeah, Florida," agrees Alvy, "that'd be cool, Florida. Any particular reason?"

Drawing out his lips, Sheppy blows a thick smokeball. "Trouble—y'know."

IT WAS FUNNY HOW WE ALL FELL IN TOGETHER, because after Alvy and Sheppy got the "nigger-cracker" stuff out of their systems, they never again used those particular words—or not personally—and if anybody had used them against Sheppy or threatened him, Alvy would have been all over them. On them like white on rice, Sheppy joked, even though, of course, Sheppy knew all along how Alvy still felt and, I guess, how he felt too, gen-erally, about white people. I only wish somebody coulda told me how *I* felt.

Sheppy's like an aerosol can, *Contents under pressure.* Pressure he almost in-flates himself so he can even get up out of bed. Pressure like a pressure suit, so his arms bow out and his palms flutter, his round face squinting and the porkpie hat just cutting his eyes. And always late. Sheppy he'd have died be-fore he ran for anybody's bus.

"That nigger's mad at the sun," says Alvy, seeing him slow-shucking down the road.

"Mad at the sun?"

"Sun's white, ain't it?" Alvy pipes up. "*Well,* if it ain't the Emperor Jones!"

"Doan even start on me, man—"

"Sorry, Jesus Christ." Wow, that tells you everything, Alvy apologizing.

The first time I saw Sheppy in daylight, I couldn't believe the scars on him. Scars on his arms and head and also, on his arm, this inky black home-made tattoo like a scar, which read "S-H-E"—maybe his Mamma or his girl, I thought—until I saw the dribbled-out "P," for "Shep." But this tattoo Sheppy shrugged off as bitty school stuff. When he pulled up his shirt, I al-most threw up. Two jagged black scars, like ropes, ripped down his hard-mus-cled chest and sides.

"What?" I cried. "Who?"

"This ole man my Mamma live wid. George."

"Old?" I ask.

"Not *ole*-ole. George jus mad she lef him. Went crazy."

"You knew him?"

"Yeah, I did. George used to beat on me an shit. Wheneva she lef him, George be on me like why doan *I* stop her? George be complainin to *me*, know what I sayin?"

And jerks his hands around in this hapless, plausible way, like hand pup-pets—he has the oldest looking hands, from all the work he did in the pick-ing fields down South. "Yeah, her new man what lived with us, Johnny, George got him right off. In bed. Chop. Right through the throat. Then I hear Mamma screamin. I half asleep. Well, I grab mah ball-bat, runs in, and here he be cuttin on her. Back and forth, back and forth—*big-assed* nigger too, boy. Ever wake up but it like you dreamin? Dreamin but you can't never move, and yo arms and legs, they all cased in like—like in cee-ment? I hit him, onct. Onct from behin, then he whip around and cut me. Here, see? Twic't so I splashin. Then I guess he figurin I be dead"—it sounds like "deed"—"so he go on back to Mamma. Wisht I was dead, too, so I ain have to hear it. Put me in the hospital near a momf."

After that he just smokes. Boy, does it get quiet. Sheppy doesn't even sound all that angry. It's way beyond that, I guess.

"So they caught this George guy?" Alvy asks finally.

"Shoot—"

"He's *loose?*" I ask.

"Yeah, he loose. People seen him. Nigger ain even hidin."

"Sheppy!" I practically shake him. "You oughta call the police!"

Sheppy smiles at me. "Thass nice, man. Nice to say."

"Right, I'm so *cute*."

"You *nice*, is all I mean. I ain said 'tupid. Cops, they ain even be concerned wif us. You kin b'lev dat."

"But wait," asks Alvy, "so George knows you're up here?"

"Sho he do. Know my aunt. Know ever'body. What kin I do? Only but so many places I kin go. Yeah, we done tied de rope, George and me, we c'nected now. C'nected fo life, and either George fin me or I fin him. 'ventually I will. Hey, I ain said I *lookin* fo the muthafucka. Not just yet I ain 'cause, face it, man, I small. Young. So, you wait. All you kin do is wait." Sheppy sighs. "Live to get bigger."

"Aaa-men to that." Alvy raises a bottle of grape soda. Probably the only white boy alive who's religious on grape, but you don't see him offering Sheppy any. "But hey, Shep," says Alvy after a minute, "this George dude comes around you let us know. We'll hide you, man. Buy you a bus ticket, get you a gun—whatever."

"*Gun?* I ain spoilin him wif no gun." Reaching in his sock, Sheppy pulls out a pearl-handled straight razor. The blade's cracked but it's more wicked for it, glistening in the sun like a piece of broken glass. Sheppy sits there stropping it on his shoe. Alvy tries again.

"Hey, Sheppy, I don't think you understand, man. I'm stone serious. Anything you want. Day or night, we're here for you, man."

That's Alvy for you. Won't offer Sheppy his soda but here he is, ready to lay down his life for him. Makes perfect sense to me.

AND THAT'S THE CRAZIEST THING ABOUT WHITES AND COLOREDS, if you ask me. Exceptions. I mean, how whities and coloreds will all make these special little side deals while on both sides everybody knows exactly how everybody still feels. Like one hot day, again Alvy has a soda, a tall, frosty grape Nehi. So not thinking, I reach it over and take a long, burning pull—when here I see Sheppy sodaless! Obviously parched, but if it's Alvy's soda, how can I give it to Sheppy? Or—admit it—even if it *was* my soda how can I drink after the kid, especially when Sheppy's not just colored but *black*. Black-black, and his big lips, they're braided like taffy, in different colors of black and pink-black and his tongue is red. I can never get over how Sheppy's constructed, *but he's dirty he'll make it all dirty you queer would you kiss him?*

What can I do? My mouth's balled out with grape soda and here's Sheppy looking at me. *Pthu!* I'd spit it out like snake poison if I could, but I look away—look down at the minnows all hot and bunched in the dried-up creek. And here's Sheppy and Alvy both watching me squirm! The bastards think it's funny, too, Alvy wondering am I fool enough to offer, and Sheppy wondering am I fool enough to think he'd ever accept. Perspiration's streaming down the bottle. I shove it at Sheppy.

"Here—"

"Naww."

"*Take it—*"

"Hey," hollers Alvy, "guzzle down my whole soda, why doncha?"

"Goddamnit, *have some—*"

Sheppy laughs. "After white boys?" And look at him and Alvy both grinning like devils! Sheppy's nervous about it himself.

"Sheppy, *drink—*"

So to spite us both, Sheppy drinks. Slathers his lips all over it, then shoves it back at me—and way too full to claim it's only spit. Well, fine! Even if it's poisoned I suck off Sheppy's spit! I pasteurize that pop bottle pure 100 percent white, then I shove it back at Alvy, and he's it! And who's laughing now, staring at the bubbles twirling up the neck? In Alvy's hand the pop bottle's like a sand clock, and each bubble's a grain of sand, a little sun that flares to life, then slowly twirls up the neck. And if Alvy doesn't drink—if he lets it go flat, I think—then either he's blackballed or I am, because hospitality, well, that's the deepest code you can violate. And Sheppy can't pretend he don't care, because Sheppy he does too care and Alvy knows it, and the bubbles and the atoms of Sheppy and me swirling in the bottle all super agitated, they all know it, just like Alvy knows it's not just nigger spit or his pride he's swallowing but a contradiction of his Dad's whole nigger-hating universe. And that's what is so great about Alvy. Truly great. Because once Alvy decides, Alvy cocks his head back and just *drains* the sucker. Nobody moves or looks. Nobody dares. Then Sheppy flops on his back, gagging. I jump up.

"What! What's the matter now?"

Sheppy busts out laughing, "*Pussy.* I *know* all y'all white boys bofe been eatin that pussy! Oh God! I gonna *die.*"

"Yeah, you'll die!"

And whooping, Alvy jumps on him laughing, and we all roll around, laughing, because Sheppy he be in us and us we be in Sheppy, and the saliva spit and the language, it all mixes up in us like spit in a bottle. And later, I sneak back and save that bottle as Old Number One, our trophy. But of course it wasn't nearly that simple, and there were still exceptions. Exceptions aplenty.

• • •

FLORIDA, WE REALLY GOT PSYCHED UP ABOUT FLORIDA.
Cheap sugar shacks and the huge boardwalks by the orange groves—Florida where it's always sunny and you can live like a seagull, raiding people's french fries and popcorn. Florida was the ticket. Tamiami, Kissimmee, all them me-me-type places. Peroxide your hair, lift weights, wear cock shorts, maybe clean some stacked widow lady's pool for her like that Dean kid in *Cabana Banana Boy*, the cock book Alvy stole off Hicks. Picture perfect, man! Except Alvy says there's no surfing. Yeah, Alvy especially is crazy about the Beach Boys who, next to Elvis and Steve McQueen, are now the reigning Coolest Guys on Earth—*ever*, to have connected fast cars and girls and surfing! And that's the only problem in Florida—no surfing—no surfing because no waves, so we figure we'll go Route 66 to California and Big Kahuna, but Sheppy he says you ain't never gonna catch no nigger on no surfboard, and Alvy says then Sheppy'll be the world's first surfin' nigger 'cause he *goin'*. Goin' 'cause he's *our partner*, because Sheppy's hopped trains and he knows the South, so that North to South, black to white, front to back, we're covered! The whole country! Meaning, Alvy says, there's no excuse ever to hang ourselves like Ronnie Bemis. No, Alvy says, if it gets that bad, you pull the ripcord—*you leave*. And if that place sucks, *you leave there*. And if that bites, then *you leave the there of that*, so that life's just an infinite egress of sun and surf, fun and girls! And laughing at Alvy, Sheppy says he ain't gonna be no kinda *Sea Hunt* nigger either, but Alvy's saying he'll learn him scuba, too, and I'm noticing that Sheppy's language is steadily getting better, while ours is getting steadily worse, 'cause like a Winston, that colored language tastes so good, like a language should.

WELL, A COUPLE OF MONTHS PASS. Then I'm walking along one day when a car pulls up and honks at me! Some guy in aviator glasses and a mustache! *A queer.* So I speed up, so he honks, so I whirl around, when I hear that asshole laugh.

"*Are you nuts!*" I hang on the door like it's electrified. "Where'd you get the mustache? And this car?"

"*I've found me the Fountain of Age, motherfucker!*" eurekas Alvy. "Theatrical store! Ain't it great? Renders you totally in-visible to adults! Cops, too. Man, I'm like an X-ray, I drive right by 'em! C'mon, hop in."

And gives me that toothy Pied Piper leer, so daring me to be insane that I gotta jump in, plus with the mustache I tell myself that it *is* an adult and he's got his license, *Gee, officer, the man just picked me up.* And as Alvy hits the gas, I'm propelled into the we-have-achieved-liftoff of the hottest, wickedest, most boner-bending freedom there is—car freedom . . . *Stolen-car freedom!* My head's spinning! And old Alvy really can drive—can shift and steer at the same time, plus do the turn signals—he wasn't lying when he said his brothers taught him to drive in the plaza parking lot. Well, good-bye, Studebaker! Cruising in the light and the wind and the speed, I'm as high as a kite, *We got us wheels again, girl.*

"S'prise!" Two black hands clap my eyes.

"Sheppy, goddamnit!"

"Hoooo-eee."

Sheppy's hiding behind the seat! And look, Alvy's heading down Connecticut Avenue. Clear down to Chevy Chase we go, down toward the Women's Club, and, sure enough, at Lanier he hooks a left, and I duck under the dash. Damn, it's her house! The big striped awnings, the urns, the perfect hedges.

"Come on, you lyin, man!" gasps Sheppy. "Frank's girl she live in *air?*"

"Paydirt, huh?" crows Alvy.

"Goddamnit, Alvy, go! Keep driving!"

It's Jessica Bayard's place, and I'm still looking up.

NOW OBVIOUSLY, I COULDN'T VERY WELL NOT HAVE TOLD ALVY ABOUT JESSICA. But then obviously, I can't just *invite* him over. C'mon! Not Alvy Loomis. At least not yet, I tell Alvy. Not until I get on a better social footing with the Bayards . . . like, with a two-story ladder.

Alvy's not fooled.

"Social-climbin' sonofabitch! God, it's in the blood with you. Christ, I cram you with poetry, my Mom dresses your sorry ass up, we give you an alibi and even cab fare, and *you can't introduce me?*"

But what makes Alvy really jealous is Mrs. Loomis being so impressed. It's just like Romeo and Juliet, Mrs. Loomis says. No, Mrs. Loomis about flips when she hears about Jessica, and especially when she hears Dad won't let me see her. Well, never fear! Mrs. Loomis goes straight into the Flies' closet and pulls out their old prep-school rags—charcoal slacks, a blue wool blazer and a striped tie from some college. And all brand new, as long as the Flies lasted at St. Bart's Latin.

But brown-and-black saddle shoes with big tassels? They're two sizes too big! Christ, they look like golf shoes, but Mrs. Loomis says they're all the rage—just what a society girl like Jessica would go for. Alvy's rolling on the floor.

"Go on, laugh," Mrs. Loomis hollers to him. "Be a fool. Frank'll go to college, not you." She beams at me. "I paid five bucks for that tie, y'know. Blue and white. Those are the actual Ivy League colors, you know."

"Yale, man," guffaws Alvy. "Yeah, those Yale locks are a bitch to bust open."

"That's right, go for the gutter. You'll find it."

"Yeah, and the gutter's right over there," says Alvy, pointing at Charlene's place. That's what Alvy's really mad about. Man, what a mess. Hicks has just moved back in, Alvy's brothers are in the army, and Mr. Loomis won't discuss it because officially *it never happened*. Pointing at Charlene's, Alvy yells back at Bunny, "Yeah, screw Yale, Maw, I'll study plumbing like old Hicks! Now, there's a lot to learn. Hot on the left, cold on the right and shit don't run uphill."

Bunny makes like to slug him. "Aww, quit tormenting your poor sister. She's pulling her life together. And what're *you* doing, staying out at all hours, quitting altar boys and falling down in your grades?" Thank God the cab honks. Running out to pay the driver, Mrs. Loomis looks ready to run away herself.

"What's the address?" demands the cabbie, "I need a house number."

"Look, just Lanier and Connecticut is fine." And I don't say another word but just lean back in my seat like a millionaire, to get in the mood. Damn this winter wool, though. It's gotta be ninety-five today. I'm sweating like a pig but here I am dreaming of Christmas—a White Christmas at the Bayards'. Big tree, the cream money of D.C. society, and I just got a scholarship to St. Somewhere. And as Mrs. Bayard is introducing me around, behind us everybody's buzzing, *"He's just so natural, so refreshing."*

"Now what's that address?" demands the cabbie.

"I already told you, I don't know the address."

Asshole. I slam the cab door, sopping sweat and my feet sucking out of these golf shoes. And when I turn down Lanier with its burly old trees, in that sudden pitch silence of money, there it is, boy—paradise. It's all we've ever pointed at and pooh-poohed and schemed about, Mamma. But what re-

ally gets me, *every lawn is done finished.* Here, you don't see anybody mowing
their lawn on Saturday. You don't even hear a mower. No, in Chevy Chase,
the Lord rests a day early, every blade barbered, and all the sweaty, invisible
old colored men who push the mowers like sleepwalkers, they've slunk off,
with their little bit of folding money, just slayed that anybody could be so
rich. I'm sleepwalking, too. I don't need any house numbers. Clear as a path
it's all laid out for me. Down two lanes of ivy and flowers I can see it all laid
out, like those dance diagrams Dad's always studying. Tassels swinging, I just
follow the footprints to the huge red door and the black-and-white striped
awnings like on a castle. I push once and four bells chime. And here's a maid,
a real maid, a big colored woman with tiny moles on her cheeks.

"Well, you must be Mr. Dougherty. Here, lemme take that jacket for you.
And a tie, too. Poor thing, you must be burnin up on a day like this."

"No thanks. I'm fine."

"You, sure? These aren't formal folks."

"Really. Thanks."

"*Jessica . . . Jess-sie.* Lemonade, Mr. Dougherty?"

Light streams through tall golden curtains. Ancient clocks tick. It's like a
museum, the quiet, and, worse, it's all *lying out,* gold watches, silver boxes, jade
Buddhas—priceless stuff. So what is this, I think, some kind of honesty test?
I'm offended, frankly. Looking around—half to see if it's real—I smear a big
greasy fingerprint on the carved table. Then, in a wisk of blonde silver hair
trailing perfume, here's Mrs. Bayard, all embarrassed to make me comfortable.

"Why, Frank, hello. Well, how are you? I didn't hear your car." She looks
around the corner, expecting to see Dad.

"Dad dropped me off. He sends his best regards and apologies, though.
He had to see an important client."

"On Saturday?"

"Well, this is a pretty, uh, powerful person. I won't mention any names, but
this guy probably owns half of downtown." Christ, what am I saying, that
my Dad shines shoes for rich people? "See, Dad's had to work more lately.
Since, uh, y'know—"

"I'm sure it must be very hard."

That's all she says about you dying, and really a look is all it takes. Unlike
all these other people, Mrs. Bayard doesn't go gushing on about you being
dead, and she doesn't duck the question either. She just looks at me like she
knows, and I know, and what more can you say?

"So your father will be picking you up later?"

"Well, no. On a job of that size"—I wince at "job"—"well, Dad'll be tied up all afternoon, probably. Yeah, he always raised me to be independent. *A self-standing unit*—that's Dad's phrase. He sends his best regards, though." Shit, I already said that.

Mrs. Bayard still looks a little flabbergasted, but she lets it go. "Please, take off your coat—I insist. Thank you, Laurie. You poor thing, you're soaked! Here, drink some lemonade. Please, come out to the porch. It's much cooler out here."

And that's when I see it, in the sitting room or pantry or whatever. A green tank of oxygen and a black mask.

"Look at you!" Blonde ponytail bouncing, it's Jessica, trouncing down the stairs. She stops in midair, seeing me all sweaty. "Frank, what did you do, run over?" She thinks this is a scream.

Well, Mrs. Bayard pops out her eyes, a habit of hers when she's excited. "Apparently, his father dropped him off— He—" She starts coughing. Jessica freezes.

"Mom?"

Mrs. Bayard waves her off. "I'll . . . I'll be fiii—"

Mrs. Bayard stops, waits. So, we wait, but again it starts, a tickle, then a raspy cough, then a wheeze, until she's coughing and gasping for air, waving her arm. Laurie, the maid, barges by me, takes her in the room with the oxygen bottle, then shuts the door. Embarrassed, Jessica eyes me, *So now you know.* And I do. Suddenly, I know exactly why they invited me. So Mrs. Bayard's really sick? *So she's gonna die too and they want me to tell Jessica what the deal is?* Well, fine! I'll explain it to Jessica. Like somebody pushed me, I butt Jessica back against the stairs. Moaning, Jessica's mouth opens into mine open with that little fun-house scream girls do—and her tongue swooshes *gosh* through the roof of my head, and I pull on her ponytail. *"Mmumphf,"* Jessica breaks away. It's Laurie. Laurie blows by us, all disgusted. Jessica doesn't care. Let her Mom be in there sucking oxygen. Jessica's eyes gleam.

"Wanna see our backyard?"

And that's the stunner, outside, in the hazy June heat. It happens like it hasn't in months. Not jacking off. Not even during Black Jump with Alvy bear-hugging me until I pass out. Pulling me along, Jessica's wanting to show me the side of the house—the cabana—anyplace—where we can make out together. But then, like a shot, I'm pulling Jessica past the swimming pool, to a little stone pond splatched with green lily pads and this frog-faced imp dribbling water. The water dances and pulses. The sun squirts like a lemon in my eye. Flirting and flashing in the sun, the black water could be six hundred feet deep, and when I lean over it—angry swirls. *Fish.* Wallowing and bloating, giant ink and white-speckled fish are fanning like giant squids. The water blurs into two nipples. Two eyes and a shining face. *Your face* blowing up out of the black water, Mamma. And young. Young as that picture Alvy had of you by the white roadster with Uncle Stephen. Vaguely, I hear Jessica calling me.

"*Frank?* What is it? Do you like fish?"

I must look crazy. Poor Mrs. Bayard inside, huffing into her rubber mask, and here you are, Mamma, beaming up at me from under the water. But not the old you. No, it's the *girl* you, Mamma, the girl my age, telling me for my penance, *Quick swipe something. Anything.*

PNB, READ THE LETTERS SEWN ON HIS STARCHED BLUE SHIRT POCKET. The "P" stands for "Preston," dontcha know.

"So! A Yale man, huh!" booms bow-tied Dr. Bayard. He's peering over his slippy black glasses. I guess he must lose them a lot, because he hangs them around his neck, on a gold chain.

"Scuse me, sir?"

"Your tie." He thinks I'm putting him on. "Blue and white. We're both wearing the Yale colors."

"*Oh* . . . yeah, Yale! Yeah, Mom always wanted me to go there."

Dr. Bayard's like a dog wagging its tail. "So, Dad's a Yalie, huh?"

Is he kidding? "No, he went to the Academy."

"Annapolis?"

I'm *about* to say the Merchant Marine Academy, but seeing this is the wrong answer, I agree with him that it was really the *Naval* Academy. Cause if you want to get along and move up, that's what you do—agree. But the other secret with adults, especially big-shot types, is to ask them plenty of *me-me-me*-type questions, to keep them all busy and gratified with themselves. Anyhow, that's what Alvy says, and he's read all of Dale Carnegie, who's right up there with Charles Atlas. Alvy did it for his Citizenship badge in the Scouts.

"So you went to Yale?" I ask.

"*Harvard.*" Dr. Bayard peers over his glasses, heh, so I nod, heh-heh, like obviously I get the joke. "So, Frank, so tell me now"—everything is "*so*" and "we" to these rich jokers—"so when did we start reading poetry?"

My heart's pounding. "Oh, that was my mother. Mom loved poetry. Read it to me for hours when I was growing up. From a baby she did."

"That's wonderful," says Mrs. Bayard. "And where did your mother go to school, dear?"

College, she means? "Well, it was a *girl's* finishing school. But it was a lot more than a finishing school. No, it was real advanced—valedictorian, glee club, pom-poms, the whole deal. No, Mom wouldn't have any college after that." At this I smile to myself. "Well, I guess you'd have to know my mother."

"And where was that school, dear? In New York? You said she was from New York, right?"

"Yes, ma'am, Westchester." (Well, Uncle Stephen lived there and he was rich.) "Y'know—way upstate."

"*Upstate?*" humphs Dr. Bayard.

"Upstate, downstate, whatever. I'm not much on maps, sir."

"Ev-i-dently."

"But, Frank," persists Mrs. Bayard, "what was the name of the school?" Man, are these rich jokers school crazy.

"Oh, well," says Dr. Bayard, rattling his ice finally, "not much on names either, eh, Frank?"

"Or dates! Or *spelling!* Lord, I am the world's *worst* speller. Well, Keats was worse."

Dr. Bayard's bow tie about pops off. "And no small opinion of ourselves either. So tell us, Frank, do you write great, badly spelled poetry or do you merely recite it?"

"Daddy!" cries Jessica.

"Recite it?" I laugh. "No, mainly I *write* it. Stories and stuff. But as for poetry, Mom and I *read* it." It's funny. You feel more vehement with a lie than you ever do with the truth. "No, Mom didn't believe in reciting. See, to her, that totally killed the poetry."

"*Killed* it, you say?" Dr. Bayard lets his glasses slip down his nose, a real card, snapping at his bow tie with his fingers. "Well, with all due deference to your mother, I was taught by reciting. In fact, if I'm not very badly mistaken, I do believe poetry began that way. No doubt because Homer and those of his ilk, those clumsy *Greeks*—well, they were all such horrid spellers." Dr. Bayard lifts his glass. "But as for us in school, it was twenty quatrains by tomorrow or whack! *Water, water, every where, and all the boards did shrink; water, water, every where, nor any drop to drink.*"

"Oh! I love that one!" Lord knows which one.

"Oh, do you?" guffaws Dr. Bayard. "But, Frank, that's mere *reciting,* isn't it?"

"Well, I won't object if you do."

Jessica shrieks. Dr. Bayard gogs. Even Mrs. Bayard is laughing, until she gives a cough and everybody stops dead. Which, to calm her down, Dr. Bayard starts reciting this whole poem. A long-assed one, too, about this guy's trying to go to his wedding and this ancient old salt who wrings this bird's neck. And even if we disagree on reciting, I sit there all enthralled, when here's Laurie.

"Scuse me, Dr. Bayard, but I got a one-word poem for y'all—*lunch.*"

LITTLE BITS OF fish on hunks of lettuce. Napkins in silver rings and ice water in crystal goblets. I look at it all and want to cry.

And later, because I'll get so vague, Mrs. Bayard, half joking, Mrs. Bayard says she thinks I've got the Negative Capability. Basically, what John Keats said about poets being invisible and going all different which-ways with ideas, so that they're anything and nothing—*something* like that. But even though I don't know *what* I'm talking about, I get all excited! I say that that's exactly how it felt in that poem Keats wrote about the Nightingale. It's all about death, Alvy says, and I guess so because he's read it to me probably a hundred times. Anyhow, I tell the Bayards that the flowers, they're at Keats's feet but it's so dark and Keats is up so high that he can finally peep over the wall and see what death is, and Mrs. Bayard glares at Dr. Bayard, *See? He's not so dumb.* But, glancing at Jessica, suddenly I hate myself for doing it—performing. Because all I can think during that first visit or the second, or ever, is *why me?*

And they aren't jerks. In fact, that's the whole problem. After that first visit, the Bayards don't grill me about Dad or you—*I'm* grilling me, foaming off at the mouth about your wedding at St. Patrick's Cathedral and how you'd served on the Olympic Committee, totally ridiculous stuff, until gently Mrs. Bayard says, "Eat." I swear I'd do anything to protect Mrs. Bayard, anything, no matter how weird. And like a spinning arrow, I sit there, feeling negatively capable and awaiting further instructions.

And sure enough, maybe my third visit, looking for the upstairs bathroom, I see Mrs. Bayard's room . . . and here's her jewelry box, wide open! So—to warn her—I stir the stuff all around. Then downstairs, as we're having our sherbet, as a final sign before it's too late, I swipe a silver spoon. Well, Mrs.

Bayard is really coughing bad that day, and I'm really feeling sick watching her, so I take it. Not to *take it* take it, understand, but more, I guess, to keep the jinx off them and Jessica, by keeping it on me.

About Mrs. Bayard, I guess she had her better days, but I doubt she ever had two whole lungfuls of air. And to tell the truth, sometimes I wonder who I come for more, Mrs. Bayard or Jessica. Sometimes, after things get too hot and heavy with Jessica or I get too obnoxious, Jessica'll go upstairs and me and Mrs. Bayard will just sit in the library paging through old books. Amazing old books. Books so old and cracked and loved and thumbed, and even signed, some of them, that I can almost imagine some person actually sitting down and writing the thing.

"Now here," says Mrs. Bayard, her voice a dry whisper, "now here's a truly great story." Slowly, she cracks the binding, then smooths back the page with those bristling rings of hers, *But Dr. Bayard couldn't afford to bury her in them could he? Fling her rings in the mud?* Mrs. Bayard's chest quivers. I feel her breath rising over her glasses, and sometimes she stops. But slowly, she reads me parts from Jack London and Stephen Crane. She even reads me those Nick Adams stories, complete with every last "bastard" and "son of a bitch."

"But Mrs. Bayard," I ask. "Hemingway couldn't actually write that, could he? He could actually write that in a book?"

"Frank, it's not a bathroom door. He wrote it as an artist."

"Artist?"

Another revelation, that you could write and be an artist. What Mrs. Bayard always hammers on, though, is that no matter how wild or made up, the story's gotta be true, with no holding back or phoniness. And no suckering people with "pretties" so a lot of prissy dum-dums can warm their hearts and say how nice it's written—like the idea, ever, is being "nice." No, she's real tough on books, Mrs. Bayard, not at all Dad's idea of a lady, much less a rich lady. And feeling like a vulture, my guts'll rumble, *Liar. You wouldn't even like her if she wasn't rich and gonna die.*

Jessica also scares me. Why do girls always have to look at boys like that? So right in the eye like that, asking, *Do you love me? Can you really be for real?* I hate that. Making out with Jessica at the bus stop, when she's all flushed and putting out that sweet chewed-grass smell of girl, it always feels like our last time. And Jessica's never really been thrown by life, so she's absolutely fearless. Little sweat beads break out on her upper lip. Athletically, she pulls back her blonde hair so the air can cool her neck. Then, sleek as a sled, she lays her damp arms across my shoulders, and down we go, down into the wind of her eyes shrieking, *Ride me ride me real fast.* And when I come up sucked breathless—when I see her so giddy, asking me did I feel it but I don't—right then, I swear I'd walk in front of a bus to save the girl. Anything to keep her from staring me to death, making me feel like such an idiot and a liar.

"So, when can I see your house?" she asks. She already knows the answer, but every visit she's gotta ask.

"Come on, my Dad's *dating.*" (I make it sound like he's on the toilet.) "Either that or he's working. Plus my grandmother's nuts. Well, do you wanna see that? Do you?"

Jessica glares. "And who says you're not lying about that, too!"

"What do you mean, *too?*"

"Oh please, Frank! You think we're all stupid?"

Really, with us it's like an adult movie, only lower to the ground and more make-believy. I can't answer her. At that moment I can't even look at her. Miserable, we wait. Then the bus shrieks up and the door swings open. Eyes welling over, Jessica calls up.

"It's really insulting, you know. We're better people than that."

Well, now at least they know, I think. Or will. Lurching down the aisle, I go clear to the last seat, then I pull it out. A ring. A girl's ring, it looks like. A big white diamond, with two red rubies and some greens and the blue whachamacallits. Slips right over my pinky, though, and I look at it, terrified, then relieved I've done it finally. Let them repossess our house! Put me in jail! Torture me! I still won't cough the ring up and I'll never sell it, ever! And here I go, crying again. Crying, because I had it too good at the Bayards', so before something worse happens, I've gotta mess it up. Christ, I think, what *is* it with me and buses?

BUT NOW TO JUMP ahead—or jump back, rather—well, Mrs. Bayard's ring gets back to the subject of Alvy and Sheppy and me. I'm talking about that day the three of us bomb over to the Bayards' house in that first car Alvy stole. Because it really horrified me, him and Sheppy all but casing the place.

"Hey, nothing big," says Alvy as we're driving away. "In fact, we *don't* want anything big—no, that'll draw attention. Just something small to pawn."

"*Steal,* you mean." Hunkered down, I feel like the cat who's swallowed the canary. (I've been hiding the ring inside the tongue of my shoe.) "God, Loomis, what a klepto you are! Who do you think you are in that damned mustache—God?"

"Pawn, not *steal*," corrects Sheppy. "Man, I tol you, pawn's jus a low-down loan. And later, if you still feeling so bad, you mail her back the pawn ticket. She get her stuff right back."

Getaway money. That's what Sheppy's talking about. See, Sheppy's really been spooky lately—about George. Just say boo and Sheppy's *gone.* Hopping a freight up to Harper's Ferry, or shacking up downtown with various kids he knows. And he's real vague about everything—him and Alvy both. No, I never knew Sheppy was so moody and secretive and superstitious, and especially when he dreams, because he is always dreaming about George. But Sheppy's not the only one talking up Florida—no, Alvy is too now that Hicks is back shacking with Charlene. And Alvy's on the warpath now that Beef has disappeared—disappeared when the dog practically never left the house except if some bitch was in heat, and even then the dog was *quick*, the way Beef could fight and climb fences. No, Alvy knows for sure Hicks got the dog. And God, did Alvy hate himself, having to smack the poor mutt whenever he growled at Hicks, not that it did any good. Ever since Hicks kicked him, Beef would bare his teeth and go for him if Hicks got too close—especially to Alvy or Bunny.

No, everybody in the family knew the truth about the dog, but of course they'd swear up and down how Beef had run off or got hit. Why, they even act like it's *Alvy's* fault, because he refused to get Beef fixed. No sir, Alvy wasn't that kind of hypocrite.

Alvy's aviators flash. "And think of it, Frank. If the Bayards finger you, all you say is you did it all to save a colored boy. Rich people love that shit."

"Aww, shut up." God, I hate Alvy's coon baiting—I hate it worse than Sheppy's acting like he's deaf to it. Now Alvy uses Sheppy to justify everything, warning me, "Well, if Sheppy goes *I* go. Then where will you be? Strung up like Ronnie Bemis? Because I can tell you, man, you're at the end of your rope."

"*Me?* I told you Charlene's the Mamma! I told you that a month ago and what have you done? Exactly nothing! And you talk about me! Christ, when it comes to Charlene, you're the biggest chicken on earth!"

"And what bout chew?" calls Sheppy from the backseat. "Cause you know yo Daddy gonna marry that ole gal." He means Dad's new girlfriend.

"Aww, come off it," I say, "Dad just met the woman."

"And introduced you," adds Alvy. "Aww, wake up, Dougherty. Has your Dad introduced you to any other woman? And what a name!" Alvy busts out laughing, "*Heidi. Heidi ho!*"

"Say whut?" laughs Sheppy. "Say she Heidi *the ho?*"

• • •

HEIDI KLOPSTOCK, HEIDI HO. Yeah, for me Heidi was the last heave ho.

One Sunday, as we're heading to church, Dad takes a sudden right. Says there's a certain lady he wants me to meet.

"I think you're really gonna like her. She's got lots of zip." Dad squeezes my shoulder with this creepy look, "I know you'll show her the wonderful kid you can be."

Now, there's an incentive. Dad's so sold, so off-to-the-races, he hardly says another word. And believe me I don't ask. Not in the car I don't. The car's the last place I'd ask that man anything.

And what a place to introduce us, right by where we bought the Bird, not two blocks from the funeral home. Even as Dad parks behind Our Lady of the Blessed Presentation, I'm getting that queasy trade-in feeling—that feeling of quick deals, incinerator blowers and shut-up-and-wait-in-the-car while he signs the warrant.

The organ's pumping. And here she is by the main doors. Blonde. Way younger than you. Long-legged in white patent spikes and a short, short to the knee, summer dress—a striped dress in the fresh "Tammy" style if you've seen the movie. She has the hottest, pinkest lips and biggest eyes. But what's with the long black veil? Is she a religious nut? And beaming. Lord, you'd think dating was a sacrament, the way her and Dad just beam at each other.

"Hel-*lo*," she says, seizing me by the shoulders. "I'm Heidi, darling. And I'm sooo glad to see you . . . " For a second, she looks like she'll bundle me up sobbing. But then, as suddenly, her eyes pop out, "Pete, *we're late.*"

And boy, is she turning the heads, with that frisky high-heeled walk and toe wriggle. Yeaaa-ah. Hanging back a half step, dapping the holy water, Dad's loving it—send this Heidi up the aisle of St. Stephen's and I guarantee there'd be a riot. And she's not a thing like you. No, that's the beauty, Heidi's the new model year. She's you totally reinvented, five inches shorter, twenty pounds lighter, eight years younger—and blonde. But wait, if she's not like you, then who were you? I half wonder. Sandwiched between them, as Dad bumps me to start praying, my head's on fire. Stop. Go. Decide, decide. But wait! I think, they'll have to get my okay before they can say I DO. Absolutely. I saw that in a movie once. I can jolt up, *I object!* Well, right?

And not only is Heidi your polar opposite, Mamma, but Dad's changed, too. With her, Dad's not one bit the way he was with you—not even close. Heidi doesn't intimidate him like Angelene, or bamboozle him like you did. Heidi's got Dad feeling ten feet tall *and what's wrong with that?* Why, they've got their own private language, Heidi dimpling up to Dad as she eyes me, *He's so precious.* And Dad furding up his nose, *I know,* then holding the hymnal out to me, *sing you jerk.* And, right on cue, Heidi cuddles in, the two of them caroling their heads off and me squashed in the middle, singing, *Loooooord on high-essst, what the fuck do I dooo?* . . .

OUTSIDE, DAD LIGHTS two cigarettes, then hands one to Heidi. They're both famished! You'd think they hadn't breathed air in an hour. At that first drag, Heidi's big eyes pop. Her cheeks completely collapse, and Dad's cigarette bounds skyward. Then Heidi announces.

"Mamma's invited you both for an early Sunday supper, you know. Oh, can you, Pete? I'd hate to spoil poor Mrs. Slattery's supper plans, but Mother's just dying to meet Frank. And Frank, lemme tell you, Mamma's pot roast is *outta this world.*"

Can we! says Dad. He barges over to the phone booth to call Grammaw. He doesn't care. Tell the old loon we're off to the North Pole. To hell. Yukking it up for Heidi he's yackity-yacking his fingers and rolling his eyes, talking to the old nut.

"Peter, stop! You're terrible!" Playing it proper for me, Heidi grabs my arm, then marvels, "Boy, are you strong! We'll have to arm wrestle, you and me. I'm really strong, too, you know. You have no idea."

"Cleared for takeoff," calls Dad.

"But Pete, is she mad? Oh, I hope poor Mrs. Slattery isn't angry."

I don't know why but, hearing this, I gape at Heidi. "You don't think Dad actually told her where we're going, do you?" Wow, it's like I've flicked water in Heidi's face. She stops dead. For a split second she almost glares.

"Well," she frets, "I certainly want Mrs. Slattery and I to get off on the right foot."

"You let me worry about that," harumphs Dad. "Frank, hop in back." Just like that! *My seat he gives her my seat.*

"Aww, c'mom," Heidi laughs, bouncing over the hump, "let's all ride up front." So then Dad's all annoyed—at me. "Oh, Pee-ter," she says, embarrassing us both, "I just know you two are best buddies. And Frank, I just can't get over it. You look just *exactly* like your Dad, exactly. And so handsome. It's uncanny." But then after the small talk, she wriggles around, sorta frimps and fools with her hem, staring at me with those big, frowsy eyes of hers. She's painted on every lash, I realize. God, how long does that take? I wonder. They're painted on like giant sex spiders.

"Well," she says, "I'm sure you'd like to know a little something about me." She bumps me with her shoulder. "Aww, gwan sure you do. Well, I'm thirty-two. Old in the tooth, hahaha. And for now I live with my mother"—she looks at me hard—"although for the past several years I've had my own place. Oh yes. And before you ask—no. For your information I've never been married, no sir."

"Well, it can take a while," I squirm.

"Well, that's right," she agrees. "It takes a long time to find a man who's not a louse." She beams at Dad. "And do you know what my problem is, Frank? I'm a lover and a truster. That's right. That's me in a nutshell, *I love and I trust too much.* But I wasn't born yesterday, and don't you ever turn on me, *newwwww-sir.* Turn on me and I'll turn on you—but quick. Oh, but I love to have fun and laugh. *I love* to be silly, but only *if* I can trust you and *if* you don't take advantage of my naturally trusting nature. And I work. Oh boy, do I work. At my job I work like a fool, a slave, but, see, that's because"—she winks—"well, there you go, Heidi girl, Miss Dum-Dum. That's because I'm too darned nice. Too trusting."

"And where do you work?" I fidget.

"At an office!" She grins. "*Curious,* huh? Raised a smart one there, Pete! Well, I'm what your Mom was, a secretary. Not an executive secretary like she was—no, I'm not the glamour type. Nope, I'm legal secretary, but strictly a backroom gal. In fact, I'm a whole legal department rolled into one. Patsy, boy, that's my middle name, and I don't mean Cline! I do the work of three men so my bosses can fool around and have their three-hour lunches. Boy, I could tell you some stories, but I won't, because I'm Heidi. No, I don't stoop to that and I don't play games—no. Stupid, maybe. But loyal, most definitely. No sirree, Heidi doesn't bite the hand that feeds her."

Did you ever read that *Playboy,* the one where Brigitte Bardot is standing sideways in the mirror? Where she's watching her long nipples jut up—*up*—like excited red lollipops, and she does that fruggy thing with her lips? Well, I probably shouldn't say it—it's sick—but Heidi's got lips like those. Okay, not *as* hot, but in that vicinity. And the most beautiful noble nose you've ever seen. A nose with this little curve, like she's French, which that Brigitte Bardot is, by the way. But with those uppity French-style nipples? I wonder. Because when Heidi nuzzles up to me, it's not all bad either. No, it's not bad at all.

• • •

HER MOM'S PLACE is an old, white-shuttered gingerbready house smaller than ours but way nicer, with done-to-a-T lawn, flowers and a white wrought-iron bench with fake bunny rabbits. Yap yap yap! Two pugs clobber the storm door like wet newspapers. Then out steps Heidi's Mom . . . and mamma-mia, all knockered out and dolled up in this tight, slit-up-the-leg, Dragon Lady thing, with the perfume pouring off her. And young. Well, pretty young, con-sidering. I mean I wouldn't have blinked if Dad had brought home Heidi's Mom instead.

"IS THIS HIM? Pete, he's adorable, ADORABLE. I'm Anna Klopstock, dahling, but you can call me Aunt Anna. Come in, come in. And look, young man, look what we have to show you today. See here?"—gliding her red nails over this white, pillowed sofa, like a giant cream puff—"And do you know why it poofs up so high? Here, sit. Sit in it. Feel the silk. Such luxury. Such gorgeous hand embroidery. Aww, go on, *sit sit*. Wuunn-derful, huh?" She hauls me by the arm.

"Okay! You've had your thrill! Never again!" At this she breaks out laugh-ing. And laughing. Man, clapping her breast, she's laughing so loud she finally buries her head in Dad's shoulder. "That always gets them—the *boys*. But who can blame them, big, healthy apes. Dah-ling," she says, patting me on the cheek, "nobody but Aunt Anna sits here. Only my bee-hind and then only on holidays, for the big *schmear*. So Frank, poopsi. *Old buddy*, you want a Pepsi, maybe?"

ONE THING HEIDI was right about—Aunt Anna does make a great pot roast. Poor Dad, though. Dad's dying for a beer or a little wine, but Aunt Anna won't allow any in her home, and she's a Catholic! Wow, a teetotaler Catholic. Grammaw's gonna hit the roof when she hears that.

And no need to pump Aunt Anna. No, just like Heidi, before you even ask, she tells you where she works (the cosmetic counter at Hecht's), where she bought it (Hecht's), and how much it cost (on sale—*always*, minus the 10 percent discount). And welcome! Welcome to *The Aunt Anna Show*, star-ring THEM, the Eighth and Ninth Wonders of the World spilling out of her blouse. ("I used to do lingerie, but no more. Awful! Not the women, the men! All the time staring at you. Disgusting . . . ") And making over Dad? Every time he stands up Aunt Anna clasps Mt. Rushmore.

"Heidi, you better keep the other girls' mitts off of *him*."

Heidi claps her own chest. "Well, I'll never have *that* to worry about." Wow, did she just say what I think she did? Heidi starts laughing hysterically and

I then see it's true. No two big Wonder Breads for Heidi. At best she's got two little slices.

"Stop!" wheezes Aunt Anna. "Pete, are you gonna let her say that? Dahling, the good Lord compensated you in other departments. Other girls, they'd die for that figure."

"Oh no, Mamma," protests Heidi. "The legs, the hands, you got them too. *And* the ooph. *And* the fabulous skin." And, looking at Heidi, suddenly I see—see almost magnified—what I half noticed in church and the car. Under the makeup, there are all these tiny holes in the skin of her cheeks, holes like those sensitive plants that close up if you touch them. These microscopic holes, they can sense anyone looking, and they do close up, too. The second they feel anybody looking, out comes the compact and the lipstick, the whole repair kit.

"Quit," bubbles Aunt Anna. "Look at her—a Mitzi Gaynor. And look at Pete, honey. *He* knows. *He's* noticed. Mamma sees the eyes you make at my poor daughter."

Dad's sitting ramrod straight, mortified. I can't help it. Crushing my hands between my knees I bust out laughing.

"Frank, *e-nough*," blushes Dad. "Frank, that's *quite* enough."

"Oh, Pee-ter," says Heidi, hugging me. And she's so young and jazzed up she has me helpless—sex helpless, like a puppy held by the scruff of the neck. And Dad, even though he's smiling, Dad doesn't like this one bit, because this woman is his, not mine. No, this time the lady is all his.

AND I ACTUALLY THOUGHT I HAD THE FINAL SAY!

After all that had happened to us, here I am still thinking I can reverse the course of life. Here I go, ready again to step in front of a bus—for Heidi, the last bus out of Spinsterville and Dad's ticket out of Misery, Maryland.

But it's not just me fooling myself. No, Dad still thinks he has a choice, too, telling himself that he'll just wait, that he'll let things develop—"naturally, in their own good time." Oh sure, Dad knew what people would think about his falling in love on the rebound, *but they didn't know*. Of course it was crazy, *and that's why it was so right*. Of course Heidi completely took over, *because she knows exactly what we need*. And of course idle minds would talk, *but we'll prove just how wrong they are*. No sir, Dad said, as a giver and a lover and a carer, Heidi would soon have everything humming in our life. "Frank," he admitted finally, "buddy, I know your grandmother and I haven't done so well in the mothering department. But trust me, this gal is different. Just give her a chance—you'll see."

But it wasn't just me or Grammaw or the neighbors Heidi needed to convince, it was you, Mamma. Straight off Heidi said she could never replace you, not as a woman or a mother, and what's more, she wouldn't even try. No, in her bruised, offer-it-up way, Heidi said she fully accepted this as her cross to bear in life, getting Dad and me secondhand. In fact, Heidi was always saying how that she prayed to God you were still *alive*. That's right, alive. And as she stared at me with tears in her eyes I could see that Heidi actually believed it—that and every other nutty thing she said.

"Bring your poor mother back?" Heidi would ask. "Frank, sweetheart, even if it meant returning to my horrible old life, I'd do it! Honey, if I could press that button and give you and your poor Dad everything you had before, my God, I'd do it. Are you kidding, I'd do it in a second. But Frank"—and her voice drops to a teary whisper—"*all that's done for, forever*. That blow-it-all life you three had and all the money and status you craved, *honey, it's all been spent, every last dime*. But now can I tell you the real secret? Honey, deep down you don't want that old blow-it-all life anymore. C'mon, we don't need to pretend to each other—I know you resent me. No, Frank, you're not the same cute little kid you were then, and your Dad's not the same guy he was then, either. And Heidi knows this. She knows this the same as she knows she'll never mean even a *tenth* to you two what your Mom did, *and that's okay*. And I'll tell you another thing, buddy boy. Your poor father doesn't need to impress me. Not me, or you or anybody—no siree. Listen, honey, if a man doesn't make it by forty, he never will. And I hate to tell you sweetie, but your Dad is well past forty now. Now, *I'll* never tell him that and don't you dare, 'cause I'll just deny it, oh yes I will. I'm only telling you so you'll stop driving your Dad into the ground with all your petty, yammering wants. Stop that. Stop it right now. Because if you don't quit it, you'll kill him."

"Kill him." "Destroy him." "Ruin him." Heidi was always throwing around such accusations, but what Heidi was really telling me, and what I heard in no uncertain terms, was that Dad was washed up and would never make it. That he was now mortally wounded and supremely vulnerable. That at this point it was cruel even to lead the poor guy on in aspiring to anything, and why when we could yip and cheer just as if he were a genuine success? And why not? asked Heidi, a pragmatist if ever there was one. Let the poor guy be happy tinkering in his shop, forever blowing bubbles. While Dad bragged about his business schemes and soon-to-be patented inventions, we—knowing better but assuming that burden—we would play the Great Man's adoring, happy family. And, like a child, Heidi sincerely believed this. And, as I say, Dad totally believed in Heidi.

Still, Julie, there was one indisputable similarity between you and Heidi, and this was Heidi's paranoia about our neighbors. Heidi, though, was more bothered by the men, especially driving her jazzy '58 Impala convertible. And being blonde.

"I see them looking," she mutters to Dad. "Especially that what's-his-name over there, fat, disgusting pig. A blonde in a convertible. Men see that and then go bonkers. Pete, I've had it, I'm going back to brunette."

"Absolutely not!" cried Dad. Nope, on virtually everything Dad went along with Heidi, but in this case he absolutely put his foot down. Nope, he'd bought a blonde and that's what he would have, a blonde in a black convertible avenging his pride with her hard, childless body. Fine! Heidi said. She wouldn't strip her hair. Instead, she'd strip beds and sheets and clean from top to bottom this pigsty we lived in. Grammaw wouldn't have to know about it, and we could save on Mrs. Eppes, a horrible extravagance, and especially when Heidi loved housework.

So while Aunt Anna took Grammaw out for a free introductory facial and the *whole spritz*, Heidi arrived in jeans and a white kerchief, dragging mops and buckets and her own surgical vacuum cleaner, which she would first sterilize with ammonia and boiling water.

"Oh, I worked like a fool," she brags to Dad and me later. "God, it felt so good. I sang, I cried, I babbled to myself. And near the end I swear I could feel Julie beaming down at me." She looks right at me. "Really, I felt like I was washing her back."

Yeah, that was the spooky thing about Heidi, how totally, blamelessly sincere she was. But spookier still was how Dad bought her every word, and the more she lied and blew things up, the more Dad had me pegged as the liar. Still, I thought, at least I knew what I was.

BUT US DOUGHERTYS AREN'T THE ONLY ONES DOING THE LIMBO DOWN AND DOWN. One day while we're alone, Mrs. Loomis—"Mom"—finally corners me, wanting to ask why Alvy only keeps getting wilder and more angry. And she's sincerely asking this when I *know* she knows why. I don't know whether to fart or cry, I've got such horrible gas cramps. Doubled over, I finally blurt out.

"Because he doesn't think you're his real mother, okay?"

"Not his real mother! Just look at him! He looks just like me. So how do you explain that?"

"Who's explaining?" I cry. God, I'm a wimp. Here I am an inch from the truth and I can't do it. "Mom, I'm only telling you what he thinks, okay?"

"Why? Because of my gray hair? Hell's bells, I was gray at thirty! And sure, I had Alvy late, but at forty-*two?* C'mon, I know women who delivered at forty-five! Forty-eight, in one case!" She grabs my arm. "But here, if you don't believe me—"

"—I *believe* you!"

"Come here!"

And dragging me to a gun-metal strongbox, she pulls out a liver-spotted photostat of Alvy's birth certificate. It feels like old skin, all greasy slick and falling apart in my hands. She's got her glasses on cockeyed, pointing with a chipped red nail.

"Look, *Alvin Christopher Loomis.* Collins Memorial. March 12, 1949, 6:06 A.M."

I'm crushed—a whole summer shot on a wild goose chase. But when I corner Alvy about the birth certificate he says it's forged.

"Forged how?" I ask. "It's got the official raised seal."

"Gullible, *God!*" Going into his Dad's study, Alvy pulls out his notary's embosser, this silver clamper, like a pair of pliers. "Here, notarize any damn thing you want."

BUT AS THE WORLD was ending, all this time, like Noah, we were preparing. Which is why it was so amazing that that movie *The Great Escape* came out then, reading our own minds. It's amazing how books and pictures will do that, because by masterminding the greatest concentration camp breakout ever, *The Great Escape* was thinking *exactly* what we were thinking. It was cherry and it was textbook, Alvy said, with just the kind of planning, discipline and organization that we needed. Best of all, it starred the coolest guy alive, Steve McQueen.

I should have known, Alvy's sudden shift to wearing dingo boots, khaki pants and a cut-off T-shirt. That was McQueen in *The Great Escape,* the hairiest American bandit ace you've ever seen! Man, busting out of prison camp on that Nazi Harley, McQueen didn't even *wanna* to escape, Alvy said. McQueen, all he wanted was the joy of the Nazi army chasing him so they could throw him back in the Cooler—solitary—with his baseball mitt and his ball to bounce off the walls until he busted out again. That was so great when McQueen got caught! Just the way he'd give the Nazis this half-assed *oh well* look—"McQueening," Alvy called it, hooting through the whole theater, "*McQueen* that Kraut mother, wooo!"

Well, finally we took Sheppy to the show. Now this was amazing, being out in public with a colored boy. (Generally, we hung out in the boondocks, mostly around the old sanitarium.) Yeah, in the theater, all the while Alvy and me, we're just watching Sheppy, wondering just how amazed he'll be at all this astounding white ingenuity and organization.

"Yeah, he cool," allows Sheppy about McQueen finally, "but Li'l Joe, he way cooler."

"You mean on, like, *Bonanza*?" Alvy can't believe it.

"You seen Li'l Joe anywhere else, sucker?"

"Hey, you don't have to get sarcastic on me. I guess I didn't figure you for the *Bonanza*-watching type." Alvy nudges me. "Here, show Sheppy how the hot-wire scheme looks." So I pull out the hot-wiring diagram that Alvy gave me to learn. All it takes is a screwdriver, a length of wire and two battery clips. Like so.

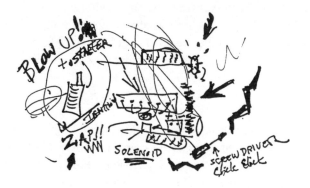

"Huh?" asks Sheppy.

"*Hot-wiring*, man." Alvy McQueens him good. "Well, it's something to learn. Even ole Frank can do it, right, Frank?"

"On his Dad's car," I add. "Man, we hot-wired that car so many times!"

"'Course Fords are the easiest," shrugs Alvy. "Solenoid's on the firewall, see?" Sheppy rolls his eyes. "I '*member* that."

"And we been stealing canned goods," continues Alvy, "and I'm the troop quartermaster, so we got the *equipment*. You catch my drift?"

Sheppy squints.

"Well, you just seen the damned movie, didn't you?"

"And how they all got caught and shot too."

"Yeah, well, check this out." Desperate to impress him, Alvy pulls out his wallet. Goddamn, it's a real driver's license! It says he's Robert Wadkins, 158 pounds, five feet nine inches, and just a month shy of seventeen—all he's gotta do is change the eyes to blue, Alvy says.

Hell no, this wasn't some soggy saltines tied in a kerchief. No, Alvy was giving me fighting and survival training and, twice now, I'd set my alarm for one o'clock—in the morning—and snuck out on maneuvers, rendezvousing at Waverly. We'd hidden all kinds of shit in this upstairs closet of the nuthouse. Alvy'd made a fake wall out of a piece of plywood, and now we're letting Sheppy into it, the whole operation. But oh man, Sheppy secretly digging Li'l Joe? With Pa and Hoss and Hop Sing? Yeah, Sheppy sure shocked us sometimes, and outside the theater, scuffing his dingo boots, Alvy's Mc-Queening all over the place, gritting at hoods if they even so much as look at Sheppy. Still, much as I hate to admit it, this escaping idea is like digging to China when you're five years old. Mainly, it's a place to escape *to*. I mean I never actually think we'll *do* it.

THEN, OF ALL THE STUPID, POINTLESS THINGS, SCHOOL STARTS. In the space of the summer, Alvy's gone so wild it's cruel. Oh, don't worry, he's outta St. Stephen's, he's outta Catholic school entirely, in ninth grade at Willard, a public junior high in hoodlumville. I'm glad I don't have to see him. I mean in *any* school, stuck in his little desk, surrounded by all these completely immature dolts his age. Crabs can grow new claws. Can a kid look older just because he has to? I wonder. Cause Alvy's a monster now. Unbelievable, the muscles he's got after lifting weights all summer. He looks a good two or three years older than fourteen—at least. No, after that first week of public school, after he's been in two or three fights, well, I know he'll never last the whole year. And sure enough, probably the third week, here he comes with his face all busted up. And immediately by the way he won't look at me, I know who did it—Hicks.

"So swear out a warrant!" I tell him.

"I told you, I ain't dragging no cops into this. Greasers jumped me. *That's* the story."

"But your Dad knows better. He's gotta."

"Goddamnit, the man fought for three years, spent five years in night school, worked his whole life and raised seven goddamn kids. He's *worn out*."

"I'll say, swilling his beer."

"Or his case of Fleischmann's, like your old man."

"Least my Dad's not watching me get my face bashed in."

"Yeah, well wait 'til December, *Ringboy*. That'll be a two-ring ceremony, one for his nose and one for yours."

THAT'S RIGHT. COME CHRISTMAS she'll be sitting under the Christmas tree. My new toy. Blonde with two big blue eyes. My new Mom.

And late, up in my room, through the heating ducts, I'll hear Grammaw and Dad in the kitchen,

Pete what will people think what?

I don't give a good goddamn what they think.

Or Frank thinks.

A lot you know. Frank's crazy about Heidi.

Crazy is right hanging all over her and her hanging all over him. It's not healthy I say.

Slam. Rumble. Bang. Then Dad's out the door—his witching hour. Mine too but then here's Grammaw, scuffling into my room, ready to start ranting about Heidi. "Lulu," Grammaw calls her.

"God, the sight of you two hanging all over each other—it turns my stomach. And I'll tell you what that Lulu really thinks of you with all her syrup about motherhood! She thinks you're a horrid, rotten brat, getting away with bloody murder. And you do, but what the hell does she know? Or your *Aunt Anna*. Shows you why her husband ran off with the Jap!"

"What?"

"Yeah, ask Lulu about *that*. That's a savory little story. After the war in Tokyo. Some Jap girl her old man took up with. Sixteen or seventeen the girl was—younger than Lulu at the time."

"But wait, I thought her Dad died?"

"Thought he'd died and gone to heaven to escape them! And you, *hanging* on her!"

"Shut up!"

"Hanging on her, I say. And her encouraging it! And I'm not the only one who's noticed. Oh no, buster, others around here have seen you two fooling around."

I jump out of bed. *"Then leave!* Goddamnit, if Dad won't tell you, then I will! Go, 'cause you sure ain't doing me any good living here! Goddamnit, *OUT!* O-U-T OUT!"

Why's it always me, having to tell women they're dead? And I can't show the old lady any mercy—not if I don't wanna drag it out. It's probably the most horrible thing I've ever done. I throw a wad of dirty underwear at her, I practically spit in the old woman's face, but this time there's no begging or blubbering—no, she just stands there, staring two holes through me.

"Go on, curse me, I don't care. For you I have no pride—none. Dump the dead old cat in a sack. Heave her in the river, but just you remember this, buster. Good, bad or rotten, *I* stick with mine. For you I'll suck up to Lulu when it suits me. Hell, for you I'll whistle 'Dixie' if I can derail this god-damned thing, because that woman is *wrong*. Oh, I know *I'm* wrong, but that Lulu is totally wrong, wrong for you and wrong for him. And not because I won't have any other woman in my Julie's place. Oh, no, your father's dead wrong there—blind wrong. And until your old man has the guts to throw me out, I'm staying put, too. Right here, mister. And as for you, *goodnight."*

AND I AM OUT TO DRIVE GRAMMAW CRAZY WITH HEIDI,

and that's not all I'm out for either, kissing and hanging on her. But how can I tell Dad this? You can't talk to slaphappiness. Worse, they gotta rub my nose in it. Riding along one afternoon, they actually break into "Oh, What a Beautiful Morning."

"Sing!" Heidi goads me.

"Sing what? It's not morning, and I hate singing."

Heidi whirls around. "You can't stand other people being happy, can you?"

And she's right, I think. At the Tastee Freez the yellow jackets are going nuts now that summer's over. *Whack! Whack, whack!* They don't even mind being killed. In fact, this one yellow jacket, as I watch him twitch his last, he's just like me, I think. He's sealed up his nest for the winter. Gorging himself on sweets and tormenting people, he's completely useless, biding his time till the first frost. And back in the car, just like these pests, here I go again, buzzing around the old Heidi pot. Half a bone on, I'm hugging on her and kissy-facing while Dad fiddles with the radio, trying as usual to ignore us both. So, cranking things up another notch, I ask Heidi one of my heavy-breather questions.

"Heidi, if you could have anything bigger, what would it be?"

She laughs out loud. "Bigger bosoms!"

"*Whoa.*"

"Heidi!" cries Dad.

"Well, it's the truth, Pete." She's like she was that first night at Aunt Anna's. Clapping her chest, Heidi, can't stop laughing.

"Well," I say, laying on another big squeeze, "*I* appreciate you, Heidi! Hey, I know! I'll call you BB! BB for *big bosoms! Oh, BB* . . . Beeee Beeeeeeee—"

Dad's arm bolos around, *whack!* The car swerves.

"Shut up, you goddamned jackass! You'll treat Heidi with respect or I'll stop this car!"

"*Pete! Watch the road!*"

Dad snorts, he stomps on the gas. "Go on, grin at me, you grinning jackass! Grin and I'll whip my belt off. I'll do you right in these headlights—"

And Heidi herself was out to prove something. When Heidi wasn't playing Joan of Arc or Snow White, she was like my kid brother, pawing at me and punching my arm and daring me to arm wrestle. But the ultimate intimidation was when Heidi would roll up her sleeve and show me her wobbly old tomboy muscle, taunting me.

"Big for your britches, huh?"

Or, "And maybe you could show me that one again, huh?"

Or, "I'll tickle more than your funny bone."

Or the bonerific, "Bet you'd like to show your father that one!"

But then as fast as the funny business starts, Heidi'll fly into a fit, whinnying, "All right, Mr. Fresh Guy, that's enough! You stop it right there!"

"Aww, don't go away mad, BB," I taunt her, "*Beee-Beee* . . . "

"*You quit it! I'm not your damned BB!*"

"Aww, BB"—ruefully rubbing my ass—"gee, don't go away *sore!*"

Boy will she be sore come Christmas.

I can't picture it.

Refuse to picture it.

Well, finally, in the backyard one day Heidi and me are really going at it, poking at each other and kinda fooling around. In that group-gropy, in-jokey, we-don't-know-what-we're-doing way, we're really going at it, teasing each other. Then, like a five-year-old, Heidi gets mad, as usual. She starts taunting me.

"Sure, Mr. She-man with his little swizzle stick! A lot you know, you stupid, snot-nosed kid."

I give her a shove. "No, I don't have your *experience.*"

It's like grab-assing with Jessica. Furious-excited, Heidi chases me around the yard, but she's so hopeless. Then she shoots back, "If you were man enough you'd Indian wrestle me! What's the problem, puss puss? Scared a girl'll beat ya?"

I can't back down, not this time. But then as we're squaring off, before I'm set, Heidi jerks me off my feet, the cheater! So pulling a ju-jitsu move I crash into her! Oops! I mash both hands into her tits.

"Hah! *Tit-titsu!*"

"Oh!" she roars, 'cause she can't stand a man beating her—any man, much less a kid. Even I can't believe it. Seizing me in a bear-hug, Heidi slams me down and pinches me hard on the crack of my butt. "There, *little* boy! Just keep it up! Just try me, 'cause I'll slap you silly!"

Furious, I bound back up. "Cheater! That was a goddamn trick! You didn't get me!"

The gloves are off now, boy. With a whoop I take her down at the knees, then leap on her chest. Heidi bucks and rips, she even tries to bite me, but I show her! Grabbing her wrists, I wrench her hands back, then chicken pin her elbows. But she won't say "uncle," the big baby. Instead, she's yelling her head off—when a hand hauls me up by the neck. It's Dad! Grabbing me by the shirt, Dad's slapping me blind, but this time it's not me. Ripping loose I drive my head into his stomach.

"Fuck you, asshole!"

Dad stumbles back like I shot him. "In the house!" He points at Heidi. *"Now!"*

"Don't blame me, Pete! Didn't you see him? He virtually tried to *rape* me, the little maniac."

"Liar! You're the one who started it, Heidi! *You,* that's who!"

Heidi rips off her engagement ring. "Here! I've had it! This is it!"

But at that exact second, the upstairs window rattles open. It's Grammaw, hollering down at Heidi.

"I saw you playing with the boy! I saw it all, you tramp! *You get out, woman!*"

"You get out!" Charging back and forth Dad's ready to scale the gutters. "You old poisoner! You I'm putting on the next plane!"

• • •

GRAMMAW GONE. FREEDOM GONE. EVEN ALVY GONE— VERBOTEN, HEIDI SAYS.

Heidi's so got Dad by the balls she even makes him quit drinking, is how desperate the man is. With a month to straighten me out Dad tells the Loomises that Alvy and me are off-limits from each other—forever. But even that's not enough for Sieg Heidi. No, with Heidi goading him, Dad finally makes me call Alvy and tell him so myself. It's like having to shoot Old Yeller. As I rattle through my brainwashed spiel, Alvy just sits there in silence. Then at last he says.

"Just you remember this, man. Just because *they've* abandoned you, that don't mean *I've* abandoned you. Same goes for Sheppy."

But what can I do? Live out in the road and starve and never go to college? It's like losing your mind and soul both, being powerless. In fact, it's the same thing. Seeing Alvy outside the High's or drugstore those next few weeks, I'm sucked breathless with the humiliation. Eyes on fire I whirl around, *But what can I do? Nothing so give up!*

Even military school would have been better. Grammaw gets two ten-minute calls a month, and only then with Dad and the Warden there. As for Angelene, she calls once to check up on me—*tries* with Heidi hovering and Dad nicey-nicing her so she'll finally get the message that she's dead to us. God, I think, she's even made Dad cut Angelene, probably the best, most decentest friend we ever had. And Jessica? Of all the luck I'm up in my cell doing homework one night when the phone rings. Then I hear Heidi calling out.

"*Young lady, I'll have this call traced if you don't put your mother on the phone. Immediately! . . .*"

It's all that floor wax and ammonia and black hair cooker dye Heidi's been sniffing. That and the Catholic hormones kicking in, now that her and Dad are in pre-Cana—"*Catholic Life,*" they call it—learning the "rhythm method" and how to work the old meat thermometer. You wouldn't even recognize Heidi now. No more high heels and tight dresses for her—no, to show the world how frugal and humble she is, it's Catholic black flats and these Simplicity pattern dresses that she makes herself. One she even made from a flowered bedsheet, giving her this holy roller look. You should see her after church, telling anybody who notices, "It's a bedsheet, can you believe it? Two dollars it cost. The price of a pattern, and I ran it off in a jiffy." Well, she's put her foot in it then. Forever more she's "Miss Jiffy," so fast in the hay, people say, that she wears her sack on her back. And here she is lecturing poor Mrs. Bayard.

"*Me??* YOU get some help, lady! What are you gonna do when the girl's sixteen? Get her *spayed?*"

AND ALVY? One day I call him secretly, but it's torture, I feel like such a wimp and traitor.

"C'mon, man, what can I do?"

"Stay tuned."

"So you finally told Charlene?"

"Like I say, stay tuned."

"And how's Buddy?"

"Missing you."

"But Buddy's okay?"

"As much as Buddy can be okay living there."

"But Hicks hasn't been smacking him around, has he?"

"Hey, you let me worry about Buddy. It's you I'm worried about."

"So what can we do, man? Kidnap Charlene? Kill Hicks? You know, sometimes I think Dad's right about us. Maybe we really are the worst thing for each other."

"Boy, have they brainwashed you."

"So what's left for us—what?"

"Oh, nothin. Just freedom. Justice. Revenge—trivial shit like that. Man, snap out of it!" His voice drops a notch. "And you still got that ring, don't you?" Mrs. Bayard's ring, he means.

"*Not over the phone.*"

"Good. Cause the seas, they *will* be rising. Now, say it for me. One time, *O what can ail thee—*"

"—knight-in-arms, alone and palely loitering? The sedge is—"

"Sedge *has*. Be precise, willya?"

"Bye—"

"Bye yourself, man. And eat your Wheaties 'cause Sheppy and me are coming for you. And soon."

• • •

SO, I'D MAKE MY BED FOR THE THIRD TIME, to get the corners straight, and Heidi would say, "See how much happier you are?" Because, like a zombie, all I had to do was please Heidi's arbitrariness and vanity so she'd please Dad—do you know how that system works?

They had a demerit system that Heidi had found in some magazine with recipes for tuna casseroles and how to make perfect kids. Say, if I leave a light on. Do it twice in one day and that's two strikes. Then all I gotta do is not square a corner on my bed, or leave out a cup, or any of a million stupid things, and I'm home free, kid—I've done my daily bread of fucking up, and I can just stew in my room with no TV, no phone calls, no nothing.

But even when Heidi's rid herself of every living rival, even this isn't good enough for her. What Heidi hasn't gotten rid of is you, Mamma. And Heidi knows this all the more as we near October 18, the first anniversary of your—whatever.

Dad sure feels it coming. Dad's gone into a clam state. Especially with Heidi badgering him how we've all gotta go to Arlington.

"That's right," she says, "we'll bring flowers, we'll pray and then, finally, we'll all get over it. Don't rattle your newspaper at me, Peter Dougherty. Yes, it's hard. For your information, Peter, *it's extremely hard for me . . . Pete!*"

"Heidi, *no,*" he fumes. For Dad to disobey is amazing—unprecedented, in fact. "Heidi, *drop it.* Frank's not ready for Arlington."

"Frank's not ready? *You're* not ready. All you're ready for is your third martini." Well, I can't stand it. I bound down the stairs.

"Hey, *butt* out, willya? Can't you just leave the poor guy alone?"

"And you mind your tone with Heidi," warns Dad.

"Aww, *tell* her, Dad. Tell her it's none of her goddamned business."

But, snorting and ruffling his newspaper, Dad ignores us both, so Heidi turns on me. "And look at you, all puffed out with yourself. You, with your big pride. You, who can't even bring his poor mother a flower on her dying day."

"Shut up!"

"Frank!" barks Dad.

"Goddamnit, Dad, tell her what a rank hypocrite she is!" I glare back at her, "Aww, boo-hoo-hoo—*bullshit,* you goddamn hypocrite, you phony! Like we all don't know you hate my mother's guts!"

But the final straw comes late one night when we're driving home from one of our weekly "family outings." It's October and it's cold, so Dad's got the heater blowing, and me, hypocrite that I am, I'm in this goo-goo state, curled up on Heidi's lap, asleep. *Whump.* I feel the bump of the drain grate in Aunt Anna's driveway. I know I should get up or at least make a noise—too late. Dad cuts the motor, then I hear him breathing real high through his nose, when he grabs her. And then it starts, with a gobbling and smacking of lips and that instant sex smell, like old socks. Are they both deaf? My heart's about to bust the glass. "*Pete?*" she pants all sleepy, and I can feel the sweat rising off her lap, "Pe pee —" "Sssh," coaxes Dad, "relax, he's out cold." Dad's belt mashes against my ear. Her stomach tightens and gurgles, her lap heaves and then real high, higher even than her nylons rubbing together, comes that weird whinnying noise I heard the day Dad caught Heidi and me Injun wrestling. And each time, as Dad weighs in, each time Heidi squeezes my hand harder, yanking and milking it so I'll wake up, *Frank please . . . God Frank wake up.* It's the Black Jump all over again—I swear I don't ever want to be a man. When I grow up, I don't ever want to do it, and in that last flicker before I black out, all I can think is why, so why if Heidi's the boss, so why is she so petrified of Dad?

BOTTOM. ROCK BOTTOM.

By then I don't have one ounce of self-respect. In fact, about all I can think of is getting Alvy's gun and killing myself. So it's lucky Dad puts his foot down about our not seeing your grave on the eighteenth of October, 'cause I would have shot myself before I'd have seen you there—or seen Heidi satisfied that she'd shown me, finally. And knowing all this, maybe for once you put in a word for me up there, Mamma. Because maybe a week later—just before Halloween—a car honks and guns its engine. It's the mustache and aviator shades! And here's Sheppy grinning at me from the backseat.

"It's White Lightning," says Alvy.

"Bull!"

"I *said* it's White Lightning."

"Yeah, it is," nods Sheppy. "Charlene, she *gone*. Just las weekend. Yeah, Alvy's Mom, she sent Alvy up to Fort Dix to see his brofers, man. *Set* him up, mo like it—"

"—so yesterday," picks up Alvy, "so yesterday I come home from Dix and find Hicks has carted Charlene off—her, Buddy, Audrey, the baby, the furniture, everything. Well, great. Here's Dad half in the bag and Mom's crying, saying it's the only way."

"Well, maybe so."

But at this Alvy revs the engine, *vrumm*. Like a ventriloquist Alvy's almost talking through the engine. "Y'know, man, you look sick. Seriously."

"So whadda we do, Loomis?" I look at Sheppy. "Like I suppose Charlene left her address."

But Sheppy's waiting for this. "Mah man, he found *out*. Had Colleen up at the diner, had her call Hicks's Mamma! Oh, yeah. Sayin she got his las check from work an axin where can she send it?"

"So, *tonight*," Alvy chimes in, "0200 hours—at Waverly. Bring your winter coat and all the money you got. *And no good-bye notes.*"

"You're crazy. I can't leave now."

"*Cain't nuthin,*" cries Sheppy. "You goin, nigger!"

"And you swore," seconds Alvy. "On your mother's grave you swore. And what about Buddy?"

"But Alvy, I got my old man's wedding." Catching myself, I laugh out loud. God, what an idiot I am! I smack my forehead. "*But guys, I'll miss the wedding!!!*"

Vrumm. "So, palm it over, Ringboy."

"Okay, okay. But where we going?"

"*Far.*" And, *vrumm*, like an ecstasy, the car bucks and shudders. Hopping on one foot I yank off my left shoe, then reach under the tongue. And don't their jaws drop when they see that rock, and especially when Alvy sees how it scratches glass.

"C'mon," I beg, "at least gimme a *direction*."

"Gone!"

"Gone fo good!"

And as Alvy pops the clutch, off with Mrs. Bayard's ring they're both Beach Boys singing, "Muthafucka, *we be gaahh—wahh—woonne.*"

WE

GONE

ONCE I HIT THE STAGING ZONE behind Waverly Alvy and Shep have the car all gassed and loaded, and I do mean loaded—food, water, packs, bed rolls, tools, gas cans, lengths of siphon hose. But right from the start there's bickering.

"So when do we divvy up the money?" I ask Alvy.

"Here he go," moans Sheppy.

"I got, like, forty-eight *cents*. So what if we get separated?"

"Man, go on." Sheppy gives me a shove. "Git *humping*."

Buckwheat's bucking for his captain's bars now! Then in the darkness I see Sheppy's wearing gloves—black gloves. "What's with them?" I ask.

"So he don't leave no fingerprints," snaps Alvy. "Remember? Officially, it's just *you and me*."

Swinging up a five-gallon can of gasoline Alvy's wearing dingo boots and a cut-off sweatshirt, his eyes like dinner plates after downing eighteen cups of coffee and two No-Doz. In his head ten thousand bombers are droning, and when he pulls down his billed leather flyer's cap, it's scary. He really does look about thirty! He's even got his hair buzzed, so he looks like a marine. Pure Steve McQueen—except for the mustache. In fact, with the mustache he's not Alvy, he's more like my big brother, *my legal guardian*. And for now he's going strictly by the book.

"We got five hours! *Five hours 'til they turn the pack loose on us*. Frank up front. Sheppy—in back. And both of you lay down. *Flat*. Totally outtasight."

"The whole time?" I ask.

"Goddamnit, just 'til we get out of *Maryland*." Teeth clamped on his cigarette, Alvy rams reverse and spins around. "Down South, once we throw 'em off our trail, Sheppy's a hitchhiker."

Black walnuts pop under the tires. It's late October—cold, the headlights swarming with falling leaves chittering like bats across the hood. Slaloming down the crumbling blacktop we go down the sanitarium road to the roadblock, crash the ditch, then gun it hard across the field to the highway, *Nyy-eerrrrr-oo))))owww*— We're off, all barking and howling and laughing in that sudden unbelievable weightlessness of *leaving*. With the air squeaking through the vent we could be cruising at 800,000,000 feet. Head propped on a balled-up coat I watch car lights sweep across the dome, maybe one a minute, then—soon—hardly any. Temples knitting, stroking that fool mustache, Alvy suddenly looks worn out—positively old for leaving, which he's fighting like friction, like gravity itself. Because even though I don't fully realize it yet, leaving is like suicide in a way. To do it you gotta be mad enough to kill yourself, or else you just disappear like the Nightingale, a peppercorn in the dark. Really, they shouldn't call it *leaving*. They oughta call it *forgetting*, and that's one big advantage I have, I guess. Forgetting, I'm a regular Houdini at that, and this'll be my greatest feat ever.

Still, I can't picture it yet, leaving, can't because mentally I haven't left, and all for the simple reason that this can't possibly be happening to me. Things like this don't happen to me and, see, the point is, *it's not me*. I'm not responsible—why, I'm not even present or, if I am, it's just as a rider. No, with Alvy in that mustache I can pretend he's the adult and that this is just an overnight, just a prank, until finally, I conk out, how long I don't know, when I startle up and remember, *Sheppy's here*. Smelling Sheppy's Kools mixed with that bacony, cabbagey smell of Sheppy, without my even seeing him, I can picture him in the backseat smoking with those knowing, heavy-lidded eyes—eyes deep with the sweet serenity of sincerely not giving a shit. It's just that whole superior attitude Sheppy wears, that colored attitude like a skin coat, and cold or hot or scared it always covers him, always. And suddenly I am so relieved that Sheppy's here. In fact, if it was just Alvy and me I wouldn't go, I just know I wouldn't. Which starts me worrying that Sheppy'll leave, then worrying why he even took off with us in the first place. Because really, when you get down to it, I still don't know the kid—I mean if you even could know him. Remember, for the past three months, I haven't even said boo to the kid on account of Sieg Heidi.

"Sheppy, you awake?"

"Oh yeah."

"So why'd you come, man?"

"Why not?"

"But George ain't been around, has he?"

"Nope." A smoke ring wobbles up.

"So why?"

Sheppy snorts. "Watch you bofe. Go somewheres, *I* doan know. Man, it mus wear you out, alwuz havin to think."

"Like you don't!"

"Sho. But wifout all yo *talk*. What is wit chu ole white boys, alwuz havin to *talk* bout what y'all think? An cain't never *think* wifout talkin. And *reas*ons! Wit chu, people's alwuz gotta be havin all these ole *reasons*."

"C'mon. Everybody has reasons."

Another smoke ring wobbles up. "No, dey don't, man. Don't nobody they *has* reasons. People, they *be* reasons."

THEN ALVY'S SHAKING ME.

"Okay, up! Time to switch horses. We need another car."

Looking up, I see foggy streetlights and railish houses—some little old country town. Alvy shoves my head back down. "Not yet. I'm circling. Sheppy, *up*."

"Whut, steal another car? Where the fuck is we?"

"Pennsylvania. Just over the border." Then Alvy's jabbering to himself, *"Come on, I need a certified* Ford *product . . ."*

"You crazy," hollers Sheppy. "Gwan, man, it's gettin light."

"Sheppy's right, Alvy. Why another car?"

But Alvy's blowing the dog whistle—S.O.P., a probing tactic—which about five hundred of these country bowsers start yowling, so we haul balls. But once we find a dog-free candidate—a '58 Olds saying "steal me"—Alvy's balking. No, the Fordman's gotta have his certified Ford product. Sheppy grabs him.

"Eithuh it's dis or nuthin. Now go on—"

"Hold on," I whisper. "Sheppy, you do the hot-wire. *Please?* I'll pay you back. C'mon, man, I gotta shit—bad."

"Oh no you don't." Alvy shoves the screwdriver and hot wire at me. "You're in it now. Up to your eyeballs. Gwan."

Sure, I'd hot-wired cars—Alvy's car—but I'd never actually *stolen* one. And hoods, I'm hopeless with hoods and latches, but Alvy does the hood, opens her up like a treasure chest, a big ol' V-8, all dewy wet, smelling of oil and cold grease. It's no Ford but Alvy shows me how to do it—in fact, he does do it, hooks it up so all I do is touch the screwdriver to the lead, *but the spark!* As usual, my hand's jittering, scared I'll get shocked. Inside the car, meanwhile, Alvy's going crazy, bouncing the car to hurry, the starter snapping . . .

click . . . click-click . . . Then, *vroom!* And I jump—*I always jump*—and *slur-rrrrrrp!* Like a string of spaghetti the fan belt sucks up the wire! Then, whanggg!!! The screwdriver rips out of my hand and, I guess, hits something. Alvy jumps out.

"What the hell was that?"

"Nothing."

Otherwise it's perfect, though. All we gotta do is transfer all the gear, but oh no. Just then Sheppy runs up. Says some paper boy's coming, so Alvy motions Sheppy to drive the Olds. Well, Sheppy stops dead.

"Say whut?"

"*Drive.* You're a country boy. You drove tractors, right?"

"*Mules.*"

Alvy goggles at Sheppy. "*Well, Sheppy, you're a driver now.*"

But great, the front seat's jammed, it's jammed clear back, so Sheppy can't reach the pedals and we can't snap the release latch to move the seat up . . . so, being commandos, we improvise. Sliding way down the seat, blind, I work the gas and the brake while, kneeling over me, Sheppy steers. It's like driving a tank, the car bucking and weaving while Sheppy hollers down.

"Gun it! Hyeah! Hole on, hole on. . . . Alvy goin in a field. Stop! *Stop*—"

Dawn's breaking out all over the place. Alvy runs up. "Quick, transfer all the shit. I'll siphon out the Ford."

Now this is slick, dick. Why, by the time Alvy yanks out the siphon hose, the Ford's so dry it barely makes the main road, when it coughs and dies, outta gas. Then—and this is so cool—Alvy lays this little "crime" scene, slaps the hood with frantic grease prints, leaves a shirt hanging out the trunk and a matchbook with his cousin-in-Ohio's phone number written inside it. But for me the master touch is the smashed bag of Fritos. Fritos ground in the carpet. Fritos stomped all over the road.

"*Friiii-tos,*" I scream. And off we tear in the opposite direction—south.

"Amateur hour," guffaws Alvy. "Yeah, they'll think we're so stupid we wouldn't piss if our pants was on fire." Oh, Alvy's high now, boy—or is until he sees Sheppy doing his wooden Indian face. "What, you don't think it's funny?"

Sheppy rolls his eyes.

"*Fritos!*" I cry, trying to keep up the yucks, the high. But even then it's closing down on us, all of us crammed in the passenger compartment, us and all our junk, because of course we've got no key to the trunk. Great. Gas cans and lanterns filling the car with fumes, and Alvy set to blow us all up. Alvy's

Zippo snaps. He looks at Sheppy. "Whass eatin you? Take care of my business, then off we go, man. *Miami*."

But Shep's looking out the window, disgusted like he'll get when you get too familiar with the future—I mean, as anything you'll *do* anything to. But instead of just dropping Florida, Alvy only talks it up, only makes it worse, so that it's hitting me hard, too—leaving. And Alvy can't stand this. Any loss of power. For us not to be excited is mutiny. To him, it's brakes, stop signs and failure. Why, it's death itself, Alvy hollering.

"*What! My foot! Oh shit my foot's stuck on the gas!*"

Valves knocking, the car rockets off, Sheppy and me yelling.

"Alvy stopit! Quit fucking around!"

"But it ain't me, it's my *foot! It's asleep!*"

And, cranking down the window, Alvy stoves his head out into the wind, screaming at the mountains, "FUUUUU-CK YOU! Look at the speedometer, boys! Ninety-five and I'm startin' to drive! . . . *110!* come-againnnn! . . . A big *120! are you getting ennnny?* Whoa, baby, I'm gonna blow my rocks!—"

BLOOM!

Rusty water splatters across the windshield. The whole bottom drops out, the muffler bladdering and steam sudsing out the hood.

"*Man!*" Alvy bucks back like he's been shot. "Man, *I blew up my first car!*"

"YOU ASSHOLE!"

"Oldsmobile!" rails Alvy. "And what did I *say!?* I said, gimme a *genuine Ford product!* Well, that's right! Any kinda Ford and this never woulda happened." He looks around. "Wow! Lucky we found this shit out now, huh?"

The hood's vaporizing. Spewing steam and burning rubber, we turn hard, then dead-stick down a rutted old forest road, weaving down the mountainside I guess about a half mile before we washboard to a stop. Scared the car'll blow up, Sheppy and me take off running, screaming back at Alvy, "Are you crazy? Don't open that hood!" But then who's in hot water? Because opening the hood, what does Alvy find but my hot-wire screwdriver sticking like an arrow through the radiator. Goddamn. It tore the fan belt clean off.

But see, that's the tremendous thing about Alvy as a born leader, because no sooner does he start ranting than he turns it all off. Blanking his mind, he sinks into a dazed, five-minute funk, looking at every possible angle. Then his eyes pop open.

"All right, I got it. We tear the plates off, then set her on fire."

"*Has yo los yo fuckin min??*"

"Cortez did it." Alvy nods. "Oh yeah he did. Once Cortez hit America, he burnt all the ships. And why? So his conquistadors, they'd *know* there wouldn't be no going back! And we're *not*, y'hear? Hell no. We get another car *and we keep going.*"

Sheppy's stomping back and forth. "Whass gotten into you, man? Bad enough we stoled it and burnt the motor up. Ain that enough fo you? Ain it?"

"*I'm covering our tracks.*"

"Set a fo'est fire, uh-huh. Thank you, Mr. Ko'tez! Good idea, bring in every redneck cluckhead for ahunnert mile!"

No sir, commander or no commander, Sheppy stands up to Alvy. And hearing his own craziness Alvy is so embarrassed—man, he's backtracking all over the place. "Haw, man, I was just pissed off, is all. I wasn't gonna set it on fire, did you actually think that?" Alvy grins and bends over. "So go on! Kick me one! *Hard.* Right in the ass." Strutting around and swinging his arms, Alvy's looking at the mountains. "Haww, man, look at us way out here! So Frank, so where's the tuna fish? Well hey, you're the quartermaster, ain't ya? Phew, I'm half starved, ain't you? . . ."

I DON'T KNOW WHAT CORTEZ'S MEN THOUGHT, but Sheppy looks at me and I look at him and I wake up, *I'm really here.*

Crows are squawking. Way up here, the leaves are a good two or three weeks ahead of ours, torrents of dead leaves taking off, funneling up into the sky. Getting the toilet paper, going behind some trees, I kick a hole, then squat down, trembling, *It's not too late. You could leave now and take a bus.* And without even looking at my watch I know it's 7:00 A.M. Getting no answer when he calls up to my room, Dad'll find my bed all made. Made perfect, with a shiny new quarter on top so he can bounce it for Sieg Heidi. God, right now, I'd give a hundred bucks to have that quarter back—anything to stop this picture of Dad rocking over himself, rocking and never making a sound, like he does, the tears pouring out of him like sweat. But c'mon, I think, Dad's got Heidi now. Dad's not desperate enough to kill himself, is he?

Then, of course, it starts drizzling. Tripping over our ponchos, dead on our feet, we hump the gear about a quarter mile, to a thick grove of pines with big drifty green boughs draping down like oldtime hoop skirts. Inside, it's pitch dark, beautiful and bouncy with soft, dried pine needles. "Deer!" cries Sheppy. White tails wave like kerchiefs in the darkness. My heart's pumping out my neck. Brushing back the darkness, Sheppy whispers, "We be just like them ole deers now, runnin all night, sleepin all day."

Then here's Hitler. "Come on, you guys, *hump*. We gotta get this crap out-asight."

I've had it. "Look, why not find a phone and *call* your damn sister?" I look at Sheppy. "Or take a bus! Well, why not? We've got the money. In fact, gimme my share."

Alvy's not laughing now. He motions at Sheppy. "Go on. Give asshole his share."

"*Me?*" ask Sheppy.

"Well, you pawned it."

"An I *tol* you, man. If you coulda *waited*—" Sheppy stuffs a crumpled twenty-dollar bill in my hand.

"Cut it out! For a thousand-dollar ring?"

"Dat's de pawn, man. Dollar be shrinkin like a muthafucka."

"Bullshit. Gimme the pawn ticket, I wanna see that ticket."

"He mailin her de ticket."

"FUCKING CHUMPS!"

Alvy snorts, "What'd you expect, *Greyhound?*"

"Greyhoun!" yucks Sheppy, "Haww! Thass de name fo Frank, *Greyhoun!* Yeah, when it get rough, ole Greyhoun be takin de bus! An leave all de shit fo us! Guck guck guck—yeah Greyhoun be wantin his taxi! Oh, taxx-ee!" Then they've both waving their pinkies, milking it for all it's worth, "*Oh, tax-eeee! Wait for meee—heeeee.*"

It's sick, everybody ganging up on everybody else. And that's the trouble with three. With two you can be honest and not have to show off, but with three you can forget it. With three there's always an audience. It's always two on one, and one seat too few, like musical chairs. And once Alvy leaves—once Alvy lets off the brake and rolls the Olds down the mountain to ditch the sucker—the feeling's totally different. The minute he goes, Sheppy stops and the teasing stops but, feeling the mountains whirling around me, my brain won't stop. It's my first bad attack—leaving attack. Bear-hugging myself, I can see me wedged inside my coffin, and as they drop the lid Dad leans down and *kisses me on the lips good-bye.*

Sheppy squats beside me. "How ya doin, man?"

"Okay." I really have to concentrate to keep from bawling.

"C'mon," he coaxes, "you doan gotta pretend bout it."

"Not with you I don't."

Sheppy's lips press out. "Man, I doan know bout Alvy. He gotta calm that shit *down*."

"I *know*."

WE'VE GOT A tin of Sterno. Bush league, I'll admit, but with a pair of pliers, Sheppy and I semiheat a can of Dinty Moore beef stew, then pass it back and forth sharing our one spoon. God, I feel proud. I almost don't once think about eating after him.

Alvy quit the Scouts last summer, but before he left he cleaned out the troop stores. We've got two whole pup tents from the army—the World War II kind with the buddy halves that button together. Still, we don't need tents here, not with these nice soft pines to crawl under. It's like a giant teepee. Crawling in, Sheppy and me lay a tent half down, roll our bags out nice, then pull the other tent half over us, and even with the cold dawn wind blowing we couldn't be any cozier. Above, through the blowing black pine boughs, pinholes of light shine like stars, and we can hear these little finchy-type birds cheeping. Wings whirr. Pine needles tinkle down like dry snow. One second Sheppy and me are both talking, and the next Sheppy's out cold. It's like a microscope, Sheppy's nustled up so close. Laying there, I just stare at his amazing hair, hair made all in little coils, like the insides of a million tiny black seashells. First, I study his hair, then his flattened nose with the notch where this kid broke it, then I get so close I can see his pores, but with none of these little sickly white plant hairs that white people get inside theirs. Out of the corner of his mouth, snuffling, comes a little white snail's dribble of sleep, and he breathes and he breathes and I think, he really must trust me with his life—well, doesn't he? To sleep so out in the open like this? Out in the world with white people, and here I'm the only living soul to protect him? And laying there, just me and Sheppy, suddenly as I look at him, it's all so cozy and alive and I'm so free that for a second I go insane with happiness! But not for long, because here's Alvy back all grumpy, staring at the empty stew can. I sit up.

"Look, there's another whole can." I feel like his wife. "Go on, eat the whole thing. We were both starved."

He looks really low.

"Look I'll *heat* it up for you. C'mon. Nobody's cutting you out."

"Save it. I'll have peanut butter." I can hear his sulky knife scraping the jar. "C'mon, *eat*. Look, Alvy, you're a really good driver, you are. But first you just gotta calm down, 'k? You're acting—well, crazy."

With Sheppy out, Alvy's grammar sure does improve. "Do you have any idea—*any*—of the pressure I'm under? And who's responsible for you two, huh?" Only Alvy. One second he practically kills us, and the next he's lecturing me on responsibility.

"Look, Alvy, you're the commander. But I'm telling you, we're not all jumping off a cliff for you."

"Well, after this it's all by the book," he promises. "No speeding. No games, just like we planned."

But this only depresses me again. "Yeah, but then what? I mean once you find Charlene—well, what can you say to her that you never said before?"

"The truth."

"And *then* what? You live with her? Take her and Buddy away—what?"

He gives me the Mustache, the four-out-of-five-doctors-agree look, "We'll see."

"Oh *okay Daddy*, I'll shut up."

But what galls me I *do* shut up. And that's the weirdest thing about that mustache. If I'm not careful, I catch myself *obeying* it, this fuzzy caterpillar of hair, like he really *does* know. In fact, when Alvy zips the thing off to go to sleep, it's like we're naked—just defenseless kids again. But when Alvy pulls off his boots, I really am scared. In the right boot he's got the 9mm and, in the left, his Dad's Hitler Youth dagger. I sit up.

"Are you nuts? Those are concealed weapons."

Alvy rolls over. "Put it on my tab."

IT'S A MEXICAN STANDOFF. We can't even get ourselves honorably arrested! In fact, I don't even want to talk about the next day except to say we nearly killed ourselves, sideswiped a truck, got screamed at, barked at, looked hard at, and chased. And that was just to get back to Maryland! Not even where we started! Just outside Baltimore the door swings open.

"So, go on, Greyhound!" sneers Alvy. "Ain't nothing stopping you. You neither, colored boy. You want I'll drop your pussy asses off at the bus station."

Well, I start to get out. Hell, I think, I've almost made it two whole days. But to call Dad from Baltimore. And then to call so soon. It's like calling "wolf." I mean, if I go crawling home now, I'll never again strike fear in them, and especially with Sieg Heidi, who you know'll be completely nuts. And what am I going home to? Military school so I can shoot myself? *Three days even if it kills you you gotta hold out for three days.*

"At least we could call," I say finally.

"They'd only trace it. And what makes you think they're so worried?"

"Oh, bullshit. I mean, if we gotta kill our parents let's at least admit it. And what about your aunt, Sheppy? She loves you."

"Love me? She love Jesus, man."

"But she does too love you. She took you in, didn't she?"

Sheppy's eyes are pained tar bubbles, and then I see I don't know the first thing about the kid—his family, his aunt, anything. And half the time I'm talking to the damn window! Shows you how the astronauts must feel, staring down on the world. First, I'll see all these little houses, lots of them pretty cozy through Maryland and southern Virginia. So I'll pick a place and pretend that I live there, but like weeds in the cracks, ugly things'll pop out. Either I'll find out about them or they'll find out about me. And then, like a dead leaf, I'll just snap off again, because once a leaf falls, that connection's broken. Glue it. Tie it. Nail it. That leaf'll never stay stuck—it can't, because the whole tree would die, and all because of that one dead leaf. The tree would actually die of the leaf.

Now, as for the rest, don't even ask me what roads we took and all that crap. *Directions*. Well, my mind shuts off. I hate 'em. Any and all directions, and anyhow Alvy's driving and the roads are so black and twisty that Alvy'll rear up. "Man, what *state* is this? God, I just drove three hours and I don't remember a damned thing."

But it's the South, no mistaking that. Virginia! Lord, Virginia's worse than Texas, this endless goiter of a state. Virginia, the thing goes on for *days*, first a riot of fall color through the mountains, and then, like an odometer, it all turns back to green, a wet, cold, dreary pine green. And then, sure enough, barns, houses, phone poles, trees, bridges, fences, everything starts to lean and slouch, *and buddy you know it's way down South in Dixie*. And paint! Paint won't stick to anything down South. Paint slides right off! In fact, about the only fresh paint you see is the white center lines of the road—that and all the billboards, hand-painted half of 'em, with whirligigs and arrows, shingled letters and reflectors, and here after they've been screaming for two hundred miles about Mammie's Fried Chicken, just when your mouth's watering, here the dump's closed or boarded up.

Yoo-Hoo soda. Mr. Softee. The white-toothed Sunbeam girl biting her buttered white bread with that hubba-hubba look. Either it's that or these signs showing fat kerchiefed mammies and bug-eyed coloreds with corn-kernel teeth. And underneath these signs, all day long, like refugees, we'll see whole families of coloreds hobbling down the road, never daring to look up as we blow by. It's horrible. I've never seen people that poor, that wet, or that drowned, ever. At night, and especially when it fogs, it's like flying over some bombed-out country. By now, we've got our permanent car, a '60 Club Victoria, and, best of all, we got the key—you wouldn't believe all the people who leave their keys in the ignition or under the mat, especially out here in the sticks. No, all we do once we hit a new state is steal us a set of new plates, that and the gas we siphon off, like a swarm of gasoline-gorging mosquitoes. Still, God help us if we ever run out of gas or break down. Down here there's nothing even worth stealing, but damned if they don't got the cops out, cops like you wouldn't believe. Actually, we've had some pretty close calls, but mainly it's lonely and boring and I'm the entertainment. Seeing another colored man wide-walking the road, I ask Sheppy one of my stupid questions, the questions I gotta think up just to have anything to talk *about*. And especially with Sheppy, who's gotten really quiet down here—weird quiet. No sir, Sheppy's a whole other kid here, down South.

"But Sheppy, they don't ever hitchhike?"

"Who?"

"The colored people."

He gives me a dirty look. "Whut, an get shot at? Or played wid?"

Then here's another colored staring into the headlights. I look at Alvy.

"He looks okay. We could pick him up."

Silence. The man vanishes, the darkness closing around him like a cyclone.

"Man," I marvel, "another dead dog!"

"You gonna count every dead dog?" asks Alvy.

"I already have. That's six today."

Alvy tries the radio again but forget that, too. No surf music. Hardly even any Chuck Berry or Elvis—all you get is twanging, screaming Jesus and static. I'm the radio announcer.

"Wow, they sure raise lots of chickens down here, huh?"

"Thass a *house*," snaps Sheppy.

"Quit it, that's a chicken house."

"Ass-hole."

Sure, I know it's a person's house. Obviously I know but for some reason

I've gotta poke at Sheppy, I guess so he'll just snap out of it. I try again. "But Sheppy, don't you wanna stop and talk to somebody?" I wait. "Your *own* people, I mean?"

"An what dey wan wif me? Trouble. Thass all I is. *Any* stranger. Doan matter what color you is. Cause down hyeah all you is, and all they see, is trouble."

But this gets Alvy worried, too. "So what was all this crap you fed us, man? How you'd get us through these colored places if we ever got in a jam?"

"Hey, I jus membering how they is, is all. Ain sayin I ain try."

"So how much longer to Charlene's?" I ask.

Alvy ignores me. I try again. "Sure would help if we had a map."

"So call AAA."

"*How long?*"

"I told you—two, three days."

"Alvy, you said that two days ago! And how do you even know where you're going?"

"How many times I gotta tell you? Sure, if I was just your *ordinary* asshole, I'd go down a certain well-known road—I won't say which—and we'd be arrested in five minutes. But we ain't taking the direct route. We ain't going the *logical* way, and that's why they won't find us. Not on their normal radar they won't. And that is why, for the eightieth goddamn time, you don't need to know just where we're going."

"But Sheppy knows where!"

"No he doan neithuh."

"Deniability," insists Alvy. It's one of Alvy's pet words now. And every state line we cross his head gets bigger than Jupiter—that nobody can deny.

"But in *The Great Escape* they gave them all maps. And compasses."

"Yeah, and they nearly all got caught, didn't they! But see, if you get caught, Greyhound, well, you can tell the cops you don't know dick. And you know what? You'll be absolutely right."

Well, I threaten a deadline—Sunday, if we ain't there I leave! "Thank God!" they cry, so what else can I do? So again I slip into that seasickness of driving, and when I come to the next morning, with the light leaking out through the cactussy woods, it's no better. Still the same cold, greasy, foggy rain blackening the pine trunks. Still the same old rain painting the road with fresh red mud.

"Look," I cry, "an eight-dollar motel! C'mon, a nice hot shower? My hair's itching me to death." But Sheppy's doing the lip, already rejected, so I look at Alvy. "So big deal—we'll sneak him in."

"Sneak who in? Like I some *dawg*."

So we pass the motel, like we pass the little breakfast joint, like we pass the dinky, peeling movie theater that looks like a bank—the theater where we see *Taras Bulba* playing with Yul Brynner and Tony Curtis. Well, Alvy's gotta do something to break the gloom, so he says maybe we'll catch the show later, after we all wake up. And as the road bows around, high on the hill on a teetering porch, here's a dozen little pickaninny kids with cotton balls in their hair, all dancing and waving, *at us*. And so happy! That's what kills me. Waiting for their ladleful of grits, they're all just as happy as hell, *happy even for us flying by*. But not Sheppy—no, through his nose Sheppy's making these snuffly, hissing noises like Kleenex played on a comb. And when I look back, either Sheppy's fast asleep or mortified into unconsciousness, although half the time now you never can tell.

HOW IS IT THAT, IN A CERTAIN STATE, you see things at the worst time possible? And not only that, I think, but *it all connects in the worst possible way?* Is that because *it's* the worst time? I wonder. Or is it because *you're* your own worst time, so you magnetically attract exactly what you shouldn't see? Because as we're looking for a place to pull over, right by the roadside, along a field, here's this, like, messy old garden. It looks like a snow-bank, dead, white carnations belted with an ankle-high white fence of the kind that comes in wire rolls. I sit up.

"Hey, what's that? A garden?"

"Thass somebody's *lan*," snaps Sheppy. "Now come on, goddamnit, I wanna *sleep*."

"Hey, wait, there's a flag. Two flags. And ribbons. And what's all that other stuff?"

"Wow, Frank, *dead* people!" Sheppy waggles his hands in disgust. "No dis-respect, man, but you shoulda seen yo Mamma's grave. Loomis! What you doin?"

Alvy's backing up. "Aww, let the kid see it." Let *him*, is more like it.

"Hey," says Sheppy, chasing after us. "You wanna get shot for desecraters? Man, down hyeah they do it, too."

Coming up on the graves, I can see why Sheppy says to keep off. It's way too real and powerful. It's not all cleaned up, hidden under grass and granite like white people's cemeteries. It's wire stakes with the names written in by hand and people's actual pictures under plastic perspiration. It's faded Styrofoam crosses and drooping wildflowers bunched in old corrugated buckets, and red mud so fresh it's caved in in places. But what really slays us is down at the very end—a white wicker Easter basket with three plastic eggs and this teddy bear with matted pink fur and two black eyes. Well, I'm overdue, I guess. One look and my eyeballs splurt. And as I spin around, here's Sheppy's own eyes like two fishbowls.

"So, you get your rocks off, man? Huh?"

"Just shut up!" I sob. "God, you talk about us white people! You never give a white person a fuckin' chance. Well, you don't. Like I really think it's *funny*." Looking strangled, Sheppy's beating back for the car.

"Mo'bid muthafuckas! I tol you doan stop. Goddamnit, goddamnit!"

What did I do? Alvy runs up, waves me off, then collars Sheppy. Hey, I wasn't disrespectful! All I did was look, but at breakfast Sheppy still won't even look at me he's so mad. Some breakfast, too, more cold beans and these pink felty Vienna sausages—greasy pink sausages like the arms of that teddy bear.

I always think night's the worst, but daytime's the absolute pits, holed up in the car, all sleeping upside down like a bunch of demented bats. Bats is right. Because when darkness falls, we all go screeching out, to fly down the roads. Nobody has the energy to put up a tent, and anyway, it would only draw attention. No, the car's our atomic shelter and as the driver, Alvy gets the "king"—the front seat—while Sheppy and me flip over who gets the backseat, and who gets the "backbreaker," the hump in the floor which, even smoothed out with clothes and trash, is pure torture. Steam's oozing down the windows, everything steeped in that wet-dog stink and my scalp scabbing and itching. Then I jump up. Something's crawling on my head! Look, it's on my finger! This speck.

"Sheppy, look! The fucker's moving."

Sheppy jerks away. "Thass just a ole hunka dirt."

"Look! It just moved again. What the hell is it—a louse?"

"How I know? Ain offa me."

First I can't sleep, then I'm sleeping like the dead, collapsed on both elbows, farting and snoring. Then somebody's screaming and punching me! Crazy people! They're holding my head underwater! Rearing up I tear at the hand on my throat, and it's Sheppy! Then Alvy pounces on us both.

"Sheppy wake up! Wake the hell up!"

"My nose is bleeding!" I start crying.

"*Sorry*," yelps Sheppy. He's more embarrassed than he was when I caught him beating off yesterday. I slug him one.

"Sorry? You busted my nose, you fucker!" But Sheppy only lays there, wheezing and snuffling, and then I know what it is. It's that little baby we saw buried in the graveyard, and that baby is Sheppy.

THE GRAVEYARD'S OUR FIRST MISTAKE. Our second is seeing *Taras Bulba* in that dinky theater we passed, the one with the hard seats and the big arrow that points to the balcony, *Colored*.

Sheppy goes in all by himself. Down in Dixie that's just the only way, pretending we don't know him—Sheppy doesn't even dare look back as he heads up the wooden stairs behind the old colored man. I guess I'd probably feel worse but the picture's already started, so I blank out, and believe me that's *all* I want, jaw dropped, stuffing my face with popcorn. Damn, though, I didn't know the show was about a Dad and his son! Yul Brynner, see, is Taras, this awful, sweaty, bare-chested, black-booted Cossack chieftain shaved bald with a topknot that he whips around. Taras must mean "terror" in Tartar or whatever. The guy's pillaging half of Europe, and Tony Curtis is his son.

I nudge Alvy. "How'd you like an old man like that?"

"Least he's decisive."

Hands hacked off. People set on fire. Men drenched with boiling oil and dancing like maniacs—half of it I can barely watch, not until Tony Curtis falls in love with this Polish girl, the daughter of his Dad's worst enemy, in the big castle. She's blonde just like Jessica. Spitting image. Absolutely gorgeous. In fact, I'll bet that's just how Jessica'll look when she's older, especially in the eyes and forehead. Taras, meanwhile, is besieging her castle, which certainly makes it awkward for Tony Curtis. Those Cossacks don't fuck around. Taras is starving them out, when the black plague hits and they start to go around with torches, piling the dead bodies on carts. What can Tony Curtis do? He sneaks into the castle to save her, but the Poles catch him, then start to burn his girl at the stake! Flames crackle. Writhing around in the smoke she looks at Tony. "Stop!" cries Tony, swearing he'll break through the Cossack hordes and get them food—anything. So wearing Polish armor and a helmet, Tony Curtis rides out with bunch of Polish knights but of course they all get creamed and Tony gets captured. The killer, though, is when Taras Bulba sees it's him in the Polish armor—when he sees his own son has sold him out.

Taras looks like he's been stabbed. "Why?" he asks, but Tony just stands there sick because, of course, there's no good excuse except that he did it. Well, Taras pulls out his flintlock pistol, cocks it.

"*I gave you life and now I must take it away.*"

Crack!

Alvy jumps. There's a black hole in Tony Curtis's armor. Just this little black hole and he stands there looking at his Dad, then slumps down dead. Plowing through the double doors Alvy looks like he's been shot himself. He lights a cigarette.

"Well, the fucker deserved it."

"*Deserved* it?"

"Hell, yeah. The kid totally betrayed him."

"Well, that's sweet! What if he was your kid?"

"What else? I'd have no choice but to shoot him."

"Your own kid?"

"In a life-or-death situation? And the kid sold me out?"

"Well, that's nice to know! Hell, you'll probably shoot *me* for desertion!"

"It was a military situation."

"He's his *kid*, military situation!"

"Hey, life's a military situation. What you think Abraham did to Isaac? And only God stopped him."

"You're sick!"

"Sick nothing. I understand necessity." At this Alvy looks at Sheppy walking just ahead, acting like he don't know us. God, it breaks my heart the way Sheppy walks down here, bobbing along all aimless and never looking up. It's not walking, it's drifting. I can't even look at Sheppy I feel so ashamed. But, loud, so Sheppy can hear me, I tell Alvy.

"I'll tell you about necessity and that's we get to Charlene's!"

"And I am getting us there. We're maneuvering."

"Maneuvering! You're driving anywhere not to get there, Mr. Military Situation."

I shut up as two men go by. It's just like *The Great Escape*, masquerading in enemy territory. Head down Alvy veers off to the restaurant on the corner.

"I'm getting some coffee."

"And your twenty-five-cent pie! And your four ten-cent donuts! And your buck for the jukebox. And what do we do when the money runs out, Mr. Commander? Well, huh?"

Christ, I think, I sound exactly like Dad. Every day I only keep getting more worried and cheap, while Alvy only keeps getting more shirking and irresponsible, every day more like Lucky. Well, there you go. Dump one family and you only create a worse one. Dump your Dad and all you get is the Son of Dad, a monster.

SHEPPY'S MY PROBLEM, NOT ALVY'S. I'm the one who has to take Sheppy into stores—to go in first and scope things out.

"Look," I try to tell him. "I'll go in for you. Just tell me what you want."

"How I know whut I want? Firs, I gotta see it." No, Sheppy's gotta show the flag—the colored flag. Besides, he says, it's the best way to see how bad a new town is. "Now go *on*. And doan be lookin back at me."

It's like having to take a little kid into the toilet, to pull his pants down for him. That whole breathless, dog-beaten tone he gets around white folks and, worse, I gotta pretend I don't notice, while he pretends nothing's changed. And where are they written—the Rules, I mean? Down here, as crazy as they are, you'd think the Rules would be written out on billboards. You'd think the Rules would be riding over the highways like the Ten Commandments but it's worse—invisible.

And they call this a store? It's more a cave than a store, with a sunken tin ceiling and a woodstove singeing your face. There's an old trailer connected to the store, all these warrens like an ant farm, and here's an old woman with her neckflesh sagging down like melted candlewax. She looks like she just woke up, eyeing me like I just walked into her living room, which basically I have. And the second the door slaps behind Sheppy, she's seething, staring at *me* like some dog followed me in.

"He wid yew?"

I blank-face her. "Not me."

"Hey, boy." She ogles around the aisle. "Out here where I can see yew. I wanna see your face. At all times, hear?"

Behind her, in the yellow light of the other room, a radio's playing—she's definitely not alone. Stepping from behind the baked goods, Sheppy's doing the dancing chicken.

"Ma'am?"

"You heard me."

"Some gum."

"Fresh out."

"Okay, Nabs and raspberry pop."

"Nabs and milk I got. Fresh outta pop."

It's incredible. The pop's gurgling in the ice-water cooler with the dust-caked fan. And there's the gum's right behind her in the slanted popcrate. Slap, Sheppy's out the door. For a split second she smiles like she's seen God.

She knocks back a dry wisp of hair. "All right. So whass fer yew t'night?"

"Twinkies. Two pops and some Wrigley's Doublemint."

"Thought you said he warn't with you?"

"And he's not."

"Lorrrd, where are you from, boy?"

"Pennsylvania."

"*Where?*"

It's like they have to taste your accent, making you repeat everything fifty times. "Pennsylvania. My Scout troop's down here. It's a jamboree." She's really looking hard at me now. "Y'know, a big get-together."

"I know perfectly well what 'jamboree' is, thank you. Scouts, huh? They teach y'all how to *bathe?*"

"We're camping." I stare at her. "You get dirty camping."

"Boy, donchew *dare* come in here asmart-assin me, Pennsylvania."

Scared she'll call the cops, I calm her down. "And I'm not sassing you, ma'am. Look, you don't wanna sell me anything, well, just say so and I'll tell the whole troop. We can take a hint."

"And I didn't say that. I jus said I won't tolerate no smartin off in my place." And, like that, she pops a bag and starts reaching things for me, just chattering away, "You know, I had an uncle up there in Coplay, Pennsylvania. You know Coplay? Near Bethlehem. Steel-makin town . . ." Man, she all but drags out the family Bible before I can get out of there. Actually, she's pretty nice, otherwise. But Sheppy has a shit fit.

"Din you see me lookin at you, *din* you? And you, sweet-facin that old cracker bitch! *Walk on out!*"

"Hey, don't blame me! I didn't invent this shit."

"Well, you cozy up to it real good, muthafucka."

"Fine! So let Alvy take you next time."

"And you keep him outta it! Shoot, Alvy, I ain goin in wid him. Not in no kinda sto!"

AND THEN I see why. The next night, even after Sheppy argues and threatens against it, Alvy hits a hamburger shack, a blaze of buttered-popcorn light in the general pine darkness. All around the red dirt lot, the yokels sit barricaded in their cars, eating out of bags and looking like the world just ended.

Well, Alvy won't listen, and Sheppy's way too proud to hide. First, Sheppy waits in the backseat, but then, feeling conspicuous or so he won't be trapped if there's trouble, Sheppy ambles out and stands by the fender—obviously *ours* in the general nigger alert. Peeping through the food hole with the bugs mashed in the screen, Alvy orders three chocolate shakes. Two come back.

"Sir," says Alvy in his all-purpose hick voice, "Scuse me . . . *sir,* that was three shakes I ordered."

The burger man flips a look at Sheppy. "Well, two's all yer gettin."

"Come again?"

"Two. You heard me—*two.*"

Which Alvy does the monkey *huh,* dropping his jaw and raising his eyebrows. Try it out in the zoo sometime. I guarantee it'll send any knuckledragger into orbit.

"I done tolt you once. 'Thass fifty cent."

Alvy straightens up. "And that ain't what I ordered."

"Yer bout to get a lot more than you ordered, boy. You ain't foolin me and I ain't servin no nigger no milkshake. Not in front, not in back."

"Fo-get it, c'mon, man," calls Sheppy, but Alvy can't believe it, and this time he can't trick it or bluff it. But, being Alvy, he sure tries.

"Look mister, we don't even *know* the kid. We just picked him up, is all, and he's starved. You act like it's liquor. He ain't gonna drink it here. So what's the big problem?"

The man snatches back the shakes. "You're the problem, that kinda attytude."

"*Attytude?*" sneers Alvy. He looks at me. "Can't speak fuckin English and he's talkin about *my attytude?*"

The man practically plows his head through the screen. "Git! Git fore I kick your ass and his monkey ass too."

Alvy patches out. "A fuckin milkshake!"

"Or candy or pop!" hollers Sheppy. "Or any goddamn thing they can hold it ovah yo head! Man, what you heah fo—fin yo sister or get us all kilt?"

"It's the principle, *he pissed me off.*" Again, Alvy gooses it. "Yeah, and what about you the other day? Weren't you jumping for joy when you saw that Freedom Rider bus!"

"*Asshole, we ain't Freedom Ridin.*"

"Who ain't Freedom Ridin?" Alvy hunkers over the wheel. "Goddamnit, get down. He mighta called the law."

"And I hope he did! Freedom! Whass at to you? *Free* to showboat? *Free* to get me strung up by mah balls? Oh, but *suh*, you gotta give this heah nigger boy his free milkshake, suh! Shoot, you as bad as all of em, wid they *pet* nigger and they *favorite* nigger!"

"So go on, colored boy! Here you go, Miloville, South Carolina! And don't say I never got you here."

"Alvy," I shout, "shut up! Shut up, 'cause I swear, if Sheppy leaves, I'm gone too!"

Well, Alvy, he hauls up the hand brake and jumps out. "So here you go, you two geniuses! See how you do without me!"

WEIRD, ALL YOU NEVER KNOW ABOUT SOMEBODY.

Using our tank-driving technique, Sheppy and I creep the car down a few hundred feet, to a clump of bushes by another little roadside dump where people have flung their old washing machines and Clorox bottles. It's just big enough to hide the car behind, so after we check the perimeter, we eat, then turn in, and early, we're so depressed. Still, looking on the bright side—not that anybody here particularly wants to look there but hey, I'm trying—well, as I tell Sheppy, the good thing about Alvy's being gone is we can spread out for once, with me taking the whole back, and him the whole front.... "*God-damn*," he cries, "*will you evuh shut up?*" Fine! I can take a hint but, God, am I itching! My hair's burning like fire, and my dipstick's tingling like an icicle at thirty degrees below zero... *c'mon Sheppy start snoring.* I bound up.

"Hey, I just thought of something. Why'd they name you Sheppy?"

Sheppy rolls around. (The faker's waiting on me, too.) "She ain't *name* me Sheppy. Name's *Shepherd.*"

"But that's a regular first name, Shepherd?"

"You out to pick sumpin?"

"Jeez, I'm only asking what it means."

"*Means?* Whass 'Frank' mean? Fuckin hot dog?"

"But why Shepherd? That's really a legal name?"

"Legal names! Man, you about an igno'ant muthafucka. *Lord* is my Shepherd. *Good* Shepherd."

"Oh, like in *God?*"

"HAH!" Rubbing his prick through his underpants, Sheppy cackles like a black buddha, "Thass me, man, the *Shepherd*. Jus watchin ovah all y'all li'l white sheeps."

STILL NO ALVY THE NEXT MORNING. Five days! Five days I've lasted and I've had it! God, I wake up totally crazed with my itching, on top of which I've been up half the night. A creek! A mud puddle! *Anything* so I can just wash my hair. Meanwhile, Sheppy's decided we'll both split up to-day—take a vacation from each other. Well, I panic. As Sheppy starts down the road I holler after him.

"This is desertion, y'know!"

"Sundown, man. You be back right hyeah."

"I got my call-home dime all ready!" It's my eject button, that precious dime. I hold it up, gleaming silver, "*I'm warning you.*"

"*Sundown, man.*"

Digging and scratching I must look like I'm flagging down cars, because just then one stops, this bull-necked man calling over.

"Hey boy, why ain't you in schoo'?"

Is he a truant officer? "Gee, thanks for stopping, sir. That's just where I'm headed."

"Well, you sure are late enough," he says as I jump in. He scowls at me. "Hey, don' be itchin' yosef in here. What you got, boy—ringworm?"

"Ringworm? What's that?"

"Contagious, is what! Shoot, health department make you shave your whole head and wear a nasty sock over it. Thass right, so them worm eggs don't hop off onto other people."

I grab my hair. "Jumping eggs?"

"Like Mexican damn jumpin' beans. Jeee-sus pee-sus, if you gimme ring-worm." He screeches up to this redbrick cannery of a school. "Now go on. Straight to the school nurse, *straight.*"

Well, what can I do? And it's no accident. I think. No, it's a positive sign from God, my winding up back at school. I tell you, if I'm not sweating Dad, jail and military school, then I'm worrying about term papers I never wrote and tests I never studied for and will they hold me back a grade, in which case I will definitely kill myself. Talk about feeling like a deadbeat turd. I mean, even when I arrive late at my *own* school, I feel like a derelict, let alone here, in a strange school. And look at this place. It never changes. Always the same worn-out bulletin board, plastered with those depressing cutouts of autumn leaves and orange pumpkins, everything designed to keep you *busy busy busy and happy happy happy*. And always that barf smell of cooked-to-death kale and yesterday's steaming Sloppy Joe. God, the men are huge down here, huge. Because around the corner, here's another puffing, red-faced guy with a whistle on a braided lanyard.

"Hey, mister. Where's your pass?"

"Gee, sir, I left it back at the office." Then like an angel told me, "I'm John Tate, sir. It's my first day but that other man he, uh, said I first gotta shower."

"Who, Mr. Stevens? Well, he was sure right there." He's looking at me hard now. "No sir, son, this is sure no way to turn out on your first day a school." He shambles around, pointing. "Well, go on now. Gym's straight down the hall. You'll find the showers."

The shower room's a mildew pit, but here's a whole stack of fluffy white towels and the water's sure hot! Man, I crank the water on scalding—*die you hopping egg creeps*. Outside, I can hear kids yelling and scuffling, bouncing basketballs. Then, as I'm slicking back my hair, here's the gym teacher.

"Who the heck are you?"

"John Tate, sir. I'm new. Mr. Stevens said I had to shower before I could go to class."

"Well, speed it up, Tate." He frowns at my clothes. "By the way, tell your Mamma we got a nice coin laundry here in town."

I sniff my shirt. Am I that bad? Quick, I switch shirts, swipe two bucks from another locker, then haul ass out the swinging doors when the lunch bell rings. Hot chow! So following the crowd, I slide into the lunch line, load up, then tell the hairnet woman at the register how Mr. Stevens said on account of it's my first day and I forgot my money that I should charge it . . . and don't ask me how but my cheezy old Kennedy accent takes over.

"Shee, at my old school," I explain, "in Mashachusetts, lunch was, uh, freeh." God it's so corny. The accent's straight off some comedy record but damned if they don't buy it.

"Well, la-de-da," says the hairnet lady. "Who'd ya charge it to, Presdunt Kenndy?"

Well, the slop slingers all have a good hoot, but who cares? The girls think I'm a teen sensation, hollering down the lunch line, "*Mary, Donna. Come hear how this new kid talks. Lak Presdent Kenndy.*" Man, it's worse than *American Bandstand*. I can't eat for the girls pushing up, begging me.

"Say *salt*."

"Shalt."

"Say *car* again."

"Cah."

"Get this, y'all. He says 'cah.' "

"Have you ever seen him?" begs some girl in this dippy little headbow and thick glasses. "Really? Presdent Kenndy?"

"Sheen him? They play touch—uh, touch *football*—on the Commons. Bobby Kennedy, tooh."

Some big lunk shoves me in the back. "You about a liar, *Boshton*—"

"Uh, noh," I stammer, backing up. "Uh, noh shit."

"Hey bub, we don't cuss in front of ladies down here."

"Shorry."

He hunkers in my face. "Hey, I got a word for yuh to try. Can you shay *ass-whopping* onct for me, please?"

And he would, too, except for the girls screaming at him—man, the girls are like my Secret Service, all protecting the famous John Tate as we troop out into the schoolyard. Ordinarily, I'd be scared to death, but that's the weirdest thing now. Down here, it's like I'm this whole other kid, wearing this whole other life. And the amazing thing is, once I'm done with it, just like my old shirt I toss it away.

"Heh, you know what?" I say to the girls. "I feel like a schoda. Is that the schtore? Over deah?"

"Huh?" they cry. "Hay, you can't do that. That's off grounds, you'll go to detention!"

But not the famous John Tate! (Shit, I shoulda said John Keats!) No, just to show that ignorant loudmouth, I stroll out across the road, all but floating up into the true, the blue, the blissful hippocream of *leaving*. Or do until this other kid hollers, "Hay! *Hay you! Thass my shirt!"*

WELL, I'M JUMPING FENCES AND CUTTING THROUGH YARDS when *HEIGH-HO, SILL-VER!* It's our car! It's Alvy with this wild little blonde. Hot too, with teased-up moon-man hair and wonderful wide jugs.

I dive in the backseat. "Go on! They're after my ass!"

Alvy nonchalants me—still pissed off. The girl peers over the seat, perky, with this toy-something face.

"Well?" she says. "You gonna lift your head up and say hi?"

I wave her off. "Don't be lookin' back here! Man, the cops are probably looking for me!" Why do I always get this stupid blowhard voice around girls? "Y'know, ace," I mutter to Alvy, "it's not too bright, you riding her around during school hours."

The girl shrugs—she's out of school, she says, tapping two cigarettes on the dash. Cigarette tapping! And for a filter! To me, that's the *height* of pretentiousness, lighting two cigarettes, then stuffing one in Alvy's mouth.

"Graduated or dropped out?" I demand.

"Let's just say *done*," she says, snuggling into herself. "Yeah, one day I went in and, just like a pan of biscuits, I just knew, *I'm done.* I didn't pick up my books, ask for no permission, nuthin. Nope, I just walked on out." Talk about a shameless self-dramatizer. Well, I sit up. *Crane* up, short as she is, and she knows why, too, the popovers she's got on her. And boy is she ever proud of them, staring back at me, *are you finished gawking yet?*

"So how old are you?"

"Sixteen."

I snort at Mr. Mustache. "*Jailbait*, huh?"

Miss Putdown glances back. "Me?? You even bait yet?"

Well, great, I think. I come a thousand miles and here I am, back in the kid seat, watching two other fools go at it. And these two, you'd think they'd been going together for ages. Next thing I know, Little Miss Putdown's swabbing out his ear with her tongue. Well, I put the kabosh on that.

"Hey, you two mind telling me what's going on?"

Alvy looks at the girl. "Gee, you never introduced yourself, honey."

"I'm Tweety," and sure enough, she's got this high, crackly, little, like, whistle in her voice, like maybe something didn't grow in quite right. "Well, go on," she prods, "so get it over with."

"*Pretty* unusual name," I snort.

"Tweety Bird. Tweety Pie, but I prefer Tweety *Bird*. Or just plain *Tweety.* Linda Bird, Lady Bird, Luci Bird—I know you hearda them. Also Angelbird. C'mon, you never heard of the famous figure skater Angelbird Carter?"

I stare out the window. "Birdbrain I heard of."

Fine, I could make a crack about her size or the chicken-plucking plant her Dad works in but the truth is, I feel bad for her—as a runt. (Being tall, I am the world's expert on shrimps, and definitely the most sensitive about how they feel.) At the same time, though, I don't want Tweety pulling a Heidi on me, suckering me with the old female sympathy. Man, I am getting depressed.

"Tweety, no disrespect," I say finally, "but mind if Alvy and me have a bird word?"

Alvy follows me down the road. "Please, don't fuck this up for me."

"*You?*"

"Hey, who dumped who last night?" I can't stand it.

"Did you get laid? Well, *did* you?"

"Hey, have some class, huh."

"*Did you?*" I whip a stone into the creek. "So what's the girl know about us?"

"Most everything. Except I'm seventeen, okay? *Seventeen.*"

I stare at him. "And what about Sheppy, huh? So what's he supposed to do while you run around? We're supposed to meet at sundown, you know."

"Why? So you can both ditch me?"

"No, to plan what we do next. Cause I've had it."

"Well, I know the plan. One last night here and we're off. Off for the final hump."

"Hint, hint, hint. God, I love you, Loomis. All free to disappear, then here I am, boys. Never fear, it's Alvy, back to run the whole show. Well, I've got news for you because you're not running everything now. And before you even start, Tweety or Twerpy or whatever her name is is *not* coming."

He turns for the car. "We'll discuss that later."

"Oh, okay, *Dad.* And it's one more day for me, Dad—a day at the most. Cause tomorrow I'm fucking leaving."

Back inside Tweety says, "Just so you know, I got no problems with colored boys."

"Yeah," grins Alvy. "Tweety thinks everybody oughta own a few."

"Honey, quit now." Even Tweety's embarrassed but I'm furious.

"Alvy, do you want me to *hate* you? Is that what you want now?"

But at this Tweety bounds over the seat and kisses me! Jams her whole tongue into my brain, *thwirls* it around, then looks at me with this crazy gleam. "Well, I know what your problem is, Frankie baby. I know jus *exactly* what your problem is."

"Oh no you don't."

"Oh yes I do. Hey, I know you like candy and I know you like cake, but *cookies?*" She winks. "Cause I know a girl by that name. She's a little older but she really might go for you. Here, hon, stop! There's a phone!"

"*Cookie?*" I ask. "So how'd she get a name like that?"

But, jumping out, Tweety only laughs, then stands there yakking on the phone, winking at me and doing the Bunny Hop in the cold. My stomach's like a flood in the Fizzy factory. Alvy yawns around.

"Oboy, Frank be getting his cookies tonight."

"No!"

"Cookies and cream."

"No! *Really?*"

BUT I'M NOT THE ONLY ONE GIRDING HIS LOINS FOR TONIGHT. After we drop Tweety off at her house—mailbox, rather—Alvy buys a bottle of Vitalis and about bathes in it, freezing his hair into hard, dark quills. Stamping and glowering at himself in the side mirror, he knows what's coming. In fact, I'm tending to think he *didn't* do it yet. He jerks some Vitalis into my hand.

"Go on. Darken your hair up. Make you look older."

"Look, I meant what I said back there. I really am leaving tomorrow."

"Okay." He keeps primping. Then, of course, I feel bad.

"Well, five days. Can't say I didn't stick it out."

"I know."

I feel even worse. "Anyhow, Tweety can go with you if Sheppy won't. Might be better, a woman. She might calm Hicks down."

"How? Stick her tongue in his mouth too?"

I start to apologize but Alvy just laughs. "Aww, forget it. Man, I was glad to see you happy. Christ, here I am, trying to show you a certain wild, cool *spirit* of life, but oh no, boy, not Frank. Show Frank any fun and he runs the other way."

"Hey, I *like* fun and I like cookies but you know, man—y'know, there's a certain *point*. I mean, your Mom—Bunny—well, she'd take you back no matter what, but you don't know my old man. I've really been thinking about it. Laugh, but it's like when a bird falls out of his nest. Cause if I don't go back now, well, Dad may never take me back, never. Especially when I ruined his wedding."

"*Not take you back?*" Rearing back, Alvy does that lusty Taras Bulba laugh which he's already added to his repertoire. "Man, every day more, every mile further, the more fear you buy. *Fear,* man. Fear's like money in the bank. Fear's fucking *respect.* Man, after this you think your old man'll ever dare treat you the way he did before? Or let Sieg Heidi jack you around. Champ, I bought you a million-dollar respect policy. After this your Dad and people will see you and marvel—marvel. *Uh-oh, watch that kid. That kid ran a thousand miles.*"

"And Dad'll hate me for it too! And the longer I wait, the worse he'll hate me!"

Alvy fires up a cigarette, blows the smoke out his nose. He gives me his deadpan doctor look. "You don't think about her much now, do you?" *You,* he means.

"We're not talking about her now."

"Hey, no fooling. Cause you never talk about her now. Never."

It's true—anymore, it's like I have an amnesia against thinking about you. "Look, it's not my fault. She changed, or *it* changed, I mean. Well, it changes, then it changes back, so lay off, will ya? It's not like I deserted her."

"Oh, no, huh? Well, just to keep you company—I mean on that *long ride home . . .*" Alvy pops the trunk, digs around, then flings a book at me. "Here— maybe this'll jog your memory."

"*What's this?*"

It's a school copybook strapped with dry-rotted rubber bands and the title *Book Reports.* No name on it. It's just a black, snow-speckled school copybook, but straight off, just from the heat, I know it's yours. Stumbling around, half crying, I almost heave it back at Alvy.

"And you've had this all this time? And *now* you gimme this? On my last fucking *day?*"

"Hey, don't blame me. You remember our deal. Because you told me, go into everything."

"Not into her personal papers I didn't!"

"So burn it—your old man almost did. Ask my Mom. We got three whole crates in our attic. Back last spring your Grammaw and me hauled it over. But hey, don't thank me just because your old man was set to burn the whole mess."

It's fizzling like a cherry bomb, that copybook. Alvy can't stand it either. He jumps in the car. "So *read* it. It's yours now and she was your age when she wrote it. I'm getting Tweety." I wave the book at him.

"That's right, cut and run! Like always!"

"*Reeeead.*"

· · ·

THE BOOK'S LIKE A BABY ALVY FLUNG OUT THE WINDOW.

Raging around, I want to chuck it in the river, when I see a picture sticking out—one of the old-fashioned kind, with the crinkly edges. It's a picture of you as a girl on a swimming float. Some lake with glinting black water and mountains all around, *But how old was she? As old as me? Older?*

All lanky and dripping dark curls, you can't be much more than fifteen in the picture. No need even to focus the camera, your face is so sharp, peering down in the water, into the reflections, with that stuck-upedness of a beautiful girl just knowing she's being looked at. But looking at it again, I see that you're mad—mad-upset. And, tacky of me, but under the black wool of your swimsuit, there's *a nipple.* And, there, in the puddle between your legs, *a fold.* Definitely. I flip the picture over.

Bear Lake, July 29, 1938. How I feel today.

And look, on the very bottom, by the white ribs of the canoe, there's the hairy knee of whoever snapped the picture. I can't stand it. Stripping off the rubber bands, I start reading.

LITTLE WOMEN
A book report by Julie Slattery, April 9, 1938

Little Women *is the second book of Louisa May Alcott, an American authoress born in 1832. I'd rather memorize the Gettysburg Address backwards. At least it's shorter.*

Tiny Women is certainly a precious gem. This particular reviewer wanted to pick up her hoop skirts and squeal Bless my little heart!

Little Women *is*

So who says you have to finish a book to write a report on it? Tiny Women *makes you* hate *being a girl. I know girls can tend to chatter but I don't ALWAYS. True this particular work was written many years ago when girls were very much nicer. Still it makes me want to vomit, the way these girls all carry on, all waiting for some dope to traipse down the garden path.*

Oh who cares. I hope you do *read this Mother, but I won't chatter. ARE YOU READING THIS? If you do, scream at me but don't tell Daddy. Daddy already has problems enough with Mr. Merryman if only he knew.*

I hate Mr. Merryman always calling and Mother always putting on more lipstick than usual and running out in her furs. We wouldn't have a telephone if it wasn't for Mr. Merryman and that would be dandy with me. Mother said I was rude to Mr. Mer-

ryman today on the telephone. She said I don't know which side my bread is buttered on. Oh yes I do, I told her. Yours too.

Uncle Stephen upset me so much tonight. People always assume I'm older because I'm so tall. Uncle Stephen says with my height and bones and skin I can be a model and I joke, A model of what? What would I ever think standing around as a model I wonder?

Stephen always liked me better than Cousin Sarah or Mary Alice, who frankly aren't so bright, or Trish who is common, or any of the boys. I find I have always preferred the company of adults and especially highly sophisticated and successful adults such as Stephen who speaks to me like one about "boys" and other adult topics. I was the perfect height for him when we waltzed at Anne V.'s wedding.

Letting me out of the car a few blocks away Stephen gives me a "note" for Mother and a dollar to keep out of trouble. Wait, he says. Embarrassed, he writes the name of a dentist who will fix my teeth and send him the bill. I jump across the seat to see myself in the window. Am I that bad? And all the time everybody saw and nobody told me? Look, they can do lots of things, Stephen says. And nix with your Mamma.

I should go upstairs but I keep walking. How could I be so stupid! I do too brush, I probably brush too much hoping the dark stuff will come off. In the light I peer in my compact mirror, then go around the block again just to feel the air on me. I'm already taller than many men, especially in my suede pumps, and believe me the gentlemen notice. Julie Slattery you are a special and in fact incredible person and everybody you meet knows this. Believe me I could say PLENTY more but I won't. Nix.

Wait, your teeth! Suddenly I remember that thing, *the flashing silver thing,* you used to wash out in the sink, with the three or four false teeth stuck to it. *A plate.* Of course, but because it was secret and embarrassing it's like I never saw it. The hollow, rattling sound it made in the water, like a girl's plastic play dishes. Once I caught you with it, but by then I was too old. You nearly caught my fingers in the door, you shut it so fast.

My stomach again. By now Mrs. Scott, the school nurse, thinks I'm either a nut or a faker. Well, the first may be true but not the second, and I don't need any doctor to tell me why.

I hate the way Mommy always protects Daddy and I protect Daddy from always feeling he has to apologize, and we both kill ourselves over who can protect Daddy more. But who will protect Daddy from us?

· · ·

When I was little I always loved to hear the story of Felix, the rat Daddy fed in the trenches. Felix was very delicate and refined for a rat, not like the fat greasy ones you see by the Hudson. Daddy says Felix ate from his hand, and for a second Daddy almost squeaks he's so happy. Daddy's the same when he talks about the sardines he used to fry in the tin he made with the wire cutters.

Why do they call it the Great War? To hear Daddy, all it was was Felix, his little brick stove and his sardines sputtering. Give Daddy a little place and he's happy. Daddy stops shaking. In the morning Mother gives Daddy his dime and then Daddy roasts his special bread crumbs. No man is neater than Daddy. He shaves. Then he puts on his cap and big shoes and his tie with his lumberjack shirt and kisses me then goes out with his big bag of bread crumbs like a respectable lunch. Some days I worry he'll drop off the end of Coney Island. But back he comes at six o'clock with the bag stuffed in his back pocket. Daddy never forgets the bag.

I hate leaving for school. Every day at the bottom of the stairs, here's Snag Lip and the other loafers giving me the business. Hey, Heartthrob, Hollywood's that way. I give it right back to them too. Boy, you guys should know, all the freaks and midgets they need out there.

Today I turn sixteen. Uncle Stephen arrives with a pile of gifts—naturally when Daddy's home. I love Stephen's red Airflow and his beautifully haberdashered suits. People sometimes think he's a professional boxer, although he really does box, plays tennis, golfs and twirls his Indian clubs.

I know Stephen can't help but embarrassing Daddy being younger and so rich. The icebox smacks. Daddy calls down the hall to Mother are we out of cheese again? Squeezing out the door Daddy escapes down the steps. Uncle Stephen always leaves fast so Daddy won't have to wait too long before not bringing anything back. We could live two months on what Uncle Stephen has brought, a gorgeous black taffeta dress, with pumps to match and a silver heart bracelet. We're both such awful beggars, Mother and I. Mother tells him he went overboard—so Stephen will always go overboard—and I cry because I want it so badly I can't refuse.

Coming back with the phony bag with the cheese in it, Daddy acts surprised Uncle Stephen is gone. Then tonight Mother will rewrap the dress so Daddy can give it to me and I'll kick up such a fuss he'll almost believe it. But for now Daddy goes back to building his toothpicks and playing the radio. All night by the radio waiting for the answer to our life.

As usual the loafers are waiting for me this morning. I should know from Snag Lip's smile that they've got something up their sleeve. Hey Heartthrob I saw your Mamma stepping out this morning. The Furs right? So who's the old guy who picks Mamma up? Is that Mr. Abe Fickelstein the Jew furrier? Snag Lip smushes down his nose and they all laugh.

Once when I was a dunce it was all I dreamed of was Sundays with the family. But now I get so sick of Uncle Tommy on his high horse just because he works for the Grand Central. Stephen says that with Tommy's railroad seniority he'll get overtime in heaven.

Why does Daddy even come? Why so they can send him to the store with their money while they all roll their eyes saying poor, poor Francis. Aunt Rose refuses to be in the same room with Uncle Stephen, not since Eleanor took Joseph and Stephen asked the bishop for an annulment. It's nothing but a white divorce, Aunt Rose says. Stephen stays only for one drink, and he's so funny, calling down the hall, All right Rose you can come out of the bathroom now! I slip out and catch him in the hallway. Stephen's huggy eyes. Pure green. He give me a big kiss and a whack to grow on. Then here's Daddy trudging up the stairs! I stand there burning, but of course Daddy doesn't see.

I jump up from the rock and look dazed at the weeds waggling in the river. I stare at the water a long time, then I flip forward, but it's only worse.

Lung stew. Creamed over toast. You loved it as a girl Mother says, but I run into the bathroom and heave. Mother pushes in behind me. You're walking funny she says. Then I realize she thinks I'm like Mary C. In that way and I look at her. What can Mother possibly think of me? I'll tell you what she thinks. She thinks I'm just like her.

IS HER DIARY THAT BAD? Tripping over roots, I'm running down the crooked river, God knows what river, following the wavy path that makes the river look almost straight. *But it's not that bad.* But shouldn't I feel horrible? *But it's not that horrible.* And the sex. But I half skip those parts. It's like if you've ever seen "fuck" written in a book—I mean, it's so blaring it bleeps itself out, *And who says that's what she was getting at?*

And poor. *That* poor, when all I had to do was open my eyes to the dump where Grammaw lives. And Grandfather Francis—so what was wrong with him walking around all day like a bum? A soldier! A war hero, Grammaw said. But here you're afraid to tell your war-hero Dad about this Snag Lip creep always razzing you? But Christ, I think, what do I *know* about Grampa Francis? You never said boo about him. Except for Grammaw, nobody did.

And what about your family, *But I thought you were crazy about them?* But then almost wanting to gag I remember the mysterious "summer bugs" that always got you during our visits, always barfing in Aunt Till's bathroom. And when Uncle Stephen did come to Croton—once in a blue moon, and never with Aunt Toody because she was way too rich and cool for us—your face broke out in weepy red blotches. *Eczema*, they said which I thought was like *Noxzema. But Mommy why does Aunt Toody hate you so bad why?*

The river rips and slithers, endlessly braiding into itself. It must have really rained because the river's really pumping. It's pumping up big clots of mud and sticks, and the water vees, the water strands into long, strong veins of water, the water that only makes more water as I stare down into the river hypnotized, hearing all this other mumbo jumbo, Dah-Duh-dum Stephen-Stephen something-something, *Frank! In bed!* It's late and the hi-fi's on—loud. The ice tray cracks. Ice cubes clink dot-dash-Stephen-Toody-you-never-Stephen-loves-me-goddamn-money-something. Then you're pounding on the bedroom door, *Pete give me my car keys because I'm going goddamnit and you can't stop me.*

I remember Angelene once said that part of your brain's in your tailbone, but with boys it's in the balls, I think. No, it's definitely the balls, because just then, staring into the I-don't-know-what-river, my balls are burning like two atomic brains, remembering how you and Uncle Stephen were always leapfrogging each other, first you getting married, then him, and then him dying, then you, *but that was really Uncle Stephen's leg in the canoe and he took the dirty picture and you let him?*

I MUST LOOK PRETTY SICK when Alvy gets back with Tweety. Motioning her to stay put Alvy runs over.

"You okay? Look, I'm sorry. Okay, I was a prick, giving it to you. Here—" He grabs for the book but I jerk it away.

"So what's so terrible in here, *what?*"

He stares at me like I'm crazy. "Who said terrible? Look, when I read it it made me feel for her more, lots more. Especially when you couldn't, uh, feel anything."

"Feel what, you fucker?" I slug him in the chest but, like you, even then I girly hit him with the heel of my fist, all halfhearted and beaten, as usual. "And all this time you *knew!* And at the Black Jumps! All your mumbo jumbo bullshit, like you were some big mind reader!"

"Yeah, and why didn't I tell you? Well, I'll tell you why. Cause you weren't ready, is why. And meanwhile, what were you doing, helping yourself to *my* house, living *my* life, wearing my clothes and calling *my* mother Mom!"

"I hate you, you goddamn liar. Fuck, I can't believe I even listened to you with those dick hairs glued on your lip."

And what's she done to him, this Tweety Bird? He's like Dad with Heidi. Alvy glances up at the car, half whispering, "Man, don't do this to me. Not with Tweety here, *please?* C'mon, you pissed me off back there. You and Sheppy both ganging up on me and freezing me out. Well, I'm sick of it with you two. And you especially, acting like I'm your fuckin' Daddy."

"Oh, no," I rail back, "it *wasn't you*, treating us both like six-year-olds. *Wasn't you*, squandering all our money, slurping coffee and playing pinball while Sheppy and me sat for hours in the car, freezing our butts off. And what now, hotshot? Blow all the rest on baby doll here?"

"She's almost *seventeen*." In the space of a second Alvy looks just exactly like what he is—a scared, worn-out kid. "*You* drive around, grand theft, no license—*you* try it on for size, motherfucker. Forget the mustache. First, you gotta *believe* it."

And now it's all collapsing around him, all the McQueen schemes. Right in front of his eyes it's all failing, and Alvy knows it. And, as suddenly, I know it too, just as hard and dead with him as I was with Dad before him. No, that kid's love impulse, it just dies of old age, laying there like our two shadows in the mud as Alvy takes off down the river. Tweety jams her door open, calling after him.

"Honey! . . . hon, where are you off to?"

"For a walk! Let the baby cry on your shoulder! He *excels* at that!"

Hell, I'd run, too, all the lipsticked, hairsprayed, bubble-gummed heat that Tweety's giving off. Tweety's changed clothes. She's wearing a dress now. Good, strong tumbler's legs, too. Snapping her gum, Tweety picks up the picture of you on the swimming float.

"That's her? That was your Mom?" She frowns. "Hey, I'm sorry. That's a bite, what happened to her, but hey, she's real beautiful." It's a superagitated, upper-brain gum chewing, studying your picture, *pop pop pop*. "Well, one thing you know. Her boyfriend took this—well, from the angle. Pretty *low*, wouldn't ya say?" She's chewing faster now, in fast, front-teeth pops. "Yeah, they had a big fight. Yeah, she's been crying—assolutely." And then, without a word, she takes the copybook from my hands, *just takes it*. Slips it off like my belt, and I stand there amazed.

"But once you read it, so you'll tell me the truth?" I ask. "*Promise?* No matter what?"

It's worse than waiting on report cards. I must walk three miles up and down the river, finally running the last stretch. Tweety jumps, she's so buried in the book.

"Look, I didn't get very far, her handwritin's so hard to read—"

"Aww, gwan!"

"Well—" A big breath. "Well, to tell the truth I didn't like her Mamma too awful much."

Of course I fly off the handle. "What is this crap, everybody always having to *like* everybody? And who even asked you to *like* them? All I asked was for you to *think* about them and tell me the damned truth."

She stares at the book. "Well, I kinda skipped around. What part was it you read?"

"*I can't read it.*"

"Well, then don't! And why the heck should you? Look, leave it with us. Yes *us*, Alvy and me—well, you're leavin, aincha? And anyways, what is it with you guys? Like, what is it with Alvy's sister? I mean, why's Alvy supposed to spend up his whole inheritance—thousands of dollars—just to send *her* kids away to some special private school? Just because her husband's a no-good bastard? And all so Alvy can enlist in the army next year?"

Huh? God knows what all bullshit Alvy's told her—I don't even dispute it with her—but what gets me is Alvy's telling her he's never going back, *Never no matter what*. So what's that supposed to mean? I worry. Alvy never told me that. Sheppy either.

Back to the diary, though, it's funny with girls. Guys if you ask their opinion, well, out it all spews, in one big, unholy mess. Not girls, though. No, looking at the picture again, Tweety's slowly picking at it, picking at it the way girls'll pick all the seeds off a piece of bread, first the seeds, then the soft center, then the crust.

"Look," Tweety says finally, "about the diary. Well at first, I thought, I could *splain* it to ya, but then I thought, 'So what good'll that do him?' Like I could splain this picture by the lake, for instance. Like I could say, that's a man's hairy leg right there, for instance, *but you already know that, right?* You know that. You know who took it, that Stephen guy, just like you know she ain't too awful proud of it, but hey, what's the girl to do? Like I'm not so awful proud a some of the things I done, but whoopee-doo—I mean, well, here I am, you know? But actually, I think this girl is pretty nice, least compared to most girls. I mean I could have been this girl's friend, for instance. Well, maybe—I'm just saying that as a for instance, understand. Or I could tell you that she probably loves whatshisname here, on account of he gave her all this nice stuff and got her teeth fixed for her. I mean, sure, I could *say* that but so what? You know what it reminds me of? It's like them 8-Ball's—y'know the one you shake and ask them the questions? Well, finally you get *a* answer. Well, up the answer floats, y'know, up in that green, inky liquidy stuff? And it says MOST LIKELY or MY REPLY IS NO. But face it, it's you that shakes the ball up, same as it's you that asks it. And when it hits you, 'Hey, it could be *any* answer to *any* question.' Cause finally, it's jus' you, y'know? Ain't it the truth. Cause in the end all there is is jus' you and you and you."

Calms me right down, Tweety telling me all this like the "facts," especially an older girl like her. God, it's just so good to be with a girl, like a big sister or something. Then a twig cracks. It's Sheppy!

"Well, well, well," he says, seeing the notebook, "Alvy finally give it to yuh, huh?"

Well, that's the kicker. Alvy, I could expect, but Sheppy knowing, when here he's about the only decent person I even know at this point? I can hardly wheeze the words out. "And *you* knew too? And you never told me? And you talk about *me* being a ghoul, nosing over people's graves! So go have a look at *your* mother, huh!" But here I've said way more than I know. Sheppy grits, he stamps.

"Hey, doan even talk to me about what *I* been lookin at today, *Greyhound*. Fuck you, boy. All you sees is that bus window back home, talkin bout what *I* been lookin at."

Tweety pulls her coat around her. "Hi. I'm Tweety."

Sheppy shrugs. He won't even look at her directly, a white girl, but peering around he huffs, "Tweety Pie, huh? So where's ole *Sylvester* gone off to?"

PROBABLY HALF OF HISTORY IS ABOUT WHO'S GETTING ANY AND WHO AIN'T. Still, as odd man out, Sheppy knows how to twist the knife—he's the champ when it comes to turning the screws. No, once Alvy gets back, Sheppy's got poor Alvy groveling, all worried is Sheppy okay. And God, I am so stupid! How blind can I be after all these miles not to know that something else is going on between them—specially considering how

Sheppy yelled at me when I accused him with the diary, and this coming after whole days of him lost in his Dixie trance. No, between the diary and this Cookie girl I don't see the half of it—yet.

"Name it," offers Alvy, pulling Sheppy's sleeping bag and pack from the trunk, all hot to dump him so we can go on our date. "Food. A bottle of liquor. Name it, man—anything you want."

"Or yo gun to blow my brains out wid?" Sheppy spins away, laughing. "Go on, man. I know of a train out dis muthafucka, too."

I wave the notebook at him. "And don't you be blaming me! Not when you *knew* about this! Like we sold *you* down the river, huh?"

"You said it that time, Greyhound! Blood be thicker than water! And poontang be thicker than bofe!"

God, can't I please just for once be a hardass, and cool? But no, at this from Sheppy, of course I start feeling like a white rat. "C'mon, Sheppy, it's my last night. I mean, I oughta have *some* fun before I get packed off to military school. Can't you at least give me that?"

"Bye, Miz Pie," he waves to Tweety, ignoring me, "an all y'all white folks, you take *good, good care* now."

Then, as I'm getting in the car—like handcuffs—Alvy presses a rubber in my hand, a boner bender called MR. MIDNIGHT. But looking at it I'm worried about the size of the *O* ring in the, like, foil Alka Seltzer wrapper, which could fit a garden hose. MR. MIDNIGHT. *And this'll sound totally stupid mister midnight but in the dark how do you know which hole is which?* But hey, I don't gotta wonder long, because pulling off the road, Alvy and Tweety are giving free sex lessons. Talk about steaming up the place. Great! Two hours to kill until we meet Cookie! Well, I slide down the seat and keep reading. Skipping whole pages—

. . . Moving day—again. This time it's the top floor—a sweatbox and a family of negroes down the hall. Only a fool would dream of somebody coming to save us, but here I am. Where's Mr. Merryman? Or Stephen I hate to say?

The family's all here. Their help feels like they're evicting us too. Depend on Aunt Rose. Mother Superior says it's high time we checked Daddy in at the Vets . . .

. . . I suppose it would be rawthar pretentious to say I "summer" in Croton-on-Hudson. Not that the Croton boys aren't just as rude as the Third Avenue variety, especially at the beach. It burns me up how completely spoiled and nosy these kids are. When they ask me what Father does, I smile and say he does very well thank you. This

awes the boys and upsets Sarah no end but who cares? Believe it or not I hate ly-
ing—stupid lying. Lying should be pure self-defense . . .

. . . I could never stand to cut myself or see blood. I think I could throw myself off a
bridge but only into water. I know I could never have a baby, or what comes before
that. Not to mention the awful stories you hear from girls . . .

. . . Stephen. I <u>love Stephen.</u> Julie loves Stephen. Stephen James Twomey, Esq. Julie
Twomey. Mrs. Julie Alice Twomey . . .

"Heads up," says Alvy, coming up for air. "Tweety wants a soda—you?"
Alvy shakes his head at her. "Look at him. Last night of freedom and here
he sits, *torturing* himself."

And they're just like Dad and Heidi—worse. When Alvy comes out with
Tweety's soda she whines, "Honnnn, you forgot the straw." God, that dumb,
sweet, eager-to-please look on Alvy's face as he runs back in for her straw.
He's like a whole other person around her.

Today Stephen "surprises" me at the beach. He is a little <u>much</u> with his gold watch,
dark glasses and straw hat. Hey, the Rivera is that way cries Sarah.

Stephen spreads his towel between Sarah's and mine. It's torture. Stephen could be
18 with that physique and what a showoff, playing ball with Jerry Cooney and the
other boys. Poor Jerry Cooney is such a nice boy, a basketball player and a senior,
funny, good-looking. So what is wrong with me? Never dreaming, poor Jerry flirts
with me while I sit there proving that I really am "stuck up." The kids know I hate
to swim, so while they take a dip I stay by Stephen—paralyzed. Better cover yourself
up kiddo he says and throws a towel over me. My eyelids burn. I can hear the motor
boats and muffled footsteps in the sand. Then dozing off I feel Stephen's hand under
the towel. My leg cramps. My stomach burns and I bolt up. In the sun Stephen's face
is whispering, Little Love, Little Little Love. I think I threw up blood later but I
couldn't look. With Bear Lake coming, Stephen and I must get certain things straight,
but <u>what?</u> What on earth am I doing?

And I can't stop reading it! I stop, I start, then again I forget, staring through
the Life Saver Tweety gave me, comparing the hole sizes with MR. MID-
NIGHT. Boy, isn't that the way in life, one too big and the other too small,
but what if it slips off? And scrunching down, like a six-year-old, I blow through
the Life Saver hole, *pheee, pheee*. Only a complete nut or a baby would peep

through a Life Saver hole, *burn the book bury it.* Then I'm back to reading again. Reading over and over this same one page.

Mother's waiting for me when we come back from the beach today. At first I'm scared she's checked Daddy into the Vets, but no. Mother says we'll have dinner out—a mother and daughter chat before I depart for Bear Lake. It's "Angelos," a candle in the bottle place, nowhere Stephen would set foot but for us it's the Ritz. $1.25 for the veal. Nuts to that—the meatballs are 65 cents but Mother reads my mind. Have the veal she says. Well why not? You're on vacation.

On the tablecloth, mother spreads out $15 for Stephen's, then gets mad when I refuse. And where else will you get the money she asks—Stephen? Sure, mother knows. She knows just like the family all knows, remarking on my "new smile" like I suppose it came from the tooth fairy. She has to know, pushing her rye and ginger in front of me. Here take a sip. Ignore those people. You're my daughter and it's high time you learned how to take a drink. Mother taps her glass to the waiter—less ice.

But she's got something else up her sleeve. I knew it! While I'm away at Stephen's, she'll be in Atlantic City for two weeks "caring for" Mr. Merryman—double pay. Mrs. Carr will look in on Daddy. God, another drink and she's making google eyes at the waiter. She starts to pant. Men love how Mother hangs on their every word and carries on. Mother will teach her kitten how to catch mice. As we leave, Mother's eyes are like two inkwells. You know sweetheart you've gotten yourself a nice little figure. And such a nice smile now that you-know-who paid to get that spinach off your teeth.

AND MY BLIND DATE WITH COOKIE? Well, that's how the Cookie crumbles. Because after another $3.53 at Ray's Lunchbucket and Alvy sticks me with the check—no show. Fine. Dump me off with Sheppy, I tell him and Tweety, but no. While Tweety takes one last look in Ray's, Alvy starts working on me again.

"C'mon, two more days. Can't you manage that?"

"Me? Look at you. You're at the end of your rope. *And* broke." I shake the book at him. "And I'll never forgive you for this, ever!" Well, Alvy almost busts into tears.

"Why you hate me so bad now—why? So *go.* Go on home. Tell 'em I kidnapped you, but just you remember, man, I've got nothing but beautiful memories of you—nothing but."

"Manipulate, manipulate. All you ever do."

And I know exactly what he's pulling—I always do—but what good does that do when the kid only believes his own lies? And even when he's half telling the truth, I catch him in another lie, because he's got a map, and all along he had it! It's a map of the whole East Coast. He's got it all plotted out, too.

"How you think we ever got this far?" he asks. "*Random,* man. Like a pinball. No fuckin' rhyme or reason. *To them.* Sure, *now* I can tell you, but when we left, well, how could I? Well, ask yourself that? Hey, those first couple days I was scared you'd crack—run off and blab everything. But damn if you haven't amazed me, man. Totally. No sir, you have totally ex-ceeded the old Frank M.O.—hell, even Sheppy says so." He points to the map. "And see here? See, here's us and here's Charlene's, *barely a hundred miles,* man. She's just over the Georgia border. Not a two-hour drive."

"*Smile! You're on* Candid Camera!"

Tweety's get her lips mushed against the window. And look, here's this Cookie girl but not a thing like I pictured, not short but tall, and not stacked but skinny, and not blonde but brunette. Brunette when ordinarily I never go for brunettes. It's not that she's not pretty—the girl's real pretty. Real pretty in the face, with smooth wide cheekbones, smooth skin and full lips. It's not even that she's poor, dressed in an old, cheap white coat with these dirty thick nubs and her faded dress spraying out like a wilted bouquet—no, it's this snag in Cookie's lip. My stomach sinks. At first I think the girl's harelip but no, it's her teeth, which—*boy,* her teeth aren't so hot. In fact, her teeth are pretty bad, dark around the edges, dark like with stuck food, *spinach.* And this'll sound crazy, but suddenly I'm so furious at Sheppy for getting screwed on Mrs. Bayard's ring. Because I swear, if it took our every last dime I'd get those cavities filled for the girl. Braces, too.

And, of course, Cookie's just staring at my teeth—my *perfect* teeth, which the girl's probably more qualified on than an orthodontist. No, with teeth like hers, you know Cookie's been put through the wringer, guys marking her way down on teeth against how she'd better put out. Well, fine, the girl's no Jessica, not by a mile. But still, she scores points for being older, plus she's got beautiful big eyes and really great lips and, when she closes her mouth, a nice smile—*a funny unstuck-up smile.* But now this invisible clock starts ticking, this, like, humiliation clock ticking, *decide, decide.* Cookie's skirts and petticoats blow upsidaisy in the wind. Under the yellow bazaar bulbs the dirty old nubs of Cookie's coat have the hard greasy look of leather, *but c'mon she could change her coat and take those stupid white clips out of her hair and get her teeth fixed.* And she is so brave, I think. Cookie doesn't do the Horse Lip, pulling down her top lip the way kids with braces do to hide the tinsel. No, with this almost curtsey shrug the girl smiles, *Hey, sorry for the teeth but it's the best I can do.*

"Hey, I know you," she says. "You're that Boston kid. Hey, they had the sheriff over t'day. After you run off? Yeah, they sure did."

I rear back and crow. "Whoh? Aftah meeh?"

"You quit!" Her eyes flicker, unsure. "You ain't from any Boston."

But in this gush of famousness I scoop my arm around her and, all shocked, she looks at me, *You're nuts,* then laughs, trembles, laughs, all super relieved that I've picked her. And it's a party! As we bomb off Alvy's passing back a fresh pint of Old Mr. Boston sloe gin, which Cookie sips, then I sip sip, *brrr!* Shudder, sip sip, *brrr!* And wham! I've sprung me a second cranium! Drunk I kiss Cookie—I kiss her hard to get it over with, the teeth, and it's like Poo the way I egg concentrate. Because peering inside Cookie's eyes, when I really concentrate, *I can't see her spinach teeth or the snag.* And boy, these country girls! Well, Cookie snorts with love and gratitude! She wriggles, and I look at her hair in my hands, *dark hair.* And I can kiss her, but if I don't stay glued to her eyes and the memory of what she could look like, well, with the liquor and all, I wanna cry that her Dad could ever let her go through life with such teeth, at the mercy of every creep lording himself over her. And if nobody ever fixes her teeth for her, well, what's the girl ever gonna do? Well what, a pretty girl like her? But just then, we both sneeze. We sneeze one of those mutual make-out sneezes, Cookie scoffing.

"*Mash*achusetts! You ain't no fifteen neither."

I pretend I don't hear. And anyhow I'm at that gabby grabby stage, pestering Tweety, "Come on, where you really taking us?"

"I *tol' you,* my Grammommie's house."

"Bullshit! And she's really deaf?"

"Stone deaf. But don't you start the dog goin' crazy."

I think this is hysterical. "But if Grammommie's deaf—well, so what if we raise hell?"

"Because she'll *feel* the dog. I'm serious. The viber-ations. She'll feel the dog butting and banging up against the walls."

"*Huh?*" I ask.

"*I said,* the vib-erations!"

"*Huh?*"

Tweety whips around, "*I said—*"

"*Gotcha!*" I holler, and Alvy and me, we both bust out laughing, screaming and laughing at my asshole joke. Why, it's just like old times! Wham-ming up the mountainside, Alvy rams second gear, and all the way up, Alvy and me, we're both romping and stomping, singing at the top of our lungs.

"Ov-er da ri-ver and through da-woods
to Gram-mommies house we go!
Da girls know da wayyyyy!
To carry da sleighh!
Through de white and fros-ty snooooo—OOOH!"

And the dog! The minute I open my door this big, bounding, slobbering lummox knocks me down, wanting to snarl and play. Then, to see if it's really true Grammommie's deaf, Alvy and me are hollering up at the window.

"GRAM-MAWWWW! WE'RE HO-OOMMMME!"

Damn, we're really showing our age, wrestling and tumbling down the hill. Well, Cookie and Tweety stomp off mad—that being the point, I guess, to delay things, like that *De-lay* salve you see in rubber machines alongside the MR. MIDNIGHT. Which I think is stupid, to slobber on that Delay, when obviously you want fast relief and as many times as possible—well, right? And what is this? As Alvy and me stop wrestling I see Tweety and Cookie butted head to head under the porch light—and look, they're both poring over your copybook! That sobers me up. I snatch it away.

"Hey, thanks for asking!"

Cookie's holding your picture. "And this is really your Mom?"

"Well, she wasn't then," says Tweety to excuse you.

"But she's really?—"

"Oh, yeah, she's really dead. Certified." Cookie stares up at me.

"Well, *sor-ree*. I mean, you said you was from Boston, too."

Tweety hooks Alvy by the arm. "C'mon, mister. You're wanted inside."

And I'll tell you what. They may be more backward down South, but they sure are more advanced in this department—at least these two girls are. It's sad watching Tweety lead Alvy into the house, off to slaughter. As Alvy looks back at me, even though this is what he's trained all his life for, suddenly I feel so sorry and scared for him, having to shoulder this too—another car to drive, another mustache or sleeve patch to wear. But this only lasts a second because pulling me into the backseat, Cookie's got the same idea. I forgot to mention that I've got my juice now, my jism egg or whatever, and there's no *delaying* it, if you know what I mean. In case I have an accident, I've stuck the copybook down my pants, under my belt buckle, but feeling it stick her,

Cookie pulls it out, then opens her mouth wide into mine—wide way beyond even Jessica. It's the Black Jump, the air hissing through her nose and that old socks smell we send up, licking and snarling—nope, it's right where Tweety left off, explaining the copybook to me this afternoon. But there's a problem beyond *Delay*. Hitting a wall, I keep stopping. My whole mind stops.

"*Don't stop,*" fusses Cookie. "Why you always keep on stopping when we just get a goin'?"

So with a squitch and a huff we start again, Cookie staring at my teeth, just craving my teeth the way people only want what they can't, and never will, have. And oh my God, Cookie takes my hand, and her hand makes my hand feel her actual tit, which I gulp and squeeze and paw at but it's like *my hand goes to sleep*. Well, Cookie fights. She snorts for air, then I feel a hand, and not my hand, rubbing me . . . *down there*. Panting, Cookie breaks off.

"Hey, talk to me like at—"

"Huh?"

"Talk like from up air. Y'know, that Boshton stuff. *Pleash?*"

So we start again, bad teeth and good teeth, Cookie and President Kennedy, humping and bumping and tangling in that pet shop smell in the back of our car. But again I stop, and not just because I'm too young but because I keep seeing you—all I can see is you staring down at the water on that swimming float, and you had the youngs and Uncle Stephen he had the olds and the camera and the money, and it's all in Cookie's mouth and in her breath. Feeling her chipped teeth on my tongue, it's an electric shock, tasting all your want and humiliation, staring through Cookie's eyes until I see the night behind them, then the darker darkness behind that, dark with those little electric flecks of actual eyes. Then I hear the dog barking. And here's Alvy tearing out of the house, Tweety flopping after him, pulling on her blouse, hollering.

"Hon, it's *okay*. Ho-ney, c'mon back in the house!"

And up in the window, goddamn if it's not her! Looking like a crazy white-haired angel in her white nightgown, it's Grammommie calling down in this turkey-gobbler's voice.

"*Baa-by-girl, thass you? Baa-by girl, who is thaat?*"

And on top of me old Cookie sees—even before I do, she sees Alvy and she bolts, boy. Grabbing the doorhandle and her pocketbook, Cookie literally dives over me, she's out of that car so fast. And as fast as Cookie's out, Alvy throws Tweety off him and locks all the doors. Then as Alvy whips the car around, half-naked in a cloud of blue smoke, here she is flopping and slapping at his window.

"Come on back here when you're *man* enough!"

"Alvy, slow down!" I holler. I'm stone sober now, the car banging and bouncing down the mountain, tearing out gravel and giant zebra-stripes of moonlight.

"What the hell happened?" I yell.

"Nothing!"

"What, you couldn't?"

"*Wouldn't!*"

"*Wouldn't??*"

"Not *in* her!"

"But wait, you had your Mr. Midnight, right?"

"*Had* it? It's still on my dick! Man, my cock was ready to explode the rubber when I thought, *One sperm! One microscopic hole.* Well, holy shit, could I ever chance putting some poor kid through that? Another Alvy Loomis? Well, could I?"

SHEPPY'S FAST ASLEEP WHEN WE ROUST HIM UP, and the next thing Sheppy knows we're twenty miles down the road. And all the way things are really falling apart, Alvy doing the big sell job on Sheppy.

"C'mon, man, didn't nobody *leave* you, so quit it. And didn't I say we'd come back? Didn't I?"

Sheppy just stares out the window. Let the sheriff see him. He's given up.

"Foget it man, ain no big deal. Mainly it was a *ride.* Dat's all this wuz to me, you wanna know the real troof."

"Just a ride, huh?" huffs Alvy, half in tears again. "And who put you back here in Miloville, huh? And who did every damn thing he could so you could see her grave today—well, huh?"

Then it clicks! Sheppy's big hurry to get away from me this morning, and Alvy so worried when Sheppy got back. I flap the diary at Sheppy.

"*Mother's* Day, huh? And how was *your* Mamma doing today? God, you both make me sick!"

Well, it was bound to happen. For the first time the whole trip, I break down crying, really crying, all furious and hungover but mainly terrified and alone. Suddenly, I feel more alone than ever. For almost a week now I'd spun myself into this white cocoon of not thinking, pretending that by leaving I was just watching, and that by not thinking I was invisible and not responsible—that I was kidnapped and brainwashed, obviously an amnesia case, besides being the youngest. But no, suddenly the trance breaks. And what really scares me now is Alvy, thinking he'll kill himself if I leave—or shoot me if I try. And make no mistake, this time Alvy really is going to Charlene's—oh no, I can feel that now, same as I can feel the doorhandle in my hand, *Eject! Jump out!*

Sheppy, I could have predicted. Head rocking back Sheppy falls into one of his sleep funks, and I'm out right behind when *whump*, I jolt awake! The car's speeding back in reverse. Then as the smoke of our exhaust clears, still groggy, I see flashlights. Two women with coats over their nightgowns are running out. Some dog's yelping his lungs out.

"What happened? Did we hit somebody?"

"Not us," pants Alvy, "this guy ahead of me. He hit this dog and took off." He yanks the brake. "Sheppy, stay with the car. Keep the motor running." Sheppy grabs him.

"Whut, you gonna get us arrested? Fo some dawg?"

But grabbing the first-aid box, Alvy's been called on high, and I'm right behind him. I've never seen an accident close up, and it really is a dog, a German shepherd with his back broken. The bone's sticking out like a broom handle and his rear paw is crushed. It's worse than a person. You wouldn't think a dog could actually scream, but God can they, worse than people. Screaming and clambering up on his front paws, it's like the dog's trying to run away from his back legs, his own life.

"Git," snaps a woman as these little kids scamper out. More people totter out but they just stand there, so Alvy shoves the first-aid box at me, then collars the dog—anything to keep him still. And of course we got a talker, this gnawed-out old man jabbering about speeders and wild strays. Which of course he zeros in on me.

"Where you from, boy?"

I point at Alvy. "That's my brother. We're heading back to base."

"*Base?* Ain't no base round here." He pokes Alvy. "Whut, you in the army?"

"Army airborne. I'm Corporal Lewis."

"Corporal? What outfit?"

Alvy glares, flicking the electricity off his fingertips. "Sir, I can't disclose that."

"Cain't dis-close it?"

Even the dog's looking at Alvy now, his chops flapping bloody slobber. You'd think Alvy had a bullhorn, glaring at all these civilians.

"Hey, *folks*, let's get this over with, huh? Who's got the gun? C'mon! Let's put the poor thing outta his misery."

"Gun?" cries a woman. "You cain't go discharging no firearms here."

Again, the dog lashes up—smacks Alvy hard in the face, painting his cheek with bloody slobber. Then here's a lady balancing a bowl of water. Alvy shoves her away.

"*Water?* Get a .22! Shotgun! Hell, I'll do it."

"You calm down, mister!" cries the other lady. "She's just making the poor thing comforble."

"*His spine's broken, goddamnit!*"

"Don't you dare curse at me!"

"Probly him done hit him."

"Well, who else? You don't see no other cars."

Alvy windmills his arms. "Hey, y'all wanna listen to this all night? Goddamnit, I'm talking about *decency!* Basic, stupid, human, goddamned *decency.*"

Now they know Alvy's crazy, the one stray with his back broken, and the other striding back and forth across his own stage. It's like Clark Kent with people watching him so he can't get into his Superman suit. And what's killing Alvy, he's got the mercy right in his boot—he's got his 9mm but he can't just go whipping it out. Well, Alvy starts back for the car. But just when I'm escaping the old man, I hear Alvy slam the trunk. And here he comes, a tent half in one hand and the pistol in the other.

"Look, he's got a gun!"

"Aww, calm down." Alvy's totally matter-of-fact about it. "Just stand back."

I'll never forget how that dog looked at Alvy, his crazy eyes like a pair of crushed jacks and his red tongue lolling out. And Alvy is so tender about it. You'd think it was Beef. Kneeling down, Alvy's stroking him, cradling his head like to explain it when, *Pop! Pop pop!*

"Go on, Jenny Lee, call the law on him!"

Alvy flops the dog in the tarp, then drags him scuffing up the road. "Hell, I'll even throw in a Christian burial. Probably rot here otherwise."

"Go on, git, you crazy filth! You trash!"

And, magically, the car roars to life. The horn honks. The lights flash on and off. And don't the earthlings stare back amazed, their faces white in our brights as us dead dog snatchers blast off from Hineparts, S.C., back to our home on planet Mars.

THAT WAS DEFINITELY THE LOW POINT, RIDING AROUND WITH A DEAD DOG IN OUR TRUNK. And samaritan that he is

Alvy is hurt. He's actually insulted at the people yelling at him, the angel of mercy, *he's actually surprised.* Let them call the cops, he says. What, *him* run off when he did nothing wrong? Absolutely not. In Alvy's mind, it's like this stolen Ford, the car which he's virtually earned by religiously checking the oil and water once a day.

"I want out!" I holler, "Stop this car right now!" I look at Sheppy but he only shrugs.

"Cops probably be long soon anyhow."

Of all the times this trip we've died seeing a cop car, or hearing a siren! And where are the Barney Fife bastards when here's a citizen in desperate need of help? God, I'm so low I'm almost missing Heidi, is how bad it is. But maybe it'll work out at home, I think. Maybe Dad'll see how bad it was with Heidi, and we'll quit all the damned finger-pointing and theatrics. Cause if there's one thing I've decided down here, it's to stop the big blameathon—you, me, God, Heidi, the doctors, everybody. No, general amnesty will be declared! Heidi can go back to living with Aunt Anna and then maybe Dad can get that Sarasota job, cut the cord and do it clean, with just the two of us again.

And you talk about blame. Gobbling No-Doz, Alvy's doing the whole Agony in the Garden—how Peter and the Apostles couldn't even stay awake when poor Jesus could hear the cock crowing, and here come the Jews and centurions with torches, ready to nail his ass. Hey, I don't argue with him. With your notebook stuffed in my pants I crawl into the backseat with Sheppy. I'll chance Sheppy punching me in his sleep. Beats going through the windshield when Mr. No-Doz dozes off.

That's the worst kind of sleep, when you can't fall asleep or wake up either. Somewhere Sheppy might have been crying in his sleep, but mainly I hear these two voices. Lord, all night long, it seems, I keep hearing this endless, stupid argument between Alvy and some guy—a guy with this slow, dixified voice and the most moronic goddamn laugh you've ever heard. Then, *poink,* I sit up! And there's the voice! And it's no dream!

It's a big, fat sailor crowded up front, a hitchhiker in a black pea coat with his collar turned up. His head is shaved white up the neck, black hair bristling on both sides, like a skunk. And thick-headed? The guy's so stupid his eyes have short-socketed. I kick Sheppy but he just lays there snoring.

"Hey, little brother," says Alvy in his put-on hick voice, "this here's Dewey."

"Hey." My heart's pounding like crazy.

"Aayyy," returns Dewey, sleepy-eyed. His fat face looks like it was punched out of some dough. "Sorry to hear bout your parents, man. Real bite in the ole ass, huh?"

I nod—God knows what Alvy's told him. And sure enough Alvy starts picking on the moron again.

"Anyways, man, don't be badmouthin the military. Been good to me, *damned good.* Specially what with this temporary hardship leave to take li'l brother here."

"Muummm." In the darkness, Dewey's head bounces like those rubber shrunken heads on the elastic bands. "Lotsa guys woulda gone AWOL." Alvy sneers back.

"But not Dewey."

Dewey's ears go back. "Hey bud, I already told you onct. I got my leave papers right here in my sea bag. I just don't feel like diggin' them out, is all."

Alvy grins. "Eeeeasy man, *I* don't care. Like I say, though, fuck all that Mickey Mouse, *See-the-World* shit. 'Lectrical school, 'frigeration. That's the ticket. Ain't nobody gonna hire your swabbie ass to tie knots. Yeah, once me and Tom here get settled, I'll be getting me my journeyman's license and—"

"—But wait," interrupts Dewey, "I thought you said you was on Hard-ship?"

"'Til my lawyer gets me out. Be different if it was some national 'mer-gency."

"Cuba."

"*Cuba?* Aww man, that's shit's long over." Alvy cranes around to me. "But I guess old Dewey missed that, down in the bilge scraping pots!"

"Fuck you too. Man, we was out at sea on the *William B. Mathers*, buddy. Full alert—"

"Yeah, and where's Dewey now when his country needs a man like him swabbing out the heads and scraping pots?" Alvy winks at me. "But *we* know Huey ain't no A-W-O-L, *right, Tom?* Naww, not ole Huey . . ."

But Dewey's got an edge to him, and I'm fast getting the feeling he's not all as stupid as he acts. Morons don't keep changing the subject like this joker does. And, sure enough, Dewey's found Alvy's Achilles' heel.

"Hey, that's one good mustache, though. *Damned* good. Specially for—what? Ten days you been out, is it?"

Alvy lights a cigarette. Fumbles it too. "Well, it's funny. Me, I can't grow sideburns! Chin whiskers either. You want chins, look in the Chinese direc-tory."

"Haw, thass good! But really, man, that is one *good* fuckin' mustache. Boy, came in superfast too, huh?"

And again Dewey changes the subject.

"So y'all goin' clear to Savannah with the jig?"

"Why not? He paid the gas."

"Hell," whispers Dewey, *"leave his monkey ass at the next station."* He looks back at Sheppy, then starts cackling to himself. God, I hate people who advertise jokes.

"Ever hear the one bout the busload a niggers? Yeah, they was all going on to—no, no, wait! they was . . . *Anyways*, they's all going along, when—oh yeah, *it crashes*. Wait! Howz the fuck it goes?—"

Alvy can't resist. "Dewey *tore* up that IQ test!"

"Wait, I 'member! Nigger dead bodies all over the place. Well, the old farmer, this good ole boy, he goes gets his tractor and buries 'em all. The niggers. Then a man—wait—*thass right* . . . a man from the *state*, so he come by and asks the farmer, 'Heard y'all had yuh a little accident?' So wait! yeah, so see the man from the state, *he* asks, *'Was they all dead?'* And the farmer says, 'I buried 'em.'"

Dewey waves his hands—he blew it.

"No! wait! Shit, that's right! No, the *farmer* says, 'Well, most of 'em was. But you know how a nigger'll *lie*.' *Haw!*"

I can't even look at the creep, it's so horrible. Alvy either. Then Dewey looks around at Sheppy again.

"Tell you what I wonder, though. What I wonder is how big his ol' thangamajigger is."

"Well," smiles Alvy, "I don't gotta wonder."

"What?"

"Back there, pissing. Had to drop his pants, horsing it out."

"No shit."

"Go an easy nine inches hard. *Thick*, too." Alvy grins. "Boy, you get some strange thoughts, doncha? In the rack?"

"Boy, you sure do. Woo." Dewey picks up the magnetic Jesus. "Thought only Catholics rode around with these things?" He slaps the dash. *"Whoa*, pull over, willya, pop? I gotta piss me a truck! Here behind that gas station, huh? Good, she's closed."

Alvy grabs Sheppy by the knee. "Hey, *Fred*. Freddy, wake up. Piss stop."

What's going on? Sheppy's wide awake. Alvy kills the lights but leaves the engine running. Then as him and Sheppy scramble out, it hits me, *they're gonna rob him*. But wait, here's Dewey hanging on my door, poking his fat face in at me.

"Hey, better come on, kid—Tom, is it?"

I clutch the copybook and face forward. "That's okay." Dewey yells to Alvy and Sheppy.

"Whoa, round back wid that, y'all. They'll arrest yer asses for that shit!"

"*Okay.*" I hear Alvy laughing this phony "come-find-us" giggle.

Fake out! The second Alvy and Sheppy disappear, Dewey grabs me by the neck. Next thing I know I'm laying dazed in the dirt.

"*Alvy! Sheppy! Quick! He's got the car!*"

Tearing around the station Alvy empties the gun at him, which he might as well chuck rocks. And what's Alvy maddest about? Your copybook. Here when I've lost the *Titanic,* panicked, I dig it out of my pants, to make sure I've still got it. And then the weirdest thing happens. Naturally, thinking it's all my fault, I start to shake and whimper—doing the old Frank number, in other words—when instead I explode. Explode laughing.

"Look! *He stole a stolen car, that dumb fuck! With a dead dog in the back!*"

That crud Dewey had delivered us, all right. Dewey was our angel and our ticket home. Only not quite yet.

WITH NO CAR WE'RE LIKE TURTLES SHUCKED FROM OUR SHELLS, not just naked but *marked,* two white boys and a Negro roaming the back roads at 4:00 A.M.

Get me a phone! I'm ready to surrender, but Alvy, all sleep-deprived and starved, Alvy is worse off than ever, raging and crying and blundering around. Already I can feel Sheppy distancing himself from us, trailing way behind, trying to light his last bent smoke with his last soggy match. Anytime I expect to see him gone.

It's cold but not too bad—luckily, we were all wearing our coats when Dewey robbed us. A light skitter of drizzly dew, drizzle like miniature spiders, is falling. The first birds are cheeping and, through the black trees, the dark is flaring into light. Behind us, talking to himself, Sheppy says.

"A cat, *he* know to find his way outta the rain."

"Fuck a cat," I call back, "find me a phone."

"*No,*" rants Alvy. "Just gimme an hour's sleep. I'll get us a car."

"Wif what? You ain got no hot wire. You ain got shit 'cept for that stupid gun."

Alvy stops. It's like when you ask a drunk how many fingers? "*Wire?* Sure, you rip a wire out of another car. The *horn wire.*"

"Aww, give it up, man."

"No, I ain't giving up! All I NEED is some sleep."

And looking at each other Sheppy and me are both thinking the same thing, *Get junior to sleep and get his gun.*

THE TRULY TREMENDOUS thing is I'm—for *me*—amazingly cool and collected. Why, in my mind I'm leading home the lost platoon.

The drizzle has almost stopped and the sun's coming up, a warm squash yellow that makes you feel warmer just looking at it. Then, crossing a wet field, we see a long, silver-roofed farmhouse with a long string of smoke teasing out of it . . . *breakfast* smoke, which starts my nose going, imagining popping grease, burnt bacon, burbling eggs. Alvy's way too gone to think of food, though. Circling like a dog, he's ready to drop, begging.

"But you're not gonna call anybody, right? I just need an hour. C'mon Frank, *one more day.* Fine, forget me. Do it for Buddy, man."

"Up hy-eah," says Sheppy steering him by the elbow. "Good dry groun hyeah."

It's a whorl of tough white grass, frosted and dew soaked on top but all plushy dry underneath. I don't know why it always gets colder at daybreak, but as Alvy plonks down, as we all squeeze in, I remember what Dad always said about themodynamics—how in even the coldest cold, there's always heat, heat in cold and now, I'm thinking, even love in hate. And that's the problem with Alvy, I realize. If I just simply loved the kid or just simply hated him, it would be easy to take his gun, turn him in and not care how he feels. But see, this also gets to how I feel about Sheppy now. Or rather, how Sheppy feels about us, since I naturally assume Sheppy's all upset about us—us I mean as white people—and not upset about saving his own life.

Even in the way Sheppy's being cold to us there's heat, but what hurts me is does he even *want* my love now, and what good is love off a white boy? I mean, food and gas you can share, and body heat and money, but love? Besides, with no car and no money—well, what can we even offer Sheppy now, and especially if all he wanted was a ride? And that's assuming Sheppy even wants to go back to Maryland, which I'm fast realizing he doesn't. No, something has definitely changed with Sheppy since yesterday—I mean even before Tweety, and especially now that Sheppy's seen his mother's grave.

But then, as I sprawl there in the field with my head buzzing and your copybook tucked under my coat like an emergency heart—well, lying there I *do* feel something move, suddenly so happy and certain I all but float up in the morning mist! And what's this? I think, picking this mushy yellow ball. It's this fruit the size of a grape from a tough cluster of field grass. What do you call them—I still don't know—these squarshy, apply, tomatoey things that you always find tangled in the stubbly field grass in the late fall? Who even eats them? Rabbits? Mice?

Tomato apples I'll call them. Laying back, I squarsh one between my fingers, then smell the yellow pulp all marshy-cold and sour. In the sharper dawn light, the yellow pulp glows like a coal and I think, *I'll always remember them the tomato-apples that aren't tomatoes or apples.* And later, when I'm all older and I do write a book (a book I hope people will fold double and paw at the pages like it's their own private dream), well later, when I really can write, I'll stick in the tomato-apples, one of those stupid trivial things that only a real human person would notice, something so trifling and stupid that it could only happen in real life, because who but a writer would ever write down such a thing—or bother? Tomato-apples! And hitting that place in the book where I planted the tomato-apple, maybe people will remember them or something just as trivial, and stopping there they'll burn for life at *something they thought only they saw and only they loved but they are definitely not crazy and they are definitely not alone.*

Well, they convinced me, those tomato-apples. Right then I *knew* and I got Alvy's gun. I got the gun and the knife, then I peeled off his mustache, too, then threw the whole mess down a groundhog hole, so deep it woulda taken a backhoe to dig them out. Sheppy doesn't want any part of this and that's fine with me. Walking back I find Sheppy leaning on his elbow, lint and straw in his hair and that smoke squint in his eyes. God, he looks so sick and miserable.

"Stay wif him," he says finally.

"But where you going?"

"See what I can scare up."

"Look, I'm giving myself up—*today.*"

"K," he shrugs. He starts walking.

"Wait! Do you know the people down there?"

"*No,* I doan *know* the people." He stands there squinting.

"But they're colored?" I ask.

Hey, I don't know! I guess I figure there's a certain *type* of colored house, like a teepee for Indians, a certain secret sign they all know, the colored people. But at this Sheppy can only shake his head, truly amazed at my ignorance yet again.

• • •

REMEMBER AS A LITTLE KID HOW YOU GO TO BED JUST KNOWING SOMETHING GOOD'LL HAPPEN? AND YOU GO TO SLEEP SO IT WILL HAPPEN?

Because here's Sheppy shaking me. And behind him is the oldest, blackest, gun-bluest-blackest Negro I've ever seen, leaning on a worn-down cane, with runny old eyes—hawk eyes—and a fine white line of saliva trickling down the left side of his mouth. Everything about him is old—old blue pants, a fraying white shirt and a brown duck-hunting coat gone at the cuffs and elbows. Sucking his toothless cheeks like he'll sneeze, he punctually spits tobacco, then wipes his mouth on the back of his trembling hand, a hand so papery old and black it glistens like a crow's wing.

"Mawnin, young man. Yeah, I *knowed* yuh'd be vis'tin me." The old man winks at me, like it's our own private joke. Then real gingerly, he pats me like a dog and stands back grinning. "Oh yes indeedy, I *knowed.*"

"You know him?" I whisper to Sheppy, who huffs back like he's presenting royalty.

"*Mr.* Sykes and *Mr.* Sykes."

Because behind the old guy is this humungous guy who looks like a football player, besides being three shades lighter and way younger—why, a positive baby by comparison. And behind them both, in an old blue car so pale and sun faded it almost blends with the sky, here's a woman, a big older colored lady just beside herself, fuming and glaring at us—"*Mrs.* Sykes," mumbles Sheppy. But mainly Sheppy's trying to roust up Little Boy Blue.

"Alvy, *up.*"

Alvy whips around, "*What the fuuuuh*—"

"Ho, easy man!" Big Mr. Sykes drops, ready to tackle him. "Yuh with friends here, boy. Friends so yuh jus calm on down."

"Uhh, sir! Yeah, sir, see . . . last night we uhh—we . . ." It's all I can do not to blurt out laughing, Alvy hemming and sirring and explaining, and not a clue. Then feeling his empty boot Alvy stops—blows his whole train of thought—then glares at me. Well, that's it for him. Gunless, knifeless, carless, de-mustached and delirious, the kid's beaten—just itching his hair and smearing his face in the sun while the big man takes over.

"I'm Mr. Don Sykes. That's S-Y-K-E-S, and this here is my Daddy, *Mr. Byron* Sykes, though y'all can—you *may* call him Daddy Sykes. *If* you nice. Me, you can call Donnie."

But it's not Donnie I'm watching just then, it's the old man. I'm watching the old man's eyes, which are such a runny, dazzled brown they look almost blue against his black skin. And as Donnie talks, all the time Daddy Sykes is nodding to the sermon like it's *him* doing the talking, his tobacco-gorged cheeks sucking like gills as Donnie goes on, "So y'all's welcome to stay. A *while*. Doan thank me, thank Daddy. It was me, I'd have the law handle it"— Wait, I think, did he say "the law" or "the *lawd*"? "So, fine!" says Donnie finally. "Y'all wanna stay couple days, come to yo senses, go back on home, *fine*. But no cussin or disrespectin. No smokin or drinkin—no crime of any kind. And just so's we *straight*, if you in any way trifle wid us or 'buse our hos-p'tality—and close you ears, Daddy—'cause I'll personally kick all y'all's punk asses, and be the rest of the day grinning fum ear to ear! So go on, man! Jus you pull some shit and toe to toe we will *go*, Joe!"—he's looking straight at Alvy—"All three at once! Shoot, doan make me no nevah min! So are we cleah, gentlemen? . . . *Goooddd*."

Man, has Sheppy gotten proper. Suddenly, Sheppy's a whole other kid, when it hits me, *I've never seen him with adults*. Adults of any kind, and espe-cially none of his own kind. But for me the strangest thing isn't being around Negroes, it's being back around adults, period—adults so my ears pop with our sudden descent into normal life and our own true scale *as* kids. Still, hum-bling as it is to feel my hand swallowed in Donnie's handshake, this is noth-ing to when the old man shakes my hand. He's positively overjoyed. I can feel him chugging and trembling like an old steam engine, *and he absolutely won't turn me loose*, not my hand or my eyes.

Look, I'm not claiming Daddy Sykes was the most regular old dude you'll ever meet—or that I was necessarily who or what Daddy Sykes maybe seemed to think I was. But the point is, with Daddy Sykes—and not that I understood this yet—but the point is that none of this stuff, worries like this, evasions like this, doubts like this, well, none of this stuff even matters. It just don't apply. And, the great thing about Daddy Sykes is he doesn't act in any way superior, doesn't pull his age or puff himself up with our despera-tion. In no way does he act like we're weird or bad or have anything to be ashamed of. In fact, he treats us as totally normal, which, I can tell you, is a real shock. And maybe, as I used to think later, so maybe Daddy Sykes was so old that he'd turned totally around, like Halley's Comet—so clear around that he could see just what it was like for us that day, dropped from the sky, helpless and excuseless, in some stranger's field. No, looking at Daddy Sykes, well, right away I knew he felt something that virtually no adult did after we got caught. The old man knew—knew as a hunter—that we'd failed in our Great Escape, and he knew, whatever else, that this was a sad thing. And, quaking and dribbling tobacco, as Daddy Sykes peers in at me with those blue-brown eyes and *he* mists up, well, that's it for me. Tears are falling on my shoes. My heart drops and my head blows open, open into light, like a ripe dandelion. It feels like my first Communion—that pure. And chugging on my hand, peering up like he's found the tomato-apple, Mr. Sykes, I just know, is feeling all this, too. He's stuttering something. Stuttering like Indian talk. Stuttering like the light, he's pulling me in like the light, trolling me in the way I'd see the light flickering through the trees at sundown when we took off on our bat rounds, and I'd be so gratefully quiet and happy as it strummed and quivered, dappled and danced. Maybe he's coughing. Maybe it's the tobacco juice gone down the wrong pipe. But then in a second happy concussion, like the tomato-apples—like something positively *historical* in my life, it hits me, *Then*. *Then* his crusty old shoes crackling superloud in the briars. *Then* the bright doorhandle of the old car, the handle burning such a fierce yellow in the morning sun that, for a second, I'm literally scared to touch it for fear I'll burn myself.

Alvy bumps me, *Are you okay? Are you just conning Uncle Remus here?* But choked up I pull away, slayed not by a heart attack but a massive change-of-heart attack. It's like lockjaw. I literally can't speak for fear I'll break it, this lump like an egg in my throat. No, at that moment I don't dare say a word, a voice inside me saying, *Shut up just get in the car and shut up.*

BUT BEFORE THEY CARRY ME OFF TO HEAVEN, here's the old man and Donnie arguing over who's gonna drive. Boy, those two! The old man practically swallows his tobacco wad, growling at Donnie, "Boy, yuh get on in, talkin all this who-do, how yuh gonna drive *mah* car."

Meanwhile, Mrs. Sykes, with her glasses on a chain and perfume coming off her in sheets—Mrs. Sykes in her felt hat and black wool coat not a speck of fuzz on it so you can't believe she's even in the same car, even in the same *state* as us—well, Mrs. Sykes is grandly ignoring all of us but most of all Sheppy, cooking in his own juice as she stares out the window. Well, Alvy can't take it. Old Dale Carnegie leans forward with his most winning grin. Out goes the filthy hand.

"Well, hello. You must be Mrs. Sykes."

And there his hand dies, too, hanging in midair. No, Mrs. Sykes goes right on bird-watching, as she does a Three Stooges on us.

"Well, hello, hello, *hel-lo*."

"I said, *Git in!*" thunders the old man. Him and Donnie are still arguing.

So Donnie squeezes his bulk into the middle and the old man, half flooring it, starts the car wallowing down the hill, the shockless old leaf springs about to rip loose, wrenching and screeching. Donnie grabs the wheel. "Daddy, *left*—" "I *see!*" fumes the old man. Then, when he's about gargling with his tobacco chaw, *sprrreeeppsh*—he whips around, thick brown juice spraying out his window! And guess who's sitting right behind him? Sheppy's coughing into his hand, laughing, but Mrs. Sykes brings his ass up short.

"Yo Mamma didn't raise no foo's, I assume." She's looking right at the middle Stooge.

"Ma'am?"

"Doan be *mamming* me, boy."

"He lives with his aunt," I offer.

"Oh, well," she sniffs, "in that case, I'm sure his po aunt hain't been worried. *At tall.*"

"*Tze-hee,*" giggles Donnie. "C'lored boy, you gonna be *dyin* to see yo aunt."

"In they own time," erupts the old man. "Send 'em back wrong, or too soon, it ain gonna take."

Leaning around, Donnie explains, "See, Daddy run off once hissef. Run off clear to Memphis and the people whut found him, they sent him on back—too soon. So, being his ole hardhead self, Daddy only run off again. Thass what he means."

"*Right,*" trumpets the old man. "Yuh *get* right so yuh go *back on home right.*" He grabs the wheel. "Donald, *off.* Boy, caint yuh see Ah'm drivin?"

Donnie covers his face. "You and them angels!"

AS FAR AS THE SYKESES' HOUSE, it is way nicer than I expect, the middle part being what I guess was a cabin once, plus a big porch and a couple of rooms they added on. Set up on a hill, the house overlooks the barn, the backs of three black hogs and the last of the old man's hunting dogs, a beagle and a baying old blue tick. Mainly, I'm eyeing the two outhouses, wondering which is the men's, when Donnie guffaws.

"Whut? Doan you know the *out*house from the *smoke*house?"

Christ, do they gotta embarrass me just because *they're* embarrassed? Like I'm worried whose chocolate butts have sat here! And look! As I tease open the door and finally open my eyes, hell, here's a pull-on light, a regular pink toilet seat and paper aplenty. And turning loose my nose, I think I should smell this—yes, do, *do*—because at the altitude where I'm at now, *this is so petty people!* so insultingly puny and utterly *beneath* where I'm sitting! . . . my pee splattering down and the great bomb-bays opening, as the cold, a deep earthen cold, comes slooshing up my butt. Finally! Alone to think! To pray, even. Craning back on the launching pad, peering up at the fume holes and the dead wasps caught in the cobwebs, I'm in my own Mercury capsule, *Revelations At Last* . . . 10 . . . 9 . . . 8 . . . 7 . . . 6 . . . But why am I so lightheaded? Why so insanely, tomato-appley happy? I wonder. Why, when I'm caught and going home and my life's still a royal mess?

And when I come in the house, opposite the dog-scratched front door, beside the fat black wood stove, here's old Mr. Sykes throned in his cracked leather lounger patched with silver duct tape, his beat-up Bible beside him and his smoldering black pipe jabbed in one black hand. Trembling, he grips the armrests. *"Well, hallooo"*—amazed I can even crowd my gigantic white wings through the door. He draws a curl of smoke across the air, his eyes burning. "Now yuh come on hyeah, *right chere.*" But then, with a jolt, again he starts that stammering, "An y-yuh is w-w-welcome in hy-hy-eahhh." He starts quoting something.

"Well, I'm really glad to be here, sir."

"An yuh know it, too! Cause yuh know, *dat stuff don mattah in hyeah. Not in dis hous it doan.*"

It's like when I got my outhouses confused—I'm scared I'll accidentally embarrass him or set him off, that I'll expose my ignorance at only understanding—at first—about his every tenth word, and especially here when I'm trying to ingratiate myself into his home, or church, rather. Because that's exactly what it is, I decide, a church. But his last pronouncement about "that stuff" seems so huge that finally I lean forward and ask him.

"That stuff, Mr. Sykes?"

"Yeeah, stuff. Dat stuff." And pulling back his frayed sleeve, he puts his hairless black arm side by side with mine all skinny white. It's so close I can smell him sweating, sweating that faint old-people's sweat, which is more breathing than sweat, like dry ice. And the walls. Above him, here's the famous painting of Jesus, the white Protestant Jesus, with the hound-dog eyes and the yellow light on his face. And, surrounding this, stacked five and six high like the hosts of heaven are pictures of black faces, some family photographs and some clipped from books or old frayed newspapers—them and pamphlets pinned open, all heavily underlined in a soft lead pencil. Mr. Sykes rubs his black skin.

"*Dat* ole stuff. Does—*that*—mattah—to—yuh?"

"Oh no, sir! *No*—"

"Well, good. Then it doan and yuh is h-h-hyeah and yuh is w-w-welcome. Welcome as good as enyah my o-own." Then he flinches away. Actually cringes, white saliva dribbling out one side of his mouth—cringes like he'd just scorched his arm on the stove and it scorched me, too. God, I feel horrible then, so stupid—stupid especially for all the time I'd spent watching other people cry, and it never made a dent. Looking into the old man's eyes, I've never seen so clearly how tears are made. Again he pinches his black arm. "Cause *dat* stuff, boy. Dat skin stuff is the *wurst* stuff."

"*Thanks*—" I croak.

"Doan thank *me*"—his loose teeth clack—"t-t-thank the Lord fo He brung yuh hyeah. To *me*. Cause it was *Him* whut brung you. Brung yuh hyeah to me an our own fambly to *think*. Thass right. To think *hyeah* 'cause, boy, *yuh know* yuh couldn do no kinda thinkin *dere*." He frowns like I obviously long, *long* ago shoulda figured out this one. "Cause why else would yuh boys have run off *but* to think? Well, right? Well, w-wh-*why?*"

"I guess not." I keep looking at that white Jesus, wondering how he feels worming his white self in here.

"Yuh guest not?"

"I mean no—I mean I guess *yes*."

"*Well, thass right*," he nods, satisfied. "An yuh in *mah* house. An mah house is yuh house now—yuh and yuh friens. An ain nobody gonna mess witchyuh, 'cause in mah house yuh gonna git yuhsef straightened out, hear?"

It's like accepting this huge trophy, more than I can possibly carry. And before I even know what I'm doing I'm shaking the old man's hand again, the hand knocking like an old motor as I blubber, "Mr.—Mr. Sykes, I am so— Mr.—Mr. Sykes, you people are the *nicest* people—"

"Stop. Right there!" Just then Mrs. Sykes rushes in from the kitchen with a folded blanket. "Off with it. Everything. Every last filthy stitch. Leave it all on the porch. Right by the wringer washer."

But our clothes aren't the only things being put through the wringer. In the kitchen, Alvy's been Samsoned. Wrapped in a blanket, hair already washed and combed, he's all ready for beddy-bye! Sheppy too! Mrs. Sykes has him bent over the sink, her fingers itching and scruffing, fussing at him.

"Boyh, you gonna have more bumps than hair you don't get this ole mess cut!" Upping the juice, Donnie turns to Alvy.

"So where y'all from?"

Alvy looks at Sheppy. "Didn't he tell you?"

"*You* I asked."

"Up North."

"Keep it up, slick." Donnie's neck starts twitching.

"Leave 'em!" thunders the old man.

"*Next,*" cries Mrs. Sykes. That's me. Hanging back, I point at the white uniform hanging on the door. "You're a nurse, Mrs. Sykes?"

"No answers, no questions."

"All right, Maryland."

Alvy harrumps his chair to shut up.

"Thass warmer," she says. "Will you look at this *hair*—"

Water gurgles down my mouth. "So, you're a bb-gnurse?"

"I *work* for a family, yes." You can tell from her voice which kind. Mrs. Sykes turns mock sweet. "Ord'narily, this is my day off."

"*Sorry.*"

"No, dahlin. *I'm* the one that's sorry."

I try again, "So you—"

"—Nope, my turn now. *Down,* keep yo head down . . ."

Delirium as her strong nails razzle my scalp. Sizzle sizzle sizzle, *good-good-good.*

"So what's in that old school exercise book I saw you hiding?"

"That's *private,* okay?"

"Set still—" Ladling warm water from the big pot on the stove. "So, what parta Maryland you from?"

"*Esther, leave 'em.*"

She flaps the ladle at the old man. "*And what then, Byron? What then?*"

Alvy's waiting his chance to get to Sheppy and me. Especially when Donnie finally takes us all outside, out to the squeaking old pump for the final douse-off. Donnie tosses us some bars of brown soap, then starts the pump gushing into a silver feed bucket. I shriek! The water's like boiling acid, it's so cold! My head's throbbing. But then the warm towels! The air! And me and Sheppy flinging water back on Donnie. Who's laughing! Who's really a good guy! Doesn't sway Alvy.

"Stall 'em," he mutters as we head back in.

"Aww, give it up. We showed 'em, we got really far. So who cares?"

"*I* care, not thirty miles from our objective! Just 'cause you got what you want. So what about me, huh?"

Back inside Mrs. Sykes holds out the phone. "Mr. Frank?"

Heart failure. "Who, me?"

"One finger. All it takes."

"Please Mrs. Sykes, can I eat first? *And* sleep?"

She turns to Sheppy. "And you?"

"My aunt, ma'am. She ain got no phone."

"Please," mealymouths Alvy, "we *really* 'preciate your hospitality, Mrs. Sykes. Specially Frank and me here—"

She points at Sheppy. "What, and *he* doan preciate our hospitality? When he done *brung* you both hyeah?"

Banging pots. Muttering to herself. Half hour later, in our rolled-up bunched-up, tied-on borrowed clothes, we file into the dark, creaky-floored dining room where the old man and Donnie are already waiting for us, them and more old family pictures hanging on long, crusty black wires that vibrate under our feet. Negro light filtering through Negro lace curtains. Negro dust and Negro smells *but how's that smell?*

"Hot stuff," calls Mrs. Sykes. "Hot stuff comin through."

And over our heads, hand over hand, here it comes, hot platters heaped with grits and country ham, over-easy eggs and hotcakes. But when Mrs. Sykes drops the last platter, Alvy and me see we've miscounted—we've accidentally left two extra spaces—but Mrs. Sykes only seizes on her chance to slide in beside Sheppy. Well, there you go! I think. Their side and our side. Their talk's different too. Completely. I've never seen people who will look at each other harder or concentrate more on a talker, or who will carry on as long without one looking at the other at all. Not that I'm listening. Knowing it's not for me, almost automatically I dim the volume and stuff my face, besides which I'm half dead. But finally, my ears do perk up. It's Mrs. Sykes. Almost casually she asks Sheppy without looking at him, "And who was it killed yo Mamma?" And without so much as a huff or a roll of the eyes Sheppy answers her.

"My faffa."

His father? And all this time Sheppy knew and he never told us? I look at Alvy but Alvy only sighs. *So Sheppy told him and never told me?* Well, Alvy lets his hands fall on the table. It's fess-up time. He looks at Sheppy and me.

"So y'all wanna tell them now?"

Well, I'll tell you, it takes real flair to lie to strangers, but the liar who can bait up the same chewed-up old lie and use it to hook his friends, well, that's a master. And out of Alvy's mouth it all sounds so noble! so sensible! so all tied up in a bow! Why, we're like the Three Musketeers, the Three Men in the Boat. Here's old Frank, trying to save his Dad from the wrong woman, and here's Sheppy trying to save himself *from* his Dad (and honor his Mamma). And last and noblest of all, here's Alvy who—it turns out—came to save his Mamma from falling back off the wagon. And looking at Alvy then, after all his bullshit, even *I* half buy it, he gives the story such a shine. Anyhow, seems that six years ago his "Dad" (whoever *he* is), anyhow, his Dad forgave boozer, runaround Charlene for the millionth time, when she ran off again. Ran off, bummed around, went to jail, then shacked up with this plumber and had two more kids.

"But see," says Alvy, "now she's *sober*. Sober a year in June. But oh no. Instead of I can just help her get straight, instead my old man gets a court injunction saying I can't see her 'til I'm eighteen, *almost three years*." He looks around the table. "Well, like I told the judge, 'Your honor, why not put a gin bottle in her hand—a loaded gun, for all intents and purposes.' And she's living right nearby. Wilkins, Georgia. You hearda Wilkins, right? Can't be thirty miles away."

"So call her," challenges Mrs. Sykes.

"And ma'am, I would if she had a phone."

Mrs. Sykes rolls her eyes. "Another one with no phone."

"Mrs. Sykes, please, you want proof?" Alvy pulls her folded address from his wallet—an address but no phone number. Smoothing it out like a page of Scripture, Alvy passes it down the table, then looks straight at Donnie. "Well? Don't you think my mother deserves a second chance?" Donnie glowers back.

"Doan look at me."

"But *if* I told her she was forgiven? Told her face to face?" Alvy turns to Daddy Sykes. "And you're right, sir. About making amends, and making things right so we can go home right. Fine, I screwed up and did some bad things, okay, that's true and I admit it. But if I can just make things right with her, then maybe I can get my Dad right. And then maybe *he'll* stop drinking."

Donnie snorts. "You say you *drove* hyeah, boyh? I'd say mo you *slid* on yo own grease."

"Now, now," says the old man, waving his pipe. But Alvy is boring straight for Donnie now.

"Donnie c'mon, you think I'd lie about this? About my own flesh? Look, I know my mother and she'll crack—absolutely, bad as she feels." He turns to Mr. and Mrs. Sykes. "Look, I know what you probably think of me. A total bum like me. Maybe *to you* I don't look like much but—"

"No," cries Mr. Sykes, "doan yuh say dat! Evuh. Ain nobody sayin whut yuh is."

"No sir, not *you*. But Donnie, he—"

"—Or Donnie. Specially Donnie. Donnie ain said dat, 'cause Donnie, he know better bout not judgin folks. Specially Donnie."

"Well, okay," agrees Alvy. "So Donnie, all I mean—well, do you know what that'd do for her? When she wants to start boozing? That *I* forgave her? Me personally?"

Donnie stares at the table.

"Look, Donnie, I understand"—about their being colored, Alvy means—"I'm not out to make trouble for you folks. Fine, we'll hitch."

"Bright idea," snorts Donnie. "Oh sho, you three."

Alvy sets the hook. "Then *take* us, Donnie. You take us. We'll pay the gas."

"Boy, what I look like—taxicab?"

Mrs. Sykes stands up.

"Well, whut you boys is doing now is *sleep*."

DEFINITELY, ALVY'S MADE AN IMPRESSION, THOUGH. No, the Sykeses are huddled up as we file out of the dining room. Then, calling Sheppy back, they all huddle with him.

Out on the porch Alvy's strung like a wire, sweating out the verdict about can we go peaceably and will they take us. Making like I drop something, meanwhile, I reach behind the woodbox, where I've stashed your copybook. Seeing me stuff it in my pants Alvy scowls.

"Well, now at least you know. C'mon, man. What's one more day?"

"And what then, huh?"

"Tell her the truth, is what. And Donnie'll take us. And he will—if you back me. The old man's right. Do it right and we all go home right. *Free*, man. Don't you owe me that much? And especially when I freed you?"

Freed me? I'm suffocating. Then the door opens. It's Mrs. Sykes saying time to come to bed. I don't know what all they said to Sheppy, but he's looking pretty woeful in the hall, Alvy looking at him, *C'mon man what's the verdict?*

But Alvy can just sweat it out. No, Mrs. Sykes marches the Cooler King into his own private room—solitary—then leads Sheppy and me up a crooked ladder of stairs, up into this baby room in the attic. What's Mrs. Sykes trying to pull? I wonder. It's this teeny old girl's room. It's barely a treehouse, practically wall to wall with this rusty iron bed with a pink frill cover. I jump! In the corner, in a play high chair, here's a big black dollie with her arms stuck out and the dust feathered like snow on her lashes. And sure enough, as Mrs. Sykes shuts the door, Sheppy falls apart, doubles over on the bed, his hands clapped in his crotch. And I thought last night was bad.

"Doan touch me."

"What is it? Your Mamma?"

The room's freezing. Squeezing in beside him, I make my little rooting noises, which secretly he'll tolerate sometimes. Finally, I roll him over, grab the old, hard-ironed sheets that peel away like soggy newsprint, then cover us both up. On the slanted dormer ceiling just above our noses are big peeling flakes of paint—or, not paint, I realize, but more old pictures. Brown pictures of pretty brown girls. Girls in sculpted, glistening black hair and brown boys in big round army hats like halos. And Sheppy can't hide it, breathing into his cupped hand. The bed's a stethoscope. Through the old mattress I can hear him crying, but real far off through the springs so he sounds like a baby or some animal dying. I shake him.

"Why didn't you tell me George was your Dad?"

"*Faffa, not Daddy.* Cock-sucka only *fucked* to faffa me."

"So it was George?"

But he won't answer, meaning yes. My head's spinning. "So what're you gonna do?"

"What *dif*'france, what I do? Be as lonesome hyeah as deah. As some othuh fuckin place. *You understand, I wish I was deed.*"

I bound up. "Stop it! Quit doin this to yourself. Look, after my Mom died, I thought I was dead, too. But hey, it goes away."

"And how long you been dead in it, nigger? A year? *Barely?* Well, try *two* on fo size. Yes'day I saw. Saw she alwuz be deed and I alwuz be deed at some othuh place wif her. An Mis Sykes axin why do I come down hyeah wif white boys? Axin are my aunt *nice?* Hey, it ain 'cause she ain *nice* or I white-boy crazy. It cause it ain fuckin mattah, not wif her or dem, or hyeah, or deah."

I start to panic. "Quit it, I'm sick of this! C'mon, Sheppy, you can't live with that kinda attitude!" Sheppy screams in his pillow.

"*Now* he figgers it out! Well, goody for you, man, *go on home.*"

I shake him again. "So, are you going off with Alvy?"

"Why not? Least dat way maybe he won die 'tupid. 'Tupid*er*."

I keep trying to hug him, revive him. "But look, they *like* you, the Sykeses do, I know they do. You could live here with them, I bet. I bet you could."

"Aww, man, I done had all these ole Holy Rollers. All my life." But soon as Sheppy says this he's furious at himself. "Aww, shut yo mouf, nigger. These

ole people worth a *hunnert* of you. An *eight* hunnert of dat foo downstairs."
Alvy, he means.

Then Sheppy's out—out cold, so that it's just me and the brown doll staring at me, wondering why I'm so screwed up. Christ, I can't even beat off
I'm so sick. No more avoiding it. Finally, I open your notebook. Random I
open it, but even paper's got a memory. No, the book knows right where I
left off—with you leaving New York City for Uncle Stephen's lodge in the
Adirondacks.

*Please, if I have to sit with anybody on the train, please make it be a man. An older
loaded type who mixes his martinis in a crystal shaker and takes long vacations.*

*No such luck. In Rye I get saddled with Mrs. Reynolds, every girl's self-appointed
guardian with two bratty boys, ages 7 and 9. I'm wearing Stephen's hat and dress,
the things Stephen gave me specially to wear so he can picture me in his mind. My
borrowed leather luggage is first class and in my purse I have almost $15. Mrs.
Reynolds asks where I go to school? St. Anne's I say and she looks terribly impressed,
oh a convent girl.*

I skip down.

*. . . Threw up twice after lunch. Even the sun on the lakes hurts my stomach. The lakes
must be a mile deep they're such a deep icy blue. And all along the road, these happy,
horribly energetic people with their little knapsacks. You'd think they were marching up
to heaven. And these grand homes. Who on earth could possibly afford them?*

*Stephen's waiting for me on the platform. With Billy McGee, wearing some nasty
old hat stuck with fishing bugs. Stephen sees I'm wearing his special dress but pretends not to notice, giving me a fatherly squeeze. As for Billy McGee he gets the tip of
my pinky. God, there's nothing I hate worse than a drunk in the afternoon.*

*Aunt Mary is waiting in the car. She hates Stephen's driving, especially on these
roads, crying, Slow down, slow down. Between Stephen's wild driving and her
grabbing my hand, they're both driving me batty. Stephen's going on and on about
the fishing, as if he'll turn me into a fisherman at this late date. That would certainly
be fishy.*

Two more pages down.

*. . . Aunt Mary is worse than mother. Banging on the bathroom door. What is going
on with you in there? Outside later Stephen grabs my arm, What the hell is wrong with
you, you brat? Damn if I ever should have invited you . . .*

And the paper does remember. It even flips the same. After all these years, in almost the same order, it flips back to the same bad parts I saw yesterday. But c'mon, it's just old blue lines and yellowed paper. It's just blots and cross-outs and crabbed handwriting. Don't call it reading. Call it more a reading form of staring. All I do is stare at the words, staring and staring like I did at that moldering pink teddy bear with the basket of plastic eggs.

Cocktails and chowder down at the Cosgroves tonight. I promise Stephen I'll be down, then retire for one of my sick naps. When I wake up, the sun's down and Stephen's over me kissing me hard. At first I sit up!! I feel so happy like a little girl kissing him but instead he yanks up my nightie and starts licking me. Wait, I say, I want to talk, we have to talk but Stephen keeps licking and squeezing me saying I'm so beautiful and I was always his girl and how he always took care of me and I finally must grow up. Trembling a grown man trembling saying such nice little cakes and I should forget all the old wivestales. He says men of a better class couldn't care less about marrying a virgin. And what better way than with an experienced man, instead of wasting it on some dumb kid? And why is he trembling? Trembling so I feel almost sorry for him, going on how I put them all to shame. Then he's mad, shaking me to stop crying, Come on, like nobody ever told you that after A comes B then C.

I get sick a little, but luckily I'm empty and he's got an extra towel. What's the use? I slap him, then I'm sorry. I want to scream but how? I can't do that to Stephen now. Forget Mother. I can't do it to Stephen or the family, and especially not to Daddy, not after all we've put the family through.

It won't "go in" anyway, so Stephen says we'll "work" on it. My new math problem. So he has me "flick it" for him and I close my eyes. Not for the reason you'd think. No, I just can't stand to see him, a grown man, making such awful faces. Isn't that crazy? After all the things you dread, the worst thing is never the thing you expect. And Stephen is right. What did you expect, kiddo? What on earth did you ever expect?

SHEPPY'S SNORING AND SNUFFLING. For the longest damn time I lay there beside him. In this crazy half sleep I just lay there paralyzed with the daylight murmuring through the faded curtains, when it hits me, *Do this last good deed for Aky and it'll all be over.* And, answering, the light murmurs through the curtains, actually rustles them *yes*, and, like the light, one cousin removed from myself, I wake up.

I guess I start hollering.

It's pitch dark and Sheppy's gone. I feel for the copybook and it's gone too! Then in the doorway, gray eyes, a woman's gray moonlit eyes and breath smoking across the freezing room. But when the gray eyes bend over me, from the younger smell and milder voice, I know right off it's not Mrs. Sykes.

"E'sy, baby," says the voice, stroking my hair, "I'm Irma, Mrs. Sykes's daughter. Din know where you was, huh, baby?"

"My book. Did you see, like, a school book?"

"Shhsssh, Mamma got it downstairs." The voice kisses me. "Sleep baby, ain nobody lookt."

How old she is or what she looks like, I've got no idea. Gray eyes. Breath. Irma's warm weight over me, and me clutching her, scared to let her go and embarrassed, to be such a baby after all this. And falling asleep then I can almost see it. All that I love, all that I once had loved, or had thought of as love, I can watch it all drifting away like Irma's smoking breath, unholdable, invisible, senseless, not even real anymore.

AND ALL THAT NIGHT, I have the longest, craziest, most upside-down sleep. It's still night when I wake up and, downstairs, I hear all these voices, *They called the cops.* Quick! Hauling on my borrowed pants I stumble down the crooked stairs, grab the crusty doorhandle, then slam into a wall of black faces.

Must be half their church congregation packed in the parlor! Men in tight suit jackets and shirtsleeves—them and plush-armed ladies sitting high on their chairs, their plump hands sitting on their laps like little presents. Propped in his big chair Daddy Sykes sure is looking grave. But not just him, because here's Mrs. Sykes, and Sheppy beside her sweating bullets. And here it comes! Next thing I know I'm facing a big, curly-haired, razor-mustached man in a white collar.

"I am the Reverend Milton Crenshaw of Mount Hope Baptist. And you, my friend, you oughta change yo name to *Lucky.* Cause of awl the homes in northern Georgia, to have descended upon this place—well, son, you have blundered upon the very best."

"Yessir," I nod.

"Lemme finish!" blisters the Reverend. "Now, I don't know many, many a'tall, as charitable as our esteemed elder, Deacon Sykes—"

"Mmm-hum. No, indeed."

"—And I'm not in *any* way shape or form gonna speak against our fine deacon, who if he have any fault be he *too* polite and kin'-hearted. So, my friend, I will take it upon myself to axe you a very hard and awkward question. And not, you understand, because we are a inhospitable people, as I trust you have seen, and seen in consid'rable abundance, at the table of Sistah Skyes. But now to git down to it, my friend, just *when* are you goin home? *Soon*, I trust? And where"—he looks all around, smiling—"now where is this other li'l boy blue sleeping in our corn? Tell me, son. Will yo young friend be, uhh, *waking* up any ole time? Oh, any ole time *soon?*"

"Oh, I could wake him up for you, Reverend!" Oh boy, could I.

"*Don't*," enunciates Mrs. Sykes.

"*Well*, young man?" booms the Reverend.

"Yessir?" I jerk around.

"I believe we were talking about you goin *home*. Speedily, safely, happily. But home?"

"Yessir?"

"Now Deacon Sykes feels obliged to send you boys home in better shape than I gather you was in when you first arrived. Naturally, we agree with the deacon on this point. And let me add that we're all very sorry. Truly sorry fo whatever drove y'all down hyeah—"

"—*Yes, indeed.*"

"—but yet and still," resumes the Reverend, "things being what they is down hyeah, well, this is highly awkward fo us."

"Oh, I know! Believe me, sir, this was absolutely the *last* place I—"
I stop dead.

"Oh my." The Reverend drops his arms in despair. "My, my, but don't the little children, as they say. Don't their very *words* betray them?"

"*Umm-umm.*"

I wave my arms. "Wait, Reverend! Everybody, hey I didn't mean *that! Like* that. Please, are you kidding? Hey, *I'm glad to be here.*"

Head rolled back Daddy Sykes is groaning up at heaven and, stuck, I'm looking around for help. Sheppy! Donnie! Anybody! But wait, I think, so where is old Donnie?

"Mrs. Sykes," I ask, "so where's Donnie?"

Her eyes blink with irritation. "*Out.*"

Beat it, I think she means! Mortified, I start to run out when she calls me back.

"Not *you*, Mr. Frank—*him.*"

" ?"

"Him! Donald M. Sykes! O-U-T, *out*. At—a—*meet*—ting. Oh Lord!" She stands up, fanning her hand under her nose. "Reverend, folks, honeybaby"—reaching over, Mrs. Sykes soothes me on the neck—"Lawd, forgive me, chile, for it has been a long, *long* day. *Irma!* Irma, honey, can you please find young Frank hyeah sumpin good to eat?" Irma stands up—look, it's my Irma, gray-eyed Irma from upstairs, and she really is the way I pictured her, soft, sweet-eyed, pretty.

"So where did Donnie go off to?" I ask Irma upstairs later. With the light out I guess I feel I can ask.

"Lord, once you latches onto sumpin. Donnie, he at—at a *prayer meetin*, K?"

"Irma, wait." Her gray eyes flicker in the moonlight. "So will your Dad and Mom let us go tomorrow?"

"We see."

"But will I see you tomorrow?"

"Maybe." Irma's soft, wet mouth crumples on my cheek. "Got five a my own but *maybe*."

But you know how that one goes. Because Irma's smoking breath glides out of the room and her feet creak down the stairs, and I never see her again either.

IT FEELS LIKE A SUNDAY THE NEXT MORNING, ALTHOUGH IT ISN'T. All night long Sheppy and me kept banging into each other, sleep-talking, snoring, kicking, tossing. Then, just before it gets light, the hair on my neck shoots straight up! At first it sounds like a dog howling, but then it drops into a lockjaw jabberty like stones rattling down a gutter. *Hooooo*, and my dog ears prick up, listening for the wolves that have long since died off. *Who* it is I know immediately but not *what*, and *who* but not *why*. Holy smokes. Again, my neck hair shoots up. *Hooooooooo.*

Even Alvy must hear old man Sykes trumpeting downstairs. When I finally get out of bed, Alvy's long been up and our clothes are dry. Peering out the window I see Alvy dressed again in his own clothes, down by the barn, picking through the pocked mud of the pig yard with Daddy Sykes. Needless to say, within ten minutes Alvy's a world-renowned expert on swine—there's a new one for his b.s. repertoire. Yeah, all inquisitiveness and gratitude, Alvy's completely rehabilitated, helping the old man feed his last three hogs, the last remnants of his farm, besides the chickens and his two hunting dogs. God, I feel so mad watching Alvy charm old man Sykes. It just makes me burn with jealousy that any kid as sick as he was yesterday can today pass himself off as normal. A block of ice, that's what Alvy reminds me of, forever melting into another new, pure white skin of forgetting. And without they even completely buy it, people buy it—or half buy it, or just plain give up. And that's the thing with Alvy, I realize, it's his crazy energy that finally defeats people. Finally, people just don't have the energy to contend with him.

Donnie sure can't. Not this morning. Huddled over his coffee, Donnie's looking pretty rough and depressed after last night's supposed prayer meeting—I can smell cigarettes and liquor on Donnie's breath as he croaks at me, "Yo clothes on top the washer. Breakfast on the stove." The door slaps shut.

"Hey, Donnie." It's Alvy, so chipper you wanna wring his neck. And he's won. When Donnie doesn't look up Alvy flashes me his toothy grin, *Now don't fuck this up for me.*

But if that's not sign enough we're leaving, as I'm finishing breakfast, here's Mrs. Sykes in her white uniform.

"Frank dear, please see Mr. Sykes in the dining room once you done eatin. And yes, he has that little school copybook of yo's."

Even before I round the corner into the dining room, I can smell his sweet, peppery pipe smoke. Mr. Sykes half rousts up, vigilant again—vigilantly *unsure,* like for a second I might be Alvy. On the table, his papery black hands glisten. Between them both sits your copybook and a wide roll of silver duct tape.

"That's mine," I say.

"I know dat."

"I don't mean mine that I *wrote* it," I add after a second.

"I know dat too. That othuh boy"—a brush of his hand, whoever—"he tol me an my wife." I doubt he ever did learn our names.

"So I can have it back?"

"Sho," he motions. "Right chere fo yuh. But firs, set on down hyeah." He motions to the chair across from him. It's real dark and quiet there in the early morning, and it's even darker and quieter with those old pictures hanging over us, dappled, pools of dark, like tree shadows.

"Then you read it?" I ask him finally.

"*Noooh*"—a pained face—"not me or nobody. Nevuh. Not in dis hous we ain. No, that young cul'd boy, he say it warnt no good. But now hole on hyeah." He winces. "Now me, personally I ain sayin *whut* it be, good, bad, indiffrunt. Ain nona my affair. But *yuh,* well, thass diffrunt. Yuh is under my roof and yuh is mah frien, which it do make it mah concern. So when I say it ain no good, what I mean it ain no good fo *yuh.*"

Then of course I fly off the handle. "And I didn't wanna see it! Did Sheppy—the colored boy—did he tell you that, Mr. Sykes? Look, I'm not saying *who* gave it to me, I'm not saying that but—"

Mr. Sykes's hand starts flipping back imaginary pages. "*F'get* all dat. *F'get it!*"

"But how? I mean I *saw* it, didn't I? And my Mom wrote it, didn't she?"

"Now hole on hyeah! Yuh Mamma wid the Lawd, right? Well, is I right?"

I half nod.

"So what yuh ain sure about?"

"About *they* weren't sure. The priests in our church. About whether she really went to heaven."

Mr. Sykes shakes his head. "An see? Yuh see, now there yuh go, thinkin all yuh ole who-do an she-do an whut-not! Thass de *Lawd's* bidness, boy! All dat whole book be *closed* an she at peace, yuh Mamma. Shoot boy, Mr. Sykes he talk to dat Ole Man up chere e'erday. So Mr. Sykes doan he jus *think*, he *know*."

I sit there with my face in my arm, breathing into it. Finally I look up, and I'm here, but there the book still is, accusing me. "So what do I do with it, Mr. Sykes, what?"

Mr. Sykes puffs on his pipe. "Could burn it. Smoke, thass holy. Then agin yuh could leave it hyeah wid me. Once yuh old nuff I send it off tuh yuh." He shrugs. "Well, somebody will, Donnie or one of the girls. Somebody be round hyeah, I spect."

"And I *do* trust you, Mr. Sykes. Absolutely. I just feel so—stupid. Like last night? With the Reverend Crenshaw? When people *thought*—well, what I mean, I felt so horrible—"

"Aww, man, now there yuh go agin wid all yuh ole she-do, I-do voo-doo! *F'get* all dat! *F'get it*, y'hear? Now pick up dat ole book. Hole it up chere. In yuh hans. Go on—"

He picks up the thick silver tape. The tape shrieks as he strips it out. A whole yard.

"Yuh listenin now? Now hole dat book on up hyeah—"

And with a shriek he belts it once, then twice around with the tape. Twice one way, then twice the other way he seals the book tight. Then on the duct tape, with an old white plastic ballpoint, he slowly draws a dark shaky ✝ and my lungs open like a flue as he makes me repeat, "*I lookt but I ain seen it—* say it!—*an now from the whol worl I hiding it an I ain evuh opening it*—say it now!—*not until I thirty or mo. Or nevuh. Nevuh, be mah advice.*"

It's amazing. Suddenly, even the old photographs look way bigger, black faces almost bowed out in their murky old glass. And here's a clunky old clock ticking. Look at that, I think. Up on the sideboard. The whole time that clock was ticking but I never even heard it! And as it ticks I don't have to apologize or explain anything, as Mr. Sykes knocks out his pipe, pulls out his tobacco, then repacks it, wadding the tobacco in with the callused stump of his right index finger. Yeah, old Mr. Sykes must wait ten minutes for it to percolate down. Then, almost remembering himself, he squints at me.

"Now, bout dat other boy—de *white* one, I mean. Well, frankly I doan knows as I b'lieve him. Not entirely. But I do b'lieve in his heart he have somethin he gotta do. So las night I heard out de Rev'rund an everybody—an I do mean *everbody*—an I thought long an hard bout it, an prayed on it too. So now I gonna axe yuh. Yuh wanna go wif dat boy today to his Mamma's? An befo yuh do answer, doan yuh even worry what *he* think. Yuh stuck it out, an ain no boy could evuh say yuh din, neithuh. So if'n yuh go, den yuh go for yuh *own* sef, an yuhsef only."

Well, I can't quit now, I think. Besides, Donnie is taking us, right? But when I say yes, Mr. Sykes still has one more concern. A big one, too.

"An the c'lud boy. Now, what bout him?"

"Look, Mr. Sykes, my Dad'll pay his way home if his aunt can't. I promise, Mr. Sykes. *Everybody* goes home—no sir, don't you worry about that. Once Alvy has his say, I'll call my Dad right away. Like, two seconds later!"

Mr. Sykes squints. "But dat white boy say his Mamma ain got no phone?"

"*Pay phone*, I mean." I whip out my call-home dime and, I must say, Mr. Sykes is still looking pretty dubious, but finally he calls everybody together.

"Mamma! Donnie! Yuh othuh boys! Y'all come on in hyeah."

MRS. SYKES SNAPS HER PURSE. She's just given us six dollars in travel money—two bucks each.

"So! *Straight* to work once you drop them off, Donald?"

Donnie rolls his eyes. "Yesss, Mamma."

"Six sharp. Mary's cookin t'night." Mary is Irma's sister. The girls take turns while Mrs. Sykes is off living in with her white folks.

"And-I-will-be-here," labors Donnie.

"Mr. and Mrs. Sykes," chimes in Alvy, dying to get rolling, "we sure do 'preciate it!" God, the kid never learns! Again, Mrs. Sykes start clucking, sucking in her chin.

"Well, 'preciate us by 'preciatin yo parents, 'preciatin-us-when-you-can-hear-me-talkin-to-my-son! And you talk about rude! Aww, hush up, Esther," she mutters to herself finally. Mrs. Sykes throws her arms out to him. "Come on hyeah, sweetheart. Alla you boys, come on hyeah an get yo hugs—"

Sharp-winged barn pigeons are blowing. Gray clouds are cutting low across the fields, plowing rivers of dark in oceans of light. I can barely face old man Sykes, not that he's happy or unhappy. No, patting my cheek, old Mr. Sykes is just as pleased as he was when we crash-landed yesterday, waving us all off, "Gwan, y'all! Git on home an yuh be *happy*, an yuh be *good!*" And as the dogs bark and the old man points us to the Greater Glory Be, so here's Donnie waving us all into the car, this time Sheppy up front and white boys in back. In her old Nash Mrs. Sykes is right behind us, too. No, Mrs. Sykes is making double sure, before she goes, that all three of our asses be gone.

Now, I know Mr. Sykes had a big talk with Sheppy, but whatever advice and encouragement the old man gave him, well, it's not working as we leave. Like a fish stuck in the corner of an aquarium, Sheppy's head is bumping from side to side, and Alvy's not doing much better. As the car finally breaks clear onto the main road, as the dust fades and the road smooths, I feel the whole car shaking, when I realize it's Alvy's nervous leg beating, *boom-bippa-boom*. God, it's torture for the kid, not having a steering wheel in his hands, the Taker being Taken. No, this isn't even remotely the movie Alvy had in mind. Yeah, that was the biggest dream for Alvy, Charlene seeing him behind the wheel, more colossal than if he'd come astride a circus elephant.

"Donnie," Alvy says finally, "c'mon man, how 'bout a cigarette?"

"And a blindfold? *Tzee-hee*." Donnie punches the lighter.

"Aww, man," sighs Alvy as they all three light up, "this is hard seeing my Mom, *hard*." He looks at Donnie. "But I guess you know all about that one, huh?"

Donnie stops short. "Which one?"

"Dreading something."

"Scuse me?"

"Well, you got a wife and family, right?"

"Who said dat?"

"Just figured."

"Well, my family's jus fine, thank you."

Boom-bippa-bippa. Boom-boom be-doom. A few miles go by. Then again Alvy starts in on him, "Gee, Donnie, I meant to ask you, man. What kinda work you do?"

Donnie waits. "Bookkeeper."

"*Really?*"—Alvy claps his hands together—"man, that's so strange, because when you said that just now? Man, I thought to myself, *that's Donnie.* No, that fits you, man. To-a-*T.* You're—aww, what's the word? Yeah, *precise.* Naww, you are, man. Your Mom too—naww, that's where you get it, man. Yeah, watching her cook I saw that. Real precise. But *damn,* Donnie, shut up all day long like that, in a little office? All them columns? Punching in all them little numbers on an adding machine going ker-chunk ker-chunk all day long? Me, I'd be ready for a drink, boy. Or *somethin'—*"

Alvy bums another smoke. He holds up the cigarette, *bappa-bappa-boom.* "Hey, Donnie, you know what goes with this?"

"Lung cancer."

"C'mon. You don't know?"

"An you do, huh?" snorts Donnie.

"Goddamnit, Loomis, please shut *up,*" moans Sheppy. But no, Alvy keeps up the Twenty Questions.

". . . Poontang? A nice cold beer? Give up? . . ." Reaching down, Alvy starts crinkling candy paper—a Hershey bar wrapper. And sure enough, when I look down, the backseat is filled with candy wrappers. Donnie snatches the wrapper away.

"Gimme dat!" Donnie's neck is twitching again.

"That's right, folks, crea-ee-my milk chocolate! Milky smooth! Mmm-mm, stickin-to-the-roof-of-your-mouth-good!" Alvy hauls out more wrappers, carnival barking, "And here I got me one Reesey Cup! And do I hear Baa-by Ruth! Something cold? C'mon, Donnie, pull over a minute. Candy bar, a nice cold Coke or Yoo-Hoo . . . *C'mon,* man, I'll buy."

But damn if Donnie doesn't stop at the next store and hand Alvy three dollars—anything we want, he says, and only Alvy can go, I guess so Donnie can watch him, and also because Donnie sure ain't leaving him alone in his car. Man, I thought I had a sweet tooth. Because when Alvy gets back, Donnie gets two big Hersheys, shucks off the wrappers, chocks them into squares, then mashes them into little chocolate sandwiches. What really gets me, though, is the way Donnie eats candy. A kid, he'll make that candy last all day, but not Donnie. No, Donnie eats it like a machine, like it's mud. What did Alvy do to Donnie? I wonder—what, to make him look so worn out and sad, and suddenly so different from yesterday? Even then, even after all I've been through with you and Dad and Grammaw, even so it's hard actually knowing these things—and especially when you like anybody as much as I do Donnie. Still, as I sit there watching Donnie cram down the Hersheys, I guess part of me knows, or half knows, what's eating Donnie but Alvy, he whole knows. Don't ask me how Alvy knows this about Donnie. Maybe he saw some AA stuff in the car or overheard something. At any rate, Alvy knew his alcoholics and he'd finally worn out poor Donnie, who's already an hour late for work as it is. A couple blown turns later we're lost and Donnie's fuming. Then Alvy cries out.

"Ho! Back up, Donnie—"

Dust flies past us. And there's the mailbox HICKS with the red flag still sticking up from yesterday. And even as Donnie turns around, Alvy's changing the story, *Boom-bippa-boom.*

"Donnie, hold on. Uh, look, Donnie, this is really awkward, man. But y'know my so-called stepfather? Well, I didn't want to go into it before. Not in front of your parents I didn't but, uhh—"

"*But what?*" Donnie's neck is spazzing out now.

"Well, my so-called stepfather, well, he's a real cracker asshole, man." Donnie bangs the wheel.

"I ain got time for this crap, *I ain got time!* You hearin this, c'lud boy?"

"Donnie," soothes Alvy, "look, he'll be okay with Sheppy, *Sheppy's a kid.* But you, man. Especially a big, strong, kick-ass dude like you? Well, you don't know what the asshole's liable to do."

"No," I jump in. "Donnie was the deal!"

"Frank," groans Alvy, "haven't the Sykeses done enough for us already? Huh?"

Then here's Sheppy's tugging on me. "C'mon, man, less go. T'night we all be on the bus back home. Hey, Donnie, *thanks*, man."

Donnie's furious. "Fine! Say y'all came by *stork!* Flyin saucer. But just you leave our good name outta it."

"Donnie," I plead, "Donnie I'm really sorry, I—"

"—Sorry?" gushes Alvy. "We're forever grateful." Why, Alvy's so flush with gratitude he pulls out the new pack of smokes that he just bought with Mrs. Sykes's two dollars. "Here," he says, paying Donnie back the cigarettes he just bummed, "wouldn't wanna leave ya short, man."

"*Short?*" Donnie's laugh is like skid marks. "Aww, gawd bless you. Gratitude! Man, I will bronze and cherish these. Sheeee-itt . . ."

WHATEVER ALVY GETS HE DESERVES IT, I think lunging up the hill. But as I turn, what kills me is Alvy's face in the light, his nostrils wide open and his glasses two glints—that weird, deep, unknowing *piousness* in him, if that's the word. Right then Alvy's a million miles from Ad Altare Dei, but even now I can still feel the heat of what won him that medal. Crazy or not, there's still that perverse fury and purpose to him, that absolute fixity, which, in spite of everything else, still makes me feel like a pygmy beside him. And of course it all goes wrong. Just as we make out the house, a dog starts barking. Alvy scrunches his nose at Sheppy.

"Today's Friday, right?"

"Yestaday was—"

"But Donnie and Mrs. Sykes?—"

"They *work* Sat'days."

"Sonofabitch! Well, we can't go up there, not now! Well, c'mon, if it's Saturday, then Hicks is here!"

But, grabbing him, Sheppy is what he hasn't been for a week—certain. "Fuck Hicks. You come dis far, now tell her, man. *Go on.*"

And never mind the dog barking or any second we're liable to get shot—stop the train, Alvy's gotta shit. Well, go on, says Sheppy, but this time he's not letting Alvy slip the collar. Leaning against a tree Sheppy just waits. Rolling a piece of stick in his fingers, Sheppy's faintly whistling, whistling in that eerie, aimless way of a hand before it knows it's a fist, before that hand even knows it's being thrown. Whispering I call over to Sheppy, but he can't even hear, he's so distracted, and the copybook, every time I shove it back down my pants, it comes riding back up, the slick duct tape sweating and itching like a boil against my belly. *Stop it. Quit it.* In my mind I keep hearing Mr. Sykes all exasperated, *F'get all dat, f'get it.* And again, as usual, here's my last refuge—feeling terrible. Terrible about Donnie and I'll never see the Sykeses again. Terrible about Reverend Crenshaw and terrible, above all, about Sheppy and what he must think of us now, as white people. No, I think, on behalf of all white people, at this whole Appomattox, I'm wanting to apologize to Sheppy for Alvy and me, to solemnly hand over the sword of us all being such white assholes. And speak of the devil, here's Alvy, hissing and out of breath.

"I just saw him—Hicks. Smart move, Frank. *Had* to take my pistol, didn't you?"

"Calm down," I tell him, "we're your witnesses. You came to *talk*, not to shoot him."

"*Who's out there, goddamnit?*"

I look at Sheppy, but with that Sheppy takes off down the hill. Dropping to his knees, Sheppy's grunting and rocking. It's a horseshoe pit. Running back to us, Sheppy's got one of the iron stakes.

"You hear me? Who's that out there?"

Alvy grabs for the iron stake but Sheppy snatches it back. *"No.* Not no gun or club—wid yo heart, man. So go on, *tell* her." All swollen-eyed, Sheppy nudges Alvy with his head. *"Hyeah's yo chance, man.* Call to him, man. And when you go down, talk and thrash round so he doan hear us, and doan you worry. Cause if Hicks start sumpin"—Sheppy holds out the iron stake—"then I be right behin him wid dis." Sheppy gives him another shove. *"Do it, man."*

"It's me—Alvy. I just wanna talk to Charlene!"

"Git on up here, boy!"

So Sheppy peels right and I peel left—flee, is more like it, down along the bushy honeysuckle fence skirting the house, and Sheppy's got the iron horseshoe stake, and I've got my mouth, to scream bloody murder at the first sign of trouble. And here he is! Not forty feet away, here's Hicks with his matted yellow hair, old blue plumber's jacket and unlaced work boots. It's been months since I saw him last and it's quite a shock. He looks terrible. Craggy. Hungover but still humungous. And definitely blocking the front door. Alvy holds out his hands.

"Look, man, no trouble. Promise."

Hicks nods. "Thass right. Get in the truck and there won't be no trouble." He looks around. "Where's that other little asshole ya run off with?"

Alvy has to stand on his leg to keep it from jumping. His head sways like a balloon. "The cops just got him—yesterday they did, but I got away. C'mon, man! Twenty minutes and I'll go, I swear I will. And how's Buddy, huh? *Charleeeene?* . . ."

"In the truck," barks Hicks.

"And I will," stammers Alvy, *"after* I see Charlene."

"And get it through your fuckin' head, she don't want no part a you! *Or* your fucked-up family." Hicks waits. "You know you 'bout killed Bunny, don't you? Don't ya even know that yet?"

Alvy's arms fly up, almost spastic. His voice gargles, "I got rights! Why are you even doing this to me? Twenty minutes, that's all I'm asking! Twenty minutes, Christ. I don't wanna fight you!"

"Yer damned right you don't, boy."

"And I don't! And I'll leave, honest to God I will. And all I came for is Charlene, okay? *Charlene, c'mon. All my life I loved you. And all my life you knew."*

It's like the silence after a gunshot. Alvy hollers again.

"Buddy! You see your Uncle Alvy out here. Now tell Mommy to come on out."

"And there's your answer!" snaps Hicks. "Now, before you really piss me off—*in* the fuckin truck!"

"*Charlene, what are you so afraid of? Your own goddammed kid?*" Again, Alvy stomps on his trembling leg. "Please," he warns Hicks, "I'm *just* going to the door, all right? *Just* to the door, and *I'll knock, okay?* And you see—you see I'm goin in peace 'cause I'm still wearing my glasses."

Hands in the air, trembling, Alvy starts toward the door, but Hicks just shoves him back. "Now stop it," warns Hicks. And to be fair, you can see Hicks doesn't want to hurt the kid—not at first, but then Alvy butts him back one. Not hard. Stubbornly, two, three times Alvy butts back and then, almost in slow motion, Hicks hammers him one, boom, right on the top of the head. "Now, thass enough!" he warns, but Alvy only jumps up, so Hicks sends his glasses flying, "*Charleeene!*" But again Alvy bounds up, so this time Hicks really cuts loose—seizes Alvy by the throat, then punches him twice with all his might. Boom. Alvy's dazed on his knees, a red rip all down the side of his face.

"*Charlene, you see this? Go on, cocksucker! You fat fuckin' pussy! Hit me!*"

Like a mallet, the hand comes down. Alvy spurts and spits, the blood running thick down his nose. *Run out, save him,* I think, but where's Sheppy's signal? And where's my courage but where it always was. Alvy clambers up, tries to run around Hicks—boom—down again, and then the real beating starts, Alvy screeching this half-child, half-animal, underwater scream, and thrashing all around. But now Hicks is getting winded. No, Hicks didn't count on this, and Alvy's a lot stronger than he was a year ago, with lots less to lose. "*You fat piece of shit! She's my mother and that's my own fuckin' house!*" Sweating and panicking, Hicks hauls him up by the belt. He slams Alvy face down but, slippery with his own blood, Alvy breaks free, then nails him one good. Gouges Hicks in his eyes. Ball-kicks him, then spits blood in his face.

"*Come on, you big fat stupid fuck! Better kill me while you still can!*"

Then here's Sheppy! Behind Hicks! Waving at me! It's the signal. Half in a dream I run out, hollering, "*Hicks,* I'll swear out a warrant! *Hicks,* I saw everything!"

All it takes is that split second. Hicks is looking at me in shock. Then Hicks and me, we both see it. Twirling. Up in the air. Black and heavy, the iron horseshoe stake lands in the dirt. And as fast, Hicks grabs the back of his leg. Like an invisible judo flip, Hicks crashes on his back, roaring, as Sheppy raises the straight razor.

"Try dat on fo size, muthafucka!"

Hamstrung. And as fast as Sheppy brings his razor up, Alvy brings down the horseshoe iron, the one beating him and the other stomping him and

Hicks bellowing and struggling up only to crumple again on his bloody, castrated leg. Then the door opens.

"Stop it! Please! Stop it!"

Without a doubt, they'd have killed Hicks if Charlene and the kids hadn't run out then. And later, that was what pained me the most, remembering how fast Alvy stopped the slaughter for her. Stopped literally the second Charlene came out. Stopped with that pathetic look of hope against all knowing, and blind loyalty against all reason, and needing against any chance of his ever being needed. No, when Alvy saw Charlene and Buddy, a switch flipped in him. Like that, Alvy was on this whole other mission, like those volunteer firemen who set fires, then go clanging off as heroes to put them out. Like that, Alvy grabs Sheppy stomping Hicks, whips off his belt, and ties off the leg. And then like a family accident, *just a normal family accident,* Alvy organizes everyone, Buddy and Audrey fetching blankets and a pillows, while Charlene backs down Hicks's prized red truck. Then on "three," we all lift Hicks dazed into the steel flatbed—two hundred pounds, a feather. "Go! Go!" yells Alvy to his Mom. The engine roars. Hicks's pants leg is sticky red like chicken liver but, incredibly, I don't pass out. Funny, I don't even remember being queasy, and there's no time, I'm so busy trying to keep the guy from sliding on the bloody, greasy steel floor. It must have been the shock. All I remember is the truck banging down the long drive, then the open road and the wind in our faces—the wind's what I most remember, the surging wind and Charlene hunched over the wheel and the kids looking back in horror, and Alvy, tourniquet belt in hand, hurtling forward like the Light Brigade. And, closing one eye, way off in the wind at that moment, it almost feels like the old T-Bird to me . . . *Nyerrrvwwwww,* a plane simultaneously mowing down and saving everybody. And only after we've flown over it, destroyed the whole toy world just to save it, only then does it hit me that it's *my* life down there, and that you and me and Dad and everyone in it, we're all so guilty and all so innocent and it's such a mess that, finally, you wonder how anybody, even God, could possibly blame a soul for it. Give it up, kid, just give it up.

But I'll tell you just how far gone I was. Because it's only when we hit the doctor's that it hits me. Holy Christ, no Sheppy!

CRACKING THE EGG

LIKE HOUDINI, YOU SPEND HALF YOUR WHOLE CHILDHOOD TRYING TO FIGURE A WAY OUT OF IT, always too young, too pig-headed or too something. And then like Dad with his easy-egg intuos—an adult like Dad and, finally, a Dad like Dad—you try to find a way back in, or at least a crack so you can peer inside, because even if it's half cooked, your egg's as done as it ever will be. Impossible, you think. The egg's done and childhood, for sure, is long, long done.

No, like the first jingle of car keys, there's the promise of true freedom now, but first you gotta break that egg open. Because even if it sucked, for better or worse, that egg's where you made your life and so you gotta love it, or at the very least accept it as what brought you this far. And it's amazing when you finally break free and see that tiny egg from the outside. It was so small yet it saw everything on earth, and saw it more or less for what it is, only exploded and rearranged, and on fragmentary, often bad, information—information that, moreover, had the incendiary ability to explain absolutely everything in creation! In fact, it reminds me of the old Mercury space capsule at the U.S. Air and Space Museum. "And the man lived in there, Daddy?" my two little girls want to know. "And he really ate in there, Daddy, and went potty there, and looked out the little window?"

And look at it, this scorched tin can with the makeshift seats and ordinary silver toggle switches—switches the likes of which you coulda bought in any hardware store back in those days. Ordinary! Why they're just like the switches that Dad and me—*Grampa* and me—used to use! A giant science fair project, is all NASA was back in those days. Heck, I want to tell my girls, that capsule almost looks like something Grampa and old Frank might have banged together down in our basement.

• • •

SO WHAT HAPPENED WITH CHARLENE?

By the time Charlene stopped the truck at the doctor Alvy and me could barely look at each other for the reviling, divorcing force of trouble. I never wanted to see Alvy again, but just before the cops come, we did agree on the need to protect Sheppy and the Sykeses. So Sheppy became "Billy," a hitchhiker we'd picked up the day before. As for the Sykeses, they never happened.

I pity the poor sheriff trying to make sense of it. Blood all over the place, a man unconscious, the doctor yelling to his nurse, Buddy and Audrey in shock, a crowd of gawkers buzzing, and Charlene yelling about "some nigger" and pointing at Alvy. But straight off the sheriff gets it.

"So this is your son?"

"Yes, I am, sir!" cries Alvy, vindicated.

Well, Charlene blows up. "I'll tell him who you are! You're nothing but a murdering, scheming little psycho, and far as I'm concerned you're *dead*. Do you hear me, you little bastard, *dead*."

DOWNSTAIRS IN JUVENILE HALL THE NEXT DAY, flipping

on the lights, the director lady leaves me alone in this huge living room, this like official *state* room, all dark and shut-up smelling, with long, greasy gold drapes and beat-up mahogany furniture. At first I feel sick to my stomach—sicker than usual—then I realize what it is. It's exactly like a funeral home, *a lying-in-state* room where kids and parents meet once the kid has returned from the dead of being gone. And sure enough, when Dad finally walks in, obviously scared to death, well, suddenly I have this on-high sense of my life, my child's life, as over, and I mean really over this time. The year before, when the phone rang with the news about you, when Dad crashed back through the living room thunderstruck to catch me tottering off the edge of the world—well, a year ago maybe I was a victim but not now. No, what I realize then—realize with a distinctly adult sense of horror—is that, whatever else, I really *did* mean to scare Dad to death by running away.

"But why did you do this to me?" he sobs. "Not to know if you were dead or kidnapped? And never so much as a call? *Why?*"

"I could't breathe! And Heidi wouldn't lay off! What difference did I make? All you wanted was her, not me. I couldn't believe you dumping me like that."

"I dumped *you?*" Dad's trembling all over, we both are. "Frank, can you imagine what it was like to lose your mother and then you, too? Do you have any idea, *any?*"

It's so pathetic. Dad weeps, then he tries to stop. Then I cry because I can't, so Dad'll know I'm sorry and terrified, which I sincerely am, and not acting, which in the sense of being fucked up I'm not, but in the sense of feeling that I'm *always* acting, I most certainly am. For a second, it's almost sweet, the awkward way Dad and me try to dance this feeling dance, neither sure who should lead, and who should follow. In fact as Dad hugs me then, suddenly I remember that story of the kid who dies and goes up to heaven, up so high the kid's overjoyed to finally see his old life down there with all his toys and the people he loved in that snowy shook-up ball that his life was once. And best of all, as the kid looks down, he can see that his old, hard-fought kid's life is *over,* draped like a set of clothes on the bed for some other kid to use. Yep, it's over and in a weird way I'm so proud suddenly. Suddenly, I'm even weirdly proud of Dad. Proud because we fought this thing together, and even if nobody won, it's over, kid, the war's over!

I'll never forget driving back home to Taverna from National. In the week we'd been gone, all the leaves had fallen, and hanging in the air was that wonderful sharp, steamy smell of burning leaves. God, Taverna was bitty as a teacup, though, and small as Taverna was, Corregidor was even smaller, the houses all so perfectly painted and organized into these little lawns. No, in the space of a week, the whole world here had changed, and as I get out of the car, here are all the neighborhood kids—them and even Mrs. Feeney and people, all waving to me like I'm John Glenn, *Hi Frank! Hi!*

AS IT TURNED OUT, I DIDN'T SEE ALVY FOR MONTHS AFTER THAT, and luckily I didn't have to see him in court once Lucky bribed off Hicks, who was also facing major assault charges. It was funny missing Alvy. Because, really, the Alvy I missed was the *old* Alvy, the crazy trade-rat Alvy who stole as much as he gave, but at least he always gave you back something.

The one I really missed, though, was Sheppy. Yeah, Sheppy I missed in that secret way you can only love a guilty secret, my biggest hope—even if it was a pipe dream—being that Sheppy had gone back to the Sykeses or maybe down to Florida to find his sugar shack. And so far as I know, Sheppy never was seen again in Taver-Shep. Anyhow, the towns were so separate that nobody ever connected his disappearance to us.

I also made a solemn vow—or what, for me, passed as a prayer in those days—never again to utter the word *nigger.* But living in this country, well, you know how far that one went. Still, I'll say this much for myself. After that, colored folks stopped being ghosts or negatives of white people. No, after that they were real flesh and blood people, and I never again saw them in even remotely the same way.

EARLY IN '64, ON PATROL IN VIETNAM, Alvy's big brother Scotty—one of the twins—lost his right foot to a VC mine.

That year I was away myself, a boarder at St. Anselm's, a Catholic school down in southern Maryland, this place that looked like a brick factory, surrounded by corn and tobacco fields and the steaming chicken barbecues that the Lions lit off every Sunday. I remember Dad handed me the creepy brochure for St. A's, asking, "So what do you think of this?" like *hey isn't this keen?* Well, I didn't argue and Dad didn't yell or wheedle, this being Dad's nice, new way of letting me know, *Well, here's where we're sending you.* And really, with him and Heidi getting married soon, Dad wasn't lying when he said it was "for the best." Which was progress, I guess. A year before I'd never have seen it, but now I don't kick about it. Serve my time. Go to college. That was pretty much my attitude then.

Anyhow, St. Anselm's was when I began to semiseriously write, and this began with writing letters. It was like being in exile, like being St. Paul or Napoleon or somebody. I loved sending these wild epistles totally out of the blue to kids I barely knew and girls I'd just met once. Jessica, Father Nivas, Angelene, Grammaw, Mrs. Bayard—they all got letters from me. Especially Mrs. Bayard, who I finally confessed the ring to in the ninth grade, two years too late.

Yeah, in the end I probably wrote everybody except the one person I should have written—Alvy. Oh, part of me wanted to write Alvy. There were even days when part of me wanted to thank him but, really, what could I have written that Alvy wouldn't have sneered at? And especially coming from a lame, snot-nosed place like St. A-holes?

Well, after a lot of agonizing about Scotty, I finally sent the Loomises a sympathy note, conspicuously addressed to "The Loomis Family." A short note. Poetic and subtle—*très* subtle and just reeking of class. Yeah, deep into the grammar and reading, I was literally *molting* new language, wanting to be either a writer or maybe a songwriter-poet—a dark-shaded John Lennon type hunkered over my twelve-string, enunciating all these twisty, angry, nasal laments. But eighty drafts to say how *very? terribly? awfully?* sorry I was about Scotty's *foot? unfortunate accident? recent armed mishap?* God knows what all I wrote. All I remember is the asshole ending, *Knowing how you all must feel, I should naturally understand if you opt not to write. Until then I think of you, all of you, most fondly. Your Frank.*

ONCE THE WEDDING BELLS RANG, Heidi started serving out her own sentence.

I remember one afternoon a few years after Dad and Heidi got married. This must have been the junior or senior year because I was back home by then. No longer a threat, I was saving Dad some bucks by going to St. Luke's, this second-rate Catholic prep school where Dad and Heidi were cutting their losses with me. And by then, except when I got drunk, I was a semi-model prisoner, mainly out of consideration for Dad who was having Heidi problems and even partner problems with his latest sidekick—but we won't go into that. Anyhow, I was old enough, and had been away long enough, that, like Moses, I could see the end in sight. Not Heidi, though. Hearing loud sobs one night I run downstairs. There she is, bawling in front of the TV.

"Look, that's my life! My whole stupid life living in this crazy house! *It's all right there.*"

She's watching the movie *Rebecca*, with Laurence Olivier and Joan Fontaine. As it opens, Olivier's gorgeous first wife Rebecca has just died and Olivier's going off his nut, all alone in this gloomy, eight-hundred-room castle, Manderley, with his creepy, jet-haired housekeeper, Mrs. Danvers. What else can the poor bastard do? He runs off, travels the world, then meets this sweet, gorgeous woman who he marries, then takes back to Manderley. Bad idea there, Larry! No, once back home, the guy collapses again, staring at the logs crumbling in the fire. Meanwhile, Wife #2 is being gaslighted by this Mrs. Danvers, always showing her Rebecca's portrait, Rebecca's clothes, Rebecca's jewels. You didn't have to wonder long who Mrs. Danvers was in Heidi's mind—Grammaw.

"But hold on, Mom"—to keep the peace, I always call Heidi Mom—"they don't have any kids."

"Quiet!" Heidi keeps bawling. "Can't you see I'm trying to watch this, you big, stupid lunk? God, always yammering at me!" Typical. I haven't said five words.

But now, as I write this, Julie, I see something else in Heidi's movie. (I just popped it on the VCR last night.) Because however warped my relationship was with Heidi, and however much you and Heidi differed (or didn't differ), what makes me squirm is to see how little things had changed in our house. Again, I was a woman's confidant and—emotionally at least—a kind of surrogate husband. And again I was a battering ram into Dad's growing inwardness and misery. Peace at any price, that was Dad's price in those days.

So we were not three but *four,* Julie. Yet if Heidi feels herself losing the man she never possessed, well, Heidi still has me, a human Ouija board through whom she can reach you, Julie. And so for my benefit Heidi explodes at the TV.

"There you go! All I ever hear, with your *Jeeew-lie* this and your *Jewww-lie* that!"

"What the hell are you even talking about?" I ask. "I never mention her to you, never."

"Not you, *your father.* I'm sick of it! *Her* house. *Her* son. *Her* mink stole with *her* initials ripped out of the lining so he can have mine sewn in! Aww go on, you jackass, staring at me! Now *go!* You *and* you! Goddamnit, all three of you, go *away* from me!"

BUT DIDN'T I EVER FANTASIZE ABOUT RUNNING OFF WITH ALVY AGAIN? Off in one last blaze of glory?

Oh sure, I guess I *thought* about it but no, this wasn't about to happen. Why, the very idea was ridiculous, as much from Alvy's end as mine.

God, what a redneck Alvy was when I really looked at him again. And him with all his brilliance! Really, the kid was a genius, but once he came home, and especially once Lucky's drinking got worse, he renounced everything, even his own brains, hanging around with a bunch of losers, half of them grown-up losers at that. Alvy couldn't stand the Beatles or Jimi Hendrix—any of that whiny, lame-assed, long-haired shit. Secretly, he was still a huge reader. (I once saw a battered copy of *War and Peace* in the backseat of his car.) But of course, Alvy would have died before he ever read a word any teacher assigned him. In fact, by sixteen, as a moral stand against everything pretentious and pussified, Alvy had absolutely decided he would *not* go to college. Above all, he hated all this whining about Vietnam—whining by a bunch of inspid, long-haired cowards whose rich Daddies could buy their way out, sending them off to college to study basket weaving. Well, fuck all that! he said. Like a greasy monk, Alvy worked at a gas station and slept with older, hardened women, some in their twenties and even older who adored him for his woundedness and mother-craving sullenness.

Finally, Lucky got a "voluntary" early-out from the VA. Alvy, meanwhile, was flunking out of high school and forever getting into crazy, suicidal fights. Just as he did with Hicks, Alvy had to trap himself, always totally outweighed, outgunned, out-aged and outnumbered. It had to be desperate. Two or three guys pounding and kicking him, holding him gurgling and choking under the water of his own will, when—snap! Ears half torn off. Crushed windpipes and spleens.

Then disaster. That fall—the fall of my junior year—Lucky dropped dead from a stroke.

ALL THE PAPERS RAN OBITS but none that basically couldn't have been written in 1945. And of course the burial would be at our favorite place—Arlington National Cemetery.

"Your mother and I forbid you to go," Dad said. Amazing. Here I am college bound but still Alvy scares him. One sniff of Alvy and they think I'll go wild again.

And I don't want to go to the funeral—are you kidding? Except for Alvy I hadn't seen any of the Loomises in more than four years. So I dither around, miss the wake, then even the mass, when I panic, skip school, call the VFW for a ride, then find myself squeezed in the back of an old tail-dragging Impala with four vets decked out in their gold-braided ice-cream-man regalia.

"You're a friend of Alvy's?" asks the man beside me, amazed at my striped tie, class ring and debating pendant. So leaving it vague, I say how Alvy and I are old grade-school pals. Fat flesh starts shifting.

"Well, sorry to tell you this," wheezes the big man driving, "but your old buddy's in jail. Oh yeah, he's in trouble big-time—assault with intent to murder."

I don't even need to hear the rest. It's almost logical. Alvy beats some marine's brains out, gets arrested, then Lucky drops dead, meaning it's all Alvy's fault. Why, even if Lucky's been swilling paint thinner, it's Alvy's fault, and Alvy, of course, will *make* it his fault, the same as Charlene is his fault and Buddy is his responsibility. *If* Alvy even comes today. All depends on some judge or psychiatric evaluation, says the driver. But then Buzz or Joe or whoever—the other fat guy beside me—well, *he* says that the judge is just their excuse, that in fact Bunny is the one behind Alvy's being banished from the funeral, which it only makes sense, he says, what with Alvy's track record of going berserk at family events. And then, inevitably, they're all onto the Vietnam War. I could already feel that one coming, just like I can see them squinting to see if my hair's so much as a millimeter over my ear, in which case I'm a pot-smoking, hippie-protester faggot. But mainly what I am is Alvy's whipping boy, Buzz or Joe or whoever telling me as Alvy's stand-in, "Look, we all know what Lucky would say. Exactly what Lucky'd say. And buddy boy, I can tell what the judge'll be hearing, and from many highly influential people too. And the message is, 'Okay, son! You love to fight, so here's your choice. Shame or honor, jail or combat duty in V'yetnam!' "

And even as I'm being sentenced in Alvy's place, even then we were crossing my old nightmare, Memorial Bridge. It's the golden behemoths wielding their massive swords, dragging their bellowing oxen and the slave women with sun-harrowed hair. And here it is, Valhalla, the great white marble gate with its screaming golden eagles and beaten golden trees. White-gloved guards salute and point the way and boy, the place is packed, a traffic jam then in 1967. Looping around the drive, we must pass a dozen funerals before we see the crowd for Lucky moving down the hill, waves of white headstones chopping like whitecaps to the Potomac. Christ, they gave Lucky a view of the Lincoln Memorial. Not all that far from JFK, in fact.

"Frank! Honey! Aww my God, look who's here!"

You can't blame Mrs. Loomis for not exactly being in her right mind. It's weird enough seeing Bunny all dressed up with no curlers, but what makes me feel crazy still, she actually looks younger—way younger than I remember, in her black chiffon and veils. And I still love her, I realize, my feelings for her haven't changed one iota. Here I'd been gone for years—I'd completely grown up—yet it's as if I'd never left. Kissing me full on the lips, Mrs. Loomis grips my arm in hers, then starts introducing me as "her other son." Jetliners whine down the river. Stumbling behind her I meet a two-star general and tons of army brass. And here are Carol and Velma—both half gray and, behind them, the famous Flies, Steve gone to pot, and Scotty even fat-ter with his mechanical leg. And Christ, here's Buddy, eight years old and acting like he barely remembers me. I'm drunk. As Mrs. Loomis pulls me along, people look at me heartened. Me, as if I can explain Alvy with my stupid blue blazer and debating pin. Me, as if I can redeem them, while you I can feel tugging over the next hill, buried at sea in what seems ages ago.

And here he comes! Ambling down the hill, with the cleft chin, squinty eyes and the same huge wrists, here's Alvy sandwiched between two powerful, stone-faced deputies. At first I think he's just being solemn but no—he's handcuffed. Bunny drops my hand. Everything stops. Escorted by the VFW commander and several army officers, Bunny hugs Alvy, then almost totters back, imploring the deputies to take off the cuffs. Forget it. Closing ranks, the deputies are threatening to leave and Bunny's crying when Alvy hisses, "Quit it. You'll only make it worse." It's a public hanging. Hands clasped together, all during the service, Alvy never looks at me, or anyone, or anything but down. Down at Lucky, another locked door and Alvy blocked again, blocked forever now, as three sharp volleys rattle down the hill.

SO TWENTY YEARS PASS. And twenty years later, even as I'm trying to write this book, my own Dad drops dead.

I'm thirty-nine and soon to be a father, and a new father at that. I'm getting off the train from New York, when, unexpectedly, here's my wife. Eight months pregnant, sore-eyed in the June heat, here's Paula's saying that Dad has just dropped dead. Just three hours ago—a massive coronary. The platform clears. And like a child, again I ask her.

"And he's *really* gone? Today? . . ."

And again that astounding coincidence-feeling I'd had at age twelve, as if my train had only narrowly missed his. Here again was that same ear-plugging, head-jarring stupefication and expulsion—that sheer *being-born* of grief, and bitterer still when I have a little girl to give him, a little Julie to make up for you, Julie, and for my running away. And again the utter selfishness and blank self-absorption of death, when the living suddenly get the news. I feel snubbed. Because my first crazy thought is, *How could he?*

• • •

AND THINGS HAD IMPROVED BETWEEN DAD AND ME.
During those last few years, for instance, every summer Paula and I had
joined Dad for a long weekend in Ocean City. Go! said Heidi, who wasn't
about to leave her "children," her dog Susie and her chestnut gelding Bart.
But really, Heidi's absence was a mercy, leaving Dad and me free to drink too
much, or fish, or pound the boardwalk—anything that effectively precluded
much talking or soul searching. And who was he now? And who was he ever,
really? God, I dreaded the boardwalk with him, the place awash with hot girls
and Dad scorching out his Ray-Bans. On the boardwalk we'd fly into this cos-
mic role reversal, the old man actually embarrassing me, muttering, "*Wow,
check the melons on that babe. Yowzah.*"

But I think Dad wanted to goose me then, wanted to communicate on
some level, even about you, Julie. Yet when he made these veiled attempts
to connect, with equal perversity I became all the more like him, ever more
passive and remote, while he became more provocative. I'd hear ominous
throwaways like "Back when your mother and I were first married..." Or
more mysteriously, "Well, you took care of all *that*." Or even more acidly, "But
then your mother died and, of course, there was The Man of Stone." Me,
he means.

So ask!

But he can't take this now.

So ask!

But this isn't the time.

But late one night out on the balcony of his beach condo, as Dad and I
are doing a two-man relay with a bottle of vodka, out of nowhere Dad admits,
"You know, after you left me"—he qualifies this—"left me *finally*" (he means
in college, when I told them both to fuck off and put myself through school),
"well, I'd sit out back under the tree and just get stoned. Just crying my
damned eyes out but what did you know? Oh yeah, gimme that noble,
wronged look! Mr. Ponytail, out smoking your dope and screwing everything
that moves! And here you *sit*, huh? And—here—you—*sit*."

I'm a rather sentimental drunk. I start to hug him but he jerks away. "Oh
sure, *now* you're sorry."

"But Dad, why didn't you ever tell me?"

"Tell you! But why should I have to tell you? *You*, of all people. You, such
a renowned expert on *feelings*. Such a *poet*. Boy, some husband you must be!
Pity poor Paula, with a Pet Rock like you for a husband!"

It's as if he's insulted you. "Oh sure, put it all on *me*. As usual. And how was I to know how you felt? Well, how with you always acting like goddamn fucking John Wayne?"

He bolts up. "And what was I supposed to do? Grovel for you? Oh, but believe me, you were that way at twelve. Cold? God, it was like staring into a goddamn blizzard with you. And what did you feel—*what? What on earth did you ever feel?*" I slam down my glass.

"Goddamnit, what do you think a kid feels at that age? Feeling—like you milk a fucking cow, I suppose! *Feeling*, like with cream in one tit, and butter in the other! Your primitive fucking notion of psychology!"

"Or no feeling! Or defective feeling!"

"Oh, sure! And some fine fucking *feeling* you had, telling me at twelve that *I* drove my dead mother to drink! Just *me*, huh? Because you were so outstanding in the *feelings* department, huh?" He bounds up.

"You see! You *see* how you are? And you'll never change! Minute anybody tells you anything, you go crazy! Belligerent! And what has changed, Mr. Kiss My Ass? Mr. Fuck You? Well, I'll tell you what, you big asshole, *good fucking night.*"

REALLY, I DON'T KNOW, AND NEVER WILL KNOW, WHY DAD DID WHAT HE DID. Or, for that matter, why I did what I did back in the old days trying to break the egg. But finally I do face it. Not long before Dad died and then twenty-seven years too late, I do finally visit your grave at Arlington.

But how will I find you? Don't be stupid, they must have a visitor's center. Why, by now they have computers and the lady punches you up, marks the site on a map, then points me off in the general direction. God, I feel so ridiculous, I feel like a *date*. Holding a huge bundle of flowers and dressed in my Brooks Brothers suit, I look like an undertaker next to all these T-shirted kids and tourists flocking to JFK's grave and the Tomb of the Unknown Soldier.

And, of course, I dawdle, following the crowds to the Eternal Flame, then up the hill to the Tomb of the Unknown Soldier. Mesmerized, I watch the sentry in his black uniform, black sunglasses and white gloves ... twelve paces down the rubber tread, *hut*, clicks his heels, then snaps the rifle around so hard the silver bayonet literally vibrates. Poor guy. It's blistering hot and I'm pouring sweat. Even with the map, I'm disoriented with all the curving drives, the great green swells and endless white stones. I must look pretty bad off, because suddenly an older man and his wife stop me. "Are you lost?" they ask. "Aww, no," I guffaw, "I'm fine," but they're not fooled. The man pulls out his map and I nod sagely, my mind blanking out after the second right turn. So after gobbling spit-warm water from the fountain, again I strike off, soon so desperate I flag down a groundskeeper in his golf cart. But when he guides me up the hill—why, Section 3 alone must be five acres! Five hundred stones and me cursing and fuming, running down the rows, when I practically fall over yours.

"Well, I came finally, Mamma."

Dropping to a squat, I'm panting, sinking into that old, fretting child's cry, which was mostly about feeling dumb, lost, scared. *Now what?* Like bandages, I pull out this packet of old pictures I brought, old black-and-whites that Dad developed, one in particular of you and me at the beach. Dad took the picture, obviously. The camera's looking straight down on us—you with your dark hair under a white sailor's cap, wearing one of those puffy flowered swimsuits that now look so impossibly old. I can't be much older than two, and I'm bawling as you hold me in a little riffle. It's just a scrim of surf. It's nothing, but a baby has no sense of scale, any power being all power, and all powerful. I squall. I kick. I'm terrified I'll be sucked away, but you, Julie, smiling in your white sailor's cap, you hold and cuddle me with a resolute calm that I honestly can't connect with you—not at least as I remember you. And let's face it. Quite possibly I'm wrong about half of this, a confused, self-serving or defective memory, but what more can I do? At last, as I stand to leave you again, I take out a picture of me and Paula, five months pregnant. So people will see you're not just another stone, I tape our picture up with the Scotch Tape that I brought, but it's quite useless. Probably the one thing Scotch Tape won't stick to is marble, so finally I wind the tape around the stone, a whole roll. Even if it blows away tomorrow, I leave our picture, loudly blow my nose, then start off down the hill, down through the bronze leaves, only a short walk from where Alvy lies beside Lucky—Alvy who, in his own way, saved me. Him and Sheppy both, staring into fixity for as long as any two kids can stare at the sun.

SGT. ALVY LOOMIS

MARYLAND

1ST CAVALRY RECON

MARCH 12 1949

MAY 21 1970

• • •

THREE MONTHS LATER, THE DAY OF DAD'S FUNERAL, I'm feeling really shaky, so I go early to the funeral home, to be off with Dad by myself.

"I'll take it from here," I tell the funeral director. But the minute I walk in and see Dad's dead face, it hits me—Georgia, a lifetime ago. The juvenile home and Dad finding me, just as I find him now, squeezed inside his little coffin. And who is this man? I wonder. It's not my Daddy, *It's not really him.* No, it's only a little mannequin, smaller and strangely narrowed, with two nose holes and that black spool inside his powdered ear where the gnat sings and the makeup ends so cruelly.

"How ya doin, man?" I ask, gliding my hand over his lapel. Weird, I think, calling him "man." "How ya doin, man? Hey man, I finally came to see you, huh?"

Adam doesn't answer.

"Aww, man," I huff, finally grasping the immensity of this last huge mess we're in, "Aww fuck, Daddy, how did this ever happen to us? What the hell happened? You never even saw my little girl . . ."

And the utter impossibility of it. The sheer unbudgeability of that egg. Desperate to somehow get *at* him, to get through to him, suddenly I see his gray but still glistening flattop, and this is real. This is intensely real. Dad's hair puts me right back in the Bird, back whooping in the wind, with the white wallop of hood and the world fleeing before us like a million startled birds. In the Bird, Dad's hair is still bristling dark and brushy with the lustrous static of life. Over the white hood, wide as the fields, Dad's hair flares out, and like the speed, his dark hair only stretches, the wind rushing into my mouth like a gigantic water fountain, gushing speed and foreverness and newness. And guiltily glancing around, desperate for that old vanquished love power—well, screw it. Because finally, right there in the funeral parlor, I skate my hand off the old man's tingly hair, "*Nyerrr-ooOWWWW—*"

Like a kid revving up a toy car, I bite my lip. Because, like that ancient kid, well, like any kid, I only want to make it go and go, grazing my hand over his hair until, real suddenly now, I gotta go myself, "*Nyyyyrrrowww—*"

The recipient of a Guggenheim Fellowship, a Whiting Writer's Award and a Lila Wallace–Reader's Digest Award, Bruce Duffy lives in Silver Spring, Maryland, with his wife and two daughters. His first novel, *The World as I Found It*, was published in four languages. He has written on subjects as diverse as hoboes, Haiti and Bosnia for various magazines. He is now at work on a new novel.